PRETTY DEAD THINGS

LIV LOWRY

For information, contact:

Liv Lowry Books

www.livlowry.com

Cover design by The Cover Collection

ISBN: 979-8-9935589-0-5 (kindle ebook)
ISBN: 979-8-9935589-1-2 (paperback)
ISBN: 979-8-9935589-2-9 (hardcover)

First Edition, 2025

For my sisters

WELCOME TO THE BELVILLE ESTATE

BY REBECCA ARMSTRONG

In the quaint rural town of Gator Springs, Florida, nestled right beside the Everglades National Park, lies a hidden gem that rivals the grandeur of Versailles. The Belville Estate, the residence of the iconic Old Hollywood actress Vivienne Belville, is now open to the public, allowing longtime fans an inside look into her notoriously private life.

The sprawling estate encompasses an impressive number of acres, with stunning gardens and century-old oak trees. Positioned at the heart of it all, her old Victorian-style manor, complete with a charming wraparound porch, overlooks a vast expanse of swampland and untouched wilderness.

The gallery, which doubles as a museum, is a dream come true for film enthusiasts everywhere. It displays an impressive collection of movie props and dresses worn in her classic films, along with her own venture into photography. The walls are covered with black-and-white photographs of her cherished Florida, her second love California, and her three young daughters.

To help guests beat the sweltering Florida heat, the estate also offers a gift shop, a café, and a popular soft serve bar featuring local flavors. Entry to The Belville Estate is priced at a modest $18 for adults and $10 for children, promising to be an affordable and family-friendly excursion for visitors of all ages.

—*Golden Era Magazine*, July 1992

BREAKING NEWS

Former *Star Sisters* child star Odette Belville (38) was found dead Tuesday afternoon in the waters near the family's famed Belville Estate in South Florida.

Authorities have listed the cause of death as drowning, but details remain unclear, and whispers of something darker are spreading fast online. 👀

A source close to the investigation tells *The Hollywood Scoop* the story is still unfolding. Fans are heartbroken and demanding answers. 💔

(Aerial photograph of the Belville Estate, with multiple police cars and vans parked on the property.)

#OdetteBelville #StarSisters #BelvilleEstate #BreakingNews #TheHollywoodScoop #HollywoodMystery #RIP

📍 Los Angeles, CA
Posted October 3rd, 2023, 8:47 PM PT

1

I WANT to strangle my mother. I picture it inside my head, wrapping my hands around her neck and tightening my grip, squeezing until I feel that delicious *pop* of her windpipe.

I'm already imagining the headlines. *Funeral at the Belville Estate Ends in Tragedy. Famous Actress Vivienne Belville Murdered by Daughter, Briar. Motive Still Unknown. Briar Taken to Mental Hospital While Awaiting Questioning.*

It's unbelievable. She can't hand over the spotlight for one day, not even at her own daughter's wake. I knock back the rest of my sweet tea like it's a shot, wishing it packed a stronger punch, anything to help take the edge off.

Oh, give me a break. Ever the leading lady, Vivienne parades around the ballroom from guest to guest, sobbing dramatically into her silk monogrammed handkerchief. She's all dolled up, wearing white. What kind of person wears white to a funeral? And it's remarkable how she's been crying all day, but her mascara hasn't even smudged.

I can't watch this anymore. Shaking my head, I navigate through the crowd, dodging my mother's pretentious Hollywood pals and snobby members of the country club. I don't see anyone here who truly mattered to Odette. No friends or work colleagues. Did anyone who was a part of her life even receive an invitation?

I hold my breath as I pass another ugly bouquet of yellow roses. The petals are already wilting. It's nauseating. Not just the smell but the fact that Odette's favorite flowers were pink peonies. Yellow roses are Vivienne's favorite. And the buffet area is filled with white fish and steamed broccoli, Vivienne's favorites again. Then there's the oversized poster of my sister in the foyer, right next to the condolence message table. Vivienne's hijacked that, too, her face taking up more space than Odette's.

Now I get why people snap.

I slam my glass on the table and snatch the black marker. I don't care who's watching. It'll be worth all the dirty looks. I scribble a curling mustache and devil horns across my mother's perfect face. "There," I say, leaning back. "That's more accurate."

Another sob rings out across the room. Vivienne buries her face into the priest's neck and beats on his chest with shaking fists. I slap the marker down on the table again. Too bad I didn't strangle her. "I need some air," I mutter before stumbling outside.

It's the middle of fall, but the Florida heat is like crashing into a wall of humidity. I can already feel it tugging at my bun, settling over me like a second skin. I move across the drive and over the front lawn, branching off onto one of the many trails. Past the graveyard, where silent crypts and the angel of death tower over the wrought iron fence, the dilapidated chapel looming ominously in the distance.

I break into a jog, curving through the thick oaks and leaning palms, the Spanish moss swaying above my head like hovering spirits. I pause beside the boathouse, bracing against the wall for support. When we were children, we used to come here all the time. Dig in the sand, explore the water. Collect snail shells, dragonflies, and snake skins.

I crumple beside the swamp, the moist sand spilling into my heels. This is where it happened, where they found Odette. The airboat had crashed into the canal, and her body was lost for weeks. The stench of the water is overpowering. Foul and pungent as rotting flesh. It's why they didn't notice her for so long, why when they pulled her out, she looked so spoiled.

Part of me wants to sink into the water, to close my eyes and hold my breath until I can't anymore. Maybe then, I could drown out the vivid details etched permanently inside my mind. The drizzling rain and the ripples across the swamp's surface. The police, with their solemn expressions and black umbrellas, gathered on the shore. The body bag that seemed too large to fit my sister. The painful groan of the gurney wheels, getting stuck in the mud more than once as they tried to transport her to the ambulance. It was almost as if she didn't want to leave.

Hugging my knees, I force back the tears. The hope I had desperately clung to that we might find her alive evaporated the moment the ambulance doors slammed shut. My sister was on her way to the morgue, and I couldn't help feeling like I had failed her. Odette was always there for me, no matter what. Where was I when she needed me most? Could I have prevented this? Saved her?

The wake is wrapping up, and mourners spill out of the house and onto the front lawn. Before anyone can find me, I run to the back of the estate and slip into the gallery, shielding my eyes as the harsh stage lights flash on.

The gramophone in the corner crackles to life, playing vintage hits from the '40s and '50s. It takes a second for my eyes to adjust. But once they do, I rush over and unplug the damn thing from the wall, letting the cord drop.

Usually, I avoid the gallery at all costs as it tends to make me uneasy. But lately, its contents have been bleeding into other parts of the house. Photographs I never knew existed—or maybe had blocked out—keep popping up, filling the halls and sneaking into bedrooms.

Always us as children.

Never as adults.

There's only one recent photograph of us, and it hangs above the mantel in the parlor. Vivienne sits front and center, of course. My sisters and I placed around her like adoring apostles: Odette and Portia on either side of her while Juliet and I kneel toward the front, our heads cast down, our eyes up. We've all been artistically airbrushed to the extreme, our perfection bordering unnatural. The version Vivienne wishes we would be. She even altered the picture to make me look thinner. Something she continues to deny to this day.

I shiver in the A/C as the sweat that's pooled beneath my dress dries and icy air blasts me from the ceiling vents. This is easily the coldest room in the house, in more ways than one. It's a mix of everything. The lack of furniture, the sterility of it all.

Rubbing at my goosebumps, I wander through the first section, a tribute to my mother's glamorous past. The walls are lined with massive black-and-white photos of Vivienne striking poses during her heyday, her eyes piercing through the lens.

I step around the glass cases that rise from the floor, holding film props and accessories like her pearl necklace, her diamond earrings, and glittering tiaras, the awards she received throughout her long career. A flicker of movement catches my eye in the glass. For a second, I think I see a flash of dark hair, a reflection that shifts like a shadow.

I whirl around, searching. "Hello?" I call, but there's no answer. Just an eerie quiet.

I hug myself as I hurry past the row of headless mannequins. They're posed under spotlights and display the gowns my mother wore to Hollywood events and charity galas, a collection of full skirts and plunging necklines. I glance at them, and then at my pale face in the mirrored wall behind them. I look so washed out by the harsh lights and my black dress, that I almost appear gray. Corpse-like.

After Vivienne's tribute, there's a section of the gallery dedicated to us. Her daughters. Stills from our '90s TV show *Star Sisters* and shots our mother took herself, enlarged floor-to-ceiling in height.

Juliet's first. Only seven years old and the newest addition to our family, twenty-five years younger than me. Vivienne adopted her long after the rest of us. I think because she couldn't bear the thought of this hollow estate without a child running through it. By then, we were all grown with lives of our own, and Juliet had the whole place to herself.

She's absolutely angelic. She has a heart-shaped face, precious Bantu knots, and wide, intelligent eyes. In the first photo, she poses on a stool in the middle of the garden wearing a colorful tulle dress. It looks like a picture-perfect post you'd find on somebody's Instagram page. But the further you move into the gallery, the more unnerving the photographs become.

Vivienne surprised us all when she started dabbling in Photoshop, and she's scarily talented at it. I mean, *really* scary. It's hard to tell where the photo ends and the digital art begins.

In one piece, Juliet is covered in flowers. They sprout from her mouth and eyes. Her ears and nose. In another, vines burst from festering wounds and wrap around her like a snare, trapping her. They're as mesmerizing as they are horrible.

I pause before my own section, my name sweeping overhead in an elegant script. Briar Rose. I look nothing like these photos. They're a constant reminder that I used to be beautiful and unique with fiery red hair and charcoal-colored eyes. Pale skin and blood-red lips. But then puberty hit.

While my sisters' beauty only blossomed, I failed to thrive. Jaw and brows a little too prominent, teeth a little too large. Something masculine about the way I carry myself, my bone structure. The fiery red hair has devolved into an average auburn. The eyes, a muddy brown. The pristine skin covered in freckles and sun damage.

Nothing special.

I move past my own section in a rush, ignoring the budding red roses and hooked black thorns that pop out at me from all directions.

Portia is next, a year older than me, with her Lucrezia Borgia buttery-blonde hair and cat green eyes. Her photographs are overgrown with giant magnolias, and she peeks out from behind the petals like a garden fairy. Her face glows with laughter as she twirls in the sunlight, gauzy dress thrown into the air like delicate angel wings.

"I didn't expect to find you here."

"Shit!" I jump out of my skin. "You scared me."

"Sorry," Portia offers weakly. It's as if I summoned her. This version of Portia is a stark contrast from her framed counterpart. Transformed by all the tears, her face pinched and puffy and flushed. She's taller and thinner now, her hair morphed into a stylish blonde bob. "Vivienne was looking for you. I don't know what she wants."

"To keep us close," I say, resisting the urge to roll my eyes. "She's been a nervous wreck ever since it happened."

Portia gazes up at the photos and I wonder what she's thinking. If she finds them as creepy as I do. "Did you come to see Odette?"

"Yes," I admit. "And to be alone."

Portia stares at the ground as she crosses her section, just like I did. "I wanted to be alone, too, but I'm glad you're here," she says as she pulls me close. "To be honest, I don't know if I could have done this on my own."

Because it's like looking at a ghost, I realize as we enter Odette's section. Being the oldest, she has the largest one. These photographs are darker than the rest, the subject bathed in hues of black and blue. Odette floating in the swamp during a full moon, wet hair glued to her face like an evil mermaid. Odette on a white pony, brandishing a sword of blue hyacinth, silver eyes ablaze, the full moon lingering in the background. An Odette-swan hybrid, white feathers protruding painfully from thin skin, limbs bent at awkward angles, lips curved into a sharp beak. Odette kneeling before a dollhouse, a perfect replica of Belville Estate, an eerie smile on her face.

Portia tries to make a joke of it. "Do you ever wonder what the adoption agency thought of all this? If they even saw the gallery? Because if it were me, I would've thought this woman was a lunatic and not fit to be around children."

I laugh, but deep down I think Vivienne has captured our sister perfectly. There was always something about her. Something hidden and mysterious. I could never quite put my finger on it. But these photos express exactly what I could never put into words. No one can deny she has a way with the camera.

"You forget Vivienne isn't a nobody. She's one of the last surviving Old Hollywood actresses. She's cinema royalty. People expect her to be eccentric."

"It's not about fame, it's about the money. It's always the money." Portia sighs and rolls her neck, her eyes narrowing as they fix on something behind me. "What is *that?*"

My heart leaps into my throat as I spin around and spot the splatters of red that mark the usually pristine floor.

It looks like blood.

We rush forward, turning a corner, and stopping before the back wall. This final section of the gallery is a stormy sea of Odette, frames touching frames with no gaps in between. Our eldest sister watches us from above like an angel of judgment about to damn us to Hell.

The back wall has been vandalized. Shattered glass is strewn across the floor. Some of the photos have been torn down, shredded, and doused in a thick, tar-like substance. The largest photo hangs right in the middle of the wall. In this one, Odette's eyes have been crossed out with sloppily smeared Xs, and at the bottom, like a signature, is a foreboding message:

DIE.

2

The gallery is wrapped in yellow caution tape as police officers investigate the vandalism.

With Vivienne's pull, they're treating it like a murder case with forensic vans and everything. They've even dispatched a detective, who's just stepped into the ballroom. Portia, Juliet, and I are positioned at the bottom of the stairs while Vivienne descends in her signature grand entrance. With a fresh touch-up to her face and her cleavage pushed sky high, she's clearly expecting the attractive male detective who handled Odette's case. To her surprise, this detective is a woman in a sharp pantsuit and practical sneakers.

"Detective," Vivienne says with a bright smile. It wavers slightly in disappointment, but she catches it just in time. "Welcome! Please, come in."

The detective is busy taking in her surroundings. When her eyes finally settle on Vivienne's white dress and the rest of us posing at the bottom of the stairs, she gets this look on her face like she's not quite sure what to make of us. I can almost hear her thinking it. *Strange family.*

I'd spied on her earlier from the window as she rolled in and parked her patrol car beside the boathouse, her sunglasses and long brown hair partially hiding her face. She'd knelt on the swamp's shore, peering out across the brackish water, a finger poised over her lips in concentration. I notice the remnants of mud on her sneakers now as she sticks out a hand to greet us.

"Detective Elena Torres with Gator Springs PD." We take turns shaking her hand, her grip firm. "I know you were expecting Martinez, but he's been reassigned. I'll be his replacement."

"A pleasure," Vivienne purrs, crinkling her nose in exaggerated delight. "Care for something to drink, Detective?"

"Coffee would be great, thanks."

Vivienne raises a perfectly plucked brow and grips the gator's skull carved into the stair railing. "In this heat?"

The detective shrugs. "Never too warm for coffee."

"Well, then." Vivienne turns to us. "Shall we, girls?"

Portia leads the way, escorting the detective to the parlor. I stick close behind, eyeing her tall, lean frame, her crisp white button-down setting off her deeply tanned skin. She removes her navy blazer and folds up her sleeves, and I zero in on the gun holstered to her waistband.

Elise bustles in from the kitchen to take the detective's blazer and serve the drinks. She's been Vivienne's close friend and the housekeeper at Belville Estate for as long as I can remember. She's always been like a second mother to us—only kinder and less toxic than the other one. I smile at her as she passes me my drink, and she gives me a wink.

"Right here, Detective," Portia says, showing her to an armchair.

"Thanks," Detective Torres murmurs as she admires the wallpaper. Every wall has been plastered with a different style of paper: the south wall with Japanese cherry blossoms, the north wall with London Park, the east wall with emerald peacocks, and the west wall with a blue-toned Caribbean scene of pirate ships and swaying palms. At the corners, the wallpaper is peeling here and there, but Vivienne says it adds to the charm... whatever that means.

I can't stand it.

It just makes me want to grab a ladder and spend the afternoon ripping the old paper away and applying brand new sheets with high-quality glue that will endure the moisture in the air.

The thought alone has me reaching into my purse and fishing out my hand sanitizer. I squeeze a glob into my palm and massage it in, careful not to miss a spot. I move on to fantasizing about vacuuming under the Persian carpet and polishing the hardwood floors.

"You're new," Vivienne says as she takes a seat, smoothing a hand over her dress.

Detective Torres nods, thanking Elise as she's handed her mug of coffee. She breathes in the steam, the tension in her shoulders loosening. "That's right. Miami, actually."

Vivienne's eyes crinkle in amusement. "You left Miami for Gator Springs?"

"I grew up here. Moved back to take care of my mom."

"Oh, hear that, girls? How lovely." Vivienne side-eyes us as she sips her iced tea. "That's a big adjustment, isn't it? Reminds me of how I traded this tiny town for Los Angeles. And once I did, I landed my very first role. You've probably heard of it." She gestures to one of the framed movie posters on the wall. "*My Fair Lady*. I starred alongside Audrey Hepburn and Rex Harrison."

It takes everything in me not to snort. *For goodness' sake, woman, you were an extra!*

"It wasn't a big part, but I'll always be grateful for it. It catapulted me to stardom!"

Detective Torres has this blank look on her face. "Sorry, but I've never seen it."

I have. Too many times to count. I could probably recite every line if I had to. Yes, instead of Nickelodeon and The Disney Channel, we were force-fed old movies Vivienne had starred in... even if she was only in it for a few seconds. Of course, any other film requests were considered sacrilege. I'm still convinced it qualifies as a lighter form of child abuse.

"That's surprising," Vivienne muses, expertly hiding the offense she's taken. "Most have."

She sets her glass aside and taps her fingers on the arm of her chair—the pink velvet clamshell chair she always sits in. Then she purses her plump lips, growing impatient.

"So, have you deciphered that gruesome scene in my gallery?"

"Not yet," the detective says, shifting in her seat. "But we do know it's not human blood. It's pig."

"Pig?"

"That's right."

"Who would do such a thing?"

"That's what we're trying to figure out." Detective Torres flexes her fingers, the knuckles popping. Her eyes dart around the room, searching for something. "What about surveillance cameras? Do you have any on the property?"

"Well, no, not anymore." Vivienne pouts. "Though if I did, perhaps I'd know who desecrated that beautiful poster of Odette in the foyer."

I tense at the mention of the poster. Portia catches my reaction and shoots me a look that says, *you're in for it now.*

"I shrieked when I saw it. I mean, have you ever seen anything so distasteful?" Vivienne leans closer to the detective and lowers her voice to a scathing hiss. "I have a sneaking suspicion it was Renaldo, my manicurist. Wicked, little snake. He's always been jealous of me."

"I'll make a note of that," Detective Torres says, trying not to smirk. "You know, a security system wouldn't be a bad idea. I know it sounds cliché, but you can never be too careful. I can recommend one if you're interested."

Vivienne sighs. "Well, alright. Briar, would you be a dear and take care of that for me? You're so good with that... technical stuff." She turns back to the detective with a wave of her hand. "She'll stare at that computer of hers for hours. I don't know how she does it. I always tell her, take a break sometimes. Go to the gym or the mall. If you'd just spend a little less time playing online games and more time working on your makeup skills, you might find yourself a new husband."

A prickle of irritation has me gritting my teeth. "I don't play games. I work," I correct her as sweetly as possible.

One of my mother's favorite pastimes: belittling my choice of career. Because I chose philanthropy over show business, it's not *really* a job. In her eyes, it's a hobby. Never mind Loving Hearts is one of the most successful non-profits in the state of Florida. We do a lot of good for low-income families. But I don't bother telling her that. It wouldn't make a difference anyway.

Vivienne flings a dramatic hand to her forehead as if I'm exhausting her. "Fine, you work. But you don't have to look like a man to prove you're a strong and independent woman."

I bite my tongue, the surface already sore. I've nearly chewed it off since coming back here. Suddenly, my lonely condo on the other side of town seems so much more appealing. I keep my mouth shut, adjusting my hands in my lap and recrossing my ankles.

Every time I visit home, I have to remember to sit like the Princess of Wales.

We all sit in the same fashion, even little Juliet. Unfortunately, she's not excluded from the *must-be-perfect-at-all-times* Belville house rule. Although I can see she's getting antsy, staring up at the ceiling, picking at one of the frayed sofa threads. She's picked it almost free, her fingers returning to the same spot.

That's the thing.

We always return to the same spot. Our assigned seats. Orbiting around our mother, so that she's constantly in the center.

Just the way she likes it.

My senses cut out as I notice a small cobweb above the mantel, clinging to one of the candlesticks. I picture myself clearing the clutter away, taking a soapy sponge to the wood, scrubbing until the paint chips. Then I'd sand it all down again and repaint it with a fresh coat. I'd have this place sparkling. I'd spend hours just...

"Briar?"

I startle. "Sorry?"

Vivienne offers me her warning smile. The one that means, *get your shit together and start acting your part*. "The detective asked you a question, dear."

"Oh, um, what was that again?"

"Have you noticed anything strange?" Detective Torres repeats.

"Um... strange how?"

"Maybe someone you didn't recognize at the wake?"

"Oh. No, I don't think so," I answer slowly. The truth is, I didn't recognize anyone at the wake. But of course, I don't say that. "No, I didn't see anything."

The detective nods, her eyes skidding past me and her leg bouncing in place.

Vivienne smiles. "You don't have to be nervous, Detective. I don't bite," she laughs. "May I offer you a spirit to help calm those nerves?"

Detective Torres frowns. "Thanks, but I don't drink on the job."

As the detective's eyes scale the wall, I realize what she's looking at. My mother's award plaques. She probably *is* a fan but not allowed to admit it. If she grew up in Gator Springs, I'm sure she toured the estate with her family when it was open to the public. Almost everyone in town did.

Vivienne pats Portia on the knee, drawing the detective's attention back to her. "How admirable. Portia here learned her lesson the hard way. I found her more than once passed out in a bar. Locked up in a jail cell. But she's been sober now for... How long is it, dear?"

Portia's cheeks flush pink with embarrassment. Vivienne loves putting us on the spot.

"Two years," Portia mumbles.

"She's come a long way," Vivienne says.

I snort. This time I can't help it. The glare I get from my mother is absolutely searing. Now, everyone is looking at me. "It's just such a huge understatement," I clarify, offering my sister a kind smile. "She's built a whole damn wellness empire on social media. She has over three million followers!"

"Language," Vivienne sings, then shifts her forced smile back to the detective.

"Good for you," the detective says to Portia. She checks her watch and drains her coffee before handing us each a card. "Look. We're going to find who did this, but in the meantime, I suggest you invest in a decent security system. Cameras. Alarms. And if anything comes up, anything at all, you call me."

Elise hurries over with the blazer and shrugs it over the detective's shoulders, the gold badge glinting in the light streaming through the windows.

Vivienne stands and clasps the detective's hands. "I appreciate you driving all the way out here to take care of us, Elena," she says as if they've known each other for years. "Thank you so much for your time."

Detective Torres wears a guarded expression. "No problem." She nods at the rest of us. "Nice to meet everyone."

I walk the detective to the door. She takes her time, eyes roaming from the floor to the high ceilings. Silently mesmerized. Would she still be so impressed if she knew about the black mold that's laid claim to the space behind the fridge, the flying roaches that nest deep within the walls, the water stains in the attic that look like spilled blood? I hold the door open for her and plaster on my brightest smile. "You have a safe drive now."

3

"Juliet, are you ready to eat?" I ask after I finish setting the dining room table for dinner.

She doesn't answer me. She's sitting by the window, her palm pressed to the glass, her fingers splayed as if comparing hand sizes with someone on the other side.

"Darling, what are you doing over there?" Portia comes around the corner with a pitcher of sweet iced tea. She motions to our youngest sister with her free hand. "Come sit."

Juliet remains silent, her eyes fixed on something outside the window. The drapes flutter around her, caught in the draft.

"Leave her be," Vivienne says, entering the dining room. "She'll join us when she's ready."

Portia starts to object but decides against it, knowing it's pointless to argue with her.

With a shake of her blonde curls, Vivienne takes her place at the head of the table. Her signature spicy perfume fills the air, stirring up a whirlwind of emotions inside me that I've learned to suppress. Despite her swollen eyelids and reddened nose tip, Vivienne looks better at seventy-five than I could ever hope to look. With hardly any wrinkles, a flawless figure, and sharp features that make her appear thirty years younger than her actual age, it's like she only gets more glamorous with each passing day. She takes pleasure in reminding me that I don't. "You know, Briar, black is really not your color. Why didn't you wear that little emerald number I ordered for you?"

"It didn't seem appropriate," I say, avoiding her gaze. "It was a funeral, remember? Besides, Portia's wearing black. *And* Elise."

All Elise ever wears is black, but she never comments on that.

"Well, they can pull it off, dear. Black looks chic on them. On you..."

"Vivienne, please," Portia interjects.

"I'll wear the green dress another time," I say, determined to keep the peace. If I let this continue any longer, we'll all start bickering, and I can already feel a migraine coming on.

Vivienne smiles, but I know there's more she wants to say to me. I can always see them, the unspoken critiques, the un-hurled insults, just behind her eyes.

Eventually, she turns to Portia. "I should have asked you both to change. This room is much too dark for everyone to be wearing black. It's depressing." The wallpaper in the dining room is a deep onyx color with silver vines that glisten in the low evening sun. A silk shawl clings to the chandelier, dimming the light. "Odette wouldn't want us to be depressed. I just don't believe that."

At the mention of my sister, I turn my head toward her designated seat. She's sat across from Vivienne since we were children. Vivienne reasoned it was because Odette was the oldest, but I suspect that was a lie. Odette was the favorite. In Vivienne's eyes, she could do no wrong. That is, until Juliet came along and usurped the title.

The thing about Vivienne is that she can never love all four of us at once. She fixates on one, neglects the rest of us. But when Vivienne chooses you, and you finally experience the love she has to give, it makes you feel like the most special person in the whole wide world.

A hand reaches across the table, unexpectedly grasping mine. It's green and blue, the fingernails bloated and bumpy like old scabs ready to be peeled off. When I glance up, Odette is glaring at me from her seat, twigs entangled in her hair, her body coated in mud. I gasp, pushing away from the table, my chair scraping the hardwood floor. "Shit!"

"Excuse me?" Vivienne cries, appalled by my language.

"Briar, you're bleeding!" Portia says, rushing to my side. She holds a cloth napkin to my mouth and when she pulls it away, I can see the bright red drops of blood.

"Oh," I say, feeling more blood spill over my tongue, tasting it. "I accidentally bit my tongue."

"Let me see it," Portia says.

"No, I'm fine," I insist. "I'll be right back."

I hurry down the hall to the bathroom and lock the door behind me, my heart still pounding rapidly inside my chest. I caress the hand Odette grasped, the skin cold to the touch. Then I swallow and shake my head. "I'm fine," I repeat, softly to myself, bracing my hands on the sink.

I glance up at my reflection and blood dribbles down my lip, smudging on my chin. I turn the faucet on and splash my face with cold water, gargling it in my mouth until the metallic taste is gone. I'm careful not to look in the mirror for too long, afraid my eyes will play another trick on me.

Back in the dining room, Elise emerges from the kitchen with a cart of fried catfish, cornbread, and collard greens. "Dinner's ready," she announces cheerfully.

"Are you okay?" Portia asks me as I slip back into my seat.

I nod, avoiding her gaze. I've only hallucinated once before in my life. My sisters and I were traveling through Europe, and after a long flight followed by an endless train ride, I was so exhausted I started imagining pigs bouncing on fluffy clouds. I blamed it on jet lag and sleep deprivation, and I haven't experienced anything like it since.

Until now.

But that's all this is. Exhaustion and grief.

Once Elise is seated, we hold hands and say grace, and then the food is served. I'm surprisingly hungry. And cold. It's like someone turned down the temperature. I shiver as I take the first few bites, the food comforting. "Everything's delicious, Elise," I say around a forkful of catfish.

Murmurs of agreement echo around the table.

Elise smiles, delighted. "Thank you! It's made with love... and a whole lot of lard!"

My tongue still throbs from biting it earlier. It's beginning to swell. I can taste the blood again, and I take a sip of tea to wash it down.

Suddenly, Vivienne claps her hands together, and everyone jumps. "What about some music? It feels so *dead* in here, doesn't it?"

Portia and I cringe at her choice of words, and Elise shifts uncomfortably in her chair, the creaking wood filling the awkward silence.

"Well? What do you say?" Vivienne pushes from her seat, raising her glass as if making a toast. Some of her drink sloshes over, splattering the embroidered tablecloth. "Let's liven this place up a bit!"

"Okay," Portia says, looking unsure. "I guess..."

Vivienne disappears into the other room, rubbing Juliet's back comfortingly as she passes by. Juliet is still pressed against that window. I wonder what she's looking at.

Music filters in from the other room. Loud and jarring. It's the local radio station. It goes silent for a moment before Fleetwood Mac's "Rhiannon" drifts into the room. It's jarring in a different sense. Odette loved Fleetwood Mac. We all do. Now, all of us sitting around the table in awkward silence, it almost feels like we're eavesdropping on the song. Doing something we shouldn't.

Vivienne dances back to the table, twirling and singing and

twisting her arms and hands in the air like a drunk belly dancer. "I love this song!"

We go back to eating. All of us quiet as Vivienne sings along, swaying back and forth in her seat. "So, I have a grand idea," she finally says, her eyes squeezed shut as she savors the music.

Vivienne's a never-ending source of grand ideas. There was the time she hauled my sisters and I to yet another Hollywood party. Not because she couldn't find a sitter, but because she wanted us to grow up accustomed to her lifestyle. The drugs, the alcohol, and the creepy middle-aged men included. All those times she called paparazzi to make sure we'd be *seen*. Pulling us out of school for six months to tour the country and perform songs in shopping malls and fairgrounds.

I can hardly help myself. "Oh, great. Now, what?"

Vivienne bats her lashes innocently. "Well, I think we ought to stick together right now."

I meet her gaze and set down my fork. A little too forcefully, so it clatters. "What do you mean?"

"Portia's already moved back home."

"Temporarily," Portia quickly clarifies. "Luke and I are separated. Again, temporarily."

Ah, yes. Luke. He's a third-grade teacher at the local elementary school. He's big on getting enough fiber in his diet, Oprah's Book Club, and biking everywhere. He's also a fan of recycling and composting. Oh, and he's in a band with his teacher buddies—well, a concert band. He plays the oboe.

For the life of me, I can't imagine why Portia moved out on sweet, safe, supportive Luke. Unless, of course, he's a closet freak? Maybe he's into necrophilia or balloons or adult diapers. The kinkiest guys always seem the most normal...

Behind us, Juliet giggles and claps, bouncing on the balls of her feet. It freaks us all out, except for Vivienne, who gives her daughter a bright smile. "What's so funny, baby?"

Juliet spins around, still giggling. She glances over her shoulder at the window. "It's a secret."

"A secret? Now, you can't keep secrets from your mama!" She reaches out for Juliet. "Why don't you come over here and eat, baby girl?"

"I can't! I feel bad."

"I know, sweetheart. I know."

"Odette says she wants to eat, but she can't," Juliet says. "So, I'm not going to eat either."

Vivienne sucks in a sharp breath like a hiss. She twists around, lowering her voice, "You see, that's what I'm talking about right there. Juliet is suffering. She needs her big sisters with her."

"Vivienne..." I say.

I *do* feel guilty leaving Juliet alone here, but we both know this isn't really about her. Vivienne has been trying to get me to move home for ages. Even before Odette went missing, she was blowing up my phone, demanding I come stay with them. Somehow she always manages to make me feel guilty for moving out. I have to remind myself sometimes that I'm an adult. I have my own life now.

"I don't know..."

Say no. Say it. What's wrong with you?

"It's what's best for Juliet," Vivienne says. "She needs her older sisters."

"I..."

"You can sleep in your childhood bedroom. Redecorate it, for all I care!"

I bite my bottom lip, thinking. Juliet is back at the window, giggling and waving, gesturing like she's inviting someone to come inside. The sight chills me to the bone. Maybe Vivienne is right. Maybe Juliet does need us.

"How long exactly are you expecting me to stay?"

"We don't have to decide that now."

In other words: *forever.*

I groan. "Ugh, I don't know..."

"Briar, have I not given you and your sisters the most beautiful life?"

"Yes, and you like to constantly remind us of it."

Portia holds back a laugh, almost choking on the cornbread in her mouth.

"All I'm asking for is your company," Vivienne says. She steeples her fingers together, her rings twinkling in the light. "And your help during this difficult time. You owe me at least that."

I bite the same spot on my tongue as before and wince. "Fine, but only for a few days, okay?"

"Sure, darling!" Vivienne grins widely, as if she knows she's won. "Oh, I'm so pleased! With this whole nasty vandalism business, I was starting to feel uneasy. It'll be so nice having my girls close to me again."

She'd have us surgically attached to her hip if she could.

I guess it won't be so bad. Lately, I've been spending less time sleeping at the condo and more time on the office couch, surrounded by paperwork, files, and empty ramen noodle cups. I even have a bag of extra clothes stashed in my trunk for nights spent at the office. A change of scenery might do me some good. Although if I had a choice, I'd prefer Paris, Tahiti, or the Seychelles. Somewhere thousands of miles away from here.

I help myself to another serving of catfish, feeling my mother's eyes burning into me. That smug little smirk still tugs at the corners of her lips. *Just a few more days,* I remind myself. *Then I'll have my life back.*

4

My childhood bedroom feels like stepping into a time capsule.

The walls are painted a pale pink, the bed strangled in dainty ribbons and draped in a white canopy. Horse and butterfly decals cover the walls, along with posters of The Backstreet Boys, Britney Spears, Prince.

A portable CD player sits on the foot of my bed and a row of Furbies line my windowsill. There's a desk, a bookshelf, an armoire, and a large circular window straight out of a fairytale with a perfect view of the stars.

I walk over to the large dollhouse resting in the corner of my room, Belville Estate in its miniature form. All four of us have one. A decades-old Christmas present. I kneel beside it, knees sinking into the pristine white carpet, turn the little silver key and crack it open. Though I haven't touched it in years, there isn't a speck of dust. No doubt my mother's doing.

I peer inside, rearranging the tiny furniture and dolls shaped like each of us. When I was little, she'd sneak in at night to fix whatever I'd moved, returning every piece to its rightful place.

I'd watch her through half-opened eyelids as she worked. It

would take well over an hour, her blonde curls glossy in the moonlight. And I wouldn't make a peep, too afraid to be scolded.

I smile, satisfied with the mess I've created. Closing the dollhouse, I twist the little key, and then I hide it beneath the base, where no one will think to look. It's a small act of rebellion, but it makes me feel good. It makes me feel in control.

Something new catches my eye. A framed photo of me and my sisters on my nightstand. We're huddled together in the grass, our awkward limbs thrown around each other, heads pressed together, our hair a tangle of red, black, and yellow. Memories flood my mind—dancing in the rain, staying up all night telling secrets, exploring hidden trails, collecting fossils and seashells, the countless inside jokes we shared.

Portia was the wild one, always pushing the boundaries, while Odette was the responsible and reliable one. She supported me through everything, encouraging me to pursue my dreams, standing by me when I dropped out of NYU.

Oh my God, I think. *I will never, ever see my sister again. She's gone. Forever. This is permanent.*

I can't just call her. Shoot her a text. Drive over to her place. Hug her. We'll never laugh together again. Watch a movie together. Go for a walk together. I can't even ask her how she's doing. But I hope she's doing okay. Wherever she is.

I don't realize I'm crying until a tear hits the glass, blurring our faces. I wipe the glass clean, and as I do, the back suddenly falls off, crashing at my feet. There's a crumpled slip of paper wedged into the frame. Curious, I pluck it free and unfold it, smoothing out the wrinkles. It's an unfinished note, the page warped by water. Or tears. The handwriting is hurried and frantic, but I recognize Odette's big, looping letters and her nickname for me. Most of the words have bled away, but I can still make out two sentences.

B,
She's not who you think.
You're next.

An icy chill breaks out over my body. I shake my head, trying to make sense of it. When did Odette write this? And who does she mean? It sounds eerily threatening. I swallow, blinking away the tears. I barely have time to process it when I notice Juliet peeking around the doorway. "Is it true?" she asks.

I quickly stash the note and the frame in the top drawer of my nightstand, photo side down. "Is what true, sweetheart?"

She blinks, bright-eyed. "Is it true you're moving back home?"

Moving back home. Hm. I wonder where she got that idea from. "Uh... not quite." Juliet deflates before I even finish. "But I am staying for a few days."

She pouts, her long lashes fluttering. "Only a few days?"

"A week," I offer because I can't resist a face like that. "Or maybe two weeks. We'll just have to see, okay?"

Juliet brightens, but she still looks a little disappointed. She prances across the carpet, twirling in her purple tutu. She practices her pirouettes in front of the towering standing mirror, tiny lips pursed in concentration. "You never come visit," she complains openly to me. Her eyes are like daggers. "Is it because you don't like us anymore?"

I'm hurt by her accusation. "No! Of course not. I love you! Why would you even say that?"

A hunch is already forming before she answers. "Vivienne says you don't like us anymore and that's why you never come visit."

Vivienne. Of course.

"Well, that's just not true," I tell her, struggling to keep my tone even. I've been trying to keep the peace, but this is really the last straw. "She shouldn't have said that to you."

"Vivienne says you think you're better than us."

I'm unable to restrain my scoff. "I don't think I'm better than you. I don't think I'm better than anyone! I adore you and I'm happy to spend some quality time with you. It's just that I'm older. You understand that, don't you?"

Juliet shrugs before going back to her pirouettes.

I sigh. "You're welcome to play here while I'm gone. I'll be right back, okay?"

She stumbles into the dollhouse, giggling, and I'm disappointed to see she didn't damage it. Right now, I'd like to destroy it with a hammer. "Okay!"

"Vivienne?" I charge down the hall and bang on her door. I know she hates that, especially when I barge in before she has time to answer. But I do it, anyway, stomping into her bedroom. "We need to talk."

Vivienne sits at her vanity, removing her makeup with a gentle hand. She doesn't look any less flawless without it. "Briar." Her reflection beams at me. "Come on in, honey. What's on your mind?"

I cross my arms, immune to her charm. "Why did you tell Juliet that I don't like you guys anymore, that I think I'm better than you?"

Vivienne chuckles softly as she swivels around to face me. "Well, don't you?"

"No!"

"It sure feels that way, Briar. You never answer my calls or texts. You never come visit. You think you're too good for us, don't you? You always did."

"What?"

"But maybe that's my own fault. I spoiled you girls too much. People warned me about that, but I couldn't help myself. Back in the day, you were too cute for your own good. Everyone thought so." Vivienne adjusts her silk kimono and turns back to the mirror. She fluffs her hair, admiring her reflection. "I don't know what happened. I keep telling you. Try a little eyeshadow. Some blush or lipstick. But you keep insisting you like the bare-faced look." She lets her delicate shoulders rise and fall. "I guess that works... for some people."

"God, I knew this was a mistake," I groan. "I'm not going to do this with you right now."

"Do what? I was being nice. Inviting you to move back home... after all you've been through... and despite *your insistence* to break this family apart." She shakes her head, exasperated, the gesture meant to relay how much of a mystery I am to her. "Us Belville girls ought to stick together."

"Vivienne, I'm thirty-two. An adult. Whether you like it or not. You can't control me anymore. I have my own life. A career!"

"You mean that little non-profit you started? That's such a waste of time!" Vivienne clucks her tongue. "Briar, dear, you're a widow. Trying to fill a hole inside your heart with philanthropy. But you need your family, baby girl. Stop trying to push us away."

The word *widow* stings, and it takes me a second to recover. The place where my wedding band used to sit feels like it's burning, the bare skin tender. Why does she always have to pull the dead husband card? I don't even want to think about Ted right now.

My sister's death makes everything feel fresh again. Ted disappeared too, his face plastered all over the evening news. Eventually, the police found his body, along with a self-inflicted gunshot wound to the head.

"Do you hear yourself sometimes?" I reply, trying to keep my composure. "Like, really, do you hear the words coming out of your mouth? I'm not trying to argue with you. If you'd just listen to me for once. Stop telling Juliet her older sister doesn't like her anymore. She's only seven!"

"She turned eight last month. We had an intimate birthday party in the garden. I called to invite you, but you didn't answer." My stomach drops, and Vivienne raises a thin brow. "Maybe if you came to visit more often, you'd remember your little sister's birthday. You are a part of this family, Briar, whether *you* like it or not."

"I..." I clench my fists. "You're lying!"

"Why would I do that?"

"Juliet's birthday is December 21st."

"Are you sure?"

I hold up a hand. "I'm going. I'm not doing this with you because honestly, you make me feel crazy. What kind of mother tells their young daughter—"

"A damn good one, thank you very much," she replies coolly. She takes her time applying a layer of expensive face cream over her smooth skin. "And how dare you imply otherwise?"

The air in here is thick, the scent of her perfume overpowering. It's her own secret blend, one she's been using for years. I saw her making it once. It looked like a witch's brew, the murky liquid stored in a crystal bottle with an orange blossom cap.

Vivienne eyes me in the mirror. "Sometimes when you speak like that, I wish I'd left you in that dirty meth lab."

She's so *full of it*. That's why the bullshit she fabricates about my past doesn't bother me. At least, not anymore...

Portia and I found our birth parents years ago. Unlike Odette, who had to fly all the way to Russia to find hers, our search was pretty straightforward. All it took was one simple DNA test on a genealogy website.

Both of our birth mothers were teenagers when they made the brave choice to put us up for adoption. Portia's birth mother lives in Kansas, where she teaches at an elementary school. She's married now—to Portia's birth father, actually.

My birth mother is a lawyer in Laguna Beach, happily married with three cool kids I follow on social media. My birth father sells real estate in San Diego. He never married, but his new girlfriend is super nice, and we talk at least once a month.

I made sure to research Juliet's adoption, too. I gathered all the information I could, saving it for when she's older and curious about her Ugandan roots.

Obviously, we never told Vivienne any of this. She'd lose it. Anytime we asked, she'd tell us horror stories about where we came from, emphasizing how fortunate we were that she rescued us from the bleak lives we would have led without her.

I almost want to call her out on it now. Catch her in an obvious lie. Rub it in her face that I've known the truth for years and watch as she unravels.

But I don't get the chance.

Once Vivienne realizes she hasn't hurt me yet, she doubles down, narrowing her eyes in my direction. "Or maybe I should've smothered you in the cradle."

That's another favorite of hers. This time I laugh, which only pisses her off more. "Great. My bedroom door'll be open! I'll leave an extra pillow by the bed just for you!"

Vivienne purses her lips. "Where did I go wrong with you?"

"Should I list the ways?"

She smashes her face cream onto the vanity, finally losing her temper. "Look what you made me do!" she hurls at me, raising her voice. "Get out! Get out of here right now, you ungrateful little brat!"

"My pleasure."

I storm back down the hall. Juliet is still in my bedroom when I return, playing dress-up with the costume trunk at the foot of the bed. The trunk is so old, it smells stale. But my sister doesn't seem to mind. A crown sits lopsided on her head, a feather boa draped around her neck. "I heard you fighting," she says softly.

"We weren't fighting," I lie, itching at the dry skin between my fingers. "We were just... having a heated discussion." I fix the crown atop Juliet's head and smile down at her. "Vivienne mentioned I missed your birthday party. I'm so sorry."

Juliet crinkles her nose. "Birthday? My birthday isn't until December!"

"December 21st, right?" I walk over to my nightstand and retrieve the bottle of heavy-duty hand cream from the bottom drawer.

"Yeah!"

I squeeze some lotion into my hands and rub it in, resisting the urge to pick at the dry patches, the small abrasions between my knuckles. If I'm not careful, my hands will end up looking as beat-up as my tongue by the time I leave here. I shove them into my back pockets, repeating the mantra my therapist taught me inside my head: I am calm and in control, I am calm and in control, I am calm and in control.

If only that were true...

"Huh," I say, turning around to smile at my sister. "That's what I thought."

THE BELVILLE ESTATE SHUTS ITS GATES
BY CAMILA LOPEZ

Bad news, film buffs! The Belville Estate is set to shut its gates to the public for good. The decision follows an unsettling incident in which an individual arrived at the estate in a white van, carrying Molotov cocktails and multiple firearms. Upon apprehension, authorities uncovered maps of the grounds and a series of love letters addressed to Vivienne Belville, the estate's owner.

The security breach has left the actress deeply shaken. While expressing gratitude for the swift response of security personnel and law enforcement, she made the difficult decision to close the estate to public access indefinitely, prioritizing the safety and well-being of staff and visitors. The closure marks the end of an era for Florida and those who once enjoyed the estate's nostalgic film memorabilia from the Golden Age of Hollywood.

—*Everglades Daily News*, August 2004

5

After a much-needed shower, I slip into something a little more comfortable, relieved to finally get out of that sticky dress. It lies in a crumpled pile in the corner of my bathroom, along with my heels and stockings, caked in mud and sand.

Brushing the tangles from my damp hair, I pick up Odette's note from the nightstand. I can't stop reading it. At this point, it's an obsession. I've probably memorized the damn thing by now.

The paper is wrinkled, the pen dragged off the page as if she'd been cut off mid-sentence. It's so damaged I can only make out a few words, the rest of them swallowed by ink.

It's just so strange.

Creepy, even.

You're next.

It's like a warning. As if she was trying to warn me about someone. Vivienne, I'm sure.

How am I supposed to know how old this thing is? There's no date, no anything. For all I know, this note could be as dated as my bedroom. But it's just... what are the chances of me finding it now? It feels like a message from beyond the grave.

I just wish I could ask her myself.

My sister could be so cryptic sometimes. She'd been like that since we were kids. Never expressing her true feelings, always hiding her emotions. Vivienne complained she was cold, but that's not fair. She was just different, more private. And after our childhood in the spotlight, who could blame her for craving privacy?

Sometimes I think that quick shot to stardom fucked us all up for life. Odette was in and out of treatment facilities for depression, on countless medications. Portia and I struggled with substance abuse issues for years. It began in our pre-teens at adult parties where drugs were too readily available. Back when we spent half of each year in California, filming, promoting, doing interviews. A lot of pressure for a young kid.

Then most of my early twenties were a blur, and it took me years to straighten myself out again. So many shady situations. Casual sex with strangers, waking up confused in unfamiliar places, still high from the night before.

We each had our own demons to battle, and it wasn't always pretty.

I trace a finger over the handwriting. It's messy, like she wrote everything down in a rush. But if she had something important to tell me, I'm sure she would have done it in person. Or at least called me, sent a text. Unless... she couldn't for whatever reason.

Stop. You're overthinking this. I know I'll drive myself crazy trying to decipher what my sister meant, so I shove the note back into the nightstand drawer and walk into the hall. I pause outside my door, touching the crystal knob and then the empty keyhole. The key is missing. There used to be a big ornate key here with a pearl grip.

I can almost hear it—the hollow click as it turns in the lock. Vivienne trapped me in here too many times to count. Sometimes when I was misbehaving, and other times just for the hell of it. I hated that sound, my freedom disappearing with a simple flick of the wrist.

I take a step back and check the floor. Maybe it fell. I don't find the key, but I do find something else. Brown stains beneath the door. I crouch down and rub the carpet. They're small and dry and look like droplets of blood.

"Briar, what are you doing?"

I gasp and slap a hand to my chest. Elise stands at the other end of the hall. In her black dress, she could easily pass for a ghost. When she walks closer, it almost looks like she's floating.

"You're jumpy," she points out. In one hand, she holds a stack of gowns set on foam hangers, her elbow slightly bent to keep them from getting wrinkled. I think back to when I was a kid and all the times I used to watch Elise perform her daily chores—ironing clothes, polishing the silver, dusting the endless clutter. I swear if this house were any smaller, Vivienne would qualify as a hoarder.

"Sorry, I don't know what's wrong with me lately," I say, embarrassed.

Elise gives me a knowing smile. "It's strange being home, isn't it? It's going to take some time to settle in again. But it would be easier if you visited more often."

"I've been busy," I reply, trying not to sound too short. I know Elise means well, but I just wish everyone would stop guilting me all the time. I touch the brown spots on the carpet, pointing them out to her. "What's this?"

Elise cranes her neck and adjusts her glasses. "Oh, that? It's only rust." Without having to ask, she answers my next question, gesturing to the empty keyhole. "From your key. I took it to my room to clean it. You know how it is. Everything in this house rusts, and you have to stay on top of it, or it just takes over." She strokes the gowns with her free hand. "Let me give these to your mother and then I'll see if I can find it for you."

As soon as Elise is gone, I search on my phone for *rust stains on a carpet*. Okay, so that checks out. Those *do* look like the same stains. Still creepy, though, that it looks so much like blood...

Once she's back, I follow her one door over to her bedroom, catching a glimpse of what's inside. It's dark, the furniture mostly veiled, like the chandelier in the dining room. Mournful opera music echoes against the bare walls. She stops me with a polite smile before I can step inside. "You wait here."

The door clicks in my face, and I exhale with a huff. Why does everyone in this house have to be so damn mysterious?

I hear her rummaging through her things, opening and closing drawers. I'm about to tell her to forget it when she suddenly opens the door and says, "Sorry, but I must have misplaced it."

I shrug. Come to think of it, that key brings back a lot of bad memories. The thought of my mother possibly locking me in my room while I'm sleeping, trying to keep me here, makes me feel uneasy enough that I'd rather not have it. "Don't worry about it," I tell Elise as I step toward the stairs.

Elise watches me from behind her cracked door. "Anything else?"

"No, that's it. I'm going to look for a snack."

I almost back right into Vivienne. Even before bed, she's dressed elegantly in a floral silk nightie and matching kimono, feathered heels, and a string of pearls. She lifts a manicured finger, looking past me. "Elise, one more thing before you turn in for the night. Please take inventory of the kitchen tomorrow morning. Briar burns through food faster than anyone else in this house. No wonder my supply is so low."

A cloud of cigarette smoke smacks me directly in the face. *Gross.* The hypocrisy of her giving me a hard time about my weight when she's smoking, as if that won't kill her even faster...

I set my hands on my hips. "I see you're back on the cancer sticks."

Vivienne's eyes rake over my body, stopping at my stomach. The look she gives me is so condescending it makes my skin crawl. "Briar, a word of advice. In my day, ladies took proper care of their figure. We avoided bread and pasta and sweets. There was a time, I survived solely on tomatoes and black coffee."

"Oh, yum. Sounds super nutritious."

"I still abide by something called *portion control*. And I refrain from eating after eight o'clock." She gives me a pointed look. "You ought to try it sometime."

God. Sometimes I can't stand her. She's clearly still mad at me about earlier, and honestly, I would just go home if not for Juliet, but I already promised her I'd stay. As much as I want to, I can't leave now. It wouldn't be right.

So, instead, I check the time on my phone and hold it up for her to see. "Did you say eight o'clock? Well, hey, would you look at that? Seems I still have ten minutes left."

Elise covers her mouth, laughing. Vivienne purses her lips so tight I think her face might break in half. Without wishing me goodnight, she slams her door shut and locks it.

"What? I'm still following your advice!" I call after her.

Elise shakes her head, still laughing. "Goodnight, Briar. Try not to press your mother's buttons too hard."

If anyone is pressing buttons around here, it's her. "Night, Elise."

Downstairs, I walk straight to the kitchen. Portia sits at the breakfast nook, hunched over her computer, eyes glued to the screen. She's also freshly showered, her blonde hair still damp. She's wearing silk pajamas with a winding monogram over the breast. So much more luxurious than my extra-large sleeping shirt. The moment she notices me, she slams the laptop shut.

I stop in my tracks. "Yeah, *that* wasn't suspicious at all."

Portia folds her hands in her lap and gives me an innocent look. "I don't know what you mean."

"What were you looking at?"

"Nothing!"

"It doesn't seem like nothing." I lower my voice to a whisper. "You're not watching porn, are you?"

"No!" Portia gasps. She places a protective hand over her laptop as if I'm going to pry it open. "Not that there's any shame in that, of course," she adds. "Every woman should engage in a healthy amount of—"

Cringing, I hold up a hand, cutting her off. "Let's not have this conversation, okay?" I make a beeline for the cookie jar. It's another mini replica of Belville Estate. A hand-painted one our mother ordered from Switzerland. Elise fills it with homemade cookies at the start of every week. This week she baked peanut butter chocolate chip. I take two and pour myself a glass of milk. "Why so secretive?"

Portia sighs, her shoulders slumping. "I fell into the rabbit hole again."

"The... what?" She opens the computer and turns it to me as I sit beside her. Then she shimmies the touchpad to life, and my stomach knots. "Oh."

Dozens of headlines, all with the same theme: **What really happened to Vivienne Belville's four husbands? Another mysterious death at The Belville Estate: Who killed Odette? Why the internet thinks Vivienne Belville murdered her own daughter.**

I nibble at the cookie as I scan through the comments of the Reddit forum she found, trying to process the toxic cesspool that is the internet, total strangers making assumptions about our family.

"Well, shit," I say once I reach the end of the thread. "Looks like we'll be dealing with a new wave of lurkers."

Lurkers. That's what we call the obsessive fans. The ones who camp out front or try to hop the gate. Most of them are harmless. But years ago, we had one pull up to the gate with a truck full of weapons and obsessive love letters addressed to Vivienne. Luckily, nothing happened and no one was hurt, but when you're her level of famous with a notorious past, it's hard not to attract some crazies. Especially in the age of the internet.

Portia winces as if the thought hadn't even crossed her mind. But then she straightens, her bob bouncing as she lifts her chin.

"We don't know that. Everything'll be fine. We just have to remain positive!"

"You're right," I say, overly enthusiastic. "We buried our sister today. Our mother's a narcissistic whack job. And it's only a matter of time before the internet sleuths come knocking at our door with pitchforks. Everything's peachy!"

Portia frowns. "Not helping."

"I know," I groan, rubbing a hand over my face. "I'm sorry. I'm being such a bitch."

I shake out my limbs, trying to chase out the negative energy. It's something our father, Robert, taught us when we were little. Whenever we felt sad, angry, or scared, he had us shake our hands and feet like we were flicking off swamp mud. We ended up calling it the happy dance because no matter how unhappy we felt at the beginning, it was impossible to finish the dance without a smile.

Robert, bless his soul, was a little loony like Portia, into all that self-improvement, spiritual mumbo jumbo. Walking barefoot to reconnect with the Earth. Drinking freshly pressed green juices. Meditating by the water at sunrise. I guess Portia picked some of that up from him.

This is the first time in my life that I've done the happy dance and not felt tempted to smile. I just keep thinking about how Robert and Odette are gone. I never imagined losing them both so soon. Sometimes it feels like this family is cursed. Like this house is cursed.

"You *are* being a bitch, but don't worry, I forgive you." Portia gets up from the table and walks over to the fridge, selecting a pint of ice cream from the freezer. "I could use a drink, but good ol' Ben & Jerry's will have to do."

I react with an exaggerated gasp and slap the table. "*The* Portia Belville, expert on all things wellness, eats Ben & Jerry's just like the rest of us?"

With a grin, she thrusts open a drawer and grabs a spoon. "You can eat whatever you damn well please as long as it makes you happy," she says, sticking her tongue out at me. "I think I'm going to go upstairs, put on a face mask, and watch something absolutely mind-numbingly stupid. Something that requires zero brain power."

"Fun," I say, perking up. "Can I join?"

Portia bites her bottom lip. "Bring the cookies."

UNSOLVED MYSTERIES: VIVIENNE BELVILLE, OLD HOLLYWOOD'S BLACK WIDOW

BY ARIA THOMPSON

Picture this. It's a sunny Monday morning in November 1998. Millionaire investor Robert Wells finishes breakfast with his family, gathers his brief-case, and kisses his wife and three daughters goodbye. He's off on a business trip to Japan. But here's the twist: Robert never arrives. From the moment he steps out the door, he vanishes without a trace, never to be seen or heard from again.

News stations pick up the story, but instead of portraying Belville as a concerned wife, they take a more sinister angle. It turns out this isn't the first time one of Belville's husbands has gone missing. Going back to the early seventies, a troubling pattern emerges.

Musician Nils Hansen in 1971. Film producer Reggie Freeman in 1980. Real estate mogul Darren Hamilton in 1988.

The police get involved, but despite growing suspicions, no solid evidence ever comes to light. Belville retreats from the public eye, shielding her young daughters from the media frenzy that ensues.

Her seclusion helps mend her reputation, but things take a turn in 2015 when Wells' siblings take legal action against Belville. They file a lawsuit alleging her involvement in their brother's disappearance. However, the lawsuit is eventually settled out of court, and no charges have been brought against the actress. Nowadays, the general consensus is torn, but the mystery remains. What really happened? Here's a detailed timeline.

—*The True Crime Chronicle*, 2018

r/TrueCrime
u/Lady-Sleuth109

The Mysterious Death of Odette Belville: Accident or Foul Play?

Giving a quick recap of the article I just read: Odette Belville, aged 38, was a former child star, a dancer with the Miami City Ballet, and a passionate conservationist based in Florida. She dedicated her life to wildlife preservation and funded various initiatives in the Everglades National Park.

Odette recently died at her childhood home, the Belville Estate. But here's where things get weird. Her body wasn't found in the house. It turned up in the swamp that surrounds the property. By the time her family even reported her missing, the body was already badly decayed. Why didn't they report her missing sooner?

I don't know. Feels fishy to me.

The coroner ruled it an accidental drowning after her airboat crashed into the shore. There was water in her lungs. Her skull was crushed in, and her left leg and several ribs were broken.

Thoughts? Curious to hear what everybody thinks.

Comments:

Username: OneLonelyNippleHair74
Idk... Think about it. She grew up there. She's familiar with the area. And those airboats are built like tanks. She would've had to be going at an insane speed and completely oblivious to her surroundings. Do airboats even go that fast? Were there drugs or alcohol in her system?

Username: DeadHousePlant

I'm devastated!!! I still can't believe it. I've been following the Belville sisters since their acting days. I own all their VHS tapes and albums, including the Christmas one!!! I feel so bad for Portia and Briar. Btw, Portia's a guru now, and she posts inspirational videos and yoga challenges on her page. Her Insta is @itstherealportiabelville

Username: cardigan_on_fire

Odette's husband passed away recently, and she's been dealing with depression for ages. I hate to say it, but I really think she just couldn't take it and killed herself. Super sad situation. She was so young.

Username: suspicious_and_fat

Just Google her mother's past, and you'll know this isn't a coincidence. I wouldn't be surprised if she's involved somehow. I'm just waiting for the story to drop.

Username: Worried_Raisin

She killed her. Vivienne did it. Case closed.

Username: terminallycaffeinated

What about Odette's wildlife conservation? It could have made her a potential target. What if her death is connected to her activism? Has anyone else looked into this and which organizations she was involved with?

Username: spicybasilhead

The lizard people are upon us!!!!!!!!!!!!!!!!!!!!!!!!!!!!!!!!!

Username: emotionallyfragilekiwi82

Vivienne Belville is sus. Four missing husbands? No one's that unlucky. She's been getting away with murder since the seventies. The police should reopen all these cases.

Username: VictorianAndroid247
Accidental death? Yeah, right. They planted her body there. Being rich and white must be nice. You can literally get away with murder. Holly-weird strikes again!!

OP: Lady-Sleuth109
Thanks, guys. So, I'm not alone in thinking there's more to the story. I'll keep up with the news, and if you know anything else or want to reach out to me, feel free to send me a DM.

6

It's 3 A.M., and I'm wide awake.

I'm reading Odette's note again. The words have lost their meaning, but I hear each one in my sister's voice, her soft inflection, followed by her throaty laugh.

Now it's just for comfort, to be close to something my sister left behind. Maybe it's my imagination, but I swear it smells like her. I hold it close to my chest, the delicate paper crinkling, and inhale deeply.

With a sigh, I turn over in bed and stare up at the Freddie Prinze Jr. poster plastered on the ceiling, the Reddit post still buzzing inside my head.

She killed her. Vivienne did it. Case closed.

Well, *Worried_Raisin*, I think you're wrong. Vivienne may not be the most maternal of mothers, but she would never try to harm us. What motive would she even have?

It's ridiculous.

I try to tune out the jumbled thoughts inside my head by listening to the sounds of the estate—the creaking floorboards, the hum of the A/C, the frogs croaking in the distance. I reach for my phone and scroll through social media, wondering if I should wait downstairs until the others wake up. But it turns out I don't have to wait long because a face stares at me from my cracked open door.

"Briar," Juliet whispers, her silvery voice sending shivers down my spine.

"Yes?"

Juliet stares at me for an unnervingly long time, her dark eyes piercing through me. "I'm scared," she says at last.

I slip the note back into the nightstand and then I sit up in bed, rubbing my eyes. "Did you have a nightmare?"

Juliet shakes her head. "No. But I need you to come here."

"What is it?" I ask, climbing out of bed. I grab my robe, tossing it over my oversized T-shirt and bunched-up plaid boxers. Juliet doesn't answer me. She takes my hand and leads me down the hall toward her bedroom.

Her room is slightly bigger than mine. Modern. There's a ladder that leads to a platform bed and a slide you can take back down again. I sidestep around a trampoline, a pair of rollerblades, a soccer ball, and a half-finished space puzzle spread across the floor. There's a corner of her room piled with colorful bean bags, a pricey-looking desk chair, and several different gaming consoles. The dollhouse is pressed against the wall, looking neglected. A stack of porcelain dolls and Barbies sits before it, hundreds of lifeless eyes watching me as I cross the room. "So, what's up?" I say, tearing my gaze from them. "Do you want me to sleep in here tonight?"

Juliet tugs me to the window. She gulps, looking scared. "There's someone out there," she says, pointing.

"What?" I yank open the shutters, searching. "Where?"

Juliet shrinks against the wall but peeks out carefully. "Over there. By those trees."

A chill skitters up my spine. "Do you mean by the graveyard?" Juliet nods, and I squint, scanning the property. There's no one out there, and none of the motion detection lights have come on either.

"I don't see anyone." Juliet stares at me, her expression unreadable. "Are you sure it wasn't an animal?"

"Can people come back from the dead?" she asks suddenly, ignoring my question.

"What?"

"If someone dies, can they come back to life?"

"Why are you asking me that?"

"Because I saw her."

My stomach clenches. "Saw who?" Juliet says nothing. She climbs the ladder to her bed and bunches the covers up around her. "Saw who, Juliet?"

"Odette," she whispers as if afraid to say her sister's name too loud.

"No." I comfort her, gripping her small hand. Her blue fingernails shimmer beneath the skylights. "Honey, that's not possible."

"Yes, it is. I took a picture!" My stomach clenches even tighter as she hands me her iPad. "Here. I'll show you."

I stare at the photo as another chill envelops me, turning my flesh tense with goosebumps. I see the outline of her first, a ghostly silhouette, white dress billowing in the breeze. You can barely see her face, it's too blurry to make out the features, but there's a whole waterfall of black hair trailing over one shoulder. It does look like our sister. I can't deny that. But even more unsettling is the fact the figure is standing behind the wrought iron fence.

Inside the graveyard.

I hand her the iPad and hug myself. "Did you photoshop that?"

"No!" Juliet says, raising her voice. "It's Odette, isn't it? It's her. She's back! She came back!"

I wander again to the window, rubbing at my arms. Whatever Juliet had captured on camera, it doesn't seem to be there anymore. "Wait here."

Downstairs, I tug on a pair of rain boots and head out the front door. The motion detection lights flash on blindingly bright, and the humidity instantly takes my breath away. For a moment, I question if I'm still in the house, dreaming, because it feels like being smothered by a pillow.

As I leave the light from the house and trudge into the darkness, I turn on my phone's flashlight and watch it bounce over the trees and the leaf-covered ground. "Odette?" I whisper into the night, feeling silly. A breeze answers me, tousling my hair. It's extra quiet tonight, and somehow that makes me feel even more uneasy.

I pause, listening. I can't tell if it's the wind rustling the fallen leaves or if there's someone moving around out here. I clutch my phone tighter, aiming it toward the swamp.

It seems to go on forever, a maze of trees and misshapen stumps. They cast strange shadows and even stranger reflections. It would be so easy to get lost out there. And it ties my stomach in knots to think about how many nights my sister spent submerged in the black water, hidden just below the surface.

I step back, suddenly engulfed in a cloud of perfume. Something like warm amber and bittersweet tangerine. My body breaks into a cold sweat.

That's *Odette's* perfume.

I adjust the light, shining it out across the water, and something cold and damp wraps around my neck from behind. Tight. Choking. I yelp and trip over my own feet, landing hard on my tailbone and dropping my phone into the leaves. Frightened, I scramble to find it. At the same moment, the motion detection lights go out, plunging me into darkness.

My breath comes in quick little gasps. My hands dig beneath the moist leaves, into the sand, desperately searching. Water splashes, and it almost sounds as if something big is wading toward me. I try to rationalize it, but my eyes make out scary shapes in the shadows. I find my phone and shine the light into the dark, blinking the tears from my eyes. The light bounces all over the place because I can't hold my hand steady.

There's nothing.

I shine the light overhead and behind me, relieved to find the icy sensation around my neck was only moss dangling from the branch above. I blow air out my cheeks, my heart rate slowly returning to normal.

I was sure I smelled Odette's perfume. So clearly, it was like she was standing right in front of me. Shaking my head, I push to my feet and dust myself off. My fingers are still trembling, my heart rate still faster than it should be. Funny how the mind plays tricks on you.

I make my way back to the path and head for the graveyard. Cautiously. Keeping my light trained on the towering iron fence. Statues observe me from the other side, engulfed with strangling ivy. Some of them are crooked or crumbling. They seem to sink deeper into the sand each year. One of them reaches out for me as if it's pleading for help.

Twigs crunch behind me, and my heart pounds in my chest. "Hello?"

There's the feeling that I'm being watched, the hairs at the nape of my neck standing on end. The crunching grows louder... and closer.

I'm not alone out here.

I swing around, aiming the flashlight at the person charging at me from the darkness. "Hey, my eyes!" Portia groans, shielding them with an upraised arm.

Relief floods me. "What are you doing out here?" I ask, lowering the light.

"Following you," Portia says. "I couldn't sleep, and I heard you banging around downstairs." Her brow crinkles as she peeks over my shoulder, searching the shadows. "Where are you going?"

"Juliet saw someone standing outside her window."

"What?" Portia winces. "Are you serious? Why are we out here then? We should call the police!"

A sound like a laugh is carried by the breeze. It's quick and harsh, almost mocking. "Did you hear that?" I breathe, swinging the flashlight back around. "It sounds like it's coming from inside the graveyard."

I'm already hurrying to the entrance when Portia whisper-shouts frantically after me, "Briar! Briar, no. Stop!"

"Shhh!" I shush her as I near the wrought iron fence. There are voices on the other side. Barely audible, but unmistakable. Laughter rings out again, this time sweeter. It almost sounds like me and my sisters when we were younger. I picture us, holding hands, running barefoot over the front lawn. My heart sinks from the memory.

After flicking off my flashlight and pressing a finger to my lips, I attempt, as quietly as possible, to unlock and pull open the gate. Inside, the voices grow louder as Portia and I maneuver between the rows of graves.

"Tell us your name," one voice says, the tone steady and formal.

Portia and I pause, ducking behind a tombstone and peering around the edge. There are three teenage girls gathered around Odette's grave, dressed in long white gowns. Each one wears a cheap black wig, the ends long and tangled, as if they're cosplaying as our sister. Candlesticks surround them, the wicks flickering and basking the area in a warm glow. A Ouija board is placed between them, their hands set upon the planchette.

"It's moving!" the first one shrieks.

The girls read out the letters together:

"O..."

"T..."

"T..."

"E..."

"R..."

The teenage girls burst out laughing. "She spelled her name wrong!"

"She's dead, give her a break!"

More laughter.

I start breathing faster, my heart in my throat. Portia looks like she's choking, and I know why. "Otter" was an old nickname for Odette, one we came up with during a movie night ages ago. We'd shouted the names at each other as they popped into our heads, cracking up the whole time, throwing popcorn. A cherished inside joke between sisters.

Odette was "Otter," Portia was "Pot Head," and I was "Bam Bam." I still have Odette saved in my phone under 'Otter,' surrounded by cute otter emojis.

"Coincidence," I silently mouth to Portia, but even I'm not sure I believe it. I try to find a logical explanation. Maybe I mentioned the nickname in one of my interviews, or maybe Portia or Odette did. Vivienne used to share embarrassing stories about us at events. Those nicknames might have made their way onto the internet. You can find anything there, especially when you search long and hard enough.

"Do you have a message for us?" the third girl calls out, adjusting her white dress to keep it out of the mud. "What do you want to say?"

The girls wait, their eyes fixed on the Ouija board in anticipation. I realize I'm waiting, too. The first answer shook me to the core, unsettling me more than I'd care to admit.

"Where are you right now?"

Probably rolling in her grave, I think bitterly. But as soon as the thought crosses my mind, a sweet scent wafts through the graveyard. It's the same perfume I'd noticed earlier. I cling to the grave, the headstone rough and moist beneath my hands.

"Do you smell that?" I whisper to Portia, but she shakes her head.

The feeling that I'm being watched returns, and I look behind me. It's so dark tonight, cloudy, with barely any light from the moon. The swamp smells especially rancid—a putrid stench like decay. But still, that familiar scent seems to settle over everything.

Portia follows my gaze, scanning the shadowy corners of the graveyard. Her whole body suddenly tenses, her eyes wide. Whatever she sees, I don't, and it takes her forever to tear her eyes away again. *It's all in your head. You want this to be real. You* want *to speak to Odette.* I clench my fists anxiously as the girls ask their next question.

"Tell us about Vivienne Belville," the third girl continues. "Is she really a black widow?" Silence falls over the graveyard. The candlelight wavers as a gust of wind sweeps through the leaves. "Did she put the bodies in, like, a meat grinder?"

"Ew, gross!"

"What? It's a popular theory!"

"I heard she dragged them into the swamp..."

"Yeah, is that why it smells so bad?"

They laugh harder. Portia and I exchange eye rolls as the girls wait for an answer that never comes. They seem disappointed. "Here, let me try again," the middle girl offers, pulling the board closer to her. "She answered me the first time."

"Go ahead, it's not working, anyway."

The middle girl lifts her shoulders and tilts back her head, her voice clear. "Tell us what happened to you," she says, her confidence growing. "How did you die? Were you *bludgeoned* to death?"

Anger rips through me. I'm about to spoil their fun when the three of them shriek, their hands recoiling from the planchette. The middle girl lets out an excited squeal, her eyes alight with the flickering fire. "It moved again! M! It's an M! Put your hands back on!"

"U..."

"R..."

"D..."

"E..."

"R..."

Fuck.

That's it.

The girls let out a terrified scream when they see me rise above the tombstone. They abandon everything. The Ouija board, the candles. One of the girls even loses her wig. They sprint past us, still screaming. "It was her! We brought her back!"

Portia scoffs, crossing her arms. "It's not even Halloween yet, and they're already out here."

I don't respond. My heart is still racing from the girls spelling out the word *murder* and the ear-splitting screams that followed. Portia blows out the candles while I rip the Ouija board in half, patting Odette's headstone as if to say, *sorry*. Sorry for all the drama. Sorry, that after a life of excessive and unwanted attention, my poor sister isn't even allowed to rest in peace. "I should have grabbed one of them."

"They're just kids," Portia says, looking sad as she blows out the final candle. "Stupid kids. Besides, I think we gave them the scare of a lifetime."

"You think?"

"For sure. They won't be back. They thought you were..."

"Yeah," I say, glancing again at the tombstone. "I know."

7

A COUPLE of sleepless hours later, I find myself in the kitchen, brewing a pot of coffee. I can hear Vivienne in her studio, the gentle whirr of the printer, the sink turning on and off. I'm surprised she's up so early, and even more surprised she can work at all. Usually, she's only in the studio when she's happy. When there's something to celebrate. It's strange she's doing it now when everything feels so messed up.

So *wrong*.

I settle at the kitchen island with my coffee and laptop, checking out the home security company the detective recommended in a text the other day. After what happened last night, there's no way I'm putting this off any longer.

I've been telling my mother for years that she's crazy not to have one. We had a full staff of people in the past, both here and in California. Professional security guards, drivers, and even a guardhouse by the front gate with an intercom and ID cards. Sometimes it felt like I was the president's daughter. Or royalty. But as Vivienne got older, she began to retreat more and more, to trust people less and less.

I feel relieved once I confirm my order. There, it's done. They'll send someone over Friday afternoon.

~

At seven, I change into my running shorts, a tank top, and sneakers. I'm craving a way to clear my head, so I hit the trails. It's a little after dawn, the sun slanting golden through the twisted tree branches. It's the most beautiful time of day, the humidity borderline bearable. I pick up my pace, falling into an easy jog. This is one of the things I've missed since moving away from home. The land here. The endless, snaking paths.

Lost in my thoughts, I end up jogging for about an hour, and by the time I'm circling back to the house, I'm so exhausted that I'm confident nothing else can bother me today. Until I notice Juliet playing with one of her dolls on the shore of the swamp. I don't know if it's because of the incident last night or my sleep-deprived state, but my adrenaline instantly spikes. "Juliet!" I shout. "Juliet, you know you're not allowed to play so close to the water!"

Juliet barely acknowledges me. She keeps her eyes on the sand and continues to dig. She's created a small hole. "I was always allowed out before."

"I don't care. Vivienne says—"

"No, *I* don't care!" Juliet shouts, cutting me off. Her little nose scrunches up, and she forces her porcelain doll into the hole until the face cracks. Now I realize what she's doing. She's trying to bury her doll. "Why won't you leave me alone?"

"You cut your finger," I notice, my heart pounding faster at the sight of blood. "Let me see it."

I reach out to inspect her finger, but she yanks away from me. "No, you... you..." Her voice lowers to a growl. "Bitch!"

I gasp, shocked and wounded. "Juliet..."

Juliet's face contorts into something I no longer recognize. "That's what *she* calls you."

"What?" I whisper breathlessly. "Who? Vivienne?"

Juliet shakes her head, her tiny fists clenched. "Odette."

The name knocks the wind out of me. *"What?"*

Juliet glances down at her hand as blood droplets spill from her fingertips. As if she's just now realizing she's bleeding. "Ow."

A million thoughts are racing through my mind. Did Odette really say that to our seven-year-old sister? Should I scold her for cursing? Or should I be understanding? Hug and comfort a child who is clearly mourning and trying to process her emotions?

"C-c-come on, let's go inside," I settle on, the words unstable on my tongue. "Let's clean your cut and get you a Band-Aid."

This time when I reach for her, she drops to the ground and cradles herself, smearing the blood across her dirty knees. "No! I can't!"

"Well, why not?" I ask, exasperated.

Juliet whimpers, leaving traces of tears on her arm. "Because I can't leave Odette."

I try to approach this carefully. "Juliet, sweetheart. Odette isn't here anymore."

"Yes, she is!" Juliet cries. "Don't you see her? She's right there!"

I turn around and look out across the water. "No, I'm sorry, but I just don't see her."

"She's right behind you!"

Despite my skepticism, an icy chill skitters up my spine. "Look. I know what it's like to see things that aren't really there. Sometimes your mind plays tricks on you. But it's only our brains trying to deal with the loss."

"Shut your mouth!"

"Juliet!"

"She's angry!"

"Juliet, this *isn't* funny."

"It's not a joke! It's for real. She's angry, and she wants you to know! She's angry with you!"

Juliet's looking past me, at something I can't see, when suddenly her eyes widen, and she lets out a bloodcurdling scream. Scrambling to her feet, she races back to the house. "Juliet? Wait!" I shout, flabbergasted. "Oh, for God's sake!"

Feeling exasperated, I trek back up the drive and slip into the house, grateful for the A/C.

Elise is leading Juliet upstairs toward her bathroom with the first aid kit in hand. "What did I tell you about being more careful? One day you're going to seriously hurt yourself!"

Thank goodness for Elise. I don't know what we'd do without her. Maybe she can give Juliet the talk about what happens when we die. And tell her that ghosts aren't real. I'm sure she'd handle it better than I would.

I fan myself with my sweaty tank top and head into the other room. Vivienne and Portia are at the dining table, chatting over coffee. Portia smiles at me as I come in, a chunk of scrambled egg stuck to the end of her fork. "There you are! I went into your room to wake you up, but you were already gone."

"I went for a run," I say, taking a seat and reaching for the tray of biscuits. "Had to clear my head."

Not that it did much good. I'm even more flustered now than before I left.

At least Vivienne seems to be in a better mood this morning. She hums softly to herself as she cuts into her egg-white omelet. The light streams in the window, catching on her luminous locks and sharp eyes enhanced by expensive liner. I'm always surprised by how young she looks, her beauty enough to make anyone sick with envy. Sometimes I think she's a vampire.

"Briar, darling?" she says, smiling at me.

I slice open a biscuit and slather it with butter and jam. "Yes?"

"I think we got off on the wrong foot yesterday, don't you?"

I look up at her, surprised. Is she about to... *apologize?* Vivienne never apologizes. I'm actually relieved. I didn't want to spend the rest of the week walking around on eggshells. "I would say so, yes."

I do want to be on good terms with my mother. Sure, she drives me crazy. Sure, she smokes and drinks too much. And sure, she can be a drama queen. She can be overbearing, narcissistic, even cruel sometimes, but she's still the same woman who took care of me when I was sick. The same woman who let me crawl into her bed after nightmares, stroking my back and kissing my forehead. The same woman who threw spa days, movie nights, and dance parties just for me. Who took me to theme parks, concerts, and plays. She always made a big production out of it, dressing me up, doing my makeup, letting me wear her jewelry, blasting music from the speakers.

There have been plenty of good memories here, too. Maybe that's why, even though more than one therapist has told me to cut her off completely, I can't.

I just can't.

Because she's still my mom.

"I know emotions are high right now," Vivienne says, interrupting my thoughts. "But I don't want to fight anymore. I'm just so happy you both agreed to stay here. It's so nice having my baby girls back home again. Isn't it just like old times? I mean, I barely see you anymore. You ignore my texts!"

"Oh, come on, we do not," Portia says.

"Oh, but you do! You can't make time for your poor mama anymore." She pouts. "I've just missed you so much!"

So... not an apology. Another guilt trip.

"We've missed you too, Vivienne," Portia says. She shoots me a look, and because I don't want to fight anymore either, I mumble, "Yeah, we've missed you a lot."

Smiling, Vivienne reaches out and squeezes Portia's hand. "Portia, dear. Sit up. What did I tell you about your posture? Ladies don't slump. And Briar, what in the world is that god-awful smell? Is there a reason you didn't shower before coming to the table?" She's an expert at insulting us with a smile on her face. "I thought I raised you two better than that."

Portia fixes her posture, straightening her shoulders. I take another bite of my biscuit and then wipe my hands on a napkin. I do smell a little sweaty. "Sorry," I say. "Should I go now?"

"Yes, and while you're up there, tell Juliet to come join us, please. I've called and called for her, but she insists on ignoring me." And only because she can't help herself, she adds, "That must be *your* influence."

I polish off the biscuit, ignoring her barb. "Fine," I say with a full mouth. "I'll be right back." I don't bother telling her what happened earlier with Juliet's doll. She'll only find a way to blame me for that, too.

I walk down the hall and climb the stairs, finding Vivienne's studio door hanging ajar at the top. It sways slightly in the draft, almost like it's beckoning me to come closer. It's normally off-limits and locked, but I swear I see someone inside, a dark figure hiding in the shadows. I hesitate for a moment before pushing open the door and stepping inside. "Juliet?" I call, looking around.

I inhale sharply, a rush of adrenaline jumpstarting my heart. Odette stands in the center of the room, looking exactly how she did in life. I'm so startled by the sight of her that I have to cover my mouth to hold back the scream. Tears spring to my eyes as I move closer to the sculpture, touching the material to test if it's made of plaster or real skin. It's hard and cold and rough below my fingers, a reminder that the real Odette is dead. That I'll never see her like this again.

At least not in the flesh.

Is this what Vivienne has secretly been working on?

Toward the back of the room, I find another sculpture. Odette in a coffin, her slender hands resting upon her lap, melting candlesticks and bountiful flowers crowded around her. She looks so peaceful. It almost feels like wishful thinking. We couldn't have an open casket. Odette had been in the water for too long, the swamp quickly and efficiently putrefying her. Half-consumed by wildlife. Vivienne had said she looked so...

A purple-mottled foot pokes out from beneath a white sheet. My heart drops as I rip the sheet away. "Jesus!" I gasp, clamping a hand over my mouth as my stomach lurches.

Odette lies sprawled across a cold, steel table, bloated and unrecognizable. Her pale skin is discolored with bruise-like patches, while in other spots, it pulls away in sheets like from a severe burn. A leg is missing, the torn bone exposed, black with rot. I stumble backward, colliding with the wall, struggling to tear my gaze away from her cloudy, sunken eyes and the gray, swollen tongue protruding from her mouth. Her abdomen is ripped open, the gases that had built up inside her belly burst through the skin, leaving plenty of jellied flesh for the maggots to feast on.

I fall over, vomiting into a nearby trashcan, my entire body heaving.

"What did I tell you about peeking at my artwork before it's finished?" I wipe the bile from the corner of my mouth, disgusted, as Vivienne steps around a large framed photograph leaning against a table. It's of the whole family, smiling together, and it looks so out of place here, surrounded by all this morbid death and decay.

"Art? This is sick," I throw back at her. "For a second, I thought it was real!"

Vivienne chuckles, her curls bouncing above her shoulders. "I'll take that as a compliment."

"It isn't real, right?" I ask softly, still cradling the trashcan. I wouldn't put it past Vivienne to bury an empty casket. Only to keep the real Odette locked inside her studio for inspiration, unable to part with her dead daughter.

Oh, no. Now I'm feeling queasy again.

Vivienne scoffs. "Can you imagine the smell in here if that were true? No amount of air freshener could ever cover it. And don't get me started on the flies." She approaches a smaller sculpture that looks like a little ghost with a white sheet covering it. She tears the sheet away, revealing a sculpture of Odette as a child. She sighs sadly, cupping a cherubic cheek. "She was such a pretty girl, wasn't she? I suppose this is my way of processing the grief."

"I'm having trouble processing this at all," I mutter as I push up from the floor, my legs shaky.

"Oh, come on," she says. "It's art. A way to express myself."

"Couldn't you have found a less disturbing way to express yourself?"

Vivienne frowns. "I thought you'd be impressed."

Her comment catches me off guard. I grip the edge of a nearby counter, staring at her as if she's lost her mind. "Impressed?"

"Well, yes. You could at least give me some credit. I've spent all my time working on these. And when I first started sculpting, I never imagined I could recreate something so perfect from memory alone." She strides over to Odette in her coffin and gazes down at her longingly. It looks like she's about to jump in. "I mean, they're exact copies. I know my girls. I study you. I know the location of every freckle, every blemish. Every sunspot and ingrown hair."

I grasp the counter, inching over to the sink. "Hold that thought. I'm about to vomit again."

"Really, Briar?" Vivienne sets her hands on her hips, annoyed. "You just don't appreciate talent. I'm certain with a little more practice, I could sculpt almost anything."

Acid bites at the back of my throat. "Can you sculpt me a therapist?" I peek over my shoulder at the decomposed version of my sister, and another wave of nausea grips me. "I'm never going to be able to unsee that, so thanks for the nightmares."

"How do you think I feel? I'm the one who had to identify her. Do you even realize how much that image has haunted me?"

Now it's my turn to scoff. "Clearly not enough. Thank God, no one else has to see this."

"Well, actually," Vivienne says. "They're going to be showcased in my upcoming exhibition!"

My mouth drops open. "Please tell me you're joking. You don't really plan on displaying these, do you?"

Vivienne tilts her head. "Well, why not?"

A surge of outrage courses through me. "Do you honestly think Odette would want the world to see her like this?" I ask, raising my voice. "After everything you put us through..."

"What's that supposed to mean?"

"You know exactly what it means." I stalk toward her, my anger intensifying. "Forcing us into acting even though we hated it. Dragging us to auditions, subjecting us to those seedy Hollywood parties where you offered us up to your producer and director 'friends'."

I emphasize the word *friends* with air quotes, fully aware of the predatory nature of those creeps who preyed on vulnerable minors, offering alcohol and drugs, getting a little too handsy.

Vivienne looks exasperated, her eyes widening as she blows out a frustrated breath. "I extended an olive branch to you, but you can't even last five minutes without attacking me or giving me attitude. Why does everything have to be an argument with you?"

"It doesn't matter. You would never understand or even want to understand because everything revolves around you and your feelings!"

"That's not true," she snaps defensively.

"Yes, it is!"

"I have no idea why you're so upset. I did all of this as a tribute to your sister's memory."

"Yeah," I say, covering the bloated sculpture of Odette with the sheet. "Real respectful, Vivienne. I'm sure she'd be thrilled."

The look Vivienne gives me could wilt a flower. She crosses her arms and taps her heel against the hardwood floor. Then, she stands up straighter, as if she's suddenly come to a decision. "I couldn't care less about what you think, Briar. I don't need your approval or your permission. The only person whose permission truly matters isn't here to grant it, and as her mother, I believe I know what's best."

I clench my fists, my blood pressure rising.

Vivienne steps closer, looking me up and down, her lip curled. "By the way, I believe I told you to shower. You look like something the cat dragged in and shat out!"

8

I SCRUB my skin so hard it hurts. The water is piping hot and high-pressure, almost knocking the toothbrush from my mouth. Why did I come back here? And why did I promise Juliet I'd stay for a week? I told myself I wouldn't do that to her. Make promises I couldn't possibly keep. I have no idea how I'm going to handle Vivienne for an entire week.

That *bitch.*

She can't display those sculptures. I won't let her.

I cover my face, trying to erase the images of my sister's bloated corpse, her rib cage exposed and swimming with maggots. I want to scream. *Go away, please just stop thinking about it!*

Feeling nauseous, I rinse the rest of the conditioner out of my hair and then turn off the faucet. The cold air hits me as I step out of the shower, the tiles freezing against my bare feet. I wrap myself in a towel and shiver, still so pissed off from my encounter with Vivienne that every little thing seems to make my mood worse. The cold tiles, the rust on my razor, the toothbrush I just stepped on after it fell to the floor.

Great. Just great!

Annoyed, I toss it into the sink. I can't deal with this right now.

I'm trying to process my own grief, and I can't do that when someone else in this house keeps pushing me past my limit.

I take a moment to de-stress and breathe. Even though I just got back from my run, I have the urge to go again—to keep running until I don't feel anything anymore. Maybe I should request an emergency session with my therapist. I definitely need one.

I move to the small window, staring out at the oak trees and the wide drive that snakes toward the front gate. There's movement near our covered porch. It takes a second for my mind to register it.

Holy shit.

There's a man on our property. Alarm bells ring inside my head. Did he jump the gate? I don't see a car. Everyone is downstairs eating breakfast, including Juliet, who has never experienced the true wrath of a lurker before.

I act fast.

Clutching my towel, I race downstairs, grab a butcher knife from the kitchen, and burst through the front door. I catch the intruder just as he's about to knock. He takes one look at me in my towel, dripping wet, slashing the knife, and he stumbles back, raising his hands. A cloth bag hangs from his thumb and I wonder if he's got a gun inside. "Stay back!" I warn him. "You're trespassing on private property!"

"Whoa, h-hey," he stutters, keeping his distance. "I'm staying—" He blinks, recognizing me at the same moment I recognize him. "Briar?" he says, breathless.

My grip on the knife weakens. "Owen?"

No. This can't be the Owen I remember. My best friend. My first kiss. My first everything. I look him up and down, barely believing my eyes. This man must be 6'5" at least, his face lined and hardened. And he's...

He's...

"You're bald," I blurt out, squinting at his shaved scalp.

He cocks his head to the side and raises a dark brow. "You're naked." An easy smile spreads across his face. "I see you haven't changed."

I lower the knife, shaking my head incredulously. "What the hell are you doing here, Owen? The last I heard from you, you were in..." I stop short, heat rising up my neck.

"Prison?" he finishes for me.

I deflate a little. "Well, yeah."

Owen nods, watching me. He clears his throat. "Last I heard, you were marrying some trust fund baby named Theodore Bolton the Third."

I swallow. The empty spot where my wedding band used to sit burns fiercely above my knuckle. I itch nonchalantly at the skin. "He's dead."

Owen's smile drops. "Briar, I didn't realize. I'm sorry." He glances over my shoulder as someone else steps out onto the porch.

Portia comes to stand beside me and smiles brightly at him. "You're back!"

I shoot her a look. *Back?* He's a regular here? I didn't even know he'd been released!

She ignores me and gestures to the cloth bag. "Hey, I love that farmers market. Their tomatoes are insane."

Tomatoes? Are we really talking about tomatoes right now?

"Girls, please. You're hogging up the entryway." Vivienne glides in between us and strikes a pose like she's found her stage mark. "Come on in, Owen. There's breakfast on the table if you're hungry." She winks at him. "How was the family reunion in South Carolina?"

"Strange. Everybody's changed so much." Owen shifts his weight, his jaw tense. "I would've come sooner, but I didn't hear the news right away. Then by the time I got in last night, it was already late, and I didn't want to disturb anyone."

Vivienne waves a hand. "You couldn't disturb a leading lady on Oscar night. Oh, and we received your lovely flowers. Yellow roses, just like I asked. Odette would've loved them!"

An irritated vein throbs in my temple. When Vivienne notices me, her eyes nearly double in size. "Do I need to place you in an institution?"

I glance down at my nakedness, my cheeks burning as I pull the sagging towel tighter around me. Elise stands in the doorway, gawking at me, and Juliet peeks around her, covering her mouth to hide her laughter.

Vivienne shakes her head at Owen. "You'll have to excuse that one. I'm not so sure she's of sound mind."

Portia drags me to the side and whispers, "Don't listen to her. After last night, no one can blame us for being a little jumpy."

Okay, even *I* know that wasn't "a little jumpy." With the way I was swinging that butcher knife around, that was more like "lock her in a padded room and throw away the key." That's what this house does to me. It turns me into a raging lunatic.

Owen gives me a polite smile as he follows Vivienne and Elise inside. The kind of smile you give to your neighbor when you pass each other on the way to the mailbox. It's infuriating!

"Nice seeing you again, Briar," he says.

"'Nice seeing you again'?" I repeat in disbelief. "Is that all he has to say to me?" I spin around on Portia. "Why didn't you tell me he'd be here?"

"Because you two have unfinished business, and you're always looking for reasons to avoid coming home." Portia shrugs apologetically. "I guess I didn't want to give you another one."

"I would've come anyway."

"Are you sure about that?"

"Yes!"

I can tell by the look on Portia's face that she doesn't believe me.

"Well, how long has he been out?" I ask.

"I don't know. I think he said ten months. Maybe a year?"

"A year?" I cry.

I can hear him inside, checking out what's for breakfast, chatting with Vivienne. Laughing with her. My heart sinks into my stomach. Oh, to hell with it. I've already made a fool of myself. I charge into the house after him, returning the knife to the block and following him out the back door. "Hey, hold it! I'm not done with you yet!"

I'm instantly blinded by the light coming off the pool, sunlight bouncing off the ripples in refractions. Owen glances over his shoulder at me and raises a brow. "Don't you want to put on some clothes?"

"No, I *want* some answers," I inform him as I hurry across the pool deck, the stone tiles scorching my bare feet.

Owen holds the door to the guesthouse open, waiting for me. It's beautiful back here, and the only part of the estate that doesn't trigger my OCD. It's newly renovated and painted a pale sea salt blue, the shutters crisp and white. Magnolia trees shade the house and delicate petals spot the winding cobblestone path. It's a charming little cottage set right beside the pool and tucked into the garden, overgrown with climbing roses and bushels of blue hydrangeas.

It usually has a calming effect, but right now it does nothing for me. "You fucking asshole!"

Owen laughs, surprised. "Wow," he says, crossing his arms. "We're doing this right out of the gate, huh?"

I resist the urge to fling him into the pool. "I wrote you!"

He looks genuinely confused. "What?"

"I wrote you letters!" I explode. I catch my towel just before it falls. "Dozens of them! I sent you Christmas cards! Easter cards! Birthday cards! I begged you to write me back! I had no idea if you were okay!" I shake my head, even more pissed off that I'm getting choked up over this. "Or how you were doing in there!"

"I never got your letters, Briar." Owen looks angry, but not at me. He scoffs, chuckling bitterly, and looks up at the sky.

"What? But that doesn't make any... sense." My heart beats faster, my mind going directly to my mother. I almost march back into the house and demand an explanation. But then I realize it couldn't have been her doing. I was already away at college when I sent those letters. My whole body deflates, the anger whooshing out of me. I rack my brain, my eyes darting back and forth, as I try to figure out where I went wrong. "Wait... Do *you* know who did this?"

"Let's just say, I wasn't exactly inmate of the year," he admits with a shrug. "I made a lot of enemies with the higher-ups."

"How could they do something like that? I should sue them!"

"Don't waste your time or energy. It's not worth it, trust me." He looks over my face, smiling. "But it's nice... knowing you wrote."

My cheeks are burning so I push past him. Inside the guest-house, I'm confronted by a half-open black duffel bag, a blazer and button-down hung in the armoire. Work boots, sneakers, and a pair of polished leather shoes are arranged beside the door.

I pad across the room, taking in the neatly made bed, the ironing board tucked in the corner, a stack of perfectly folded shirts set on the nightstand. I peer into the kitchen, surprised at how clean it is, the dishes washed, the countertop sparkling.

This is an entirely different Owen than I'm used to—that shy boy from deep in the swamp with wild hair and thrifted clothes that barely fit him, covered in mud, his laugh louder than the singing cicadas.

When I turn around, he's still watching me, curious. It *has* been almost fifteen years since we last saw each other...

Despite everything he's been through, he looks good. He's dressed casually in jeans and a black T-shirt, a thick silver watch wrapped around his left wrist. Roman numerals curve along the length of his forearms, some of the tattoos on his biceps so rough and faded I can barely make out what they are.

The bald head suits him, as does the five o'clock shadow. He smells nice too, like leather and musky cologne. I can't tell what he's thinking, his expression stern and unreadable, his intense blue eyes making my pulse spike even higher.

Oh, right. I came here for answers, and I'm not leaving until I get them.

"So, what?" I persist once I've found my voice again. "You're just living here now? In my mother's guesthouse? Like, you two are besties or something?"

Owen's eyes twinkle in amusement, and for a moment, I see the old him shining through. But there's still a slight edge to his voice. He's way quicker to offend than before. Or maybe that's just how he sounds now. Like he's constantly on the defense. "Besties?" he repeats.

I nod, standing my ground. "Yeah."

"Sure," he concedes, stepping closer. "We stay up late, binge-watch reality TV, braid each other's hair." He runs a hand over his shaved scalp to emphasize that last comment.

"Are you sleeping with her?" I whisper, suddenly scandalized by the possibility.

Owen releases a noise between a choke and a laugh. "You're joking, right?"

A wave of relief washes over me. I tug my towel higher and cross my arms over my chest. I already feel the hair on my shoulders drying, curling into chaotic ringlets. "It's just... given our history... and everything I've told you about her..." I shake my head, irritated. No one thought to say anything to me. And after all those years I spent crying to him about my mother, he chose to go to her instead. Part of me wants to beat him with that black duffel bag of his. It *is* big enough to fit a body.

"Look," he says gently, putting up his hands. "When I got out of prison, no one wanted anything to do with me. All because of a stupid decision I made as a kid."

A first-degree felony, with a sentence of fifteen years to life for drug possession and intent to sell. I saw it on the news when it happened, not long after I left for NYU. I was about to embark on my freshman year while he was awaiting trial in a jail cell. I remember I begged him to let me pay for an attorney and post bail, but he refused. And not long after that, he refused to speak to me at all.

I did help out his grandmother, though. The woman who raised him. Every now and then, I sent her some money to cover groceries and those ridiculously expensive arthritis meds—ironically, Owen's main reason for getting into trouble in the first place.

I just can't get over how strange it is to see him again. Not only does he look like a completely different person, but the way he carries himself has changed, too. It's intimidating... and not just because he's massive and hulking with scary prison ink everywhere. It's like he's always on alert, his shoulders stiff and his hands curled into fists, ready to jump some guy if he has to.

I soften a little, trying to put myself in his shoes. It must have been rough in there. Fourteen years behind bars is a long time.

"How did you get out early anyway?" I ask. "I'm guessing it wasn't for good behavior. You've always been better at breaking rules than following them."

Owen's mouth quirks, but there's no humor in it. "My lawyer argued I was wrongfully convicted. It took years, but I guess someone finally decided to cut me a break."

"Well, good," I say. "I'm glad."

"Me too."

We're quiet for a moment. There's something in his eyes I can't quite read, and my stomach does a small, traitorous flip. I pull the towel higher over my cleavage, heat rising up my neck. "So you *are* living here?" I say. "Did she reach out to you or...?"

"I ran into your mom in town, and she was nice enough to offer me work around the house. Patch things up here and there, fix the leaky roof." He gestures to his bag on the sofa. "She's letting me crash here until I finish building the house."

"You're building your own house?"

Owen nods. "Should be move-in ready next month."

"That's incredible, Owen," I say, genuinely happy for him. "I'd love to see it sometime."

"Sure."

A stretch of awkward silence follows. My neurotic brain breaks it. "Are you sure you're not sleeping with her? I mean, you can tell me if you are. Vivienne never does anything without strings attached."

"To the best of my knowledge... no." He studies me as I wander around the room. I'm genuinely impressed by his cleaning skills and the fact that he actually uses an ironing board.

My gaze shifts to the work desk behind me. It's organized with papers, notebooks, and photographs. "Oh, my gosh. Owen, are you writing again?"

He tucks his hands into the back pockets of his jeans and nods.

"Short stories?"

"A novel."

"Wait... seriously?" I say. "What kind of books are we talking about here? Political thrillers? Horror? *Romance*?" My eyes land on a picture of me and my father at the zoo. "Hey, where'd you get this?"

Before I can reach for the photo, Owen hurries over to the desk, shuffling it out of sight. "Sorry about the mess."

I laugh. "What mess?" I quickly find the photo again and turn it over, checking for my mother's delicate cursive on the back. *Robert and Briar at The Bronx Zoo. 1995.* "Did Vivienne give this to you?"

"That's the book I'm working on," Owen admits, clearly uncomfortable. He holds the back of his neck. "Vivienne asked me to help her with a memoir."

My mouth falls open. *Oh, no. I found the strings.* That's so typical of Vivienne. She's always been weird about strangers. She likes to avoid outsiders, keeping the ones she trusts close. Like Elise. She's even reluctant to hire maids or landscapers, afraid they'll take advantage of her. No wonder she asked Owen to ghostwrite her memoir. It gives her full control over the narrative and ensures no renowned ghostwriter or journalist steals her thunder on the cover.

God. She's so predictable.

I think about warning Owen and explaining how manipulative

Vivienne can be, but it feels like overkill. Owen's a big boy now. He can protect himself. He knows what he's getting into. I just never thought he'd agree to work for her after everything I told him.

"And how's that going?" I ask instead, trying to keep my tone non-judgmental.

I fail miserably, but Owen politely ignores my skepticism. "Good, so far." He shrugs. "It might be a way to get my foot in the door."

I give him a look. "Owen, I've read all your short stories. You don't need my mother to open any doors for you."

We exchange a smile, and I hand him back the photo. "By the way, I'm sorry. You know, for my not-so-warm welcome."

"Already forgotten."

I glance down at my towel and sigh. "I should get dressed." I feel awkward as I stand there considering whether or not to give him a hug. It's like I don't even know how to act around him anymore. He's a stranger, and I have to get to know him all over again.

I walk to the door and then offer him another small smile. "I can't get over how weird this is... but I guess I'll be seeing you around. Just let us know if you need anything, okay?"

Owen fidgets with the photograph, his thumb running over the glossy finish. It looks like there's more he wants to say, but he returns my smile instead. "Will do."

Selected Diary Entry from Briar Rose Belville

Written on Sunday, May 20th, 2008

Dear Secret Keeper,

You won't believe what happened!

I thought I'd be freaking out, but weirdly, I'm super calm. Like, I know I made the right call, even if it seems crazy. It's as if my whole world is about to change, but in the best way possible!

Okay, let me rewind a bit. I'm going to try and write everything down exactly as I remember it, starting Friday afternoon. We were in my room, and Vivienne covered my eyes and led me toward the bed. Even though it was supposed to be a surprise, I already knew what it was. My prom dress! The one we'd picked out together at the mall. I was bouncing in place as she moved her hands away and my vision adjusted.

My heart fell into my gut.

I was speechless.

I could feel Vivienne's eyes burning into me. She was relishing every moment, and I was trying so hard not to give her the satisfaction. "It's not the dress," I said.

She actually tried to act all innocent. Maybe it would have fooled someone who didn't see right through her. She shrugged, pretending to be shocked as she inspected the dress closer. "What do you mean it's not the dress? This is the one we picked out together."

I was breathing faster, and I could feel the tears coming, but there was no way I was about to cry in front of her.

"This isn't the dress I tried on. It's too small. You returned the other one, didn't you? And bought the one that wouldn't fit me. To make some twisted point!"

She fluttered her stupid eyelashes, still pretending to be shocked. She isn't as good an actress as she thinks.

"The dance is tonight! You do know that, right?"

Finally, she admitted the truth. "Briar, I can't help you if you refuse to help yourself."

"What?"

"I've told you for months now to start dieting, and you never listened to me. If you'd kept track of calories and fit in a couple of salads every once in a while, you'd have a dress to wear to prom tonight."

I expected to be mad. What I didn't expect was to feel so helpless. My own mother just shattered my heart, and all I could do was burst into tears. I'd never felt so low in my entire life.

So, I ran. Because I needed to be as far away from her as possible.

I pushed past her and ran, sobbing all the way down the stairs and across the lawn. I couldn't stop running, even when my lungs were burning so fiercely I was certain they'd catch fire. Not until I saw the brown shack on stilts and Owen sitting on the dock. His legs were dangling over the edge, his dark hair ruffled, a Polaroid camera raised to his squinted eyes.

It wasn't until I got closer that I realized he was taking pictures of the spoonbills. There were three lined up perfectly in the water, searching for dinner, and my muddied bare feet stomping over the creaky wood panels of the dock startled them away.

Owen blinked at me, lowering his camera into his lap, noticing my distress. He exhaled, his brows knitting together in concern, as he pushed to his feet. "Briar," he said. I could barely hear him above the cicadas, but I could read his lips. I broke into a jog again, the tears still falling, and Owen dropped his camera.

He reached out for me, and I hit him so hard we both spun around. He held me against his chest. "It's okay," he whispered into my hair as he embraced me. "Tell me what happened."

The sunset was blurry. One big glob of orange and red smeared across the sky. It was beautiful and intense, like being caught in a wildfire.

I didn't know why I felt so safe there. Or why I felt like I could tell him everything. But it poured out of me all at once, the words seeping into his shirt along with the tears and snot. "I was looking forward to the dance for months, and you know me, I don't even care about stupid dances like this, but Vivienne seemed so excited about it. It was all she was talking about. She took us for a spa day, and we got our nails done, and she let me pick out any dress I wanted, no matter how expensive. I thought we were having a good time. I thought she cared about me, that she loved me. But she only wanted to hurt me."

I've replayed our visit to the department store a hundred times inside my head. When I walked out of the changing room in that dress, did I misread her expression? Instead of pride, was it jealousy? Did she only make a big deal out of the dance to be cruel?

I just don't get it!

Somehow we ended up sitting on the dock. I was half in Owen's lap, my head resting on his shoulder, and he was cradling me. He stroked my hair lovingly with gentle fingers that tickled my scalp and sent shivers down my spine.

He was quiet that night. "You're shaking," I realized. I lifted my head to look at him, surprised to see how angry he looked.

"You know I'd do anything for you, right?" he said in a low voice, his fingers trailing down to caress my cheek. I nodded as his thumb wiped away one of my tears. He gripped my chin, his blue eyes boring into mine. "I mean it, Briar. I'll always protect you. No matter what."

"I know."

"I'd kill for you."

I nodded. "I know."

"You could come live here. With me," he said. "You could run away. No one has to know where you are."

I couldn't believe he offered it to me, Secret Keeper! Living with Owen would be amazing. I'd never cry myself to sleep at night again. I'd finally be happy for once. I'd never have to deal with Vivienne ever again.

But some dreams are just too good to be true...

"You don't think they'd find me? Vivienne would have every news station on our front porch if I don't show up by tomorrow morning." My lower lip quivered. "She may like to bully me, but she also likes to keep a tight rein."

"You're not happy there." He was so angry that his cheeks had gone all red. "I see what she does to you. It's like she's draining the life right out of you." I was shaking then too because I knew he was right. "It's not only how she treats you. Or the names she calls you. It's having to worry every day she's going to drink and terrorize you. Aren't you tired of it?"

His thumb caught another tear, and I gripped onto him like a lifeline. He was the only thing keeping me from drowning. "Of course, I am. But I can't leave my sisters. You know that." He nodded, holding me close. "I know you're trying to help, but I just can't."

"Then I'll be here for you," he promised. "I'm here."

He held me until the sky turned purple and the stars peeked out. I watched the reflections on the water. The ripples the swamp snake made as it slithered across the surface, the sawgrass as it swayed on the shore, the baby gator as it swam between the cypress trees. I was so exhausted from crying that I didn't even bother swatting the mosquitoes that swarmed me. I didn't care enough to fight them.

Owen stirred, rousing me from my depressive reverie. "I have an idea."

I twisted around, watching curiously as he padded down the dock toward his house. He glanced over his shoulder at me with a crooked smile. "Close your eyes, okay?"

"What are you up to?"

"It's a surprise."

I smiled and covered my eyes. It felt like an eternity had passed.

I could hear him walking up and down the dock. "How much longer?"

"I'm just about..." There was static and then music played. Bonnie Raitt's "Angel from Montgomery." "Ready."

I opened my eyes and turned around. "Oh, my gosh," I laughed, my mouth falling open. "Owen, you didn't!"

The whole dock was lined with white candles and rusty lanterns! He had even turned on the string lights that hung criss-crossed above us, dotting the water with luminescent, rippling orbs. It was like the spirits hidden within the swamp had risen to watch us dance. My eyes welled up. This time they were happy tears. He had done all this for me?

Owen grinned. He ran a hand through his dark curls, looking satisfied. "You like it."

I couldn't stop smiling. I'm still smiling now, even as I write this.

"I do."

He extended his hand and cleared his throat. "Ahem. Care to dance, miss?"

I laughed. "You bet!"

I grabbed his hand, and he pulled me close, twirling me around. We stared into each other's eyes, grinning like idiots. "Why, Miss Briar Rose, you just might be the prettiest girl at prom!"

I threw my head back and released a belly laugh.

"You're such a dork!"

Owen's laughter joined mine. We were hugging more than dancing, swaying and spinning, our fingers tightly intertwined. "But you make me so happy," I admitted, surprising myself.

That's just how it is with him. I can tell him whatever is on my mind. No matter what.

"You make me feel like..." Owen hesitated, his eyes sparkling in the light. Without warning, he lowered his head and kissed me. It was so romantic.

Obviously, it wasn't the first time we ever kissed. We've made out plenty of times before, even came close to going all the way, but

I always told him I wasn't ready yet. This time, though, felt different.

"You make me feel like I can do anything. Like I'm invincible." He said it so seriously that I didn't know how to respond. I stared up at him as he brought my hand to his mouth, his eyes not leaving mine. He nibbled at the corner of my finger before kissing the spot his teeth had just grazed.

"Marry me."

"What?" I gasped.

"I want you to marry me."

"I heard you, it's just..." I shook my head, my heart suddenly thumping so hard I could barely hear myself think. "We're too young!"

"We'll be eighteen soon."

"What about school? I've been accepted to college."

"Then go. But come back after. We can live here." He stroked my cheek. "And I'll take care of you. I'll make sure you always feel loved and protected."

"Owen."

"I'm serious."

"I know you are."

"So, marry me."

I laughed and cried and then kissed him harder than I ever had before. "You're supposed to drop down on one knee, silly."

Owen laughed. "Is that a yes?"

I beamed as he covered my face in kisses. "You already know it's a yes."

This morning, I had breakfast with my sisters and Elise. The sound of Vivienne grunting in her sleep filtered through the house. She had passed out by the pool again, wearing one of her designer dresses and a tiara, cradling an empty bottle of vodka with a thick circle of red lipstick staining the neck. Sometime later, I hitched a bus to Macy's and returned the dress, requesting cash. When I handed it over to Owen, his eyes widened. "I can't take this," he said, forcing it back to me. "This is more money than I've ever seen in my life."

"It's two grand. Enough money to buy your grandma's medication." The pain from Willa's arthritis is sometimes too much for her to bear, and they don't have insurance.

Owen shook his head. "I can't take this from you, Briar. It's too much."

I sighed, growing impatient. I'd buy the medication myself if I had to. "Please. Just this once."

Owen didn't look at the money. He held eye contact with me. I could stare into his eyes all day long.

"Fine. But I swear on my parents' graves, I'll never take anything from you again. I have something else lined up, and I know it's going to fix everything. All I need is you." He lifted my chin and kissed me, and then we just couldn't stop kissing each other.

I love him. I love him. I love him.

I LOVE OWEN AND OWEN LOVES ME! I'm sorry, I sound so stupid and crazy, but WOW!!!!!

I'M SO EXCITED! MY LIFE IS ABOUT TO START!

A new life. A better one.

God, I can't believe it. I'm not going to be a Belville anymore. I'm going to be known to the world as Briar Rose Greene!!!! Doesn't that sound perfect?

I know we're young and dumb, but I've never felt so sure of anything or anyone in my entire life. ~~And I have so much more to write you about that night and what Owen and I did after, but I'm already so afraid Vivienne finds this and reads everything, and it kinda felt like someone was watching us in the woods when we were having sex.~~ I have to be so, so, *so* careful...

With all my heart,

B.

9

ALL THESE OLD memories leave a bitter taste in my mouth. Owen proposed to me only a few weeks before I left for university. He crafted a ring out of twigs, promising that he'd find a way to buy me a proper one someday. By any means necessary.

I kept it after all these years, tucked safely in the back of my jewelry box. Whenever my marriage hit a rough patch, I'd take it out and think about happier times, wondering what might have been.

And even though I know I wasn't the one to push him into doing anything illegal, I still can't help feeling that I was partly to blame.

I'm in my bedroom now, the towel tossed aside, trying to figure out what to wear. Originally I was going to opt for sweats and a T-shirt, something comfortable to lounge around the house in, but with my ex here, as pathetic as it sounds, I'd rather not wear anything baggy. Especially when he looks like... well... *that*. How did he spend his days in that cell? Constantly doing crunches and pull-ups?

My closet's a disaster. It looks like someone's been digging through my clothes and trying stuff on. Portia used to steal my clothes all the time when we were teenagers. But if I touched anything of hers? All Hell broke loose.

Sisters.

With an annoyed sigh, I pluck the emerald dress from its hanger, the one Vivienne ordered, and hold it up in front of me, mentally trying it on. I'm still triggered by the memory of my mother sabotaging prom night, but all my nice clothes are at the condo, and this dress is all I've got.

I slide the dress on and study my reflection in the mirror, shifting from side to side. As expected, it's not really my style. It's too long, too lacy, too grandma. It's like wearing a doily. I wouldn't mind showing a bit more skin, maybe some cleavage, or just a hint of it. Well, at least this time, she got the size right.

I don't *hate* this dress. But I do shrug on a black leather jacket and slip into a pair of studded ankle boots to make the look a little edgier. Hmm, not bad. And not totally off from what I'd actually wear. Satisfied, I head downstairs.

"Wow! You look good!" Portia says as I swing around the banister. She's just got back from dropping Juliet off at school, her short hair combed into a perky ponytail, her gym clothes on. She sets her purse and keys in the foyer, then looks me up and down, impressed.

I strike a pose. "Thanks! I wanted to make an entrance."

We move into the kitchen. Vivienne turns to look at me and her eyes brighten. "The color suits you so well," she compliments, her lips curving into a genuine smile. Then she ruins it. "So much better than black, which entirely washes you out. The only good thing about black is that it's slimming." She puckers her face at my jacket, her disapproval evident. "But what's this?"

"What?" I ask innocently, batting my lashes at her. "Don't you like it? I thought it was a nice touch."

"On you, no. On a hooker, maybe. A hooker that doubles as a trashy biker chick."

"Vivienne!" Portia gasps.

I ignore the rude remark, flipping my hair over one shoulder. "It's okay. I know I look good."

"Dressing up for anyone in particular?" Portia says with a smirk.

"No! I just didn't want to look like a total slob."

Portia laughs. She mouths to me, *You lying slut!*

I widen my eyes in mock outrage. "Excuse me?"

"Come on, admit it," she says. "Your old flame is back, and you've got the hots for him. Again!"

"I mean, sure, he's not bad looking. But that's not the reason I dressed up."

Portia walks over to the window by the back door and peeks past the drapes. The other women gather around her. "He's giving serious villain vibes. All he's missing is a black turtleneck and a fluffy white cat in his lap. Very James *Bond*-esque," she says.

"Or a hitman," Elise offers. "A sexy hitman."

We all look at her, surprised, like we didn't even know she had ovaries.

"I don't know what you two are talking about," Vivienne says, running a red nail across her bottom lip. "I think he looks deliciously rugged, like he knows his way around a car or a motorcycle."

"Yeah, I'm sure that man can change a tire," Portia agrees.

"I'll tell you what," Elise says. She makes a show of patting down her silver Bettie Page bangs and taking off her red-framed glasses, pretending she's wiping off the condensation from the lenses. "He could change my tires any day of the week. I wouldn't mind at all."

They're all giggling together.

I stare at them like they've lost their minds. "What does that even mean?" I explode, stomping toward the window. I slam the shutters closed and draw the curtains, ignoring their barrage of protests. "Can we please stop objectifying the poor man?"

"Oh, right. He's not your type anymore," Portia says bluntly.

"You like the *assholes*. Guys who'll treat you like a doormat. I guess Owen's too nice for you."

I'm insulted, but mostly because what she's saying is true. I open my mouth to respond, but nothing comes out.

She gives me a look. "Please. You know I'm not wrong. Would it kill you to be interested in someone friendly for once?"

"You shouldn't speak ill of the dead," Elise chastises her.

"Why not?" Vivienne says as she sits at the breakfast nook. She parts the drapes, her eyes on the guesthouse. Elise and Portia join her, fighting to see. "Her late husband was a very bad man."

"Just because Ted didn't like to hang out with his father's crowd, doesn't mean—" Elise starts, but is quickly interrupted.

"It has nothing to do with social status or connections. He was an ass, and even Briar can do better than him."

"Wow. Appreciate that," I mutter.

"It's true. I never understood what you saw in him. It was a blessing what happened to him. A blessing in disguise, but a blessing all the same."

"You're right," I admit, surprising everyone. I lean against the marble island, glaring at Vivienne. "It *was* a blessing in disguise. But I don't have to tell you that."

"He's coming!" Elise cries suddenly, and all three women dive away from the window, pretending to busy themselves. Elise grabs a broom and hastily sweeps the floor. Vivienne pops open the fridge and taps her chin, picking up a jug of milk and checking the expiration date. Portia starts a pot of coffee.

I roll my eyes.

Owen sees us through the glass and steps inside. He's holding the cloth bag from the local farmers market.

Everyone greets him, smiling, as he sets the bag down on the counter. "I almost forgot. I picked you up some oranges, mangoes..."

"They're so ripe!" Vivienne gasps, admiring them as he unloads the bag into the fruit bowl. "You spoil us."

See? Friendly, Portia mouths to me, and I narrow my eyes at her. "Yeah, thanks, Owen," she says, turning away from me and plastering on a sweet smile. "Can we repay you with a cup of coffee?"

"No, thanks. I'm going to get started on the yard before it gets too hot."

"Be careful now." Vivienne strokes his bicep, grinning. "Wouldn't want you to wither out there."

"I'll be alright." Owen's eyes briefly connect with mine, but not before I notice the little pause, as if he didn't *want* to look away. I feel a thrill in the pit of my stomach, an electric shock I haven't felt since I was a teenager.

Vivienne catches it too, but instead of commenting on it after he leaves, she frowns. "Actually, Briar," she says, pulling out her compact to touch up her makeup, scrutinizing her reflection in the mirror. "I've changed my mind." She struts toward the parlor, her stilettos tapping along the wood floor. "I think black suits you much better."

10

THAT NIGHT, I startle awake with the feeling I'm not alone. I sit up in bed, the damp sheets tangled around my legs. My heart is racing, and it pumps even faster when I realize there's someone standing in the doorway. I can see the outline of them in the darkness, as if they were watching me in my sleep. "Vivienne?"

The door slams shut, sending my heart into my throat. There's no sign of retreating footsteps. It's like whoever's out there is waiting on the other side.

I throw off my covers and reach for my robe, chills prickling my skin. "Vivienne?" I call out louder. "Is that you?"

For whatever reason, I have the horrible feeling it's not Vivienne.

I jump out of bed, tie the robe around my waist, and reach for the door. I'm seconds away from touching the handle when footsteps thunder down the hall, causing the little hairs on the nape of my neck to stand on end. I jump back as if I've touched something hot, frightened, before tearing open the door and flicking on the lights.

There's no one.

No one's out here.

I move slowly down the hall, fists clenched at my sides, peering over my shoulder. I can't shake the feeling I'm being watched. "Hello?" I call. I know I saw someone. I heard someone. And it wasn't a rat or the floorboards. "Portia?"

The sound of fingernails trailing over wallpaper fills the hall. I watch, terrified, as the door to Odette's childhood bedroom swings open and slams shut. *This can't be real. You're dreaming. You* must *be dreaming!*

As if in response, the door opens again and wavers in the draft, trying to lure me inside. I clench my fists tighter, approaching cautiously. "Odette?" I whisper as I peek inside, the door hinges creaking violently.

My searching hands find the light switch, and the room brightens. It's robin's egg blue with elegant white Parisian-style furniture and touches of silver and ebony. A ballet barre against one wall holds a collection of worn pointe shoes with delicate pink ribbons.

The estate's dollhouse sits to the side, the doors hanging wide open, well-loved and often used. An ornate standing mirror reflects the room where she performed hundreds of pirouettes. I graze the cold frame as I take in my own reflection. Frizzy, disheveled hair, wrinkled pajamas.

There's movement in the mirror—a flash of long black hair—and I whip around. "Are you trying to tell me something?" I whisper, feeling ridiculous. Like those teenage girls who performed the séance on my sister's grave. I don't believe in ghosts. I've always considered myself a lifelong skeptic. "What are you trying to tell me?"

Of course, I get no answer.

I nibble at my bottom lip, questioning my sanity. *It's just the grief*, I reason. *You're not losing it. You're not crazy.*

I planned on coming in here, anyway. I just haven't been able to since Odette passed. But she had moved back home six months ago after the death of her husband, and if there's anything in here that could help explain what happened, I'm determined to find it.

First, I rifle through her vanity. There are dozens of used tissues stashed in here, covered in mascara and blotches of porcelain foundation. At first, I think she just forgot to throw them away after doing her makeup. But they're everywhere. Crammed into the drawers of her nightstands, wedged between the layers of her bed, even beneath her silk pillow, staining the white sheets.

There's something poking out from under the bed. A pair of plastic feet. I take hold of the ankles and pull it into the light. It's the *American Girl*-sized doll from our TV show, *Star Sisters*. They were these popular special edition dolls that came out near the end of the series. This particular one is Odette, though I can't really tell for sure just from looking at her face.

She's smashed it in, either with a fist or a rock, distorting the features and erasing the color from the eyes and lips. I can, however, tell from the lengthy black hair, the denim jeans and jacket, and the clogs which were all the rage in the '90s.

Odette *hated* clogs.

I think of all the times I sobbed in the dressing room in that hideous plaid dress they made me wear, the one with the lace that itched at my neck and upper arms, causing rashes and welts. And Vivienne would do nothing but keep urging me to smile. "Show the cameras your dimples, Briar!" she'd say, pinching my cheeks with her sharp claws.

I shove the doll back under the bed and slump onto the carpet. Something had been wrong with Odette. I don't know how I know that, but I can sense it. I can *feel* it.

She'd been crying enough to accumulate a small mountain of tissues. She'd been thinking of the past, remembering our cringy acting days. She'd even gone into the barn, the area of the estate that used to serve as a gift shop and brought her doll doppelgänger back to her bedroom with her, only to angrily smash in her own face. And she'd never come to us, her sisters, to talk about it. She'd been completely alone.

My gut twists with guilt. I should've been there for her. I

should've asked her if she was okay. She lost her husband. She was grieving. Why didn't I reach out more? Why did I just assume she'd be okay?

There's one last place I haven't checked yet. I move to her desk and slide out the long drawer beneath the workspace, pencils and pens rolling across the wood. A burgundy leather journal with a silver clasp sits inside, my sister's initials beautifully monogrammed across the front. *Oh, my God. Is this a diary?*

My excitement fades when I realize this is probably a workbook from therapy, similar to the one I have, and it fades even more when I discover I can't open the damn thing. I tug at the clasp, trying to pry it open, but it doesn't budge.

It's missing a key.

Shit.

I dig around some more, checking beneath the mattress, inside her pillowcases, the empty designer purses hanging on the closet door. They release her scent as I shake them and it's almost like she's here with me, as if she's just breezed through the door.

Feeling defeated, I return to the journal I'm unable to open. I'm sure it's from therapy. I have one just like it, though a little less flashy. I chose the one issued to me by my therapist. Odette was the kind of person who would go out and buy her own. Monogram it. She liked to monogram everything.

I'm tempted to take scissors to the spine and snap through the binding, but I resume my search of the key instead, checking her antique jewelry box—the sapphire, egg-shaped one with the gold trim—and the row of dusty books that line her windowsill.

I'm lost in my own thoughts when something outside draws me closer to the glass. At first, I think it's my own reflection, the sight of my hand as I shuffle through the books, but then I realize what I see is not a reflection at all. There's a woman standing below the window.

She stares up at me, frightened, clearly not expecting to be seen. I press up against the windowpane, trying to get a better look, waiting for my eyes to adjust to the dark. I can barely make out her face in the shadows, but I know she's there. I can see her white nightgown flowing in the breeze.

"Hey!" I yank at the window, trying to wrench it open, suspecting the trio of teenage girls have returned for yet another graveyard séance. But then I notice the slashes of red through the bushes. Is that... *blood?*

"Hey!" I shout again, struggling to open the window. It's jammed and won't budge. The woman is backing away, her feet muddied as she stumbles back into the trees. I shove the books aside and they topple to the floor. It takes all my force to finally pry open the window. But once I lean out over the sill, searching, the strange woman I thought I saw is already gone.

Transcript from *Rise and Shine, America*, interview with Vivienne and Briar Rose Belville, hosted by Gwen Morgan, aired December 14, 1996

The camera zooms in on Rise and Shine, America *host Gwen Morgan. The background is a beach scene at sunrise. Gwen wears a cobalt blue skirt and blazer with black pumps. Her platinum blonde hair is cut in The Rachel hairstyle. She smiles at the camera.*

Gwen: Rise and shine, America! Our next guest requires no introduction. She's an icon of Old Hollywood, an Oscar winning actress known for her unforgettable onscreen performances. Let's give a warm welcome to the legendary Vivienne Belville!

Vivienne smiles and waves as the camera pans over the cheering audience.

Gwen: And today, we have the pleasure of sitting down with her adorable daughter, and one of the talented young stars of the popular TV series, *Star Sisters*. At only six years old, give it up for Miss Briar Belville!

The audience cheers louder.

Gwen: Welcome, ladies!

Gwen turns to her guests and smiles.

The camera zooms out.

Vivienne Belville and her young daughter, Briar, sit on the sofa beside Gwen. Vivienne flashes a gorgeous smile and smooths her billowing plum dress with a graceful hand. Her feet are crossed at the ankles. Briar sits the same way.

Vivienne: Thank you for having us!

Gwen: I know. I'm happy you guys could make it, and you both look so lovely. Briar, I love your dress! It's beautiful!

Briar hops off the sofa and twirls in her floral dress with the oversized white collar. She shows off her lacy socks that peek out from her patent leather Mary Janes. The audience applauds and cheers for her.

Briar: Thank you! My mama picked it out.

Gwen: Well, she has good taste, doesn't she?

Briar nods in agreement and gives her mother a thumbs up. The audience laughs.

Gwen: *Star Sisters* has taken the world by storm, and you, little missy…

Gwen wags her finger at Briar.

Gwen: Your spitfire personality has won the hearts of millions! How does it feel to be part of such a successful show?

Briar gives an exaggerated shrug.

Briar: We get to sing and dance a lot! Last week, we had a monkey on set.

Gwen: A monkey?

Briar covers her mouth and giggles.

Briar: Yeah, he was pretty funny.

Gwen: Well, it sounds to me like you're having a blast. Was it always your dream to become an actress like your mommy?

Briar frowns and kicks her feet anxiously against the sofa.

Briar: Umm... well... not realllly.

Laughter.

Gwen makes a surprised face and then laughs with the audience. Vivienne joins in.

Gwen: But you still enjoy it, don't you?

Briar: I think my sisters like it more than me...

Vivienne sets a hand on Briar's knee and leans in with a smile.

Vivienne: Unfortunately, Odette and Portia couldn't be here today because they're still filming their Fourth of July special.

Gwen smiles back at Vivienne.

Gwen (talking about Briar): When did she start getting interested in performing?

Vivienne pats Briar's knee and squeezes it affectionately.

Vivienne: When she saw my very first movie. We sat down, the four of us together, and watched *My Fair Lady*. As soon as the credits rolled, Briar shot right up and told me she wanted to be a star like me.

The audience claps.

Gwen leans forward and rests her head on her hand, looking interested.

Gwen: So, tell me, Briar, what are your favorite things to do outside of filming? Do you have a lot of hobbies?

Briar lists her hobbies on her fingers.

Briar: I like fishing, catching snakes and lizards, climbing trees, making bug traps…

Gwen: Bug traps!

The audience laughs.

Vivienne: My girls are constantly outside, and Briar here is the very definition of a tomboy. She's always tracking mud into the house, or I'm plucking twigs out of her hair. But she's sweet as sugar, isn't she?

Gwen: She's simply adorable! Can I take you home with me? I'm going to steal her from you, Vivienne!

Audience laughter and cheers.

Briar giggles and hides her face. Vivienne beams.

Vivienne: I'd like to see you try! Briar and I are two peas in a pod! We do everything together. My girls are my world. If they could stay with their mama forever, I'd find a way to make it happen.

End of transcript.

Lost Behind-the-Scenes Footage of *Rise and Shine, America*

The dressing room is bright and clean. Briar sits on a chair, looking tired and uncomfortable. She rubs her eyes and shields them from the light. Vivienne stands nearby, a cold expression on her face. It's ten minutes until showtime.

Briar: Mommy, I want to go home. My stomach hurts, and I'm tired. Can we please just go home?

Vivienne: I'm not going to tell you again. If you don't behave like a perfect little princess and do exactly as I say, I'll leave you on the side of the road when we drive home. There are dangerous people out there, Briar. Terrible people who hurt children.

Vivienne leans in, gripping Briar's arms, causing her to gasp.

Vivienne: You'll end up being kidnapped by someone like them, and then the police will have to search for you. But they'll never find your body.

She raises her voice to a vicious shout.

Vivienne: Only a bloody shoe in some dumpster in the middle of nowhere! And I'll be on the news, crying, pleading for them to bring my precious baby girl back home. Do you want to make mommy sad?

Briar starts hyperventilating. Tears stream down her face.

Briar: No, Mommy, I'll be good, I promise!

Vivienne suddenly notices the camera filming them from the doorway. The cameraman retreats, but Vivienne chases him into the hallway.

Vivienne: Get out of here! How long have you been standing there? Don't you know anything about privacy? You'll be sorry when you hear from my lawyers!

The camera abruptly cuts out.

End of transcript.

11

THE SECURITY CAMERA blinks at me from above the front door. It looks like something out of a sci-fi movie. White, modern, and sleek with an ever-watchful black eye in the center. There's one installed above every entrance now, but I'm not sure it makes me feel any safer.

It's why I keep checking that they're working, why I keep bugging the customer service line with questions the tech who installed the cameras answered the day before.

I'm just so sure I saw someone, I think, remembering the white gown, the blood stains. I know it was early. I know the lighting was bad. Actually, come to think of it, the lighting was practically nonexistent. I hadn't even had my first cup of coffee yet. But I was so sure...

I pause in the drive, still watching the camera, and open the SecureHome app on my phone. The screen flashes blue with the little white eye logo, and then there I am, captured in real time, staring down at the phone clutched anxiously in my hand. If only they had installed the cameras a couple of days earlier.

I flip through the different vantage points, my thumb hovering above the screen, before selecting the guesthouse back door, the camera that faces the stretch of woods beyond the estate.

The rosebushes sway softly, along with the moss hanging from the branches above, and a squirrel darts across the screen. The birds are singing, and they're chipper this morning. The total opposite of how I feel right now.

I squint my eyes, obsessing over every movement, every shadow and change of light. Then a rush of adrenaline surges through me. A flash of white jets through the trees. My heart is racing as I try to zoom in, but I'm not fast enough. The controls are still new, and I end up turning the camera too far to the left.

"Damn it!" I groan as I punch out of the app, giving up. I pocket my phone and sprint around the side of the house, and then farther into the woods. Past the stretch of glittering pool, the garden, and guesthouse until I've almost reached the gift shop.

It could have been a bird. But then again, it was too low to the ground.

Too big.

I think of the woman, the frightened expression on her face right before she disappeared into the trees. The way she hurried to get away. I'm sure this time it was real. And not a trick of the eye.

My toe connects with a fallen branch and my ankle twists, sending me hurtling into the rosebushes, the thorns tearing at my skin. I gasp in pain as the barbs prick me from all directions and dribbles of fresh blood streak down my forearms.

After untangling myself, I crawl from the bushes and collapse beside them. I've dropped my phone. It must've flown out of my pocket during the fall. It lies on the ground a few feet away, half-buried in dead leaves and facing upward, the SecureHome app still running onscreen.

I feel like a complete idiot. A complete *paranoid* idiot with a busted ankle. I sit forward and draw up my knees, inspecting the damage. It feels sore to the touch and the area around the joint is a little red. I hope I can walk on it. Before I try to get up, I wipe at my arms, the blood staining my palms pink.

The sight of it gives me déjà vu, conjuring images inside my brain. Another memory dislodged from somewhere deep. I'm playing dress-up inside Vivienne's walk-in closet. Somehow I've gotten my hands on her red Oscars gown, dragging it over my head, stepping on the train.

The next thing I know, Vivienne is shouting and yanking me by the hand—out of the bedroom, down the grand staircase, across the drive, and into the trees. I'm screaming and crying because I know what's about to happen. It's happened many times before. Vivienne tosses me, her small daughter, into the rosebushes to teach me a lesson. She stands there watching, with a sadistic grin on her face, as I fight desperately to escape the thorns.

I'm still staring at my bloodied palms as the memory fully resurfaces. *Did that really happen? Was it so traumatic that I blocked it out?*

My fingers are shaking as they travel up the length of my arms and hover above the pale crescent-shaped scars that fan out around my elbows. I could never remember how I got these. Or maybe I didn't want to.

Tears blur my vision as footsteps approach me from behind. I straighten and twist around, another blast of adrenaline surging through me.

"Briar?"

12

"BRIAR?" Owen repeats, jogging toward me.

I quickly wipe away my tears, embarrassed to be caught in such a vulnerable moment. I give him a wave, wanting to tell him that I'm okay and don't need any help, but I can't find the words. My throat is constricted with emotion. I'm still so shaken by the memory.

He leans down to grab my phone and dusts it off before handing it to me. I take it from him, noting the white basketball shorts he's wearing. It was him on the camera. "Thanks," I say, pocketing my phone.

Owen removes his AirPods, a podcast blaring from the speakers before he cuts the episode short. He extends a hand, helping me up. "Are you okay?" he asks, concerned. I never noticed how crystal clear his eyes are. Almost electric blue. It's like they've brightened over the years. Or maybe it's the lack of hair that really makes them pop.

I swallow and nod, relieved I can apply at least some pressure on the twisted ankle. "Yeah. I guess I slipped."

"Is that blood?" Owen asks, his concern rising. He looks me over, searching for the source of the blood.

"The bushes have thorns," I explain with a wave of the hand, as if it's no big deal that I have cuts all over me. I look away, flustered. "It was my own fault. I fell. I can be pretty clumsy sometimes, and I guess I wasn't looking where I was going. But I think I'm okay. It's just... my ankle."

"Can you walk on it?"

"Yeah. I'll be fine." I take a step forward and my ankle gives out from under me.

Owen catches me, and I blink up at him, surprised. "Come on. I'll walk you back and we'll get you patched up."

"Patched up?"

"Yeah." Owen offers me his arm and I gratefully shift the majority of my weight onto him as he nudges me along the path toward the guesthouse. "You should keep it elevated. I'll whip you up an ice pack to help with the swelling. I played a lot of sports in my day. Twisted ankles, pulled muscles. Taking ibuprofen helps. Even if you're not in a lot of pain."

"They give you ibuprofen in prison?"

"It's about the only thing they give you."

"Ah," I say, nibbling on my bottom lip. "Well, it sounds like you're an expert."

Owen chuckles. "I kind of am."

Once we make it to the guesthouse, Owen lowers me carefully into one of the wicker chairs in the garden. He lifts another chair, swinging it around in front of me, and instructs me to rest my injured leg on the cushion. I do as he says and then he disappears into the house, and I hear him rummaging through the kitchen.

I use the time to fix my disheveled hair, combing it free of any tangles and debris like twigs and moss. I know I'm a mess. And I'm so tired of trying not to be a mess that I can hardly hide it anymore. Like when you're told to clean your bedroom as a teenager and instead of *really* cleaning it, you just stuff all your clothes into the bottom of your closet, and you keep doing it until it can barely fit anything anymore. Until it's about to explode.

Sometimes... I feel like that closet.

The humidity is choking today. It hangs over everything, mixing with the scent of sweet flowers and chemical chlorine. The pool is in need of a thorough cleaning, much like the rest of the estate, but it looks pretty the way it reflects the trees hanging overhead and the clouds speckling the sky.

Owen returns with paper towels, both dry and damp, and a sandwich bag he's filled with ice cubes. "Here you go," he says, handing me the paper towels and gently setting the ice pack on my wounded ankle. "How's that?"

"Perfect," I admit, savoring the relief I feel as the coolness seeps into my tender muscles. "Thank you."

Owen shrugs. "No problem."

I wipe the blood from my arms and hands, balling up the dirty napkins and handing them back to him. He doesn't even flinch at the gore. He gathers them up, tosses them in the trash, and drops into the seat across from me.

He looks different from the other day. Maybe it's because he seems softer now, like he's finally loosening up around me. I keep wanting to think about him as the Owen I knew from before. But I know we've both changed, and not just physically. We're different people now. And somehow, that's scary and exciting at the same time.

I give him a quick once-over. He's shirtless, the sweat on his chest highlighting the broadness of his shoulders and the firm ridges of his abdomen. There are even more rough tattoos marking his skin—a collection of numbers in his chest hair, a large crucifix over one pec, Xs slashing across his lower obliques.

Realizing I've been staring for too long, I clear my throat. "You're up early," I point out, trying to keep my gaze from falling below his shoulders.

"I'm an early riser."

"How's the guesthouse treating you?"

"It's comfortable *and* spacious." He stands and nods at the door.

"How about I make us a pot of coffee? I'm usually on my second cup by now."

I smile. "Sure."

I spend the next five minutes scrolling through work emails, answering what I can, and scheduling meetings for later in the day, trying to ignore the SecureHome app. I can smell the freshly brewed coffee even before Owen returns with two mugs, a pair of spoons, and a pint of Half & Half. He's swapped his basketball shorts for blue jeans and a clean shirt. "I wasn't sure how you like it," he says as he hands me a mug. "I'll grab the sugar."

"The Half & Half is fine," I tell him, unscrewing the cap and adding a dash to my coffee. I take a long sip, then another. "Wow, this is good."

Owen sits across from me again, smiling. "Thanks. Not bad for someone who's barista career lasted only a single shift." He takes a sip and adds, "Guess I should've stuck with that."

Another pang of guilt hits me. I don't know what to say, so I dip a spoon into my coffee and stir. "I'm sorry. I didn't mean to cut your jog short."

"I was on my way back."

"Still."

Owen nods at the dry patches that speckle my hands like ugly bruises. "Stressed?"

"Oh." I hold out my hands for him, showing him the coarse skin. "They don't look as bad now. You should've seen them the other day."

"You pick at them?"

"I wash my hands a lot. It's a nervous tic I have. It always happens when I come back here. I don't know... I think it has something to do with all the clutter inside the house, the dust, the *termites*."

"Is it OCD?"

"Maybe." I shrug. "I've never been officially diagnosed."

Owen studies me. "What triggers it?"

I lower my hands, tucking them below my thighs. He takes this as a sign I've grown uncomfortable. "Sorry," he says quickly. "You don't have to tell me. I shouldn't have asked."

"No, it's fine!" I shake my head, flustered, trying to string the right words together. "I guess, nerves. Anxiety, maybe." I don't want to get into all the reasons, so I change the subject.

"So, um," I say, scratching at the corner of my nose. Why the hell can't I figure out what to do with my arms? I keep moving them, and if I don't, it's like they just hang there awkwardly. I play with my hair instead, tugging at a strand. I don't know why he's making me so nervous. We used to do everything together, know everything about each other. I clear my throat. "What podcast were you listening to?" Owen blinks at me, and I clarify, pointing to my ear. "I heard it when you removed your AirPods."

"Oh."

"Come on. What is it? Conspiracies? UFOs and tinfoil hats?"

"I'm not that interesting..." Owen pulls the podcast up on his phone and shows me the screen. It says *Where Motive Lies*. "True crime. My guilty pleasure."

"Do you watch the Netflix documentaries, too?"

"I've seen all of them."

We laugh.

"Should I be concerned? You're not secretly an ax murderer, right?"

"Oh, no," he assures me. "Axes are too messy. You had the right idea with the butcher knife."

I reach out and punch him playfully on the arm. "Hey!"

He gestures to his phone. "This podcast is about my cell mate, actually. He *was* an axe-murderer. Slaughtered his whole family. The county sheriff."

My mouth drops open. "What?"

Owen gives me a look. "I'm kidding."

A full minute later and I'm still chuckling into my coffee. Owen leans back and stretches, smiling at me. I tear my gaze away from him and study the house. It looks better in the early morning light, the imperfections hazy. It almost comes off as charming rather than run-down. "Hey, you should have breakfast with us," I say, realizing I've missed this. Him and me. The way we used to laugh. "I mean, if you want to..."

"I wouldn't want to impose."

I shake my head vigorously. "It's not an imposition."

Owen smiles. It's boyish and crooked, but somehow it comes off totally genuine and charming. "Okay, then. Sure. Can I help with anything? I'm not bad around the kitchen."

"I'm sure Elise would appreciate the..." I want to say *help*, but the word gets lodged in my throat. Vivienne is watching us from her bedroom window, a hand drawing back the heavy drapes, one thin brow cocked. She doesn't even try to be discreet. It's like she wants to be seen. Owen spots her and waves. She smiles, waving back flirtatiously, but her eyes seem dull. Disappointed. And when they fall back onto me, they almost appear angry.

I know why.

Owen is here for her. He's her guest. And she expects all the attention to be focused on her and if anyone else tries to steal that away, even for a moment, she views it as a threat. Competition. And it definitely doesn't help Owen is so attractive, and his butt looks *really* good in jeans. Not that I've noticed...

The drapes swish shut, and I'm left with a bitter taste in my mouth. My stomach is in knots. We don't need any more drama in this house, but Vivienne is always on the lookout for more. My ankle throbs and I adjust the icepack with anxious fingers. Owen notices. "You okay?"

I try to play it cool. "Yeah. I'm good."

"Can I get you more ice?"

The ice has mostly melted, but I shake my head. "Thanks, but it's still pretty cold." Owen seems to be thinking about something. "What is it?"

He massages the back of his neck, looking unsure. "You don't have any pets, do you? A cat, maybe?"

"No," I say. "Vivienne's allergic."

"But Juliet plays out here, right?"

I tilt my head at him, not sure where he's going with this. "Yeah, why?"

"There's hemlock in your garden." After taking in my clueless expression, he points out the plant to me. "Do you see those white flowers over there? By the trellis."

I nod. "Yeah."

"They're poisonous."

"Are you sure?"

"Deadly."

"I had no idea. I don't exactly have a green thumb."

"Just thought I'd mention it. They're fine as long as no one eats them, but I'd still recommend putting up a fence or tearing them out completely. Not worth the risk, if you ask me."

"Huh," I say, frowning. Of course Vivienne never bothered to check if the pretty plants in her garden might be poisonous to children. Sometimes I think it's a miracle we made it to adulthood. "Thanks for letting me know."

13

"Owen!" Vivienne gasps excitedly. "What a pleasure! I'm so glad you finally decided to join us for breakfast!"

Everyone stops what they're doing. She looks *that* incredible. Portia and Juliet stare from their seats at the table. Elise almost drops the pitcher of ice water, the ice cubes clattering on the embroidered tablecloth. I accidentally bump into the back of Owen as we come out of the kitchen.

We spent the last thirty minutes helping Elise prepare breakfast and set the table, talking and laughing and listening to music. It helped take my mind off everything, but the sight of my mother in that scarlet dress as she steps into the dining room sets me right back on edge.

It's form-fitting and slips suggestively off the shoulders, accentuating her cleavage. She's given herself a salon-style blowout, along with a red lip and black Louboutin heels. I'm well aware of the way Owen stutters, the scrambled eggs close to slipping off the pan, the effect she has on him. On every man she waltzes past. It's like her beauty momentarily reduces their minds to mush.

I know exactly why she's so dressed up. This is about me and Owen talking in the garden. This is her way of asserting dominance, putting me back in my place. She won't allow anyone to upstage her. *Well, she's done a pretty good job at it*, I think, suddenly feeling insecure. I quickly adjust my white tank top and ripped jeans. Then I try to scuff some dried dirt off my Converse.

Vivienne strides confidently over and sets a hand on Owen's arm, her eyes shining. "You cooked for us! You're such a gentleman."

I shake my head, annoyed.

Owen gives her that charming smile. He follows her to her side of the table and pulls out her chair, serving her eggs. "It's the least I can do."

Once we're all seated, we hold hands and say grace and then everyone dives into the food. "Mmm, these eggs are so good," Juliet cries, her twists bouncing on her shoulders. "So cheesy and buttery and gooey!"

Vivienne beams up at Owen, flashing her teeth. "Oh, I don't doubt they're delicious!"

I ignore them as the food is passed around the table. Owen sits beside Vivienne, still smiling at her, until he tastes the grits I've whipped up. "Wow, Briar. I'll be having a second serving of these."

Vivienne's smile falters. She narrows her eyes at me. Then she laughs. It's fake. I can see right through it, and I know what's coming next. A sweetly concealed barb meant to make me look bad. "Yes, Briar, these grits *are* delicious. I didn't even realize you cook. You're always so busy playing on your laptop."

I nearly choke on the ice cubes in my drink. "I think you mean *working*."

"I don't know what you do on that thing all day," Vivienne says, waving a hand. "All I'm saying is that I'm surprised. You're such a strong and driven businesswoman. Not the domestic type. But when you do find the time to step away from your busy schedule and help out, your cooking isn't half bad!"

Portia stops chewing. She sets down her fork, sensing the undercurrent of tension. Elise sucks in a sharp breath, anticipating an explosion. Owen remains oblivious, helping himself to more food.

I lean back in my seat. "Well, grits aren't too hard. I could show you sometime, you know, the next time you ever feel like setting foot inside a kitchen. Poor Elise here does most of the work, anyway. I know she loves the help."

"I don't mind cooking for your mother," Elise says, hoping to calm the oncoming storm.

Vivienne nudges at my grits with her fork as if it's toxic waste. "Briar, didn't you give your late husband food poisoning?" She laughs louder, glancing at Owen. "I swear that wasn't what killed him, but it was a close call."

"Vivienne!" Portia snaps angrily.

I narrow my eyes at my mother, and she gives a little shrug. *Cut the crap*, I'd spit if not for our guest. *What are you trying to pull, you wicked witch?* I nibble on a slice of bacon. "Are you going somewhere, Vivienne? You're so dressed up!"

"I'd rather be overdressed than..." She gives my choice of clothing a disapproving once over, "...under."

I laugh at that and then we all do. Owen looks up, blinking, as if he's missed the joke. I turn to him, brushing my hair over one shoulder and tilting my head to the side with an innocent smile. "How do you think I look, Owen?"

I feel bad for putting him on the spot. It's this weird competitive nature Vivienne riles up inside me. She's always trying to outdo me. Bully me into backing down. She claims she wants me to do well, to be better, but the second someone pays me the slightest bit of attention, or something in my life finally starts going right, it's like it threatens her. And then she gets cruel. She always does. She has to put me back into my place.

Well, I'm sick of her steamrolling me. Tired of being her perfect puppet that does whatever she says. It's about time I fight back.

Vivienne's expression hardens. Owen chuckles nervously. "You're beautiful," he says earnestly, then clears his throat and adds,

"You all are. I'm a very lucky man, sitting at a table surrounded by beautiful women."

What a good, diplomatic answer.

More laughter.

Vivienne leans in closer to him. "It's okay. You don't have to tell us what you're really thinking. Besides, you must have a special lady in your life."

"Not yet," Owen admits.

"But you must want to settle down eventually?"

"Yeah." Owen shrugs. "Eventually."

"Look at your bone structure!" Vivienne trails her fingers along his jaw. "Have you ever considered modeling?"

Owen laughs, turning red. "You're too kind."

"You should consider it. You would make a killing. Oh, and your arms. Now, I know you work out..."

"Speaking of working out," I cut in. "I thought we could go for a walk together, Owen. You and me. Catch up since we haven't seen each other in a while."

He sits up straighter. "Sure, that sounds—"

"He'll hardly have time for that. There's much work to be done on my memoir and I won't allow for any *unnecessary* distractions." Vivienne's eyes are like daggers. "Besides, I noticed you were limping. Did you hurt your leg? I'm surprised it took this long for you to injure yourself.... with all that extra weight you're carrying."

My mouth falls open, the bacon dropping into my lap. Portia quickly cuts in, breaking into a funny story to help lighten the mood. But I don't hear anything she's saying because I'm so fixated on Vivienne and her smug smirk.

"What's your problem?" I blurt.

The story stutters to a stop and everyone falls quiet. Elise sets her fork aside, and Portia and her exchange exhausted sighs.

Vivienne blinks at me, her long lashes fluttering. "Excuse me?"

I raise my voice, losing my temper. "You said I was the difficult one. But *you've* been giving me a hard time since I got here, and I want to know what your problem is!"

"There is no problem, Briar, aside from the one you're creating," she bites back. "Finish your breakfast and stop making a fool of yourself... if you're capable of it."

"Why is there hemlock in the garden?"

Vivienne purses her lips. "Pardon?"

"Hemlock," I repeat, louder this time. "It's poisonous!"

"Yes, I know. It's mine. I like to admire the beautiful but deadly blooms."

"Well, it's a safety hazard!"

"That hemlock has been in that garden since you and Portia have been sucking on pacifiers. Juliet's not dim. She knows not to just stick anything inside her mouth. I can't say the same for you."

"So, Owen," Elise says, interrupting our back and forth. "Do you have any plans for the future? How's your house coming along?"

"Oh... uh..." Owen clears his throat, obviously uncomfortable. "Well... not bad... I started working on the patio area..."

Still fuming, I lean back and cross my arms. Owen, Elise, and Portia talk for the rest of breakfast with occasional chime-ins from Juliet. Vivienne and I glare at each other. It's a staring contest I refuse to lose.

"Owen?" Vivienne catches his attention as he goes to clear the plates, her eyes not leaving mine. "The girls will do that. You're our guest."

"I don't mind," he assures her.

She sets a hand on his arm and bats her mascara-coated lashes. "Please, I insist. We should get started on the book. I'm sure there's a lot more you want to ask me. Shall we continue in the guesthouse?"

Owen sets the plates down. "Yeah, alright." He glances at me, and Vivienne tightens her grip.

When she eventually saunters over, she pauses beside me, and her nose curls at the small bacon grease stain on my thigh. "Briar," she says, her fake-nice voice back on display. "It's never too late to start acting like a lady."

I clench my fists as she drags an apologetic-looking Owen out of the room. *Whatever you say, you washed-up, trussed up...*

Portia exhales once they're gone. "I smell drama," she sings as she picks up the plates Owen left behind.

"What? No!" I say, collecting our dirty utensils. "There's no drama. We're just... trying to get used to having each other around again."

I limp into the kitchen and Portia trails behind me. She puts the stack of plates on the counter and after wiping her hands on her yoga pants, she starts unloading the dishwasher. "Why are you giving her such a hard time?" she asks me.

"*I'm* giving *her* a hard time?" I say incredulously.

"Just do what I do. Ignore her."

"She can't," Elise says, addressing Portia. She grabs the dirty dishes and washes the excess food into the sink. "They're cut from the same cloth. If I were you, I'd stay out of it and let the two of them hash it out."

"Hash it out? No one is hashing it out!" I load the utensils, scoffing at their nonsense. "That was just a little blip! She clearly has a problem with me, and all I'm trying to do is get to the bottom of it."

"You're right," Portia agrees, nodding, ignoring what I just said. Elise nods right along with her, like they've figured everything out. "It's why they're always going at each other's throats."

"Like I said, let them hash it out."

I throw my hands into the air. "You do know I'm standing right here and can hear everything you're saying, right?"

Elise unwraps a pod and sticks it into the machine. She moves over to the sink and wets a sponge before wiping down the counter. "They'll either come to a solution together or..."

"Kill each other," Portia finishes with a knowing smirk.

I can't do anything but roll my eyes.

14

After the kitchen is clean, I pop two painkillers for my ankle and spend the rest of the morning attending Zoom meetings. It's difficult to stay focused on work, even after consuming enough caffeine to substitute the blood in my veins. I'm doodling in my notes and drawing frowny faces on my arm. *What kind of adult still doodles on herself?*

I'm exhausted and can't stop yawning, which isn't a good look for the boss. Everyone keeps asking if I'm sick.

I'm mainly trying to avoid thinking about the woman in the white dress. The childhood memories I've blocked out. Owen alone right now with Vivienne.

It's nearly 3 p.m. when I decide to call it quits. I relocate to the kitchen and throw together a cheese and turkey wrap with pickles and a side of potato chips. I eat it in the breakfast nook, staring out the window at the guesthouse. I can see them moving around in there. I wonder what they're talking about. Is he asking her the hard questions? The juicy bits internet sleuths have been obsessing over for years. What happened to your husbands? What happened in the days leading up to their disappearances? Why haven't you ever addressed the rumors publicly? Did *you* kill them?

I wonder if she's sharing her entire life story with him, and whether it's the truth or her own version of events. If there's one thing I know about Vivienne, it's that she loves to twist the truth.

Something else has been bothering me lately. The idea that the gift shop might be linked to the note Odette left me. It's been shut down for decades, but she still went out there, still brought back that doll. Was that what she wanted, or had she been searching for something else?

I finish my wrap and chase it down with some freshly squeezed orange juice left over from breakfast. Then I head into the foyer to grab my bag and sunglasses, fully expecting them to be on the side table where I left them. Only... they're not there. I pause, mentally retracing my steps, before finally checking the coat closet. They're sitting on the top shelf.

That's odd.

I was certain I left them on the table. Elise must've put them away for me.

Or maybe it was Odette, her spirit restlessly wandering the house, moving things out of place to let us know she's still here. A floorboard creaks somewhere upstairs, my heart skipping a beat. *It's probably just the draft stirring up the old floorboards,* I tell myself. *Or Elise tidying up the second floor...*

But still, I don't wait around to find out. I snatch up my things and hurry for the door, anxious for some fresh air.

It's time for a little excursion.

~

THE GIFT SHOP is a trek from the main house. I follow the signposts that point me down the right trails, eventually coming to the butterfly garden. It's still well-cared for, and it's my favorite garden on the property. I love the colors. There's a whole collection of vibrant blooms, small signs naming each one: lantana, hibiscus, blue sage, and swamp milkweed. This path in particular is lined with towering sunflowers that guide you all the way to the shop, which sits at the tail end of the property.

When it was in full operation, there was a soft-serve bar and café positioned around a grassy field with large, family-size picnic tables. Now, the picnic tables look moldy and water stained, the gastronomy options have been removed, and the gift shop sits boarded up and deserted. I pause in front of the little wooden house, shielding my eyes from the brutal afternoon sun, and take it all in.

I can already see that someone has removed the boards that were nailed across the front door, securing it in place. Odette, most likely. I still can't get over why she'd come all this way just for a doll... Was it an exercise assigned to her by her therapist? Some odd therapeutic ritual in the name of emotional healing?

I limp over to one of the picnic tables, press on the wood to test it won't collapse on me, and then take a seat to rest my ankle. Or maybe I'm stalling. I don't really want to go in there. Now that I'm seeing it up close, I'm remembering what's inside. All those pieces of our past piled up ceiling high. What if it triggers another memory? My mind worked hard to forget my traumatic past. Maybe it did so for good reason.

I sigh, shifting in my seat, the damp wood groaning beneath me. *Okay, you hobbled all this way. At least look around before you hobble back again.* Pushing up from the table, I limp to the front door and grasp the twisted handle. There's a long rectangular window at the top of the door, but it's too dark inside to get a good look. I can, however, make out the outlines of cardboard boxes propped against the walls, and stacks of shelves studded with outdated merchandise.

A twig snaps in the woods behind me and I gasp. Pivoting around, I push my sunglasses on top of my head and search the trees with frantic eyes, but there's no one there. I have to remind myself that there's a lot of wildlife out here. Not to mention, the last time I let my paranoia get the better of me, which was only a few hours ago, I almost broke my leg chasing after an imagined intruder. I'm not about to let my paranoia control me again. Not if I can help it.

I inhale steadily before forcing the door open and slipping inside. Geez, I forgot how musty it is in here. The whole store smells like an old cellar, and I'm sure there's mold crawling up the walls somewhere. It looks like a hoarder's paradise. There's not only gift shop merchandise stored here. All our old childhood toys Vivienne couldn't bear to throw away are stashed here, too. Rocking horses. Porcelain dolls. Miniature luxury cars in hot pink and cherry red.

That's the spookiest part. All this junk from another era stuffed into one room like a giant, fucked up blast from the past. I stare across the shop, waiting for my eyes to adjust to the low lighting, and all I see is a forest of dolls and mannequins and ghostly white sheets.

My hand finds the light switch on reflex, but there's no power and I remain frozen in place, blinking in the dark. The only light comes from the afternoon sun, which slants through the boarded-up windows, casting harsh shadows. It does nothing to calm my nerves, the silhouettes of the mannequins on the opposite wall warped and contorted, their limbs bent out of shape.

I venture further into the shop and look around. There are cobwebs everywhere, clinging to the autographed prints of Vivienne, the copies of my sisters' and my headshots with our twirly, girly autographs and cheesy catchphrases: *Never stop believing in yourself! From one shining star to another! Best wishes and plenty of kisses!*

I can't help but cringe. Cringe at the claustrophobia-inducing amount of cheesiness radiating from every corner of the shop. Cringe at the collection of VHS tapes from our TV show that line the walls, including the holiday specials. Cringe at the dolls. The mini versions of Portia and me, in our matching blue overalls, pigtails, and white sneakers dotted with pink flowers. I think of

Odette's doll upstairs in her bedroom, the face smashed and unrecognizable. I'm almost tempted to do the same to these.

I spot something on the ground beneath the shelves. It's a VHS tape, lying there, seemingly forgotten. I reach down and brush off the layer of dust, revealing a bold red marker scrawl on the homemade label: "Anti-Fan Club."

Oh, my gosh. I remember this! My sisters and I started an anti-fan club in Vivienne's honor. I smile. Well, would you look at that. Suddenly, I'm in the mood to watch a movie. I stick it into my small crossbody bag, praying the VCR in my room still works.

I turn around, crinkling my nose at the awful odor that hangs in the air. What *is* that? One of the mannequins suddenly shifts forward, and I almost scream. I slap a hand to my chest, cursing, stumbling back. "Hello?" I choke out.

The mannequin's flat eyes stare back at me. I take a steadying breath as I search the shadows. But just as I look away from it, the mannequin jerks to the side as if it's come to life, the motions violent and wooden as it knocks into the others, sending them toppling over like a row of dominoes. This time, I can't stop the scream that forces its way out of my throat.

A mannequin head rolls across the splintered floor and bumps into my shoe. The eyes are slanted up at me, the mouth hanging open as if in mocking laughter.

I kick it away and something else in the corner falls over, making me jump. "Juliet, is that you?" I call, my heart beating fast. "You can come out! I promise I won't be mad."

The silence that follows is eerie. Fed up, I stomp to the back of the gift shop and shove the pile of mannequins aside. A large cotton rat scurries away, disappearing into a hole in the wall.

It was *feeding* on something.

I cover my mouth, trying not to gag. There's a dead crow. *Well, I guess I found the source of the smell.* It's been killed recently, fresh blood staining the floor around it like a morbid halo. The chest cavity has been ripped open and cleaned out, the heart removed.

There's nothing left except strands of flesh that cling to the delicate gray rib cage and the crooked spread wings. Black, glossy feathers lie everywhere, and by the look of the poor thing, it put up a fight.

I'm pretty sure it was an owl because I know they can be vicious, using their large talons to rip apart their prey, usually decapitating and devouring the head. Its nest could be here, somewhere in the rafters, and there are probably plenty of other carcasses and tiny bones scattered around the room. But still, the way the rib cage has been dismantled and the organs removed, almost in a ritualistic way... it's strange. It feels more like the work of a human. With my heart hammering in my chest, I quickly backtrack to the door.

15

ONCE I'M in my bedroom, I make sure the coast is clear and then I quietly shut my door. I don't know why I'm suddenly so nervous or why my stomach is revolting like I've chugged a gallon of spoiled milk. It's a painful sensation—a constant twist and stab.

I clench my stomach muscles, trying to ride this wave of nausea as I plop onto the floor before the VCR. I fully expect it not to work anymore, to be unplugged or broken. But like everything else in this room, it's in perfect condition, pristinely preserved in time. I feel like I'm ten again. Like I'm about to spend the afternoon watching *Jurassic Park* with a PB&J sandwich and a Capri Sun.

All I have to do is turn on the VCR and insert the tape. I hold my breath as the screen lights up blue, the machine whirring as it comes to life.

I hit the play button.

THE ANTI-FAN CLUB VHS TAPE FROM 1997

```
PLAY — -:--:--
SLP  — 0:00:00
```

Odette, aged 12, blinks at the camera, the frame so close to her face, only a portion of her eye and nose are visible.

Odette: Testing, testing. Is this thing on?

Portia (off camera): Give me the camera!

Odette zooms out. Her entire face and upper body are visible now. She's wearing a denim jacket and a denim bucket hat decorated with fabric flowers. She has pale skin, thick, dark brows, and pencil-straight black hair.

Odette: No, I'm the director.

Portia, aged 8, tries to push her face into the frame.

Portia: Why?

Odette: Because I'm the oldest, of course. Stand back. I'll make the introductions.

The camera pans around, filming Portia and Briar, aged 7. Portia strikes a pose. She's wearing pink knee-length shorts, an oversized striped T-shirt, and a green headband. She has tan skin and bronze-colored blonde hair.

Briar covers her face. She wears a maroon velvet dress, green stockings, and a black headband. Her red hair is hip-length and tangled.

Odette: Sorry about that, Briar's shy!

Briar removes her hands and laughs. She twirls around.

Briar: Yeah, sometimes.

Portia breakdances. She knocks over a music box from Briar's dresser, and Briar laughs loudly. Odette shushes them.

Odette: Guys, stop! I don't want her to wake up!

Briar: Yeah, she's drunk.

Briar snatches the camera and runs downstairs. The camera bobs up and down. It captures Vivienne, aged 49, on the sofa in the parlor. She's sleeping and snoring loudly. She hugs a wine bottle to her chest. Briar sneaks back into her room.

Briar (whispering): She's still sleeping.

Odette: Praise the Lord!

Portia: We made a fan club for Vivienne, but we call it the anti-fan club.

The three girls giggle.

Briar: Yeah, she's mean to us, and we're done with her crap!

Portia: Everyone thinks she's the greatest mom ever, but she's not. She's a total B-word!

Odette: I've got an idea! Let's sneak into her room!

Portia (squealing): I want to play with her makeup! Briar, let me do your makeup!

Briar makes a face.

Briar: Ew, no.

Portia jumps up and down.

Portia: Please, please, please!

Odette shushes her sisters, and the three girls move into their mother's bedroom. It's decorated with antique furniture and glamour shots. It looks like it belongs in a magazine. Briar finds a red bustier on the chaise lounge and holds it up to her own chest. She poses for the camera.

Briar: Ooh, ooh, ooh! Look at me. I'm fancy like Vivienne!

Odette: Oh, my gosh. Cut it out, Briar.

Portia digs around in her mother's vanity and laughs at her sister. Her smile disappears and she suddenly looks horrified. The camera zooms in on something bloody in her hand. She squeals and drops it onto the floor.

Portia: Ew, ew, ew! What was that?

Briar: Is that a finger?

Odette: It's a movie prop, you guys.

Portia: But it felt wet!

Odette: Let me see.

The door opens and Elise, aged 42, walks in. She appears exhausted and there are dark shadows beneath her eyes. She's outraged at finding the girls in their mother's bedroom.

Elise: What are you three doing in here?

The girls scream.

THE TAPE ENDS THERE. I stare at the screen, rewinding it and watching it from the beginning, wishing there was more. Was that really a finger? I doubt it, but I curse the grainy footage and my sister's amateur directorial skills. When I reach the end, the screams make my heart pound. There's something haunting about seeing the film unfold in the same exact spot I'm sitting now, and to see my sisters so young again, to see Vivienne and Elise, how they used to look, almost twenty years erased from their faces.

I eject the tape, and the screen falls black, reflecting another face staring back at me. Now it's my turn to scream. "Vivienne! What the hell!" I gasp, twisting around, a hand on my chest. "You almost gave me a heart attack!"

How long was she standing there? This is why I always wanted a lock on the *inside* of my door. She stands by the bed, a tight smile on her lips. I never even heard her come in. "Feeling nostalgic?" she asks.

I answer her question with a question. "You finished working on the memoir?"

"For now. Owen's a wonderful listener. I see why you two were such good friends back in the day." She takes a second to admire her manicured nails and pick at her nonexistent cuticles. I sense she's stalling. With a little sigh, she clears her throat and turns her attention back to me. "I guess I should apologize to you for earlier. I was rude and you didn't deserve that."

I raise my brows, surprised. "Wait, really?"

"Yes."

"You're apologizing to me right now? I don't think you've ever apologized to me before."

"That can't be right, Briar," she says, crossing her arms. "I've apologized to you many times before!"

"Not that I remember..."

My comment irks her, but she chooses to let it slide. "I suppose there's a first for everything."

I stare at her, waiting for the catch. Expecting it. There's always a catch with Vivienne. "Is that all?"

"Well, don't you have anything you'd like to say to me?"

I let out an incredulous laugh. There it is. "You mean, an apology?"

Vivienne lowers her head slightly, giving me a look.

"Oh, come on." I shake my head. "You can't be serious."

"If anything, you owe *me* the apology..."

"What?" I almost crush the VHS tape in my hands, the plastic crunching. "You've been rude to me since I got back here!"

"You've had some pretty harsh words to share with me, too. And the way you behaved so disrespectfully at my dining table, under my roof, and in front of my guest. It's unacceptable. You embarrassed me."

"Like I always do."

"Excuse me?"

"You constantly criticize me! I can't do anything right."

She presses her hands to her chest and raises her voice like she's delivering a rehearsed monologue from one of her movies. "I criticize you because I love you! I want you to be the best version of yourself!"

"As long as I don't outshine you, right?"

Vivienne recoils like I've slapped her. "I wouldn't point out your flaws so often if there weren't so many areas for improvement, starting with your level of maturity," she says, her upper lip curling into a sneer. "Then there's your unsightly clothes, your unkempt hair, your inability to properly maneuver a makeup brush!"

"I'd love to tell you what you can do with *your* makeup brush." I smile at her.

"I should smack that filthy mouth of yours."

I chuckle softly, rubbing at my temples. "Are we done with this back and forth? Because if you haven't noticed, I'm kind of in the middle of something."

"Not until I hear my apology," Vivienne counters. "Your rude, thoughtless behavior has absolutely mortified me, and I thought I would be the bigger person by coming in here and making amends, but it appears you're too bullheaded to even consider—"

"Fine, fine, fine!" I explode, covering my face. "You win! We both were mean to each other. Happy?"

"That's not much of an apology, Briar," she says, narrowing her eyes at me, "but I'll accept it for now. I'm sure I'll find a way for you to make it up to me later."

I force air out my nostrils, trying to rein in my temper.

"I only came up to tell you that dinner will be ready soon. We're having meatloaf and roasted potatoes, and Elise whipped up a batch of homemade raspberry lemonade."

"Sounds delicious," I reply flatly.

Vivienne pauses at my door, staring at me for an uncomfortably long time. Eventually, I meet her gaze and give her an expectant look. To my surprise, she's back to being nice again. Her voice turns sugary sweet and she pastes on a motherly smile, the actress in her making a reappearance. "Despite everything, I really am grateful you decided to stay, Briar."

I can't tell if she's being genuine or not. But I force a smile to match hers, my cheeks aching from the effort. I just want to get rid of her. "Sure, whatever. I'll be down soon, okay?"

Vivienne nods. She turns to go, but glances over her shoulder, at the VHS tape in my lap. "Don't be too long now."

16

"You've been quiet tonight," Portia says as I scroll through the SecureHome app. It's dark outside, and the cameras have switched to night vision mode. I'm waiting to see a pair of glowing eyes staring at me from the shadows or a ghostly figure drifting between the trees. Something ghoulish and super cheesy like a monster from an old *Goosebumps* episode.

"Sorry." I close the app. We've already had dinner and changed into our pajamas. I sit on the edge of my bed, my knee bouncing anxiously. "I guess I just have a lot on my mind."

Portia stands in my doorway, brushing her teeth. "Want me to lend you one of my self-improvement journals?"

"I don't know. That's not really my thing." My stomach churns. It's been getting worse by the day. After dinner, I was literally kneeling over the toilet with cramps so bad I wouldn't wish them on my worst enemy.

She moves down the hall to her room, then into the bathroom. I follow and watch her in the mirror as she gargles.

I don't know what it is about coming home that makes you slip right back into your old habits. Portia's stuff is everywhere. Makeup, lotion, and perfume bottles clutter her vanity, and there are even smudges of foundation and mascara streaking the mirror. But while Portia's turned back into her messy, scatterbrained self, what I'm turning into is so much worse. Someone who worries and obsesses over every little thing. All the confidence I built during my years away from here is rapidly dissipating. This house and this family always seem to transform me into an uncertain and insecure mess. I rub my temples. No, I won't let that happen. I won't be that person again. I'm different now.

I'm *better*.

But even as the thought crosses my mind, I open the app again. The little white eye logo flashes onscreen, and I'm flipping through the different vantage points, studying the ghostly outlines of trees and the shadowy drive.

Portia runs a brush through her hair and leans against the sink to look at me. "Meet anyone new lately?"

"Excuse me?"

"You've been glued to your phone all night!" she points out, gesturing wildly with her hairbrush. "So, who is it?"

"No one!"

"Oh, come on."

"Trust me. There's nothing but cobwebs down there."

Portia pouts, her green eyes brimming with sympathy. She brings me in for a hug, but I know it's really to take a peek at my phone. She seems disappointed when she realizes I'm scrolling through the security cameras again. "Wait, hold on," she gasps, stopping me. I pause, my thumb hovering above the screen. Owen is swimming laps in the pool.

"Hello, gorgeous!" Portia says, resting her head against mine. "You should go say hi!"

"What? No."

She nudges me. "Why not?"

"Because I don't want to bother him. He's working out, and I already ruined one of his workouts."

"You're not bothering him. He likes you!"

"Not like that. Not anymore."

We watch the screen as Owen climbs the small silver ladder, water cascading off him. He doesn't have a towel. Portia dashes to the linen closet and thrusts a fluffy white one into my arms. "Here! Take this to him."

I groan. "Why are you always trying to set me up?"

She drags me downstairs, her arm draped over my shoulders. "Because I care about you and you've been lonely."

"Only a little," I lie.

Portia pats me on the cheek. "Briar. You're my sister," she says with a sweet smile. "I know when you're lying." She unlocks the sliding glass door, pulls it open, and shoves me out onto the lawn. "I ship you two!"

"Do you even know what that means?"

"It means my sister hasn't seen any action in over a year, and as her number one wing woman, I'm invested in making that happen."

"Portia!"

"Have fun!" She shuts the door and gives me a thumbs up through the glass. I roll my eyes and make sure she can see it. It only makes her laugh. She points in the direction of the pool. "Go!"

Owen's headed to the guesthouse when he notices me approaching with the towel. He grins at me. "Hey," he says, wiping the water from his face. "How's the ankle?"

"Better," I admit, returning his smile. "The painkillers helped. And keeping it elevated."

"Good. I'm glad." I hand him the towel, and he takes it gratefully. "Thank you," he says as he wraps it around his hips. I avert my gaze, trying not to linger on the muscles of his arms and back. "I forgot mine."

"I noticed."

Owen cocks a brow. "You watching me?"

"I'm watching the house," I correct him, enjoying deflating his ego. "The security cameras." I point them out. "We had someone break in recently and vandalize Vivienne's art gallery. Photographs of Odette. Probably a stupid teenager."

"That's awful. I didn't know." Owen frowns. "Look, I never got the chance to tell you how sorry I am about your sister."

I hold up a hand. "Thanks, but if one more person offers their condolences to me, I think I'll lose it."

Owen looks down, rubbing the back of his neck. "I get it."

I sigh, my gaze drifting over my shoulder. Portia stands in the kitchen, spying on us. I shoo her away. "I'm sorry," I apologize, turning back to him. "That came out a lot harsher than I meant it to."

"Don't worry about it."

"It's just... Odette's been on my mind a lot lately." I follow Owen as he pads toward the guesthouse and sinks into one of the chairs at the garden table. I sit across from him. "We weren't as close as we used to be. We stopped talking not long before... it happened. And now I can't help but wonder what she was hiding."

He raises a brow again. "What makes you think she was hiding something?"

"A hunch, I guess."

"Look, your sister was an introvert. In all the time I knew her, we barely exchanged two words. But being introverted doesn't automatically mean someone's hiding something." Owen leans back, stretching his legs out. He crosses his arms over his chest, studying me. "But if it's bugging you, I'd look into it. Investigate. What did Odette do in the months leading up to her death? Who was she close to? What was going on in her life?"

"She bought a new house with her husband. Not far from here, actually."

"Then I'd start there. Go to her house, her old hangouts. Maybe you have to figure out what she was about. It might help you come to terms with her passing."

"Yeah," I say, sitting up straighter. "That's not a bad idea."

Owen grins. "Happy to help."

17

It's drizzling by the time I reach Orange Blossom Drive, the picturesque cobblestone roads of Odette's old neighborhood glistening in the rain.

It's so unbelievably perfect. Like one of those miniature model towns that hobbyists take years to complete, painstakingly hand-painting every last piece. The houses are all two-story cookie cutters done in preppy pastels. The roads are bordered by vintage street lamps, and the lawns are perfectly manicured, the sidewalks wide and shaded by lush oaks.

Odette's house is a classic brick colonial with white pillars and black shutters. It's right at the end of a cul-de-sac, towering and austere. I can't help thinking how out of place her former home looks compared to the rest of them. Maybe it's because I know it's been empty for months or maybe it's because all the windows are dark. The other houses are already decorated for the holidays. They look so cheery while this one sits in mourning.

I unbuckle my seatbelt and grab the mini umbrella from my glove compartment before stepping out into the rain and sprinting to the front door. I use the key to let myself inside. It's empty, the furniture cleared for the next potential buyer. But there's something nagging at me that we've missed something important.

So I start checking everywhere—kitchen drawers, cabinets, even the garage. I'm hoping to find a hidden compartment or forgotten lockbox, anything that might hold some answers. I go through linen closets, the pool house, and the shed. But all I find is a foam cooler and a couple of shiny fishing lures.

I disinfect my hands as I slip back inside the house and then make my way upstairs, feeling a little hesitant about going into Odette's old bedroom. But I force myself, the door creaking open in a way that's unusual for a house this new.

It's large with a sweeping view of the whole neighborhood. A clean smell lingers in the air, and you can still see the vacuum lines on the white carpet. They're perfectly parallel, a soothing sight for my OCD, and the walls have been recently repainted, a dainty custard color. I remove my shoes before crossing the room, and then I search for hidden spaces in the carpet or subtle folds in the wallpaper where a secret safe might be stashed.

No such luck. I go back to the hallway and try the other rooms. Thirty minutes later, the search turns up nothing, and I feel silly for even trying.

It's still drizzling when I lock up the house and head back to my car, the drive slippery beneath my heeled sandals. I'm trying not to step into any puddles, eyes on the ground, when I smack into someone.

The woman drops her shopping bags onto the wet pavement, a pack of Halloween candy landing in the street. "I'm so sorry," I gasp, bending down to help gather her things. "Are you okay?"

"Briar?"

The woman looks up at me from her crouched position on the sidewalk and I instantly recognize her. It's Odette's sister-in-law. "Sophia," I say, surprised. "I didn't know you lived here."

"Down the street. We bought the place a few months before..."

Sophia stands, her bright smile dimming. She adjusts her shopping bags and takes the candy from me. "What are you doing here?"

"I... uh..." I try to think up some excuse, but in the end, I don't have to.

She glances up at the sky and motions for me to follow her. "Come back to my place. We'll catch up there."

~

Sophia's house is painted bright canary yellow with white columns and a brick porch. As we step inside, the foyer gets flooded with this gorgeous warm light from the empire chandelier that sparkles overhead. I look up, admiring it, and then catch a glimpse of myself in the entryway mirror. My hair is a mess. I run my fingers through it, hoping to tame the frizz. This weather is definitely not my friend.

Three cocker spaniels race to the door, their tongues lolling out and tails wagging. I remember their names because Odette adored them. Archie, Aidan, and Alexander. She was planning on bringing home a cocker spaniel puppy around Christmas. She'd already spoken with the breeder, and her name was added to the top of the waiting list.

Sophia removes her tartan Burberry coat, her light chestnut hair as luminous beneath the chandelier as the strand of freshwater pearls draped around her neck. I shimmy out of my own coat, shivering from the rain, and she places it on a hanger next to hers in the wardrobe along with our umbrellas.

The dogs are still going crazy. I kneel to give them some extra attention, scratching behind their ears and rubbing their tummies —mostly to avoid standing there awkwardly. I haven't seen Sophia in ages. Not since the wedding. My sister didn't have the greatest relationship with her in-laws. And that's putting it lightly.

"Can I get you anything?" Sophia asks, twirling the bow of her cream-colored sheath dress. "Coffee? Tea?"

"Coffee's fine, thanks."

We move into the kitchen, all white marble and dove gray cabinets. The floor plan is open, the separate rooms connected, even the little nook by the front windows where the grand piano sits shining below a sea of skylights.

I wander around, pausing before a framed wedding photo. It's a massive print of the wedding party. Sophia and her husband at the center. The flower girls and ring bearers stationed at the front. The groomsmen on one side. The bridesmaids on the other. I take a closer look, focusing in on the edge of the photograph where a sliver of shoulder is barely visible in the frame. They *cropped* Odette out of the picture.

Sophia clears her throat, startling me. She gestures for me to sit. I turn around, a little bit annoyed on my sister's behalf, and settle on a stool at the kitchen island. Once the coffee's done brewing, she pours us each a cup. She keeps her distance from me, choosing to stand on the other side of the island, her lips pinched into a thin line. "Look," she says, the tension in the room mounting. "I'm not very good at this small talk thing and I know we've had...problems...in the past."

I nod, lifting my chin. "You mean when your family accused my sister of murdering your brother, had her tailed by a PI, and then tried to sue us?"

She holds eye contact with me, probably wondering if inviting me back here was a mistake. I half expect her to throw me out for being so blunt. Then she swallows and tilts her head at me. "I'm sorry about your sister. After I heard what happened, I thought... Well, I thought..." She shakes her head and takes a quick sip of coffee. "If my family played any part..."

"Because you were harassing her?"

"Well, yes," Sophia chuckles wryly. "My family can be pretty merciless. I didn't want to destroy her reputation or drive her to... kill herself. If that's what happened." She has her voice lowered to a whisper as if the thought alone is scandalous. "But when you grow up in a family like mine, it's hard for their ways not to rub off on you."

I bring the little silver spoon around the edge of my mug, chasing air bubbles. "I get it," I say. "I really do. And I don't think your family had anything to do with my sister's death, just like I don't think my sister had anything to do with your brother's."

Sophia nods. She seems relieved. "It's easy to get caught up in the headlines."

I wince at her choice of words. Isn't that the truth? The media dubbing us the 'Belville Black Widows.' First, with my husband's death, and then Odette's husband, Ryan. A sudden, fatal heart attack in his late thirties. It was rare enough to raise suspicion. The autopsy revealed an enlarged heart, likely caused by prior drug use. But still, with the tragedies so close together, and with Vivienne's mysterious past, it made for a sensational story.

The press and the internet ate us alive.

"Speaking of your sister," Sophia continues, swirling a packet of stevia into her drink. "I've been meaning to talk to you about something."

I straighten up in my seat, interested. "Oh?"

"Did you happen to notice that your sister seemed... different?"

"Different how?"

Sophia hesitates. I'm afraid she's changed her mind when suddenly she says, "It wasn't only the headlines that had my family so freaked out. Odette changed quite a bit in the months leading up to my brother's death. She stopped attending family functions. She withdrew from friends. Became secretive. I couldn't help but suspect she might be having an affair."

I think about the last time Odette visited me, a year ago when she came to stay at the condo after my husband died. That's around the same time I noticed the unusual late-night phone calls, her whispered conversations that she'd hastily end whenever I walked into the room.

Sophia's brow creases with worry. "I even caught her with a man once, but when I confronted her about it, she denied everything. She warned me to stay out of her business, or in her words, I'd be sorry."

"Odette had a boyfriend?" I murmur. It's hard believing she used to share everything with me and Portia. What changed? And how could I not have known this?

Sophia nods, retrieving her cellphone from her bag. "Yes. Give me a minute. I'm sure I have a picture somewhere."

I wait as she scrolls, her determined brown eyes scanning the screen. "Here," she says, turning the phone to me. "Look."

I take the phone from her, my heart aching at the image of my sister. She's with a man I don't recognize at all. He's tall and slender with sharp, angular features. His head is covered by a gray hoodie, but a portion of his wavy blonde hair peeks out. "You took this through your window," I say, noticing the parted curtains at the corners of the photo.

"What? No." Sophia blinks, feigning innocence. "Okay, yes. But I was concerned." She switches to a video. As the man approaches Odette, he glances over his shoulder, and she does the same, as if they're afraid to be seen together. "And," Sophia adds with a sigh, "I was looking out for my brother."

I watch the video intently, observing their body language. They seem nervous. But not in a *we're-lovers-and-could-get-caught-any-moment* way. They don't kiss. Or hold hands. There's nothing intimate about this video at all. I hand the phone back to Sophia. "When was this taken?"

"Eight months ago, maybe. Not long before Ryan passed."

"And you said that you confronted her about it?"

"I tried, but she'd just get angry. In the end, I decided to let it go." She frowns into her mug. "I didn't want to drive her away."

"Did you ever find out who he was?"

Sophia shakes her head. "No, despite my best efforts. As you know, my family has a lot of resources at their disposal, but unfortunately, our mystery man remains..." She gives a defeated shrug, "...elusive."

18

THE HOUSE SMELLS delicious when I get home. Like the inside of a bakery. Warm and sweet and mouthwatering.

I make a beeline for the kitchen. Juliet and Elise are sitting at the table in the breakfast nook, decorating cupcakes. The table is covered in rainbow sprinkles, edible heart-shaped confetti, and bowls of pastel-colored icing. Juliet has it all over her face and stuck between the gap of her two front teeth.

Elise is taking decorating very seriously. She has her red glasses pressed firmly to the bridge of her nose, her silver bangs brushed back with a cheetah print headband, her mouth puckered in deep concentration.

They're wearing matching pink ruffle aprons, including Owen who dons a pair of kitten oven mitts. He's just taken a second tray of cupcakes out of the oven.

"What's all this?" I laugh.

"We're making cupcakes!" Juliet announces excitedly. She kicks her legs, slides out of her seat, and runs a fully finished cupcake over to me. It has my name and everything. Spelled out in silver beads. "This one's yours!"

"Oh, my gosh! Did you make this?"

She smiles wide. Then she folds her arms behind her back and nods.

"I love it! Thank you so much!" I pull her in for a hug and plant a kiss atop her head.

"Try it!" she urges as she wraps her arms around me and hangs from my waist. She's so strong, she almost knocks me over.

I take a bite, savoring the moist fluffiness of the cake and the creamy sweetness of the buttercream. It melts in my mouth. "Mmm, it's delicious."

"Owen baked them," Juliet informs me, smiling shyly at her new friend. He returns her smile as he sets the cupcake tray on the kitchen island to cool. "But I helped."

"We baked them together," Owen tells me. "And with her help, they're the best batch I've ever made." He moves over to the breakfast nook and slaps a hand to his mouth, looking impressed. "Wow. You've got mad decorating skills!"

My heart warms at the sight of my little sister. She's absolutely glowing from the compliment. She runs to the table, picks out her favorite cupcake—the one with the most sprinkles—and hands it to Owen. "You can have this one!"

She watches with happy eyes as Owen takes it from her and goes on about how fantastic the cupcake looks. He takes a big bite. "Wow, Juliet. This is a winner!"

Juliet jumps up and down like she's won the lottery. I think someone's developing a little crush. But then again, who can blame her?

"Can we bake cookies next, Owen? Sugar cookies?"

He nods. "We can bake whatever you want."

"Once I finish decorating these, I'll decorate the other ones too," Juliet decides, tapping her chin. She points at me. "And Briar, you can help me!"

"I'd love to," I say, grabbing an apron and dropping into the seat beside Elise. Owen and I exchange a quick smile as Juliet skips over to his cellphone. It sits on the kitchen counter, charging. Disney's

Encanto soundtrack is playing. She pokes at the screen, trying to unlock it. "Owen!"

"Yeah! What's up?"

"Can we listen to Judy Garland now?"

He doesn't even question it. "Sure!"

I suspect Juliet is the only seven-year-old diehard Judy Garland fan. Her favorite song is "Get Happy," and she plays it on repeat.

Elise hands me a cupcake and I select the blue icing, spooning a dollop on top and smoothing it out with a butter knife. I'm in the process of adding sprinkles when my phone vibrates against my left butt cheek. I drop everything, hoping it's Sophia with more information about Odette.

I'm disappointed to find a push notification from the Secure-Home app instead. There was motion detected by the front gate. I don't know if it's from all the craziness that's gone on lately, but as I tap on the notification and the camera footage stretches across my screen, I'm hit with a surge of adrenaline. It climbs even higher when I see a flash of red behind the hibiscus bush. "Everything okay?" Elise asks, noticing my panicked expression.

I relax once I shift the camera angle and find Claire standing beside her jeep, looking startled at the sight of the lens. She breaks into a smile and gives a timid, little wave. "Yeah, it's just Claire from the ecology center."

Elise raises a brow. "Odette's friend?"

"Yep." I promptly buzz her in and go to meet her at the door. "Hey, come in. It's been forever!"

"H-hey," she stutters softly, standing there awkwardly on the porch. She hesitates like she's afraid to come inside the house. She wrings her hands and squeezes her fingers together. "I see you've upped your security game," she says once she's brave enough to step inside. "I didn't notice last time."

"Oh, you were here for the funeral?" I ask, surprised, certain I hadn't seen any of my sister's friends there.

Claire fidgets with her purse strap, swallowing. "Actually, I wasn't invited," she admits, offering me an apologetic glance. "I dropped by the other day before work, but when I spotted you through the window, I guess I got scared." She lets out a self-deprecating chuckle and nervously brushes a strand of hair behind her ear. "I kind of ran away."

I chuckle too, but at my own stupidity. It was *Claire* I saw the other morning, not some ghost in a bloodstained dress. She must've been wearing the same uniform she has on now, the crimson polo with the ecology center's logo on the breast, the crisp white pants. "So, that was you, huh?" Claire nods, and I internally curse myself. "I thought I was seeing things."

"Yeah, sorry about that." Claire cringes. "The gate was open, so I drove in and parked, and then I had this moment of realization like, 'Claire, what the heck are you doing? Showing up unannounced, without even calling or emailing first.'" She shifts nervously. "Kind of like I'm doing now. When I got to work, I realized I didn't have anyone's number except Odette's, and I really need to talk to you guys."

"Seriously, it's no problem," I insist, shuffling her into the parlor. It sounds like she might know something, and I can't chance her running away again. "Please, sit. Make yourself comfortable. I'll grab us some refreshments." I hurry to the kitchen and pause before the door. "By the way, would you like a cupcake?"

I catch Claire gazing up at the family photo on the mantel, her eyes lingering on Odette. "Sure, that sounds great."

"Just so you know, the cupcakes are blue."

"Even better."

I whip up a tray of herbal tea with cream and sugar and put together a small platter of cupcakes. Then I find Portia upstairs and drag her to the parlor. I'm sure she's just as curious as I am to find out what this is about.

Claire's hand trembles as she takes a sip of tea, the delicate porcelain cup rattling against the saucer. Purple shadows ring her eyes. It looks like she hasn't slept in days. She clears her throat, her petite frame shaking like a frightened chihuahua.

Portia looks worried. "Hey, are you...okay?" she asks.

"You don't have to be nervous," I cut in with an encouraging smile. "We can handle anything you came here to tell us."

"I guess you already know the first part," Claire says, speaking into her tea. She peeks up at Portia. "I mean, *you're* the one who suggested she see a hypnotherapist in the first place."

I make a face. "A hypno-what?"

"A hypnotherapist," Portia answers, way too enthusiastically, and I mentally prepare myself for a lesson on alternative medicine. "They help others by using hypnosis, a state of focused relaxation. They work with the person's subconscious mind to promote personal growth or healing or even help them get rid of bad habits."

I blink in surprise. "You encouraged our sister to pay a stranger to mind-roofie her?"

Portia widens her eyes at me in mock offense. "That's not it at all, Briar. It's actually very helpful for many people, and I sent her to a highly reputable therapist. Mason Montgomery, the owner of The Hypnosis Group. He's all over YouTube!"

"Yeah, about that," Claire interrupts gently, setting her tea aside. "Odette told me she was being blackmailed by your... um... reputable therapist. Yeah, so... Apparently, he secretly recorded sessions with his wealthy clients and used the videos to extort money from them."

"What?" Portia and I say together.

Claire covers her face with her hands. "I know I should have spoken up earlier, but Odette made me promise not to say anything. Then after she died, I thought, 'Oh no, I knew all along what was going on, and I could have done more to help her. I could have reported him. And now it's my fault she's gone.'"

Blackmail? I grip my teacup, my heart beating faster. What

could he even use to blackmail Odette? She was practically a saint. "You think she killed herself because of it," I realize.

"Maybe," Claire says. "I just don't believe it was an accident. It's strange to me that Odette would drive an airboat. She felt that they damage our local flora and fauna. And she was extremely cautious in the field. She prioritized safety. Do I think she crashed? Absolutely not. I checked the weather for that day and visibility was clear. No fog. Trust me, the only way she could have crashed that boat is if she intended to." She fights back tears, staring up at the ceiling. "Honestly, I think she hoped no one would find her. I think she was so desperate it was just a split-second decision for her."

I don't want to believe it. I'd rather cling desperately to the last shreds of denial.

Portia shakes her head as if she's having trouble keeping up with us. "Hold on, let's back up for a second," she says, a line forming between her brows. "You're saying Mason Montgomery was blackmailing his wealthy clients. But why would he do that? And how come nobody else ever accused him?"

"Hm, I wonder why someone who's being *blackmailed* wouldn't want to accuse the *blackmailer*," I say, giving her an incredulous look before turning back to Claire. "Do you know what was on those videos?"

Claire shakes her head. "I have no idea. Something bad. She only told me how scared she was. She never told me *why* she went to the hypnotherapist in the first place, other than that she was having some trouble remembering things from her childhood. She felt like she had some kind of mental block in place."

Sounds familiar.

Claire gazes over her shoulder, her eyes glued to the window. It's like she's stuck in a trance, a deer-caught-in-the-headlights expression on her face. I peer out the window but see nothing.

"Are you sure you're okay?" Portia asks again.

"Yeah, I've just been feeling out of sorts lately."

That sounds familiar, too.

When she turns back to us, she seems even more stressed than before. "I'm just really freaking out right now. I keep feeling like someone's following me," she says, her voice strained. "Stalking me, you know?"

"What?" I say, looking back out the window.

"I don't know if I'm just imagining it but..." She swallows, her breath quickening. "The other night, I woke up around 3 a.m. and I thought I heard someone moving around downstairs. There was banging. Like they were going through my things... maybe looking for something. I don't know. It scared the hell out of me! So, I grabbed the baseball bat I keep in my closet, and I walked downstairs and I thought I saw..." Claire's eyes shift to the photograph above the mantel. "Her."

"Odette?" I say in shock. Suddenly, I'm freezing cold, the draft biting at the back of my neck.

Portia shakes her head. "No, no. That's..."

"Impossible? Crazy?" Claire supplies. "Yeah, I know. I thought I saw her standing in the middle of my freaking living room, but it was so dark, I don't know." Her lower lip quivers and she sniffles, wiping her nose on the back of her hand. I give her a quick squirt of hand sanitizer and a napkin. "Thanks... Anyway, by the time I made it to the light switch, she was gone. I'm not even sure I saw anyone at all." She leans in closer, searching our faces. "Do you believe in ghosts?"

"Yes," Portia says, transfixed.

At the same moment, I say, "No." But it's not with as much conviction as I usually have.

"Sometimes I think Odette is haunting me because I didn't do more to help her. It's why I keep feeling someone is... *there*. I can't explain it." She shakes her head, worry contorting her features. "But I know."

I think of my conversation with Sophia, the video she showed me. "Are you sure it was a woman you saw? And not a man?"

Claire's shoulders droop. "It was dark, so I'm not a hundred percent certain. But I could've swore it was her. I screamed. I screamed so loud and dropped my bat. Afterward, I called the police, but they searched and couldn't find anyone."

"But it could've been a man?"

Claire sips her tea, mulling it over. "Yeah, I guess. Maybe..."

"Was Odette seeing anybody?" I ask. "Did she have a boyfriend?"

"Boyfriend... I... Didn't she ever tell you, guys?" Claire laughs breathily, her cheeks turning pink. She stares into her tea again. "Odette didn't have a boyfriend. She had a girlfriend." When she looks up at us, she wears an anxious but excited smile. "Me."

19

The waiting room at The Hypnosis Group is packed with people. Portia and I snag chairs in the back, sandwiched between an older couple and a woman who looks like she just got back from a yoga retreat. I crane my neck, checking out the reception desk. It's swarmed with patients, the receptionist holding onto her coffee for dear life.

Portia selects a magazine from the table and absentmindedly flips through it. "It looks like we're going to be here for a while," she says, opening an organic perfume sample and rubbing the whole magazine against her neck. "Maybe I should've tried reaching out to Mason over Instagram first. It doesn't look like he'll have time to talk to us today."

"We're not here to talk," I reply in a discreet whisper. I avoid the magazines and cover my hands in disinfectant. This whole place is probably crawling with germs, but as usual, I came prepared. "We're going to find out what's on those videos."

Portia shifts uncomfortably in her seat. She snaps the magazine open to a different page. "You never mentioned that. I thought we came here to confront Mason, not get thrown into jail."

"Hey, no one's getting arrested, okay?" I hold out a finger. "Pinky promise." It's something we did all the time as kids, especially when we were up to no good, and it feels fitting now. And I choose not to share with her that I fantasized about beating Mason half to death with his own computer on the ride over here.

Portia rolls her eyes at me, but she does it, anyway. The sun catches the glimmer of her diamond ring as we connect fingers, blinding me. I blink, trying to get the dancing spots out of my eyes. "Hey, can I ask you something?"

"Sure, hit me."

"What happened between you and Luke?"

I can actually see Portia visibly clam up. She sinks deeper into her seat and flips faster through her magazine. "Why do you want to know?"

"Because you're my sister," I say with a sigh. "It's just... I don't know... Sometimes it feels like I didn't even know Odette at all. I had no idea she was dating anyone, let alone a woman."

"Don't feel bad. I didn't either."

Shifting in my seat, I playfully swing her arm around like the pesky little sister I am. "Yeah, but isn't that sad? We're family. We should be able to share anything with each other." I stare earnestly at her, prodding at her arm, as she tries to hide behind her magazine. Then her shoulders drop and start to shake. I'm horrified to see she's crying. "Portia?"

She slaps the magazine down on her lap, revealing an article about celebrity moms and moms-to-be. "Luke wants to have kids," she whispers, a mascara-streaked tear dripping off her chin.

I'm frantically searching for a tissue and find a wrinkled pack of them buried deep within my purse. "And you don't?" I ask, handing her one.

"No, I do. I really do." She takes the tissue from me and dabs at her eyes. She looks around self-consciously and then lowers her voice. "I'm just fucking terrified, you know? That I'll mess them up, that I'll fall off the wagon and start drinking again. I think that's why I've been pushing Luke away. Every time he brings up the baby thing, I find myself sitting in my car, gripping the steering wheel, trying to resist the urge to drive to the nearest liquor store. I'm so afraid of putting our kids through what our mom put us through, and I refuse to let that happen." Her face crumples again. "I already love them too much."

"Oh, Portia," I say, bringing her in for a hug. "You're not our mother."

"I know that," she says as she pulls away. She blows her nose into her tissue, and a few heads turn our way. I'm sure everybody's eavesdropping, but this is a therapist's office, so I feel like tears aren't so out of the ordinary here. This waiting room has probably seen much worse.

"But this fear is embedded in me," Portia goes on. "And I can't shake it, no matter how hard I try. It's like everything else in my life. Everyone seems so happy. Like they're moving forward. Having the perfect wedding, going on the dream honeymoon, starting a family. And it doesn't matter what milestones I achieve or how many personal victories I experience. I still feel unhappy. Like I'm just permanently... *stuck*."

"In the past?"

"Yep." She pops the 'p' at the end, looking miserable.

"That's called emotional baggage," I inform her. "You should know this, right? Miss enlightenment?"

Portia smiles through her tears, playfully swatting at me. She tries to make a joke, but it's only half-hearted. "Shh, don't let anyone know. I have an image to maintain."

I mock surprise. "Wait, you mean you're not the ultra-perfect self-help guru 24/7?"

She gives me an exhausted look. "If you knew how hard it is to act like you've chugged a bottle of Percocet with your morning smoothie..."

We both laugh.

"Thanks, Briar. I do feel better now."

"Better than writing in your daily manifestations journal? Or whatever it's called."

"Much better."

"Don't worry," I assure her. "You'll figure things out with Luke. I know it."

"I know it, too." She reaches for another tissue and glances at the reception desk. "Should we just go up there?"

"Actually..." I stop Portia before she can wipe her face. "Hold off on that. Keep looking sad. I have an idea."

I make my way to the front, where the receptionist is having a heated discussion with a patient. "I had an appointment at nine, and I've been waiting for 45 minutes already!" he says, raising his voice.

"I understand, sir. If you'd prefer to reschedule..."

"I don't want to reschedule! I want to see my therapist! Where the hell is he?"

I slide in beside the man, flashing a polite smile. "Excuse me, but we're kind of having an issue." I nod at Portia, still sitting over there with her magazine, sniffling and dabbing at her eyes with the crinkled tissue. "Do you know what time Mr. Montgomery is supposed to arrive?"

The receptionist, clearly flustered, looks at me. Her shoulders and jaw are tense, and she seems close to her breaking point. "Like I told this gentleman..." She says the word *gentleman* through clenched teeth. "Mr. Montgomery is running late today."

"Is there another therapist available, maybe?" I ask, trying to figure out if anyone other than the receptionist is here. "It's an emergency."

"There is no other therapist," the receptionist says slowly, her teeth still clenched. "This is Mr. Montgomery's office. But you're more than welcome to use the restroom while you wait. There are more tissues in there."

"And where's that?"

The receptionist picks up the phone and dials a number.

Covering the receiver with her hand, she nods her head to the left. "Right down the hall."

"Okay, thanks." She seems happy to be rid of me, and the *gentleman* doesn't seem like he's going to leave her alone anytime soon, so I stride down the hall, gesturing for Portia to follow.

"What did you say to her?" Portia asks once she catches up to me.

"Mason seems to be running behind this morning," I say as we pass the bathroom and turn a corner. "But that also means his office is currently unattended..."

"Are you suggesting we sneak in?" Portia says. "Briar, I'm pretty sure this is illegal. And you promised we wouldn't leave this building in handcuffs!"

"We're not going to get caught." When we reach Mason's office, I quickly unlock the door with a bobby pin and crack it open, happy to see the skills Owen taught me as a teenager are still paying off.

"I can't get into trouble! Nothing about prison screams wellness! That would be so off-brand for me. Unless... hey, do you think I could get into Camp Cupcake? Martha Stewart went there. And you know how I feel about Martha Stewart. I would *so* be her prison bitch."

"We're not going to get in trouble!" I whisper-shout. "The receptionist has her hands full, and we'll be in and out before Dr. Scumbag arrives."

Portia chews on her thumbnail. "Are you sure?"

I nod. "Positive. But on the bright side, if you do go to prison, think of all the new clients you'll have!"

Portia crinkles her nose at me. "Very funny."

We step inside and quietly shut the door behind us. The space feels cramped. There's a desk, a sofa, an armchair, and shelves stocked with stress relievers. A Zen garden, a Newton's cradle. Framed certificates and diplomas hang on the back wall. I pick up a framed photo on the desk, my pulse quickening as I take in the man's strawberry-blonde hair and distinctive features. Mason

Montgomery is the same man from the video Sophia showed me, the man she suspected my sister was having an affair with. But I was right. There was no affair. Odette had looked nervous in that video because this two-faced crook was threatening her.

Portia picks up another framed photo, this one shaped like a dog's paw. A German shepherd sits in Mason's lap, with the name *Princess Pecan Pie* written over the top. I move to his computer and jiggle the mouse, typing the name into the password field.

Portia sidles up to me, giving me a skeptical look. "Yeah." She snorts. "Like that's going to work."

When the computer unlocks, she chokes.

"Now, that's just embarrassing," I mutter as I drop into his swivel chair. I open the folder titled "sessions" and then click on the video labeled "OdetteBelville_Session03.mp4." This video was recorded two months before her death.

Portia and I exchange a glance.

"Well, what are you waiting for?" she groans, gesturing impatiently at the screen. "We don't exactly have all the time in the world here. Open it!"

I open the file and hit play.

OdetteBelville_Session03.mp4 transcript from The Hypnosis Group

Odette Belville appears onscreen. She lies on the office sofa, her hands folded in her lap, her fingers tightly intertwined. Her foot bounces nervously. She wears a simple black pencil skirt, cardigan, and flats. Her hair is greasy and unwashed. Mason Montgomery sits off-screen, his voice soft and soothing.

Mason: So, Odette, when you're ready and comfortable, feel free to close your eyes and take a deep breath for me.

Odette squeezes her eyes shut and inhales deeply.

Mason: What I want you to do is relax and forget all your troubles. Remember that safe space we discussed in our last session? The island with the beautiful palm trees and the hammock that swings out over the ocean?

Odette: I remember.

Mason: I want you to return to your safe space.

Mason has the patient practice breathing exercises, guiding her into a relaxed state.

Mason: Have you reached your safe space yet?

Odette's voice is low and monotone, like she's in a trance. Her expression is serene.

Odette: Yes.

Mason: Good. Keep swinging there for a moment. Enjoy the breeze. The clear sky. The lapping sound of the waves. And once you're ready, I'm going to have you take me back to a point in your childhood when you felt happy.

Odette's mouth tugs into a soft smile.

Odette: I'm with my sisters. We're singing a song together and dancing by the pool. We're making s'mores.

Mason: Tell me more.

Odette goes into more detail about the memory.

Mason: You're doing amazing. But next, we're going to try something a little more difficult. I want to explore a time in your childhood when you didn't feel happy. Maybe you even felt sad or angry.

Odette falls silent, frowning, but her body twitches and trembles. She looks like she's having a nightmare.

Odette: I can't… I don't know if I can.

Mason: You can, Odette. I know you can.

Odette: No, I can't. There's too much.

Mason: Too much what?

Odette: Blood. It's everywhere.

Odette thrashes harder, striking the sofa. She groans as if she's in horrible pain.

Odette: I can't! I'm so ashamed.

The armchair creaks as Mason leans forward in his seat.

Mason: Ashamed of what?

Odette: I can't live with myself anymore.

Odette begins to sob, thrashing so violently she almost looks as if she's convulsing. She knocks over a lamp, and it crashes to the floor, shattering.

Mason: I think that does it for today. Let's return to your safe space. Return to the island for me. The hammock. Remember that you're shielded there and nothing can harm you.

Odette begins to calm down and gradually reemerges from the trance.

Mason: Take a deep breath for me. Inhale… exhale. Now slowly open your eyes.

Odette's eyes snap open and she shoots upright. She's visibly distressed and rubbing her chest.

Odette: What happened?

Mason: You were in a deep state of relaxation. We explored some memories and emotions. It's normal to feel a bit confused after coming out of the trance.

Odette: I feel more than confused. I feel…

Odette looks uncertain.

Odette: I'm feeling a little woozy, actually.

Mason: That's completely normal. Take your time to process everything. You did great today. Lie back if you need to and rest for a moment.

Odette lies back onto the sofa, shaken. She wrings her hands in her lap.

End of transcript.

Portia and I stare at the screen after the video ends. My heart feels heavy in my chest, and my stomach twists. It sickens me to think this man, this "so-called" professional, recorded our sister with the sole intention of using the footage against her in the end.

Portia turns away, shaking her head. "I should've never sent her here. I should've done more research. Or at least gone with her. If I had known he was an extortionist..."

"It's not your fault," I say, looking over my shoulder at her. She paces around the room in tight circles, her fists clenched. "You didn't know." I click out of the video and search for the next one, but can't find any.

There *has* to be other videos. If Mason was really blackmailing our sister, Odette never mentioned anything incriminating in the video we just watched. And where is session one and two? Maybe the other videos are in another folder. I continue my search, clicking through files and folders and various apps, even the trash bin.

There's nothing.

That bastard must have wiped them from the computer. Or maybe he was storing them somewhere else.

"Help me check the drawers," I instruct Portia, and we rifle through his desk, fingering through folders and notepads and letters.

Just then, the door bursts open and the receptionist marches in, an angry expression on her face. She glares at us, hands planted firmly on her hips. "Excuse me, but you're not allowed back here."

"We only wanted to speak with Mason," Portia says with a disarming smile as she circles around the desk. "You see, me and him are super close friends and I'm sure he wouldn't mind us waiting here for him."

I doubt the receptionist would count following each other on Instagram as being super close friends, but I let Portia do her thing. I don't want to be escorted out of here in handcuffs, either.

"Well, that's fine and dandy, but Mr. Montgomery is running

late, and I haven't been able to reach him for two whole days. He's not answering any of my calls. So, unless you can get him on the phone right now and he can give me the green light, I'm going to have to ask you to leave." She crosses her arms. "Or I can call security. Your choice. What's it going to be?"

Portia and I exchange a glance. "We'll go," she says.

Outside, the bright sun does nothing to raise our morale. We sulk all the way to the car, our spirits low. "I had no idea what she was going through. Or that she was in such a dark place," Portia says. "You don't think she... took her own life, do you?"

I slide into the passenger seat and fasten my seatbelt, trying to avoid speaking out loud what's been running through my head. Portia gazes at me expectantly before starting the car. "I don't know," I say, distracted, picking at a small scab on the back of my hand. "After watching that video, I don't know what to think anymore."

That's not true, and I know it's not true. Because after seeing my sister looking absolutely terrified on that sorry-excuse-for-a-shrink's sofa, I'm starting to think that maybe Claire was right. Maybe Odette's death wasn't an accident.

20

You'd think the lack of sleep would start getting to me, but as I follow one of the many footpaths of the estate, I'm wide awake.

I clench my fists, exhaling, as I approach the swamp's shore. After what happened, I thought I'd never want to come back here. But as strange as it sounds, it makes me feel closer to my sister. I don't know how, but it does. It's oddly comforting.

Dropping onto the cool sand, I stare up at the full moon, hugging my knees close to my chest. The sky is clear, the stars blinking at me.

At night, the swamp really comes to life. There's a constant chorus of frogs, crickets, and cicadas. The black water gurgles and a hazy fog swirls over the surface. The cypress trees sway in the breeze, and it smells so clean and fresh now that it's cooled off. This sweet tropical scent.

My sister and I share... shared... a lot of good memories here. Taking the boat out on the water, searching for iguanas and otters. One time we spotted a herd of manatees and Robert had us jump in and feed them a head of lettuce. I remember their skin being so thick and slimy. Smooth like blubber. Their snouts and whiskers wiggled as they pushed against us and tried to eat our hair. I rest my head on my knees, smiling at the memory.

A lot of locals are scared of this place. The swamp and its waterways. There's a lot of lore in this town. Superstition. Handmade crosses staked along the roadside in an effort to ward off evil.

Legend has it that a rogue wave carried a pirate ship deep into the Everglades. Whenever a full moon rises in the night sky, the undead crew trudge helplessly along the muddy banks. They drag anyone who dares cross their path into the depths, drowning them, trapping their souls here forever.

I've never bought into all that stuff, but when a twig snaps somewhere behind me, I hold my breath and listen, every muscle in my body tense. I hear footsteps, and they're headed my way. I scramble to my feet, searching the darkness. "Hello?"

Another twig cracks, loud, in a different direction. My heart races faster. The woods are a noisy place. I hear animals trampling through the brush almost every night. But whatever this is...

It sounds big.

Human.

I take a timid step back, bracing myself, as the bushes shake.

"Hey," Owen says, stepping into the moonlight.

I breathe a sigh of relief, my heart still pounding in my chest as Owen comes closer. "Hey," I manage weakly.

Owen knits his brows together. "Sorry. I didn't mean to scare you."

"You didn't," I lie, my heart rate slowing, but not completely returning to normal. I search his face. "What are you doing out here?"

Owen rubs sheepishly at the back of his head. "At the risk of sounding creepy, I followed you," he admits. "I was outside having a drink when I heard someone. I thought I'd check it out."

"That's noble of you." I smile. "Or stupid. Wandering into the woods in the middle of the night because you thought you heard something. That's a mistake side characters in horror movies make right before they die."

Owen cocks a brow. "So, I'm a side character?"

"Like I said, a noble one."

Owen chuckles, blowing air out through his nose. He kicks at the dead leaves scattered over the ground beside the path, his hands stuck in his pockets. Something about the action makes him look younger. As if I'm standing here with my childhood friend. He's just hidden somewhere beneath that burly exterior. When he looks up at me, his eyes are kind. "Couldn't sleep, huh?"

I shrug. "Nope."

"Insomnia?"

"Yep." I sink back into the sand, swatting at the mosquitoes. "It's a fairly recent problem."

I pat the spot beside me, and Owen takes a seat, releasing an easy sigh. I can't help noticing how good he looks, even in flannel pants and a loose T-shirt. There's something so edgy about him. Like he's not a good guy, and he *knows* he's not a good guy, but there's a bleeding heart tucked behind those rock-solid pecs of his.

"Do you want to talk about it?" Owen asks, tilting his head to look at me.

"About what?"

"Why you can't sleep and why you're sitting out here in the middle of the night at the same spot your sister..."

Breaking into chills, I avoid his gaze and study the dark reflec tions that reach out across the water. "No, I'd rather not."

"I heard about what happened today."

"Oh," I say, embarrassed. "Did Portia say something?"

"Yeah," Owen chuckles. "She had a *lot* to say."

I roll my eyes. "She exaggerates."

"Maybe. But it was my fault. I told you to dig around, and I shouldn't have done that."

"It wasn't *your* fault. It was mine. I just... I don't know where my head's been at lately. It's, like, I'm… I don't know. Never mind. Forget I said anything."

He watches me a moment longer before gazing up at the moon. "I'm going to share something with you I've never shared with anyone before." I can hear his breathing quicken, sense his discomfort. "My father took his own life and I'm the one who found him."

I'm looking at him now. He has my full attention.

"No one expected it," he goes on, his voice low. "Sure as hell not me. And I was angry and confused for a long time after."

"I can understand that," I whisper, sympathizing with the young Owen and the equally distraught version sitting beside me now. "How old were you?"

"Seven."

My heart breaks. He's never opened up to me about his father before. I reach out and touch his arm. "Owen, I'm so sorry."

"He was my best friend. That's why I was so shocked. Never in a million years did I think he would…" He drops his head, shaking it. "I didn't realize he was unhappy. He never said anything. Never acted depressed. And I kept thinking, if he was so unhappy, why didn't he say something to my mom or grandma? How could we have missed the signs? If there were any…"

I give him a reassuring squeeze. "There was nothing you could have done to change it."

"I know that now. But at the time, his suicide felt like a big *fuck you* to me. I started getting into trouble at school. Into fights. I couldn't focus. Couldn't commit myself to anything." He closes his eyes. "It took me a long time to come to terms with the past. I forgave my father eventually, but only because I realized something."

"What was that?"

"He thought he was doing the right thing. For me. In his own warped brain, he thought my mother and I were better off without him. All those years I spent hating his guts, blaming myself, blaming him for abandoning us. But he was sick. Like any other illness, he was sick. You'll drive yourself crazy asking *why*. Their reasoning doesn't look the same as ours. It can't be explained... rationally."

"I get it," I say, hugging my knees tighter. "I'm glad you're in a better place."

"You'll get there, too," Owen promises.

"Thank you for telling me that," I say. "It helped. Really."

"Good."

"And I'm sorry for what happened."

"It was a long time ago."

"Still, I'm sorry."

Owen holds my gaze. He takes my hand suddenly and gives it a gentle squeeze. "Yeah. I'm sorry, too. For him, and for your sister."

My heart beats faster, and this time, it's not from fear.

THE HOUSE IS dark when I slip back inside. It's almost morning and dawn is quickly approaching. There goes another night without any sleep, and I'm already wondering how many cups of coffee I can safely guzzle before breakfast.

I consider heading upstairs to my room, falling into bed, trying to get in a few hours before everyone else is up. But I'm certain if I did, I'd be stuck lying there, staring at my ceiling, bored, replaying my conversation with Owen.

We'd talked for hours. About everything. I told him about my time in university, how Ted and I met, and eventually married. What life was like as newlyweds, back when everything was still fresh and fun.

I told him about how I first started my non-profit, Loving Hearts, and how many TV interviews I had to do, and how nervous I was starting something of my own that wasn't tied to my mother or my *Star Sisters* fame.

He told me about how difficult it was adjusting to life now that he'd been released from prison, how the last year was one of the hardest of his life, how lost he felt at first, overwhelmed by everything that had happened in the world while he was in there.

He told me a few stories from the inside, all the drama between gangs, just like cliques in high school. Like the time he got jumped by three guys because he took the last popsicle from the cafeteria freezer. And the time he collected paperbacks beneath his bed, lending them to his buddies, starting a prison book club.

He always makes me laugh, and he's a great storyteller. He also has a special way of getting you to open up, to allow yourself to be vulnerable. He makes it feel safe.

Once my ankle feels better, we plan on jogging together. It'll be fun to finally have a partner.

My mind is racing. I'm so wired right now, even more than before. I guess I can forget about sleep. Coffee, it is. I change directions, walking to the kitchen.

"What are you doing, Briar?"

I jump. Vivienne sits in her armchair, legs crossed, bathed in shadow. Her eyes narrow at me above her sharp cheekbones, illuminated by the moonlight slanting through the windows. They burn into me, glittering like gemstones. "Jesus," I gasp, clutching a hand to my chest. "You scared me. What are you doing down here alone in the dark?"

"I was waiting for you. I always know when you're awake." She runs her finger along the arm of her chair. "Couldn't sleep?"

I shake my head.

"Me either. I had a nightmare about Odette." Her voice is strained, still shaken. "She was standing at the end of the hall, and black blood was pouring from her mouth. It bubbled up her throat, soaking into her dress. She kept trying to speak to me, reaching out, but the sound just wouldn't come. The blood kept pouring, and she looked so *desperate*, like if I could just hear her, everything would make sense. It was almost like she was trying to warn me about something." She exhales, uneasy. "But I couldn't. I just stood there watching her drown in it."

"That's awful, Vivienne," I breathe. "But it was just a nightmare." A disturbing one, but that's all it was.

"Do you know why she would want to warn me, Briar?"

"No?"

"Are you sure about that?"

I hesitate. "You've been under a lot of stress lately. Maybe it's just your mind—"

"My mind? So, I'm crazy now?"

"That's not what I said." I sigh. "Look, I really need a coffee. Do you want to talk about this in the kitchen?"

Vivienne snorts, shifting in her seat. "I saw you."

I cross my arms, growing impatient. "I don't know what you mean."

"With him."

"Owen?"

She nods.

A scoff escapes my lips. It takes everything in me not to roll my eyes and walk away. Why does she always try to start drama out of nothing? "Okay. So?"

Vivienne leans in closer, the chair creaking and snapping like bones beneath her weight. Her eyes take on an otherworldly glow. "Have you been talking to him about me?"

I'm already exhausted with this line of questioning. She clearly thinks I've been feeding Owen information about her missing husbands. She's paranoid… and jealous. "No. We weren't talking about you at all."

Not everything is about you, Vivienne.

"Sure, you weren't, Briar." She stands, coming closer, the beautiful silk kimono trailing behind her. "You're not going to sabotage this book for me."

"I'm not trying to," I respond evenly.

"Must I remind you he's my guest? I'm the reason he's here, and

I don't appreciate you trying to use your feminine wiles to seduce the man writing my memoir."

"Seduce?" I repeat, laughing at the ridiculous accusation. "We were only talking!"

"Yes. In the dead of night. While everyone else is asleep. I don't know. It comes across a little desperate."

"For your information, he followed me out there. It's not like we planned to meet. I couldn't sleep, and he just happened to be there."

"Briar, you're embarrassing yourself. What would he ever see in you?" When I frown, she laughs, clearly pleased with herself. "Oh, lighten up. I'm only kidding."

I can feel my blood pressure rising, my thumbs aching from how hard I'm squeezing my fists.

Vivienne has a cruel smirk on her face. She enjoys taunting me. Driving me crazy on purpose, and she knows exactly how to push my buttons. She shrugs her delicate shoulders, circling me. There's something savage in her expression. Something predatory. Like a carnivore cornering its prey. "But, on that note, I thought I raised you to be a lady. To never chase a man."

"Really?" I bite back, just as vicious. "When you've been chasing men your entire life? And you want to talk about *desperate*..."

Vivienne pauses, her face screwed up in surprise. That's right. Two can play this game, and I learned from the best. "How dare you," she growls, obviously insulted. "How dare you speak to me like that under my own roof?"

"Oh, lighten up, Viv. That's just how we kid, remember?" I smirk as she stomps toward the stairs. She never likes it when we stick up for ourselves. Never likes it when we challenge her. "Hey, where are you going? Don't you want to spend some quality time with your daughter who never visits?" I go to the banister, the gator's skull sneering at me, and hurl a final line after her in the most innocent voice I can muster. "Was it something I said?"

21

OWEN and I jogged together every day last week.

I find myself sleeping better, waking up excited to start the day. We jog every morning at 6:30 for about an hour, choosing a footpath at random and exploring a different part of the estate each time. Afterwards, we return to the house and have a cup of coffee before breakfast. Owen's become a regular guest now.

I've decided not to leave yet. Partly because of him—I like the quiet routine we've fallen into—but also because I'm not finished here. There are still things about Odette's death that don't make sense, and the longer I stay, the more I feel like the answers are somewhere in this house or buried in the swamp. I like spending time with my sisters, and Vivienne apologized again after our last little tiff. She's been pleasant lately. Well, as pleasant as Vivienne can be.

But it's nice, just having my family around again. It feels like old times.

Owen and I plan to go jogging again today. I feel pathetic as my eyes settle on the clock above the stove. It's 6:50 now. He's late, and I wonder if he's slept in. I sit at the kitchen island, answering work emails. I'm already in my workout clothes, my hair drawn into a ponytail and a baseball cap tucked over my head. I have a lot of meetings lined up this afternoon. That's another thing about my new jogging partner. He's forced me into this new routine, and it's done wonders for my productivity. I've stopped obsessing over the security cameras and started focusing more of my energy into work.

I finish typing another email and hit send. I'm about to start another when I hear muffled laughter coming from upstairs. I'm pretty sure that's Owen. I shut my laptop and follow the sound.

It leads me to Vivienne's studio, the door slightly ajar. I lean in and peek through the crack, transfixed by what's going on inside. Owen sits on the edge of a stool in front of one of the photo backdrops. His T-shirt has been tugged down slightly, so that you can see a hint of muscle, a smattering of moles and chest hair. Vivienne hovers over him, too close for my comfort, snapping shots with her camera. "If this doesn't kickstart your modeling career, I don't know what will..." She lowers her camera and shakes her golden locks out over her shoulders. She's in one of her kimonos, and when some of the silk droops down her shoulder, I realize she's wearing nothing underneath. "But I have to admit, I'm surprised. A man that looks like you. Your age. But no wife. Not even a pretty little girlfriend you're seeing?"

Owen chuckles. I can tell by the way he's smiling that he's enjoying the flattery. "I don't know. Getting my life back on track is my number one priority right now."

"But if the right woman comes along?" Vivienne prods.

"I'd probably tell her to run."

Vivienne bites her bottom lip. "If I were thirty years younger, I'd be all over you," she admits shamelessly.

Yikes. I'm seconds away from rescuing him.

"But back in my prime, believe you me, I would have made you forget all about your troubles with the law..."

I believe it. She'd done it her entire life. She was a true maneater. A new partner every week until she finally settled on one she liked enough to keep around a little longer, only to end up running around on them, too. And the ones she liked enough to keep were truly kept.

Locked up in this house with us children, made to watch us, take care of the chores, and fawn over Vivienne whenever she was bored enough to stick around.

I try to picture Owen locked up in this house, her new sexy boy toy. Any hope of a career retired, and eventually his personality, too. Becoming whatever Vivienne wishes him to be. When it comes to men, it's always the same story with her.

"Come on," Owen says, interrupting my thoughts. "You're beautiful."

I know he's being polite, but it's like a stab in my abdomen. I shouldn't care if Owen is attracted to Vivienne. And I mean, look at her. Why wouldn't he be? But still.

It stings.

Vivienne lets out a girlish giggle, batting her lashes. "Boy, you're blind. I'm not what I once was. The imperfections are starting to take over."

"I don't see any," Owen says with that heart-fluttering smile.

"I'm too old for you, anyway," she adds with a little hopeless shrug, the sleeve of her kimono sliding further down her arm and exposing half her breast. She shakes her glossy curls out some more. "I know you're just saying that."

She reaches out, stroking his five o'clock shadow, her long manicured fingernails grazing up to his skull. "I think you ought to grow this out a little more. I've always loved a beard on a man, and you have just the face for one. You're so..." She leans in closer to him, her lips hovering above his. "Rugged."

I suck in a breath as their mouths nearly collide, and they startle at the sound of my gasp, pulling apart as if they've been caught doing something much worse. The little side table next to them topples over with a crash, adding more chaos to the scene. I back away, embarrassed to be caught eavesdropping and even more embarrassed that I feel so wounded and betrayed.

"Briar!" Owen curses, shooting out of his seat and chasing after me. "Briar, wait!"

I return to the kitchen and debate whether or not I should jog right out the door. I don't have enough time to decide. When Owen reaches me, his eyes are frantic. I've never seen him like this before. "I don't know what that was back there, but I swear it's not what it looks like," he says earnestly, taking my hand.

I flinch at his touch. "It's fine," I hear myself say. "I was just heading out actually."

I can't get their faces out of my head, the way their lips were only a breath apart. He didn't even try to push her away...

"Can we talk somewhere?"

"I don't know what there is to talk about."

Owen opens his mouth to answer but no words come out. His eyes remain on me, even as I shrug away from him, grab my car keys, and jog for the door. As I pass the stairs, I notice Vivienne standing in her studio, hidden in the shadows, listening. A cruel smirk contorts her features as she relishes in my distress. All too happy to see me running away.

22

The weather is beautiful today. Part of me wants to ditch work and spend the day sunbathing by the pool instead. I'm trying to remember if we have the ingredients for a piña colada, but my mind keeps drifting to the awkwardness between Owen and me.

There's been a lot of avoiding each other. Brief and flustered greetings. Polite smiles. Casual small talk that feels shallow compared to the way we were oversharing before. It took me a while to process how I was feeling. My brain knew I was being ridiculous. But sometimes my brain and emotions don't align. And I know I had no right to be mad at him, but every time I pictured Vivienne running her nails over his skull and him smiling up at her, I wanted to wring both their necks.

Of course, resorting to mindless violence would be a massive overreaction, so when Owen catches me at the front door after picking Juliet up from school one day, I put on my friendliest smile. Juliet wastes no time kicking off her shoes and tossing her back-pack on the floor before dashing upstairs to her bedroom.

Owen leans against the doorway. He slides his hands into his pockets and returns my smile with a hopeful expression. "Hey."

I'm in the middle of gathering Juliet's things, transferring them neatly into the coat closet. "Hey."

He comes closer, kneeling beside me, helping. "Would you want to go see the house?"

By house, he means *his* house. The one he's building. He's trying to win me over, but he doesn't have to. I've already made up my mind to smooth things over with him. Things have been too uncomfortable around the house. The others are picking up on it. And Vivienne loves it way too much. I don't want to give her the satisfaction. "Sure. I'd love that."

~

I FORGOT how gorgeous this wetland is. The brackish water blanketed in vibrant green duckweed, the gnarled cypress trees that tower overhead, their pale bark decorated with lichens. Witch orchids rise up from the banks, their petals quivering in the humidity like salivating tongues.

Something splashes in the shallows, and a sizable gator dips its head below the surface, while above us, a wood stork takes flight, its gray head like a skull against the hot Florida sun. It's just *so* stunning. And easy to feel like you've time traveled, back to when the Native Americans explored these maze-like waterways with their dugout canoes and animal hide kayaks.

I love it so much. And I fully understand why my sister was so passionate about it, why she wanted to preserve it, to protect the ecosystem here, the wildlife. I'm so grateful for all the good she did while she was alive.

I'm thinking of her as I navigate down a narrow path, remembering the way by heart. Out of respect to Odette, we've chosen a canoe over an airboat, and it's more fun than I expected. We're both struggling, our arms sore as we steer around stumps and logs like an obstacle course. We're closing in on the shore. I see a shack in the distance, and beyond that, the start of something bigger that makes my heart speed up in anticipation.

Once we dock, Owen climbs out and helps me up. He nods in that direction, taking my hand. "Careful. Watch your step."

The dock is rotting. Whole planks are broken or missing entirely, the dark water burbling below. As we come closer, I gaze up at the wooden shack on stilts with the tin roof, algae and mussels clinging to the decaying walls. It takes me back to when I was seven years old, after I met Owen for the first time. He found me crying in the garden about my parents fighting and he took me by the hand and led me here.

There was an old woman sitting in a rocking chair out front, and she leaned forward when she saw us coming through the trees, her face brightening. "Well, aren't you the prettiest girl I've ever seen!" she cried out, reaching for me. She grabbed ahold of my arms, her hands warm and comforting, and spun me around to get a better look. "Look at that flaming red hair!"

I blushed.

"Owen, darling. Are you gonna introduce me to your girlfriend?"

Neither of us corrected her. "I'm Briar Rose," I introduced myself, politely shaking her hand, the way I'd been taught.

The woman grinned at me. Up close, I could see just how old she was and that she was ill. Her fingers and toes were as splayed and twisted as mangrove roots. I tried not to stare at them as she talked. "It's a pleasure to meet you. You can call me Willa. I'm Owen's granny. Now, do you have a sweet tooth, Briar Rose?"

I nodded vigorously.

"I think I might have some pralines left over for you. How does that sound?"

She got up and went inside, and we followed her. Inside the shack, I saw a tiny kitchen with mismatched pots and pans hanging on the wall. There was a worn-looking sofa and a wooden crate for sitting around and eating. There was a checkered curtain that hid another part of the room, and I wondered if that was where they slept. Willa handed me a tin of pralines, and I broke right into them, already forgetting the reason I had been so upset.

Owen showed me a cardboard box. "You ever play checkers?"

"A few times."

We sat together on the ratty rug and played a couple of rounds. I had the sneaking suspicion he was letting me win. "I like your home," I told him.

"It's nothing like yours."

"I know. That's why I like it."

I never thought I'd be back here with him so many years later, the both of us all grown up. "This is crazy," I tell Owen now, voicing my thoughts. "Everything looks exactly the same, like nothing ever changed."

A lot has changed, though. Not only Owen and I, but Willa passed away around six years ago. When I heard the news, I spent almost a week confined to my bed, crying and depressed. It was the last time I tried reaching out to Owen, desperate to hear his voice, to see how he was doing. I never heard back from him.

"I thought about this place a lot while I was locked up," Owen admits, taking a moment to pause and take in the scenery. He rests his hand on a strangler fig, his palm moving up the web-like bark. "I missed the sound of the cicadas singing," he says, smiling fondly at the thought. I smile with him, knowing the exact sound he means. "Sometimes when I closed my eyes long enough, I could pretend I was here."

"I bet you're happy to be back."

"You have no idea." Owen gazes up at the drooping canopy and then maneuvers around the thick roots. "Just being outside, being able to go wherever I want to, *whenever* I want to." He moves forward, shaking his head. "I'll never take it for granted again."

I nod, following after him, wanting to ask him more, but not wanting to pry. Did he get used to it? Did he ever think he'd be a free man again? "I can't even imagine what that must've been like,"

I settle on instead, and judging by Owen's sudden silence, I'm glad I didn't prod. It's a sensitive subject, a heavy one, especially for us. I'll let him open up gradually to me, share whatever stories he wants. But I'll never force him before he's ready.

I can see another waterway, Owen's house perched right on the edge. He smiles over his shoulder at me. "Well," he says, gesturing to it. "Here it is!"

I laugh because it's so Owen. I don't know why, but I expected a classic Southern-style home, complete with a wraparound porch and rocking chairs. But this house is surprisingly modern —almost entirely made of glass, like a giant mirrored cube sitting in the middle of the woods. There's an observation deck on the roof with a telescope, a patio, his own dock and boat, a small but well-maintained vegetable garden, and a hand-painted chicken coop.

"This is amazing!" I say before I've even been inside. I walk to one area, and then another, not sure where or what to look at first.

"Come on," Owen says, leading me inside. "I'll give you the grand tour."

The interior blows me away. The house is absolutely flooded with natural light. It's still pretty much a construction site, and there's practically no furniture, but the bare bones are breathtaking. It's geometric in shape with a floating staircase and a worn rug that he's probably thrifted to help warm the place up. One wall is stacked with bookshelves, the covers a colorful and chaotic mess. In the living area, there's a half-finished coffee table set beside a workspace and table saw, and I can see right away that he's chosen cypress and likely sourced the wood himself. I follow the skylights down the hall, my mouth dropping at the sight of the atrium he's created, brimming with ferns and water lilies and palms. Part of the house even appears to hover above the water, the floor made of thick glass or plastic, so that you have a clear view of the aquatic life thriving below.

"Holy shit," I keep repeating. I cover my mouth and laugh.

"Owen, this is... *insane*. Like, actually, insane. How can you even afford all this?"

"Compensation from the state. I'd already served over a decade, so..." Owen shrugs. "It wasn't much, but enough to get me a fresh start and build this place."

"Well, it's way better than I imagined," I admit. "I don't know what I was expecting, but this was not it. No offense, but I mean, just, wow!"

"You haven't seen anything yet," Owen says, his eyes bright and passionate. "You should see it at sunset. The way the light hits the water." He shakes his head. "It's like there aren't any walls around you."

I'm breathless, running around like a child in a candy store. "I bet it's extraordinary." I run over and bring him in for a hug. "I'm just so happy for you. Everything you've accomplished here. It's going to be so peaceful."

He smiles down at me. "It is peaceful."

I sense he wants to share more, but he's holding back, not wanting to come off as boastful. He takes a deep breath, running a nervous hand over his scalp. "Got my GED and a vocational certificate in construction and design," he says, speaking casually like it's no big deal. "I planned the whole layout years ago, and it turned out just how I wanted, with some extra stuff here and there. Still working on the plumbing and trying to piece together the furniture."

"It's perfect," I say as I continue to explore.

He sets his hands on his hips, smiling. "Thought you might like it."

"Like it? I want to move in!" As soon as I blurt it out, I'm embarrassed, but Owen's smile only gets wider.

I can feel his eyes on me as I pause before the bookshelves, fingering through his impressive book collection, listing the authors out loud to distract from what I've just said, but it's pointless because Owen holds onto it. He uses it as a segue to say something that's been on his mind. "You know," he begins, coming closer to me. "I did a lot of thinking when I was away. Not just about the past or my plans for this house. But about you."

I keep my back facing him, but I can feel him ebbing closer, every nerve ending in my body catching fire. My adrenaline rises, my heart racing. "Me?" I whisper, holding my breath. I focus intently on Flannery O'Connor's *A Good Man Is Hard to Find*, flipping through the pages, inhaling that sweet old book scent.

He comes to stand beside me and nods. I steal a glance at him, swallowing. "I thought about you a lot too," I admit. "Every day. I tried calling you. Writing you letters... that never even reached you, anyway."

"Even if they had, I wouldn't have written you back."

"Why?" I shake my head, upset, thrusting the book back onto the shelf. "Because I moved on?"

"Yeah, that's exactly why." Owen furrows his brow. "You don't get it. I threw my whole life away. My future." He stops, hesitating, but then pushes forward. "*Our* future." My heart quickens as he reaches out and gently takes my hand, rubbing circles over the rough spots with his warm thumb. He turns it over, tracing a finger along the lifeline that cuts across my palm. "I didn't want you waiting around for a deadbeat like me."

His touch on my skin takes me back to when we were sixteen. We would hide away in the graveyard chapel, our own little slice of solitude. It was so quiet and cold in there compared to the choking humidity outside, the constant cry of the wailing birds. We laid on the leaf-strewn altar, staring up at the branches tearing through the ceiling, the vines strangling the walls and bursting through the windows. Just talking. For hours. About everything and anything. Out of nowhere, he'd propped himself up on his elbow and traced my bottom lip with his thumb, the sensation intoxicating. I closed the gap between us. It was our first kiss.

He peers earnestly into my eyes now. "I felt like you deserved better. I wanted you to move on with your life and be happy."

I close my eyes, trying to process this. "Owen..."

"But I never meant to hurt you," he goes on. "So let me apologize now for that and let me apologize again for what happened with Vivienne."

I open my eyes, sighing, not wanting to talk about her right now. She always seems to find a way to butt into every aspect of my life, weasel into every layer. Owen gulps, leaning in. "I realize what that must have looked like the other day. But I'm not interested in Vivienne that way, and nothing happened other than a bit of friendly flirting. I never meant to lead her on, and I already talked to her about it. I let her down. Gently."

What I would've given to be a fly on the wall for *that* conversation... I search his face, a breeze rustling the trees outside. "Owen, stop. You don't have to explain yourself to me. You did nothing wrong."

"I was late for our run. You were waiting for me."

I shrug. "It's okay."

"No, it's not," Owen says, frowning. "It won't happen again."

"Okay."

"Now, are we good?"

I smile, pulling away from him and walking toward the stairs. "Not until you show me that observation deck of yours."

Owen smiles back.

23

Vivienne is peeking out the drapes, and she looks like she wants to murder someone. And by someone, I mean, me. She watches Owen and me with daggers as we embrace one more time before parting ways, her nostrils flaring. She shuts the drapes so violently I think she's ripped them straight off the rod.

My heart pounds as I approach the house. I can hear hurried footsteps, and I hesitate before opening the door. Once I've stepped inside, I want to run away again.

"Oh, Briar. You've arrived home just in time!" Vivienne cries. She shuffles me into the dining room and forces me into a chair, making me wince. The best china is laid out, along with the silver utensils, the handles shaped like twirling vines.

"What's all this about?" I ask. My nose twitches at the fresh-cut yellow roses used as a centerpiece, the stems crooked and ugly, hideously bent to accommodate the heavy thorns.

Vivienne fluffs her blonde curls and shoots me her movie star smile. "Now, I know how much you love my famous key lime pie, and I made one real special. Just for you."

She disappears into the kitchen, clattering pots and pans, dropping things on the floor.

"Need any help in there?" I call.

"Oh, no. You just sit right there, and I'll serve you a big, juicy slice of this delicious pie!" My stomach churns uneasily as Vivienne returns with a large knife. It glints in the light of the chandelier, reflecting my own worried expression. "Oh, no. Why the long face? You should be happy. I took the time out of my day to make this for you." She pulls out a cloth napkin and cracks it in the air like a whip. "Blood, sweat, and tears."

She leans in close to me, attaching the napkin to my dress like a bib. I can smell the alcohol on her breath. The scent mingles with her perfume, making me dizzy. I narrow my eyes suspiciously at the key lime pie. It looks edible, the meringue topping toasted to perfection. But Vivienne's insistence that I have a slice has spoiled my appetite.

"I'm not so hungry," I admit as Vivienne dips the knife into the pie and cuts me a piece. It lands with a wet smack onto my plate, the pale custard-like filling jiggling from the impact. I lean in closer, trying to nonchalantly sniff at it. I can't tell if something's amiss. Smells like any other pie Vivienne's ever made.

"Oh, you're going to eat it," Vivienne says, pointing the knife at me.

I double down. "I said I'm not hungry."

"You're always hungry."

"Well, right now, I'm not."

"Eat the damn pie, Briar!"

"No!"

Vivienne jabs the knife in my direction. "Eat it!"

"No!"

Vivienne grabs a handful of the pie and shoves it in my face, smearing the filling into my hair. I can feel it squish between my teeth, splatter my tongue. It tastes like piss. Or dog shit. At least I *hope* it's dog shit. I gasp for air, clawing at the woman's hands until she releases me. "What the fuck, Vivienne?" I shout, choking and sputtering as I wipe graham cracker crumbs and chunks of filling from my chin and neck, shaking it off onto the floor.

It's on my dress, stuck between my breasts. The smell of the pie is totally off, and the citrus burns my skin. I don't know what the hell else she mixed into it, but I'm not sure I want to know either.

"What exactly is going on here?" Elise asks, coming around the corner. There's a mixture of concern and anger on her face. Like she wants to know what all the fuss is about and then beat whoever's causing it with the broom.

I push back from the table and rip the makeshift bib from my cleavage. "I have no idea! I think she's trying to poison me!"

"You're the one doing the poisoning around here, isn't that right, Briar?"

"What?" I shout, losing my patience. "What are you even talking about, you crazy woman?"

"You're poisoning him against me!"

"Who?"

The knife clatters across the table. Vivienne whirls around and sticks an accusing finger right in my face. "You were with Owen again. Throwing yourself at him!"

"I was not! Have you lost your damn mind?"

"I saw you, Briar. Hanging onto each other like lovers." She grips her curls, pacing now, clearly outraged. "I know I'm getting old. I find a new wrinkle every morning. My hair's thinning, my skin's dry, my body isn't what it used to be."

She laughs bitterly. "Do you have any idea what that feels like? To walk into a room and be invisible? To smile at a man and realize he's not smiling back? To be constantly overlooked?" She slaps a hand to her head in disbelief. "He'd rather have you. I mean, honestly—really? *You?* What does he even see in you? Obviously, you're no beauty, but I suppose you're young and fresh. So is that all that matters now? What about me? What happens to me now? Is it all over for me?"

I say nothing, hurt. I don't even know how to respond.

"Where were you two all day?" she shouts, startling me. "Answer me!"

I move away from her, but she follows, trailing after me around the table like a rabid dog.

"You're trying to poison him against me. Air out our dirty laundry. Expose all my secrets. This house's secrets, that I've tried so long and hard to keep!" Vivienne gains on me, her whole body shaking with rage. "I know you, Briar. You've been trying to tear this family apart since the very beginning!"

"What are you even talking about?" I shout. "Don't you hear how paranoid you sound?" I turn to Elise for help. "She's been drinking again!"

Vivienne scoffs. "I have not!"

"I thought you quit! I can smell it on your breath! No wonder you've been acting like a lunatic lately!"

Vivienne waves a hand. "Another lie for Owen. Go on. Fill his head with ideas and sabotage my memoir. Destroy my reputation. It's been hanging on by a thread for years, anyway."

She's never done this before. Gotten plastered when she knows we have a guest staying with us. She's been tipsy before at the country club, but never to this extent.

"I'm not out to get you, Vivienne. Owen and I weren't even talking about you!" It's not *entirely* true, but I'll say anything at this point to get her to calm down and leave me the hell alone.

"What's next? You're going to climb into his bed?"

I let out a frustrated groan.

Vivienne turns to look at the kitchen. "Speak of the devil. Maybe I should warn him!"

Owen peeks his head into the dining room. He looks at Vivienne and then at me, having no idea what he's just stepped into. "Everything good here?" he asks, sensing the tension. I'm sure he heard our shouting from outside.

Vivienne laughs cruelly. "Be careful with this one," she warns him, throwing a thumb in my direction. "Don't get too close. She's more dangerous than she looks. Ask her what happened to her husband."

"Vivienne," Elise snaps. "Stop this. I think you've said enough."

"Go on. Ask her. Lord knows we've all been wondering." She turns back to me and that cruel smile grows wider. "I think I know why you're my least favorite. You remind me too much of myself. My husbands went missing, too. Of course, they never found mine..."

"Vivienne," Elise snaps, gripping her arm. "Stop!" She glances nervously at Owen. "We have a guest. Remember?"

Vivienne yanks away from her. "Take your hands off me!"

I look at Owen, feeling helpless. "I'm so sorry," I apologize. "She's drunk."

"Sure, Briar. I'm drunk. But at least I know what I am." She turns to Owen, waving a finger in his face. "Listen here, boy. It's unwise to get involved with women whose husbands end up dead. Be careful. You might be next."

I shake my head, backing away from her. My vision blurs, tears threatening to spill. "Sometimes I think I *hate* you."

Vivienne chuckles. "Honey. The feeling is mutual."

I glance at Owen, embarrassed that she's doing this in front of him. Embarrassed by the pity visible in his eyes. Angry that I've placed myself back into this toxic environment again. When I moved away, I promised myself that I'd only come back to visit Juliet, and not for long, either. Now I remember why I couldn't stand being in this house, why I was so desperate to get away.

I need distance and I need it now. The room spins as I sprint for the door.

"Briar, wait!" Owen calls after me.

But I don't stop. I burst out the door and head for one of the trails, legs pumping as hard as they can beneath me. The humid air envelops me, weighing me down, but I push against it, and keep pushing until I can barely feel it anymore. I've run this path a thousand times, so I don't have to think about where to go. My mind is someplace else, an old memory finally breaking free.

24

I'm eight years old and I'm terrified.

I'm dreaming that hands are reaching out from under my bed, tearing at my clothes and limbs, trying to pull me apart, to dismember me.

I wake up crying for Robert. Never for *her*. It's always Robert, who is kind and thoughtful and everything Vivienne isn't.

Robert usually comes running when I cry for him, but this time is different. I know there's something wrong because I hear them arguing downstairs, their voices loud and angry. Angrier than I've ever heard before. Part of me is afraid to interrupt them, but the other part of me is still swept up in my nightmare. I can't stand to be alone in the dark, staring at my own frightened reflection in the mirror.

I hurry out of my bedroom and tiptoe down the hall, my nightgown tickling my bare calves. Halfway down the stairs, I crouch and peer through the bars as Vivienne tears across the ballroom toward the foyer, lunging at Robert as he reaches for the front door. "Stop!" she screams hysterically, hitting and tearing at his clothes. "Have you lost your goddamn mind, Robert? Think about the girls!"

"I *am* thinking about the girls, and I think they'd be a hell of a lot better off with me."

"You'd take them away from the only mother they've ever known?"

Robert circles around on her. "Don't pull that with me. Nothing you can say is going to change my mind."

"No, Robert!"

"Vivienne, let me go!"

"No! You can't go to the police. You can't do this to me. Please promise me you won't say anything. Please!"

"Let go of me!" Robert tries to untangle Vivienne from his shirt, her fingernails pinned to his collar, scratching at his chest and drawing blood. He manages to pry her off him, shoving her away. He fixes his clothes, his expression turning stony. "I can't promise you anything."

Vivienne is trembling. She cries so loud it makes me cover my ears. I watch in silent terror as she removes a long blade hidden in her robe and plunges it straight into his chest. Quick and smooth, like she's done it before.

Robert opens his mouth, his eyes wide. But nothing comes out. And when Vivienne removes the blade, his whole shirt turns dark red. He collapses at her feet, gasping for air, a substance like grape jelly bubbling out of his mouth.

Vivienne falls to the floor and cradles his head in her lap, his body becoming still. Stiller than when he practices meditation by the swamp. Or when he takes naps on the sofa in the parlor after yoga. Or when he's in the pool with me, supporting my back as I float lazily over the surface. I'm thinking about how he makes French toast with me on the weekends and crying harder than I've ever cried before.

I'm scared.

I have *no* idea what to do.

I run upstairs, taking two steps at a time, crouching in the hall like a frightened animal. I can't move. I can only shake uncontrollably, my teeth rattling inside my skull, my jaw tight and painful. I hear footsteps and turn my head to find Odette, the gauzy fabric of her nightgown flowing around her ankles. "What are you doing out of bed?" she asks, her fingers gently grazing the knobs of my spine.

"I-It's Robert," I whisper, the words a struggle to push out of my chattering mouth. Goosebumps break out over my skin. "He's..." I don't want to say the 'd' word. *Dead.* Because I've never seen a dead body before and I don't know if he is or not. I just keep picturing that knife in Vivienne's hands and that feral expression on her face as she drove it into his chest. "He's b-b-bleeding. He needs a hospital."

"What?" Odette breathes, her light eyes turning stormy against the shadows. "Wait right here for me."

At thirteen, Odette is much braver than I am. She charges ahead, right down the stairs.

My whole body hurts from shaking. I can feel my beating heart against my curled-up knees that I'm hugging to my chest. I know Odette wants me to go back to bed, but I can't make myself. Not after what I saw. I need to know if Robert is going to be okay. I crawl across the landing and cling to the stair railing, peering down at the ballroom floor, which is now covered in a large puddle of blood. Robert isn't moving and my gut twists.

Vivienne lets out a shrill cry when she sees Odette. "I don't know what happened. He was threatening me. He was threatening our family."

"Shhh," Odette shushes her. "You're going to scare Briar and Portia. Is he dead?"

"I killed him," Vivienne moans.

I cover my mouth and my whole world spins. I think I'm going to be sick. My heart is painful like it's about to explode out of my chest.

Odette's voice is low, almost a hiss. "Why, Mama? Why would you do that?"

"He was going to take you girls away from me," Vivienne sobs, covering her face. She wipes her tears, mascara smearing across her temples. "Help me clean up this mess."

Odette stares at her and Vivienne latches onto her wrists. "Please."

"How?"

"Help me carry him to the kitchen."

Odette shakes her head. She holds up her hands and backs away. "Mama, I can't."

"Yes, you will!" Vivienne cups her cheeks and peers into her eyes. "You're old enough. You will help your mama cover up this mess and you won't breathe a word of it to anyone. Do you understand me?"

Odette says nothing, only nods. I can't see her face, but I imagine she's crying just as hard as I am. Somehow I find the strength to move down the stairs and watch as Odette takes hold of Robert's ankles and Vivienne takes hold of his arms. They drag him into the parlor and then the kitchen, a trail of blood forming behind them. I feel sick as I follow it like a trail of breadcrumbs, stopping outside the kitchen, too afraid to go any closer.

I hope I'm still dreaming. I hope this is part of my nightmare.

Elise stands in the kitchen, her face buried in her hands. It takes me a moment to realize that she's crying, her shoulders shaking violently. "I can't do this again," Elise gasps in between tears.

Vivienne drops Robert to the ground, his head hitting the floor with a sickening crack. "Stop that!"

"How could you do this again? How could you do this to your girls?" She gestures wildly at Odette. "Now, you've brought your own daughter into this mess. You're ruining them, Vivienne. You're going to turn these girls into monsters, and I won't be a part of it!"

"Quiet!"

"No!"

"Yes! You'll shut your mouth right now! You helped with the

others, you'll help with this one too. Talking to the police is only going to hurt us. So, we have to take care of this. Together."

"What... others?" Odette whispers.

The adults ignore her. Elise wrings her hands. "God help me."

"Don't you dare bring him into this," Vivienne hisses. "He knows that I had to do what I had to do. There was no other way. I'm not letting anyone break up this beautiful family I created."

Elise shakes her head as she picks up the sponge I saw her use on the dishes earlier and fills a bucket with soapy water. She doesn't acknowledge me. She walks right by, drops to the floor as if her legs give out from under her, and begins to scrub.

I turn my attention back to the kitchen. Vivienne is looking right at me. She's steaming, her hands planted firmly on her hips. "I thought I told you to go back to bed," she says, her anger palpable.

I fear I'm about to get spanked when Odette suddenly charges over and takes my hand. "Briar, you can't be here," she says. I've never seen her look so frightened before. Frightened for me and what I'm witnessing. "Don't worry, Vivienne. I'll take care of this." There's a protective look in her eyes as she leads me toward the stairs. "I told you to wait for me!"

There's something sticky in her grasp. I can see it oozing out, feel it trickling down the length of my fingers and dripping onto the stairs.

Blood.

My hand flies to my mouth once I realize, and then I taste it. The metallic bite of it. My head swims, and my stomach lurches. I'm sure I'm going to be sick. Panicking, I rush out the front door and into the rain. Lightning crashes overhead and I scream. My sister races after me. "Briar, no!" she hollers above the tropical storm. "Come back!"

I don't know how far I run, but eventually, I collapse, the flooded lawn swallowing me up to my waist. I use the wetness around me to wash away the blood, submerging my face, my ear canals filling with mud. Odette grabs me, her white nightgown sullied with dirt, blood, and rain. I gasp for air when I resurface. "It's not what you think, Briar," she keeps repeating as she drags me back to the house. It's a warm light in a sea of stormy darkness. "Daddy's fine. *We're* fine."

Later that night, I stare out my window at the stars, replaying the scene over and over inside my head. I don't even realize I'm trembling until Vivienne comes into my room early the next morning and hugs me until the shaking stops. "There, there. My precious girl. Everything's okay," she whispers, stroking my hair. She smells clean like she showered, and her hair is freshly styled. But I can still see something like rust caked beneath her nails. "You've had another night terror. A bad one. But that's all it was. A night terror."

"Is Robert...?"

"Your daddy had to go to work, remember? That business trip he told you about? He just left a little early, that's all. But don't you worry, sweet one. He'll be back before you know it."

I sniffle, melting into her hug, forcing myself to believe her.

As the memory loses its grasp on me, I collapse on the shore of the swamp and allow the tears to fall. Then I stomp into the murky water, outstretching my hands, feeling.

"What are you doing?" Owen shouts at me from the shore, panting. He rips off his shirt, getting ready to jump in after me.

I turn to Owen, the memory making my heart race. "If you really want to know the truth about Vivienne, then you should dredge up this swamp."

25

"SHE'LL NEVER FORGIVE you for this," Portia says as more cop cars pull onto the property. They've been searching the swamp and surrounding woods for hours, their forensic tents lining the shore. It took them less than a day to arrive once the call was made.

Portia and I stare out the window at them. They've been at it all morning and we're still waiting to hear word from Detective Torres. She stands beneath the shade of a tent, a walkie-talkie held to her lips. She surveys the area, her eyes squinted behind her mirrored aviators. Harsh lines mark her face, a sign of restless nights that I'm all too familiar with. She has a thumb hooked in her jeans and the big black gun on her hip is more than a little intimidating.

She pulled me aside when she first arrived and asked me questions. I didn't tell her about the night of the murder. Just that I thought I saw a body floating in the water during my morning jog. Skeletal remains.

"Whereabouts?" she asked me. She turned and looked across the water. "Can you point it out for me?"

I took her to the area behind the boathouse. I just picked a random spot.

"You have good eyes," she noted. "You picked out something in the water, behind this shed, while you were jogging on that trail... *all* the way over there?"

I'm such an idiot, I thought. "I stopped by the shore," I said, thinking quickly. "I always do. I don't know why."

The detective studied me. It felt like she didn't buy my story. And maybe she didn't. She interrogates people for a living. I'm sure she can tell when someone isn't being a hundred percent truthful. It felt like she could sense I was holding something back. "Okay, we'll start here," she said finally.

She watched me for a beat, then turned to her right. "Hey!" she shouted. A woman was attempting to record on her phone through the gate. The detective marched over. "This isn't a movie set. It's a potential crime scene. If you don't want me to slap cuffs on your wrists, I suggest you pack up and head home!"

When she returned, she offered me an apology. "Sorry about that, Briar."

"It's fine." I waved a hand. "Believe me, we're used to it."

"Animals," she spat in disgust. "We blocked off the whole road, but somehow, somebody always manages to slip through. Another fan of your mother's or maybe someone who loved the show..." She snapped her fingers, trying to remember.

"*Star Sisters*," I supplied a little too forcefully, and then felt like a jerk. *Who cares if she knows the name of the show or not?*

"Right. So," the detective said, moving on. She squinted against the sun and flipped her sunglasses over her eyes. "You said by the boathouse?"

I nodded. "Yeah, but that was the other day. There's a current, and I don't even know what I saw. Maybe if you could check the whole area..."

"I plan to."

"Good," I sighed, feeling relieved.

I close the curtains now, turning away from the window. Honestly, I'm not sure if they'll find anything at all...

Vivienne's been icing me out all morning. I half-expected her to blow up when she found out what I'd done. Throw my things out the front door. But instead, she's scarily calm and collected. She's sober as a judge and dressed to the nines in a bright yellow shift dress, a white fur-trimmed cape, and peep-toe pumps.

When I got back after dropping Juliet at school, I found her strutting around outside with a lacy parasol and silk gloves, turning on the charm for the detective. She even draped an arm over the detective's shoulders, complimenting her sleek ponytail and tactical vest.

Now she's sitting in her pink velvet chair, sipping iced tea and reading *Eat, Pray, Love*. She told Portia this morning that she plans to read more and broaden her horizons. She's trying to make a point, but she might as well wear a big "I'm unproblematic" sign plastered to her Botox-ridden forehead. Just the looks she keeps giving me scream, "I'm the sane one. You're the one overreacting."

But I need proof. Solid proof. Her little ploy is working. She's too relaxed. Too at ease. And I'm doubting myself again. Maybe the murder I thought I saw *was* a night terror. Maybe I'm jumping to conclusions. Maybe I *am* overreacting. But then I think of Odette's cryptic note I found in my room.

B,

She's not who you think.

You're next.

No, I have to trust my gut here. My heart pounds faster as I suddenly remember something. Odette's journal. I almost forgot about it. I still haven't tried to open it and see what's written inside.

I silently slip away, stealing a pair of scissors from the kitchen drawer. The house is unnervingly quiet, save for the ticking of the grandfather clock and the roar of the excavator outside. I can see Owen speaking with the detective, his eyes on the digger as it churns up tangles of algae and dead logs.

"Briar, where are you going with those?" Vivienne asks. She narrows her eyes at me as I pause at the bottom of the stairs.

Why does she care? I'm caught off guard by how nervous she

looks, the muscles in her arms suddenly tense as she grips her paperback. Is there some reason she doesn't want me going upstairs?

I don't have to explain myself to her. I sprint to my bedroom, find the burgundy leather journal with Odette's shiny monogram on the cover, and I cut open the spine, tearing out the pages. They scatter over my bed, and I desperately try to piece them together, reading greedily through the entries, my heart soaring and then sinking as I consume the content.

I was right. It *is* a therapy workbook. She must've stopped turning it in once the memories started coming back, because Odette had recorded every piece of her childhood, each memory more damning than the last.

The more I read, the more my own memories come rushing back. I'm sobbing when I reach the last page. Odette left a final message. I'm assuming right before she took her own life. It reads:

I feel so alone. I can never get over what I did and how I helped her. I can't go on like this. Can't live with this much guilt inside me. I'm so sorry.

My heart is broken. I've never been this upset in my entire life.

I storm downstairs with the papers crumpled in my hand and grab a mallet from the kitchen. Now all three women are looking at me. Without a word, I charge back upstairs and straight into Vivienne's studio. Marching right up to the sculpture of Odette lying in her coffin, I bring the mallet down onto her head. The blow shatters her face, crushes her collarbone and arm. Crying out, I unleash my anger on the other sculptures, plaster pieces of Odette flying around the room in miniature explosions.

It is beyond satisfying.

"Briar, stop! Have you lost your mind?" Elise shouts as she flies into the room. She chases after me, trying to pry the mallet from my hands, but I swivel around, annihilating Odette's bloated corpse, a maggoty foot bouncing off Elise's head.

"It's fine," Vivienne assures her, clutching her cape. "Let her do whatever she feels she needs to do. I couldn't stand looking at them anyway."

Once everything is destroyed and the whole room is covered in broken bits of my dead sister, I hold the journal entries up for Vivienne to see, the pages flapping.

Portia steps cautiously into the room, taking in the mess. "Briar," she whispers, covering her mouth. "Briar, what are you doing?"

I know how this looks, but I want her to understand. I'm not crazy, even if I'm holding up a mallet, sweating and panting like a madwoman.

"She's off her meds again," Vivienne says.

"I'm not on any meds," I snap.

"Well, you should be!"

"Read these," I urge Portia.

She reluctantly takes the wrinkled pages from me. She shuffles through them, her brow furrowed. "What is this?"

I point my mallet at her. "Just read, okay?"

Elise tries to wrestle it from me again, but I hold it out of reach. She glares at me before storming out of the room. "You're officially banned from my kitchen," she hurls over her shoulder. "And from every utensil in it!"

Portia covers her mouth, her eyes widening as she reads. Eventually, she can't read anymore. She's too disgusted. Too triggered by the gory details, the images flashing through her brain.

I know the feeling.

"I have no clue what's inside that book, but whatever it says, it isn't true," Vivienne says coolly, crossing her arms defensively over her chest. "It's a work of fiction. Lies. Odette loved creating trouble. She was much like you in that regard, Briar."

"Stop insulting her," Portia snaps, holding up a hand. "You've said enough."

"Excuse me?" When neither of us respond, Vivienne bites nervously at her manicured nails, the tendons in her neck protruding. "So, what? Are you girls going to turn me in? Is that what all this is about?"

Portia and I stare at each other. We don't answer.

Vivienne breathes faster, panicking. "Girls, I am your mother." She grabs onto Portia, shaking her by the shoulders, and then takes me by the chin, forcing me to look at her. "Remember what I always tell you. We're a family. We're best when we're together! After everything I've done for you. *This* is how you repay me? Where is your loyalty?"

"This is different," I say, pulling away from her.

"How?"

"We're sick of your lies. You said you were innocent, but you haven't been honest about anything!" My pulse thuds heavily in my ears as I lift the mallet again. Vivienne jerks back, frightened, as if I'm about to bash her brains in. I narrow my eyes at her. "Odette knew where you hid the bodies, and they're *not* in the swamp."

I charge past her, back to my bedroom, zeroing in on the ornate standing mirror. It towers over me, the doorframe, almost reaching the ceiling. I swing the mallet into it, the surface fracturing. Again and again, until the whole thing crashes down. Glass rains over the carpet, shimmering in the early afternoon sun that streams through the windows.

"Holy shit," Portia whispers as she comes up behind me.

Robert's face is recognizable but shriveled. His cheeks are sunken in, the skin wrinkled. He looks like he's been shrunken and dried, all the moisture sucked out of him. Like he's been trapped in a bog, his emaciated body wrapped in torn yellowed bedsheets. The gray hair still there, wisps of his salt-and-pepper goatee.

I open my mouth, but no sound comes out.

"Please tell me that's a Halloween decoration," Portia whispers.

The reality of the situation doesn't sink in. Not until I've crashed through every mirror. Mine. Portia's. Juliet's. Odette's. It's only when there's nothing left to break that I realize I've finally found Vivienne's missing husbands. Their shriveled bodies stored in the coffin-size mirrors she had custom made for us, like so many other things in this house. I never thought anything of it. To think they were tucked away for decades in our bedrooms. Just on the other side of the glass.

Vivienne lingers behind us, gauging our reactions. She clears her throat, rousing us from our shocked state. "You have to know I was happy with them, but in the end, it just didn't work out. Nils, that Swedish bastard, chased women almost as much as he did drugs. I caught him running around on me one too many times. Of course, back in the seventies, everyone was running around on each other. But he didn't like me having male friends or admirers. He was the jealous type. And I didn't like being told what to do."

She gives a simple shrug of her shoulders, a distant look in her eyes. "Reggie was already sixty when we married. He made sure I was cast in plenty of his movies. You could say that relationship was mutually beneficial. But I grew tired of bending over backwards for him—literally."

She crunches a shard of glass with her heel. The sound is grating and sets my nerves on edge. "Darren was gorgeous *and* wealthy. But he couldn't handle my success. He wanted me to take a step back from acting. Be a real homemaker. I asked him as I plunged that knife into his chest, 'Well, why the hell can't I be both?'"

"But Robert," she continues, sadly. "Robert was the only one I regret. He was a good husband and father. But he found the bodies... when *Briar* broke one of the mirrors the first time. Kicking a ball around the house. How many times did I ask you to not do that? But you never listen, do you? Naturally, your father went to clean up the mess and there was Nils, one eye peeking out from behind the shattered glass. What could I do? He was going to take you girls away from me. I had no choice."

"Why do they look like that?" Portia demands as she stares at

Vivienne's second husband Reggie's body, planted deep within her standing mirror, a trembling hand covering her lips.

"Baking soda and salt, among other things," Vivienne replies. She talks so flippantly about it you'd think she was discussing Juliet's latest science project. "Elise promised it would preserve them. I couldn't bear the thought of my handsome men being reduced to bone, mere shells of their former selves. The thought alone haunts me."

"You're sick," Portia spits. "You're a sick, sick, twisted woman!"

Between Portia and me, something snaps. We break down, sobbing our hearts out, clinging to each other. It feels like we've been holding back these tears for ages, and once we start, we can't seem to stop.

It's not even the fact that she killed them. I always suspected she did. I knew she was capable of murder. There was just something about her, something dark. But what gets me is that she kept them in our bedrooms, lying to our faces for years when she already knew the truth.

This is the last straw. I'm done with her lies, being traumatized every time I set foot in this house. When we finally manage to pull ourselves together, I glare at Vivienne.

She tenses, swallowing. "I don't know what you girls are crying about. I thought you'd be happy. A decades-long mystery finally solved." I shake my head, wiping the snot from my nose, ignoring her. "And what about Juliet? What happens to her when I'm locked up? Where will she go? Are either of you ready to raise a child? If you ask me, the answer is no."

She's trying to manipulate us, but I can hear the strain in her voice. The panic. The jig is up and she knows it. We're going to turn her in and there's nothing she can do about it.

I'm surprised when she doesn't even try to stop me. I shoulder past her, picking shards of glass from my jeans as I jog down the stairs. Portia is right behind me, gripping my hand, our fingers tightly intertwined.

I'm reaching for the doorknob when something sharp pricks me right in the neck. "Ah!" I gasp, clutching my throat and chest as a burning sensation spreads across my body. "What the..."

My head swims with vertigo, and I collapse at Elise's feet. She stands over me, a long syringe grasped in her hand. "What..." I whisper. "Did you... *stab*...me with that?"

I can't feel my legs.

It's like someone rubbed numbing gel all over my body.

Portia crumples beside me. A stream of drool trickles down her chin and seeps into her shirt.

"We have to move them into the other room," Vivienne says from the landing. I can feel my heart pounding inside my head, in my skin, making my entire body vibrate. She comes down the stairs slowly, her hand stroking along the polished railing. "You take Briar. I'll take Portia."

They drag us into the kitchen, letting us drop onto the cold floor. Portia and I stare at each other, wide-eyed and blinking, but unable to communicate. Vivienne has Odette's journal in her hands, the pages stuffed between the broken covers. She strides over to the oven and twists one of the knobs, turning on a burner. "Portia," I gasp, my throat tight and constricted. But she doesn't answer me. Her eyes close and her mouth sags open. "Portia..." I groan desperately, hoping to rouse her.

Vivienne and Elise stand beside the oven, where Odette's journal crackles above the stove. My nose twitches as the smell of burnt leather and ink fill the air. It makes me feel sick and sweat beads across my forehead and prickles over my scalp. I try to shift around and crawl to the door. The detective is on the other side. Owen is out there with her. Help is so close. If I can just make it there...

My head droops and my vision cuts in and out, the edges dark and blurry. *I'm getting weaker*, I realize. It's coming over me in waves. I flop onto my back, groaning in discomfort, as whatever they injected me with courses through my veins. Elise stalks over and yanks me back, dropping me beside my sister.

I moan, rolling over onto my side, feeling like I'm about to vomit everywhere. Bright spots block out everyone's faces, except for one. "Odette," I whisper as she watches me from behind her ruined journal, the pages warped and blackened by the fire. Her long hair is matted and dripping with dark water, and her skin is a sickly shade of bruised green. Thick tangles of moss cling to her throat, her arms. The putrid stench makes me choke. She's as clear as day, and even though I know she's not real, I'm frightened. When I'm finally able to speak again, my voice sounds miles away. "Help us."

26

ODETTE STANDS at the foot of my bed. She's deathly pale. Shadows ring around her eyes and twigs stick in her damp hair. She holds out a pruney hand for me, the fingertips dripping with moisture, the slender wrists wrapped with algae.

I sit up in bed, and it takes everything in me to gather the courage to speak. "Odette, why did you leave us? We need you. We're in trouble!"

"Shhh." She shushes me, the sharpness of it sending needle-like pinpricks down my spine. "Come with me."

I'm hesitant to take her hand, to feel the iciness of her palm. Another reminder that my sister is gone. "I can't," I cry, lurching away. "I just want you to come back. Please come back!" Odette slowly raises a finger to her blue-tinged lips and moves soundlessly toward the door. "Wait!"

I slip out of bed and chase after her, making it to the hallway in time to catch the tail end of her nightgown as it swishes around a corner. The hall goes on forever. My hurried footsteps thunder in my ears, matching the pace of my heart. The photographs on the walls stare down at me. They're from the gallery. Me and my sisters.

The strangeness of the artwork is exaggerated like someone has positioned them in front of funhouse mirrors. My sisters are crying. Begging me not to go after her, but I ignore them. I keep moving. I have to catch up to Odette.

The hall ends in a tangle of brambles, the thorns long and sharp and fleshy. I weave through them, climbing and crawling, until I reach the other side. My sister glides down the stairs, disappearing into the shadows below, and I stumble after her, taking two steps at a time. "Odette?" I gasp.

A sliver of light creeps in from the parlor, accompanied by deep, seductive laughter. I hug myself as I wander closer, the air so frigid I can see my breath. Vivienne sits in her armchair dressed in a sexy black dress, her legs spread wide open. Owen is on all fours, crawling toward her. She runs her long fingernails over his scalp and down his neck, her lips pursed as she toys with him. "Good boy," she purrs, her grip tightening as she forces his head between her thighs. "You know that's just how I like it."

"Oh, my God," I breathe, stumbling away.

They look up at me, revealing the ugliest smiles I've ever seen. They're mean. Sadistic. Owen jumps up and comes at me, his face transforming. As his strong hands clamp onto my shoulders, I let out a frightened cry. "Ted?"

Ted's malicious grin widens. He shakes me, my head jolting violently on my neck. "What did you do, Briar?" he shouts in my face. "What did you do?"

He shoves me backwards into the dark. "Ted!"

There's a wisp of breath at my neck, tickling my earlobe. "Briar, help me!"

I'm desperate as I whirl around, searching. My heart is racing even faster now. "How?" I shout. "How can I help you?"

A stage light flashes on, illuminating the ballroom. Odette twirls effortlessly around the room with Portia and Juliet. They're dressed in leotards and tutus, doused in sparkles and feathers and gemstones. They dance in circles around me, fading in and out of the shadows, as I struggle to keep them in my line of sight. Tchaikovsky's *pas de deux* plays somewhere in the distance, the tone slightly off, the music low and haunting. "Go away from here," Odette whispers as she breezes behind me, rustling my hair. "You're not safe."

"I can't!" I cry out, stumbling after them.

Odette's voice thunders, echoing off the walls. "I keep trying to tell you!"

She sounds *so* angry.

"Tell me what? Is this about the note?"

"You never listen!"

The spinning quickens until my sisters twirl into one, a blur of freakishly conjoined arms and legs, shooting out in all directions, crooked and morbid and wrong. When they inevitably collapse, it's at the center of the ballroom, and only Odette is left, hunched over and sobbing into her tattered tights.

I sprint over and kneel beside her, placing a gentle hand on her bare back. "Odette?"

Odette whirls around and envelops me in a chillingly tight embrace, thick globs of mud streaking down her face like smudged mascara. It dribbles over her lips and hangs from her chin. "I tried to warn you," she whispers, her eyes wide with terror. "But it's too late now. It's too late!"

The stage light cuts out, and I drop to the cold ground. My sister evaporates into the air, sinks into the ground, turns into swamp water. "No!" I shout angrily, trying to collect the fluid in my hands. "Come back!"

My sister's voice thunders in my ear. "It's too late!"

WHEN I JERK AWAKE, her words are still ringing in my ears. I try to sit up, to kick away the heavy comforter, the damp sheets, but I can't move. All I can do is lie there, staring up at the speckles of water damage on the ceiling, the worn-out wallpaper curling at the edges, the dusting of black mold. My heart beats faster once I realize where I am. What the hell am I doing in Vivienne's bedroom?

My eyes dart frantically around.

The room is filthy. There are piles of clothes everywhere. Designer gowns strewn across the ottoman and chaise lounge, silk scarves draped over dimly lit lamps. I almost squeal when I see a palmetto bug scurry below the bed and then again, when I notice the big one floating in the water glass on the nightstand, bloated and dismembered, an antenna clinging to the side like an overgrown eyelash. The water has turned a murky brown. Frustration and disgust surge through me, not just with this house but also with all the infestations my mother has ignored. I can almost hear the roaches crawling through the walls.

Nesting. Laying eggs.

I'm still stuck in the nightmare, I think. This must be sleep paralysis. I'm only dreaming, and that's why I can't move. I try to force myself awake, so I can run to the bathroom and shower, shake off the heebie-jeebies. I'm covered in a film of sticky sweat. It prickles at the small of my back and beads above my upper lip. I absolutely hate sweating. I can't stand that constant dirty feeling—like being coated in toad slime.

Just sit up. Kick off the covers. I can hear Juliet playing outside, right below the cracked open window. She's humming some song, probably playing with her dolls, and I try to call out to her. But I can't even open my mouth.

I'm starting to panic now.

Get up. Just get up! Why can't I get up?

"Look who's finally awake!"

I cast my eyes toward the door. Vivienne steps into the room in a full linen ensemble and a pair of beige-heeled sandals. She looks as if she's about to spend the day relaxing at the beach. As non-threatening as a person can look. But my pulse spikes anyway.

Because I remember. *Everything.* My memories. Odette's journal. Calling the detective to search the property. The bodies in the mirrors. Elise... injecting me... with something.

What the fuck did you do to me? I want to scream. My insides are writhing. Squirming. I'm fighting so damn hard just to move my pinky finger, but no matter how hard I try, nothing is working.

Vivienne is glowing. She leans against her vanity, throws her head back, and laughs. "Oh, you look so scared. But don't you worry. Mama's here now."

She comes closer and her slender arm swoops overhead like a bird of prey as she lovingly strokes my hair. "My delicate rose," she coos, twirling a damp curl around her finger. It gets snagged in her diamond ring, tugging at my scalp, and I die a little inside—both from the pain *and* the nickname.

"You're burning up," she notices, frowning. "I know it's stuffy in here, isn't it? The A/C isn't working right. But it's old. It was only a matter of time before it croaked." She pinches my cheek, grinning at me. "We'll just have to make do, won't we? The temperature should reach the high 90s today. With the humidity, it'll feel like 110."

What's wrong with me? I'm internally screaming. I think my blood pressure has reached its max limit.

Vivienne throws the covers off me and I stare down at the pale blue dress I'm wearing. No wonder I'm burning up. It's ankle-length with long sleeves, a high collar, and dozens of black buttons. And it's made up of at least five layers of lace. I've been dressed up like an old-fashioned porcelain doll. Even my hair is curled and tied with baby blue ribbons.

My pinky finger twitches and Vivienne frowns. She slaps the finger down onto the mattress. "I see it's time for your next dose."

My pinky finger shoots up again and Vivienne leans in close to my ear. "There's no point, Briar. You're paralyzed from the tippy top of your head down to your itty-bitty toes." She snaps her fingers, singing, "You can't run. You can't leave. You can barely even breathe!"

My shallow breathing quickens. It sounds like I'm gasping for air through a straw. Drool dribbles down my chin and Vivienne catches it with her silk handkerchief, then rubs it over my brow to wipe away the sweat. "You said something to me when you first came back here. If I recall correctly, you told me that you're a grown woman now with your own life. Funny how things work out, right? Because I get to keep you here. With me. For as long as I like." She leans in closer, fixing my hair and giving me a tender kiss on the temple.

"I get to dress you however I want. Do your hair, your makeup. And you can't talk back, either. Isn't it wonderful?" Her eyes are twinkling. "The truth is, Briar, I don't trust you *or* your sister. You were ready to turn me over to the police in a heartbeat. And that wounded me deeply. I thought if I taught you girls anything, you'd know that family comes first."

Is Portia... okay? Is she trapped here, too? My thoughts feel sluggish. Slower and delayed, somehow. Like I've caught a serious case of brain fog. I'm trying to fight through it.

Vivienne goes to the door. "Elise!"

Moments later, Elise hurries into the room with the same bottle and syringe she'd used on me earlier. I fly into another panic, but it's like my body is stuck inside a cage and I can scream and cry and fight as much as I want but there's no escaping it. Without saying a word, she comes right over to me and injects the leaden liquid into my arm.

I wince at the stinging pain. Or at least I try to. Vivienne stands behind Elise, watching, a satisfied smile on her face. She thanks her before asking, "Would you be a dear and help me lift her? I want her to sit at my vanity. And I hope you gave her enough. She needs to be as still as a sleeping baby."

Elise wags the needle at me. "Trust me, she's not going anywhere."

I can *feel* whatever it is she just injected in me already working. It's like someone has arranged heavy weights all over my body. My eyelids grow heavy, and my brain slows down even more. I care less, and I don't want to care less.

I want to fight.

More drool dribbles down my chin as the two women hoist me up from the bed and sit me into a chair, then roll me over to the vanity.

"There, just how I wanted her," Vivienne says, smiling widely at Elise. "Now fetch me a cool rag. Poor Briar here is dying from the heat."

"Of course." Elise nods. "I'll be right back."

Vivienne presses her cheek to mine, grinning at our reflections in the mirror. "Look at us. Mother and daughter. Two perfect little peas in a pod." She stands, quickly undoing the ribbons from my hair and setting them aside. "You have a case of bedhead but I'm going to make you beautiful again. You're finally going to look like a lady!"

She grabs a golden brush and drags it through my hair, the bristles yanking at my curls. The pain is enough to make my eyes water. "I could brush your hair for hours," she purrs into my ear. "I know you don't believe it, but I do love you and your sisters. More than you'll ever know. You'll understand that one day when you have children of your own. A mother's love is stronger than anything."

Elise returns with the rag and hands it to Vivienne. She presses the cool cloth to my sweaty forehead and my flushed cheeks, dribbles of water trailing down my neck and soaking into my collar. I'm grateful because it cools me down instantly. I close my eyes as she sets the rag aside and finishes my hair, giving me a loose braid and tying the ribbons back into place. I open my eyes when Vivienne grips my chin, turning my face to look at her. "You know what I can't stand? All these damn freckles."

She grabs her makeup bag and plasters my face with chalky foundation, too white for my neutral undertones. It washes me out.

Makes the dark circles under my eyes pop. I stare at my reflection in the mirror, thinking I look like a corpse.

"I never understood why you always insisted on wearing lip balm instead of real makeup." She slathers a thick layer of lipstick onto my bottom lip, then the top. It feels like candle wax. "This pretty pink shade will brighten up those dull, muddy eyes of yours!"

Fuck you.

She coats my lashes in mascara, humming happily to herself as she works. "I'm going to tell you a story now. So, just sit back, relax, and listen. I think you'll find it very interesting."

She gives me another kiss on top of my head before jamming eyeliner onto my waterline. She's not gentle, and I'd give anything to pull away from her, to jam that liner straight into her eye socket.

"I was fifteen when I met the love of my life," Vivienne begins, a nostalgic expression on her face. "Right here at Belville Estate. He was the gardener's son. Scandalous, I know. Long story short, we shared a passionate, whirlwind romance, and before I knew it, I was knocked up and desperate for help."

This is new. I've never heard this story before. She pats my face with a pale powder. I don't even look like myself anymore.

"My mother was shocked but supportive, being the loving person she was. She stepped in and organized an abortion at my request. Unfortunately, in those days, it had to be performed illegally, and it left me without the ability to have children of my own. Though in the end, it brought you and your sisters into my life," she says, placing a hand on her heart and giving me a sweet smile.

"When my father found out, of course, he was livid. Furious at me for engaging with someone from a lower social class. Enraged at my mother for going behind his back. For speaking up to him when he felt she shouldn't. He said he couldn't tolerate her defiance any longer. She had challenged him one too many times, and in response, he had her committed to an institution, where she underwent a lobotomy, something he personally requested. When she returned, I hardly recognized her. She deteriorated so rapidly..." Vivienne closes her eyes and shakes her head at the painful memory.

My stomach churns. Just the thought of a husband forcing a medical procedure onto his wife, one that involves thrusting a metal instrument through her eye and scrambling her brain, is traumatizing. All because he couldn't stand her having a mind of her own.

"She was never the same woman again. My hatred for my father grew so much, I ran away from home that very year." Vivienne sighs heavily, a faraway look in her eyes. "I don't even know why I came back here after all those years. Maybe I missed it. Even with all the terrible things that happened, a part of me still considered it home. California is beautiful, but it doesn't hold a candle to the South."

I follow her gaze out the window as she admires the centuries-old oak trees with their tangled branches, the Spanish moss waving with the breeze as if acknowledging the compliment.

"But my parents were still alive, and I couldn't live with them. I wanted to erase them, along with all the bad memories. I wanted to make this place my own. Mine." Vivienne shrugs. "So... I killed them."

My heart skips a beat. Vivienne dabs the drool from my chin. She organizes her makeup in silence, as if she didn't just let that bomb drop. She plucks her favorite perfume from the vanity. It's a slender glass vial with an orange blossom topper, the fluid inside as murky as the swamp water that surrounds the estate. She spritzes her décolletage and wrists, daintily dabbing the excess behind her ears, in the coils of her hair.

The curtain of perfume reaches me, irritating my eyes. I want to choke out a cough, but I can't. It sits inside my lungs and burns, especially when she sprays it in my direction.

"You wanted to know why I keep hemlock in the garden," Vivienne remembers. She holds the vial up to the light streaming in through the window and reflections bounce off the opposite wall, catching on the collection of blades. She has a whole wall dedicated to them. Antique weapons from four different continents, including a blade rumored to have belonged to the female Dracula, Elizabeth Bathory.

I recognize it now as the murder weapon, the knife she drove into Robert's heart, and I break out into a cold sweat. I imagine her plunging the same blade into my chest, driving it in deeper and viciously twisting it. I think I'm going to pass out.

"It's my secret ingredient," she continues dreamily as she studies the dark liquid inside. "I think it adds a certain spice to the fragrance. A hint of danger. In small doses, it's harmless, once you've built up a tolerance. And I suspect it does wonders for the skin."

Maybe you pickled yourself, you old witch.

Vivienne smiles brightly at me as she sets her perfume aside and holds up a pair of cuticle scissors. They glint dangerously in the light. "Time for your nails. I've been dying to manicure them for the longest time. All they require is a little trim." She takes my hand, grasping it unusually tight. "A simple snip to get rid of the dead skin cells."

My breathing quickens as she snips around my left thumbnail, just a little too close for comfort.

Snip, snip.

"In larger doses, and once ingested, hemlock can prove fatal," Vivienne explains. "For my mother, it was an act of mercy. I made sure to give her enough poison to make it quick. The symptoms of ingestion mimic a heart attack, and she was already poorly, so no one questioned it when she didn't wake up in the morning. We buried her in the family plot."

I think of my grandmother's name on the marble Mother Mary tombstone. I remember it because I used to play hide-and-seek with my sisters around the graves.

She moves onto my pointer finger. *Snip, snip, snip.*

"But for my father," Vivienne continues, her gaze darkening. "I administered only trace amounts, enough to prolong his suffering. He became ill and then one night I had Elise cook him up a big feast. His favorite food was pork chops with gravy and mashed potatoes. We laid it all out for him, and he gobbled it right up. Too bad he didn't know about my secret ingredient because he was dead before dessert." She smirks, as if recalling the memory fondly. "He used to say I was too soft. Can you imagine that? He would call me all sorts of names, and I would cry and cry. Well, when I pulverized him and fed him to the gators, I kept thinking, Who's soft now, Daddy?"

She cackles.

"His funeral was a private affair. Everyone thinks he's buried next to his beloved wife, when really he was swamp stew!"

I think I'm going to be sick. She clips my middle finger. *Snip, snip, snip, snip, snip.*

The cuticle scissors slice into my skin, drawing blood. It drips off the end of my finger and splashes on the floor. Vivienne covers her mouth. "Oops!"

I draw in a gasp, unable to react to the pain or this horrible story, which somehow makes it a thousand times worse. Vivienne mistakes my reaction for fear. "Don't worry. I'm not going to kill you if that's what you're thinking." She grins at me, snapping the tiny scissors open and close. "And certainly not with cuticle scissors."

She ignores my bloodied finger and moves onto the ring finger. *Snip, snip.* She's a little too loose with them, not looking where she's going, opening them too wide, letting the sharp edge graze my skin. *Snip, snip, snip.*

Sweat drips down my back and beads at my hairline. I keep my eyes on those scissors, terrified.

"Hemlock isn't going to paralyze anyone, though. What you have in your system is something far worse. It's a new strain I've been cultivating. One of my garden experiments. I've created all sorts of flowers over the years. One that blinds you, another that causes hemorrhaging. I call this one Sinister Beauty. It's distantly related to Devil's Breath. The Soviet Union used it as a kind of truth serum back in the day."

She lifts a small vase from her vanity, showing me a trumpet-shaped flower with sharp violet petals and spiky leaves. She's preserved it somehow, but I can still smell the rancid odor coming off the broken stem.

"Just a tiny dose of Sinister Beauty causes hallucinations, feverish dreams, and amnesia. A stronger dose renders the victim completely immobile, unable to speak or save themselves." She chuckles, pointing the scissors in my direction. "Elise and I had to increase you and your sister's dosage because we've been giving it to you since you were children. Made it into a tea, slipped it into your grits. You both have built up quite the tolerance. It helps make the brain pliable, erasing memories. Even the scary ones, like witnessing a murder."

I stare at Vivienne, shocked. *The repressed memories.*

It was *her.*

She was the reason.

Odette was also missing large chunks of her childhood. It's why she had asked Portia to recommend her a hypnotherapist in the first place...

"Oh, I seem to have forgotten your rouge!" Vivienne straightens and searches the vanity, so I'm not expecting it when she suddenly strikes me in the face, a hard slap across the cheek. The pain is absolutely searing. She grasps the arms of my chair, getting down to eye level, and jerks me closer to her. "That's for forgetting where your loyalties lie," she says through clenched teeth.

Tears streak down my face and she catches them with her handkerchief. "Quit your crying. You're going to ruin your makeup."

Vivienne notices all the blood running down my hand. "I'll be right back." She wags a finger at me. "Now, don't you move a muscle. I'm going to get the first-aid kit."

I stare at my tear-soaked face in the mirror as she disappears out the door. I'm freaking out but I look brain-dead, my eyes glazed over and spittle glistening at the corner of my mouth.

"Owen, what a surprise!" I can hear Vivienne say in the hallway.

The sound of Owen's voice fills me with hope, and I fixate on the cracked open door, urging my legs to cooperate, to propel me toward him. But no matter how hard I try, I can't make a sound, not even a whimper. All that fills the air is the soft pitter-patter of blood as it drips onto the floor.

"I wanted to check on Briar. I know you mentioned she was under the weather, but I brought her some pralines." I hear the rattle of the tin container, and I know he brought ones just like his grandmother used to make.

"What a thoughtful gesture," Vivienne says in a tight voice. "But unfortunately, Briar went home. So did Portia. In fact, you just missed them."

She's lying! Don't listen to her!

"As you can imagine, we got into quite the fight after the police left," Vivienne continues, sounding troubled. "What with Briar making up all those ludicrous stories! She has quite the imagination. Maybe she should take up writing like you." She gives a little laugh. "Anyway, they both just stormed right out of here. Oh, you look so disappointed! I'm sorry she left without saying goodbye..."

"Do you mind giving me her number? I'd really like to call her."

"Elise will write it down for you." She quickly changes the subject. "You know, I was wondering, maybe we could work on my memoir again tonight?"

"Uh... Sure. But I meant to talk to you about something else. My house is finished. I won't be staying in the guesthouse much longer."

"No! Not you, too. I'll be so lonely here!"

"We're neighbors. I'll still come by to visit. Fix things up around the house."

"I certainly hope so. You've always been so handy. Speaking of, would you be a dear and clear off the vines from the front porch? They're driving me mad."

I focus on trying to move my legs, but it all feels so pointless.

"I'll get started right after I talk to Elise," Owen promises.

"You're a gem!" Vivienne cries. I can hear their voices fading, the floorboards creaking as they move farther away.

No! Don't go! Don't leave me here with her! Eventually, I don't hear them at all anymore.

27

TWENTY MINUTES LATER, my cellphone buzzes on the nightstand. I watch it vibrating towards the edge, the screen brightly lit. I'm agonizingly close, and if I can just...

Vivienne rushes into the room and snatches my phone from the nightstand. Holding it up, she smirks, "Owen's calling already? He must really have it bad for you." She uses my face to open my phone and thumbs over the screen. "Please stop contacting me," she reads aloud as she types. "I think we should part ways. We're too different."

I imagine tackling her to the ground.

"Sent," Vivienne chirps as she grins at me, clearly satisfied with herself. "I hope we haven't broken his heart. But if we have..." She pinches my cheek. Hard. "At least he'll have *my* shoulder to cry on."

All I can think of is breaking that shoulder *and* that smug face.

Vivienne drags my chair to the window, so I have a front-row seat to the show. "Oh, stop looking at me like that, Briar. I'm only trying to help you. Owen's no good for you. He was ready to jump into bed with me the moment I started batting my eyelashes at him. He's a greedy opportunist. A user. You don't see it yet, but you will. I know I have an unorthodox way of showing it, but I'm trying to *protect you*. From rotten, dirty, no-good men like that." She pats me on the head like a dog. "You're just not pretty or smart enough for this big, cruel world. You're safer staying here with your mama. I'm all you and your sisters need."

I can see Owen below. He's clearing vines and fallen branches from the drive and porch columns, the aged white paint chipping, the cracks like tangled black veins. He's in a white tank, sweat breaking out across his brow, the muscles flexing in his arms and back as he works.

He stops to check his phone, frowning at my mother's text. My cellphone buzzes as he responds, and then again. I'm dying to know what those messages say. He looks down at his phone for a long time, waiting for me to text back. Obviously, I don't. Vivienne's already left the room, and I can hear her singing happily as she heads downstairs.

Owen shoves his phone into his back pocket and goes back to clearing the porch.

Just look up, I want to shout. *I'm right here!* I will my arms to move, to force them up so I can bang on the window until he notices me. But they lie limp in my lap, unresponsive.

Elise sweeps the pebbled drive, her eyes on Owen as Vivienne glides down the porch with a glass of lemonade. She shoots him her movie star smile and rests a hand on his bicep as he knocks it back. Is it my imagination, or does Elise look... jealous? Of Vivienne and Owen?

She sweeps faster, almost agitated, and then charges into the house. I can hear her downstairs, banging around in the kitchen.

For a split second, I think Owen sees me sitting here half-hidden behind the curtains. He looks up at the window as he lowers his glass, locking eyes with me.

Oh, please.

Please, please, please. I need help!

I'm right here!

Please!

I'm panting, struggling to lean in closer to the window, and I end up drooling all over myself in the process. Just when I thought I might catch Owen's attention, he turns to grab his garbage bag and Vivienne gazes up at me instead. She waves her hand and flashes me a taunting smile.

It's hopeless.

I'VE BEEN TRAPPED inside this house for six days. Vivienne spoon-feeds me. Bathes me. Shaves me. Dresses me. Worst of all, changes my diapers. It's humiliating. And I've cried more than once out of pure frustration.

I should've left when I had the chance. Why did I stay so long? How could I let this happen? But I think I finally have an escape plan. Elise comes every morning to administer the next dose of her poison. But there's a short window right after I wake up that I'm alone and the effects of the flower have started to wear off. I can wiggle my toes. My pinky fingers. Even lift my head a little if I really concentrate.

It wasn't until a few days ago that I noticed the more water I drink, the faster the poison flushes out of my system. If my plan works, I might be able to gather enough strength to get to my phone or hide somewhere before Elise jabs me with her syringe again.

So yesterday when Vivienne set me in front of her vanity and brushed my hair, I would show her with my eyes that I was thirsty, pointing them in the direction of my water glass. She obliged and thought nothing of it. And when Elise brought me a fruit smoothie for dinner (the more liquid, the better), I would do the same thing. She would give me water or refill my glass, without suspecting a thing.

I was so nervous about my plan that I barely slept last night, afraid I'd miss the moment. But now that I'm lying here, I realize I feel different this morning. Stronger, somehow. Not only can I wiggle my toes and lift my head, but I can sit up. My heart races as I spot my cellphone on the vanity. Vivienne left it there to torment me, so I can hear it buzzing any time someone texts or calls me throughout the day, and then before bed, she replies to each one, reading her responses out loud for me. She wants me to understand that no one's coming to save me or my sister, at least not anytime soon.

Summoning every ounce of energy I have left, I manage to swing my legs around and shift toward the edge of the bed. My mouth is bone dry. My tongue feels like sandpaper. Black dots speckle my vision, and I press a shaking hand to my forehead, closing my eyes for a second. I'm so woozy. Being stuck in bed all the time has taken a toll on my body. *Please don't pass out, please don't pass out...*

As soon as I recover, I take a deep breath and rise to my feet, keeping a hand on the headboard for extra support. Once I'm confident enough, I take a step forward, then another. My legs wobble beneath me and then my knees buckle, slamming onto the floorboards.

Shit. I bite my lip, my eyes tearing from the pain.

I freeze. My eyes move to the door when I hear muffled voices somewhere below. My pulse picks up. I feel like I'm choking on it.

Footsteps rush up the stairs. I'm holding my breath, waiting for the door to burst open. I have two options here. I can try to make it to the phone in time, or I can climb back into bed. I swallow, thinking, running out of time. I don't trust my body to make it there, but what if this is my only shot?

The footsteps are closing in, growing louder. Pushing off the ground, I fling myself back onto the bed and pull the covers over me. I close my eyes just as the door swings open and try desperately to relax my face. Elise glares at me from between my cracked lids, her blurred figure lingering in the doorway.

It's a challenge to keep my breathing even, especially with my heart moving so fast. I swear she can see it pounding through the comforter.

When the door finally shuts, I breathe a sigh of relief. My whole body is tense, drenched in sweat. I wipe at my forehead as I sit up again. This time, I need to be more careful.

I slip out of bed and lower myself onto the ground, the muscles in my arms aching. As quietly as possible, I start crawling to the vanity. My limbs feel like lead weights, but I urge myself to go faster. My bruised knees scrape against the wood floor, and my palms are on fire from the friction.

Oh, thank God. I make it to my cellphone. I'm shaking even harder now, and I'm not sure if it's adrenaline or withdrawal. I can barely keep my phone steady.

I use Face ID and go to the keypad. *9...* My sweaty fingers slip across the screen, hitting the wrong button. *4...*

Frustrated, I erase the extra number and try again. *9... 1...1...*

The footsteps return and my heart leaps into my throat. The door slams open and Elise runs in, syringe in hand. It's too late. She snatches the phone from my grasp, pockets it, and grabs a handful of my hair, yanking me down to the ground.

"No!" I plead, my voice hoarse and strained. This isn't happening. I refuse to stay here! I refuse to go down without a fight!

I kick my legs and swing my arms, landing a blow to her stomach. The air whooshes out of her and she doubles over. I lunge for her pocket, but she stops me from grabbing my phone. I could have easily taken her before, but now she's so much stronger than me.

"Briar," Elise warns. She straightens and rubs the sore spot on her stomach. "You're making this harder than it has to be."

She doesn't look angry like I expect her to. Instead, there's a hint of guilt in her eyes, which only pisses me off more. She's the one doing this to me, going along with whatever my mother tells her to do! She could help me, save me, but she chooses not to.

"Please, I don't want to hurt you," she begs, her steps faltering as she edges closer with the syringe, the sharp tip glinting in the pale sunlight. "Just do as I say, and it'll only be for a little while longer," she says, exasperated. "Why won't you behave?"

She reaches out for me, jabbing with the syringe, but somehow I catch her arm and ram it into the vanity. Tightening my grip, I do it again and again. She sucks in a pained gasp, and the syringe falls, bouncing and rolling across the floor.

We lunge for it at the same time. I'm on top of her, my arms locked around her neck, trying to choke her out. But she has way more strength and energy than I do. I can't hold her down for long, and her fingers are already inching closer to the needle.

So, I do the last thing I can think of. I open my mouth and bite down on her arm. Elise screams, and it's like music to my ears. She swats at my head, but I don't budge. I bite harder, tasting blood. It fills my mouth, dribbles down my chin.

It's disgusting. Salty and metallic. But at this point, I'd do anything to get out of here.

Elise screams louder.

Out of nowhere, a sharp pain pricks me in the neck. It happens so suddenly I almost don't realize it—not until my jaw loosens and my muscles relax, a warmth spreading throughout every vein in my body.

"She bit me!" Elise yelps, jumping up. She quickly backs away and nurses her wounded arm.

I spit her blood out onto the floorboards, coughing and groaning.

It didn't work. I failed.

My vision blurs as I roll over onto my back. I can just make out the empty syringe clamped in Vivienne's delicate fist. She frowns down at my crumpled body, and the last thing I see is my own dazed reflection in her shiny black heels as she towers over me. "Looks like someone's been a very bad girl..."

28

I DRIFT in and out of consciousness.

I peel one eye open, and then sometime later, the other. My tired eyes struggle to focus. For a moment, I swear I see a figure standing at the foot of my bed, their dark silhouette looming ominously in the shadows.

My breath catches in my throat. "Detective," I whisper hopefully, but when no one answers, my heart sinks. "Vivienne..." I barely manage to get the name off my tongue. Drool collects in the corner of my mouth. The figure slowly fades away, making me doubt if it was ever there at all. "Odette?"

My brain feels like mush, my body a sluggish mess.

I continue to drift.

I lose track of time and the days and nights begin to blur together.

But eventually, the heavy fog seems to lift. As time runs on, Vivienne starts keeping me company, telling me stories I've heard hundreds of times before about her time in Hollywood, shamelessly name-dropping actors she may or may not have crossed paths with—Lauren Bacall, Olivia de Havilland, Marlon Brando. It's so mind-numbingly boring. If she wants to kill me, I wish she would just do it faster. Listening to her drone on about how fabulous her life was and how her fabulous famous friends adored her is torture.

At least my brain is taking ten times longer to process everything. Since my little escape plan failed, Elise has been coming into my room extra early every morning, shooting me up with that disgusting concoction and waiting beside my bed until she's certain it's working.

They've got me surviving on liquids alone, and I'm pretty sure I've already shed a good chunk of the weight my mother won't stop hassling me about. Which is infuriating, because I never wanted to lose it in the first place. I've always been content with my body. Always.

I pass the time by fantasizing about brutally murdering them, ramming Elise's head repeatedly into the glass cases holding Vivienne's knife collection, plucking that massive blade with the golden hilt off the wall, the same one she used to kill my father, jamming it deep inside Vivienne's throat. After that, I'd save my sister.

I figured out Portia is being held hostage inside Elise's room. Right next door. Vivienne goes back and forth, traveling between us. Probably boring my sister to death, too. I can't stand that she's so close but I'm unable to call out to her, see if she's okay.

It's the same for Juliet. I often hear her playing outside. Singing and laughing and screeching. Sometimes I hear her racing down the hall, her footsteps thundering outside the door. At least I know she's safe and happy, but for how long? How can I be sure our mother won't do the same to her?

I've never felt so helpless in my entire life.

My head throbs from the gramophone sitting in the corner, an upbeat '40s jingle trumpeting from the sound horn. Vivienne reaches out and grasps my hand, squeezing. "And then Cary said to me..." she continues now. "That's Cary Grant, by the way. Well, he said to me, 'Vivienne, you are one of the most beautiful women to ever grace the silver screen'."

I would snort if I could.

The door bursts open and Elise stumbles inside, looking panicked. She still has a bandage covering the arm I bit, and I can't help but feel a twinge of satisfaction every time I look at it. She slaps a newspaper onto Vivienne's lap. "Read this."

Vivienne lifts the newspaper, holding the headline up to the light. She squints her eyes as she reads, "Mason Montgomery of The Hypnosis Group reported missing."

Oh, my fucking God. Did she have something to do with that, too?

Vivienne barks out a harsh laugh. "This is nothing we haven't dealt with before. So, what? He's been reported missing. They have no way to link us to him other than Odette, and she's been dead for months."

Vivienne digs in her purse, retrieving a packet of cigarettes with shaky fingers. "I know I keep telling you I quit," she says with a guilty smile. She lights up, the cigarette stuck between her teeth. "But I quit a lot of things, only to take them back up again." She tilts her head, chuckling softly to herself, and I catch a glimpse of the bottle of chardonnay behind her.

"You didn't read it," Elise protests. She snatches the paper back and waves it around. "They have a description of me. They caught me on video!"

I blink rapidly. The only way I can communicate my distress to anyone. Vivienne notices and groans, rubbing her temples. "Oh, stop. You're scaring Briar. Take that away. How many times do I have to say it? It's nothing we can't handle."

"Fine." Elise lowers her head. "Whatever you say."

I stare longingly at the door as she exits the room.

Vivienne sighs. She takes a couple drags of her cigarette. "Elise discovered Odette was being blackmailed. She's my extra set of eyes and ears."

I know. I remember all the times I caught Elise eavesdropping on me as a teenager, the creaking of floorboards just outside my door whenever I tried to secretly smoke pot. Somehow the fact she wore dark colors made it worse. She was a constant shadow. Always creeping around.

"Mason Montgomery was just one of many who threatened to expose our secrets. It had to be done." Vivienne gives me a look. "We're telling the truth now, remember? No more lies."

How many people has she hurt? Did she kill him? No one deserves that, not even lowlife blackmailers like Mason Montgomery.

She takes another long drag of her cigarette, her thin brows knitting as she draws the smoke into her lungs. "Don't look at me that way," she says, blowing it into my face. It makes my eyes water, the vindictive expression on her face blurring. "I had Elise follow Claire. Odette's pretty, little girlfriend. She was going to take care of her too, but the girl didn't seem to know anything of importance. But we would've killed her… if we had to."

I stare up at the ceiling, feeling desperate. The gramophone in the corner crackles, pausing before it plays the next song. The happy-go-lucky vintage music makes me want to scream. I feel like I'm living in a horror film.

Vivienne senses my unease and adds, "I do wish you'd come around, Briar, and realize that everything I do is for the good of this family." She takes another hit of her cigarette, enjoying the buzz. "I would eventually like to let you and your sister go. You have no idea how much work it is to care for the two of you… not that I don't enjoy taking care of my babies." She blows another cloud of smoke over my head, then taps the ash away. "Once I trust you won't spill our secrets, well, I'll stop all this nonsense. But I just don't see that happening anytime soon."

I wish I could run away. Someone has to realize I'm missing eventually. I don't care if Vivienne is pretending to be me. I'm very involved with my work. I attend multiple meetings a day, and that's obviously drastically changed. Someone is going to realize something is up eventually.

And what about Luke? Is she also writing Luke and pretending to be Portia? That might be easier since they're separated, but she can't pretend to be us forever.

Can she?

I WAKE up to shouting going on downstairs. It's Vivienne and Elise, arguing. I've never heard them argue before and definitely not like this. It sounds serious. I hear the word *police*, and I wonder if this means we're finally going to be rescued.

I remember the look on Elise's face when I tried to escape. There was a flicker of remorse. Pity. Guilt. It was quick, but it was more than the blank face she usually gives me.

My heart races as I sit up in bed, and thunders even faster when I realize I can move.

I have no idea what time it is, but I figure it must be early afternoon. Elise should've already been here to give me my next dose. And Vivienne should've come with my breakfast smoothie.

I reach for my phone on the nightstand, my arm heavy and weak, but it's not there, and it's not on the vanity either. I take the half-empty water glass beside me and chug it down, streams of it flowing over my chin and soaking into my dress.

I set the glass aside and throw off the covers, then slowly move my legs out of bed, touching my bare feet to the floor. I manage to stand upright, using the bed and nightstand again for support. I'm searching the room for my phone as I trudge toward the hall.

I look both ways to make sure the coast is clear. They're still fighting down there, still shouting. The voices exchanged are vicious. I can hear things breaking and shattering. It sounds like they're tearing each other apart.

I drag my feet to Elise's room, and my heart instantly drops. Portia lies still in bed. Her mouth is slack and her lips are pale and chapped. "Portia," I say, collapsing beside her. I shake her shoulders, trying to wake her, but she doesn't move. I check her pulse. It's there, but dangerously faint. "Don't worry," I promise her. "I'm going to get us help."

I push to my feet, my knees wobbling. I'm out of breath, lightheaded. Most likely from not eating enough. I inch back to the door, forcing my weak legs to move faster. Elise's room is much smaller and darker than the other rooms, the furniture simple and the walls bare—except for a stunning headshot in a heart-shaped frame that hangs above her dresser. It's of a young Vivienne in the early days of her stardom. She's reclined on a bed in a backless dress, her blonde curls done to perfection, her pouty lips a deep red. Her brows are lifted and pencil-thin, and her eyes are heavily lidded as she seductively stares down the camera.

I wonder how many times Elise has stood in front of this dresser, preparing for the day, admiring her employer. The lengths Elise goes to keep Vivienne happy, worshipping the ground she walks on, doing all her dirty work. They're a match made in heaven.

Or Hell.

I'm about to turn away when I see something. A corner of an envelope sticks out from the top drawer, wrinkled and worn. I recognize my handwriting right away, and somehow I know what this is even before I tug it free. "No, no, no, no," I whisper.

My letters I sent to Owen while he was in prison. All of them. Stashed in a box in the top drawer of Elise's dresser for over a decade.

I grip my stomach, in pain, fighting the tears. This feels like the final blow, the last excruciating twist of the knife.

It was them. They were the reason he never got my letters. I rifle through the envelopes, my horror growing. Each one is sliced open, every intimate line read, every page reeking of Vivienne's awful perfume.

I'm *so* angry. Filled with rage. I shove down my emotions and slam the drawer shut, steadying myself against the wall as I retrace my steps to the hallway. I'm headed for the stairs when I hear an ear-piercing scream and three distinct gunshots, one after the other after the other.

I stop dead in my tracks. I almost turn back when I hear a low moaning noise coming from downstairs. Taking a deep breath, I start inching along, my legs getting stronger the farther I push myself. When I reach the end of the landing, I find Vivienne.

She lies at the bottom of the stairs, the back of her dress covered in blood. There are two gunshot wounds—one on her side and the other below her right shoulder blade. She looks up at me and opens her mouth to speak, but dark, coagulated blood gurgles out instead.

Shocked, I remain rooted in place, gripping the stair railing.

She tries to push from the ground but winces in pain. There's a large crimson puddle spreading out beneath her. She reaches out for me, her fingers splayed. "Briar, please. Help me. Elise has lost her mind. She shot herself. She shot me!"

I close my mouth and clutch the railing tighter. I step back.

Vivienne drops her arm, growing weaker. "Briar." She clenches her teeth. "I'm dying!"

"I see that," I say, surprisingly calm.

"Well, call for help!"

My heart thuds low in my chest. "I found the letters, Vivienne."

"What?"

"The letters! You know which ones."

Vivienne exhales shakily as she stares up at me. For the first time in my life, I think she looks afraid of me. "Briar..."

"Is that all you have to say?"

"Briar, I'm sorry! Please, if I explain to you why I did it, will you call me an ambulance?"

I chuckle softly, then shrug. "Sure. Why not?"

Vivienne looks relieved. She sighs, trying to muster the strength. "Elise. It was Elise," she pants breathlessly. "She followed you that day into the swamp, spied on you and Owen from afar. She told me he proposed and that he wanted you to run away with him."

I'm shaken by this new information. Because at the time, I was so sure someone had been watching us. I'd taken Owen's hand after he proposed and led him deeper into the woods. We went all the way for the first time and spent the whole night in each other's arms.

At one point, I heard a twig snap in the distance and was convinced I saw someone watching us from behind the trees. It spooked us so much that we hurried back to Owen's house without checking to see who or what it was. My skin crawls at the idea that it was Elise, and that she'd also run home, only to tell my mother everything.

"He wanted you to live there in that dirty shack of his. He wasn't good enough for you! He was involved with drugs, getting into trouble with the law."

Her eyes roll back as if she's about to pass out before focusing on me again. "I'm good friends with... the warden. All he had to do was withhold the letters... and return them to me." She spits up another wad of blood. It clings to her chin, dripping onto the floor. She coughs violently as if she can't get any air into her lungs. "I thought Ted... would be a better match. That's why I introduced you two in the first place... at the club. But he was an even bigger disappointment."

I wipe away my tears. "Thank you for telling me that."

Vivienne nods, reaching for me again. "Now, darling, please, will you help me?"

"No," I reply. I laugh a little, sniffling. "No, I will not."

"What?"

"No one is coming to help you. You're going to die here," I inform her as I cross my arms over my chest. I remain very still, the tears still falling. "And I'm going to watch." I laugh again, the sound unhinged. "I'm going to watch and enjoy it!"

Vivienne's eyes widen in horror once she realizes I'm serious.

She manages to push herself off the floor out of spite, but only for a couple of seconds before collapsing and groaning in pain.

She writhes around, her fingers twitching. More blood gurgles out with a noise that sounds like my name or maybe an insult. It takes her a surprisingly long time to die, and it seems painful. I watch as she chokes on her own blood and drowns in it, her whole face turning purple, then blue.

Eventually, she falls still, her eyes wide and staring.

I don't move for a long time after. Then, finally, I tread slowly down the stairs to make sure she's really dead. There's no pulse.

I stare in quiet shock at her lifeless face.

It's a shock because I guess I thought she'd never die. That she *couldn't* die. But now all that bite, all that bark, is finally gone.

And I feel nothing but relief.

With bloodied hands, I push off the banister and stumble into the grand ballroom, following the trail of blood. Elise lies motionless in the center of the room, a gunshot wound to her temple. In her hand, there's a typed confession on my mother's stationery, and in the other, a gun.

It's an antique pistol from the 1930s, but I can see our family's shotgun abandoned nearby, and I'm sure that's the murder weapon she used on Vivienne. I had planned on grabbing it for my own protection if I had to. Well, not anymore.

Kneeling beside Elise, my body trembles as I reach for the slip of stationery. The metallic smell that hangs in the air makes me feel sick, and I'm afraid that as soon as I touch the paper, her eyes will spring open, and she'll have the gun to my head, her thumb on the trigger. But she doesn't budge as I try to take it, and the page slips into my lap.

I start reading.

Gator Springs PD Evidence Files

ERN: 0507845
Recovered by: Detective Elena Torres
Description of evidence: The following is an excerpt from Elise Dowell's confession discovered at the scene.

...eyes on her first. She laid eyes on me, and it wasn't like a tap on the shoulder, but a violent shove. Her gaze was physical. Intense. Fiery hot...

...looked so dove-like, with those clear hazel eyes, fair golden strands, and baby-soft skin. I thought it looked soft—that's the very first thought I had—how beautifully soft her skin looked. It was as if it were painted on by Leonardo da Vinci himself. She was an oil painting, the first flower to blossom in spring...

...an all-consuming sinkhole. I knew I'd follow her anywhere, that I'd do anything for her. You know how they say you see the light before you die? I died that day. Though those feelings were never returned, I was no more than an extension of her...

...murdered the following people: Nils Hansen, Reggie Freeman, Darren Hamilton, Darren Hamilton's friends Billy Prescott and Walter Coogan, who were in the wrong place at the wrong time. Robert Wells, Robert's secretary, Eleanor Perry, when she became suspicious, and Mason Montgomery, when he blackmailed our family...

...burned most of the bodies except for Vivienne's husbands, which we preserved. They are in the boathouse. We kept them in the mirrors of their daughters' bedrooms until they were found. I knew exactly what I was doing, and there was a part of me deep down that enjoyed it, that felt...

...and I'll never forgive myself for what I put those girls through. I couldn't bear standing by while she tortured them, while she tried to convert them to our wicked ways...

...and Briar found the bodies. Vivienne and I held her and Portia captive so they wouldn't go to the police. We drugged them and confined them to their beds. They had nothing to do with any of this...

End of excerpt.

I'm so transfixed by the puckered bullet wound in her head and the contents of the letter that I barely react when I hear the front door being kicked in, the alarm blaring in the background. Someone grasps me from behind, and I scream.

"Briar, it's okay. It's just me." I turn around and look at Detective Torres with wide, fearful eyes. She grips my arms, reassuring me as I hyperventilate. "You're okay now. You're safe."

My fingers smudge blood onto the detective's crisp white shirt. I stare at them, and then at my hands, holding them up to my face.

"Elise called the police and told us everything," she assures me. "What she was planning to do. What she did to you and your sister."

"My sister," I say, remembering, pointing to the stairs. "My sister!"

"We'll get her help." She ushers me outside where dozens of flashing lights blind me.

There are police cars, trucks, ambulances. Crime scene techs remove Vivienne's husbands' preserved bodies from the boathouse, gingerly loading them into body bags on the shore and then hauling them away. Owen stands with Juliet in the distance, and they both look relieved to see I'm okay.

I take a deep breath as I'm taken to an ambulance, staring down at the blood that's caked to my body, this dress I'm already trying to tear myself out of. I'm okay, and I'm free.

I'm finally free.

Excerpt from the transcript of episode 64, "The Belville Murders", from *Femme Fatales with Lacey Black*, uploaded to YouTube on November 17, 2023

The host, Lacey Black, has dark hair with pink streaks, a nose ring, and colorful tattoos. She sports comfortable loungewear and sits behind a large, hot pink microphone. There is a fluffy pink wall behind her with a white sparkly skull.

Lacey Black: Hey, guys! Welcome back to my channel! This was one of my most popular video requests. A lot of you reached out to me to cover the case of Old Hollywood actress Vivienne Belville, and let me tell 'ya, this one is wild! This is one of the most chilling and horrific cases I have ever covered. And I mean that, you guys. So, brace yourselves, because the truth is truly stranger than fiction.

She takes a quick sip of her matcha latte, and her bedazzled black nails shimmer in the ring light.

Lacey Black: Let's cover the basics here. Vivienne Belville is a massively famous actress from the golden age of Hollywood. She starred in *Doctor Zhivago, Once Upon a Time in the West, El Dorado, Fahrenheit 451.* She was a Bond girl at one point. A Hitchcock blonde. She was on Broadway.

Multiple photographs of Vivienne at various ages are displayed onscreen.

Lacey Black: She retired from acting in the early '90s and eventually returned to her childhood home, The Belville Estate, in Florida. Obviously, she comes from a very wealthy family. We're talking old money. Her great-grandfather was Louis Antoine de Belleville. Born in 1854, he was a French industrialist engaged in mining, steelmaking, and railways. He would later emigrate to America and expand his empire there. By the late 1800s, he had amassed a fortune worth over 100 million dollars. So, yeah, we are talking stinkin' rich. And there is a lot of dark history involving child labor and exploitation, but that's a whole other video...

She readjusts her microphone and glances down at her notes.

Lacey Black: Now, Vivienne is no stranger to scandal. This woman had not one, and no, not two, but four husbands go missing. Yes, you heard me correctly. Four! And this went unsolved for almost fifty years. Everyone suspected Vivienne to be responsible, but she lawyered up, and no one could prove anything.

Lacey leans in and stares directly into the camera. The ring light reflects in her brown eyes.

Lacey Black: Until now. On November 2nd, the police received a phone call from The Belville Estate's long-time housekeeper, Elise Dowell, who reported she was about to end both her employer's life and her own. When police arrived, they discovered that Vivienne had been keeping her adult daughters, Briar and Portia—known as the star sisters from a popular children's TV show that aired in the mid to late '90s—heavily drugged and severely incapacitated. She had been holding them captive for *weeks*.

Photos of Briar, Portia, and Vivienne appear onscreen. Lacey cups her matcha latte with her hands and shakes her head in disbelief.

Lacey Black: Why, you ask? Well, it gets crazier, people. Let's back-track a little...

End of excerpt.

29

It's been three weeks since it happened.

I set the table, arranging the plates and silverware. Owen brings in the Chinese takeout he picked up, and I give him a grateful but tired smile. Between that psychopath holding us captive and the whirlwind of Vivienne's post-death drama—the will reading, deciding who will take care of Juliet—I feel exhausted.

It's been endless meetings with our attorney and Vivienne's estate manager. We haven't even discussed what to do with the house yet, but I know I want to sell it. Or maybe bulldoze the place to the ground. Vivienne's fortune was split equally between the three of us, but Juliet's share will be held in annuities until she's eighteen, and that comes with its own flurry of decisions. Portia has temporary custody of Juliet for now, but she'll need to attend a court hearing in a few days to finalize everything.

The media circus has mostly subsided, thank goodness, but journalists keep reaching out to Portia and I about making a statement or doing an interview. They keep throwing around words like *brave* and *inspiring*. I don't feel brave or inspiring. But on the plus side, I'm feeling a lot better. No more hallucinations, stomach pain, or strange dreams.

I've asked Owen to stay a bit longer, at least until things settle down. Having him here makes me feel safer. Last week, he even punched a lurker in the face for trying to shove his way through the gate during the private funeral we held for Vivienne and Elise.

We only did it for Juliet. Portia and I would have gladly cremated those monsters and thrown their ashes in the trash.

No, that's not entirely true. I hate myself for the conflicting emotions, but I know I'm also devastated over the loss of my two mothers. Part of me is glad Vivienne is dead, though. The thought of her wasting away in some cold jail cell in a hideous orange jumpsuit... I can't even picture it. And that wouldn't be the ending she'd choose for herself either.

I stop at the head of the table, looking at my mother's empty seat. I'm trying to be strong for my sisters, to hold it together. But I break down, tears rolling down my cheeks.

Owen moves closer to me. "Come here," he says, taking me into his arms.

I melt into the embrace and he wipes away my tears, catching them with his thumb. I rest my head against his chest and he holds me longer, comforting me.

"I'm sorry," Portia says, coming around the corner. She hesitates as if she's not sure whether to stay or leave. We break apart, awkwardly. Owen adjusts his watchband, trying to keep his hands busy. I rub at my arms, my cheeks burning. "Didn't mean to interrupt."

"You're not," I assure her, casting an apologetic glance at Owen. "I was actually just going to wash my hands."

I head down the hall, his cologne clinging to the ends of my hair, and it makes me feel so heady that I don't even notice Juliet's school bag on the floor. The toe of my heel connects with one of the straps and I stumble forward, almost colliding headfirst into one of my mother's framed glamour shots.

I groan and charge back toward the stairs. "Juliet! How many times have I told you not to leave your backpack on the floor?"

"I'm busy!" she answers, unbothered, her soft voice carrying down from the landing. I see her peering at me through the railing, her dark eyes testing me.

"I don't care. Come down here!"

I hear her hurried footsteps as she retreats into her bedroom. "No!" she shouts before slamming the door shut.

"Excuse me, missy—" I release a frustrated sigh, deciding to let it go for now. This month has been tough enough, and I can discipline her later. I'll just put the backpack away myself. *Sometimes, getting through to a kid feels harder than communicating with the dead...*

As soon as I think it, I flinch and tighten my grip on the bag. Something squelches between my fingers, and I make a face as I examine the sticky brown substance. It's coming from the zipper, oozing out in wet globs. Disgusted, I rush into the spare bathroom and drop the bag into the sink, quickly washing my hands. Using a towel for added protection, I reluctantly open the zipper. *What in the hell?*

The sink swirls with mud and sand and hair ribbons as the bag overflows with water. Splashes of brown sludge splatter my dress. I turn off the sink and drain the bag, scraping the muck out from the bottom. "Ouch," I hiss, bringing my wounded finger to my lips and tasting the blood. A cool, smooth object protrudes from the cut and it's not until the water completely drains that I realize what it is. Juliet's porcelain doll—the one she buried near the swamp. She must have dug it up again.

I exhale shakily as I clean the gash in my finger and gather the broken doll, trying to determine whether this is normal behavior for a grieving seven-year-old girl or something to be concerned about. In this family, it's hard to tell.

Once I'm finished, I wrap the doll in the towel and stash it in one of the bag's pockets. There's something already wedged into the bottom of it. I fish it out and let out a shriek, dropping it into the sink. It hits the porcelain with a sharp crack. It's...

My heart drops into my stomach.

It's a bird's skull and there's a tiny black feather poking out of the gaping eye socket, dried blood stuck to the quill. "What the actual fuck."

I clean everything up, return her bag to the coat closet, and then head upstairs. "Juliet, I really need to talk to you. Like right now."

I enter the room and freeze. Juliet is crouched in the corner, against the wall, scribbling with her markers. She's drawn a family portrait. Only it's horrible. Like something Vivienne might've imagined.

There's me, Portia, Odette, and Vivienne, and a sixth figure, too, hovering in the distance, shadowy and dark. I have no idea who or what it's supposed to be.

The whole thing is gory. Blood, everywhere. I can see where she pressed extra hard with the marker, the color seeping into the wallpaper in big, ugly blotches.

She drew the funeral. The estate's graveyard, the little chapel. Vivienne's headstone and burial plot, her body visible beneath the dirt. And cradled in Vivienne's arms, with a happy smile on her face, is Juliet.

She looks up at me, her eyes taking on a strange light, and mimics our mother's voice with eerie perfection. "What did I tell you about peeking at my artwork before it's finished?"

I'm too stunned to speak. Alarm bells are ringing inside my head. I'm no expert, but there's no way this is normal seven-year-old behavior. Coloring on the walls is one thing, but this level of blood and guts and gore? "Portia!" I yell out the door, holding onto the frame for support.

"What is it?" she calls as she rushes upstairs.

I open the door wider for her, stepping back, letting the picture speak for itself. Portia's mouth pops open. She recoils and then squeezes her eyes shut as if not looking at it will make it go away.

"Do you like it?" Juliet wonders in an innocent voice, twirling the red marker playfully between her small fingers.

I grasp Portia's arm and tug her into the hall, dragging her out of earshot. "I need to talk to you."

Portia widens her eyes. "What the heck was that in there?"

"Forget the drawing, there's something even more concerning than that." I lower my voice to an urgent whisper. "I found a bloody feather and *a skull* inside Juliet's backpack."

"A skull?" Portia repeats.

"A whole ass skull! Like, a bird's skull!" I tell her, trying to keep my voice down. "And there was another dead bird in the gift shop. Its ribcage had been ripped open, and its heart was *missing*."

Portia gasps, her hand covering her mouth. "What are you suggesting, Briar?"

"What do you think?" I explode. Even though the A/C has been repaired, I'm covered in sweat. I wind my hair into a messy bun and fan nervously at the back of my neck. "Okay, well, I don't know for sure," I admit. "But it's strange, isn't it? How the hell did she get *that* and why?"

Portia peers over my shoulder to make sure Juliet isn't listening. "You can't seriously believe Juliet would purposefully harm an animal. That's crazy. She wouldn't hurt a fly."

"Kids are curious," I say. "They want to dissect things and figure out how they work!"

Portia shakes her head, clearly unconvinced. "Yeah, future serial killers. Juliet's idea of fun is playing with dolls and cuddling with her stuffed animals. Not an impromptu biology lesson with a dead bird!"

I gesture wildly to our sister's bedroom. "Hello? Did we not just see the same thing? Are you not at least a little bit concerned?"

"Maybe a little." Portia frowns, bouncing in place, her blonde hair swishing above her collarbone. "Okay, a lot. A really freaking lot."

"Good," I sigh, relieved that she's on board with me. "Then maybe it's time we consider a shrink."

30

"Do we have to go back again next week?"

I glance at Juliet in the rearview mirror. We're sitting in my car at a red light on the way home from her first therapy appointment. Dr. Harper tried for the better half of an hour to get Juliet to open up, but she just sat there, picking at the chipped purple polish on her nails, looking bored and distracted. Dr. Harper cut the session short, determined to give it another shot next week.

So, yes.

We *do* have to go back again next week.

"Our next appointment is on Friday," I reply, trying to sound enthusiastic. Like we're headed to Disney World instead.

Juliet kicks her legs, whining. "Aw, man," she sighs, slumping into her seat. "What a bummer."

"Come on. Don't you like Dr. Harper?"

Juliet grunts in response. "Can I play on my iPad now?" She reaches for her backpack in the passenger seat and I hand it over to her.

"Sure." I study her in the mirror, trying my hand at a good old-fashioned bribe. "And if you answer all of Dr. Harper's questions on Friday, I'll take you out shopping after and you can buy a new toy."

I expect her to jump on this golden opportunity but instead she ignores me, totally absorbed in her iPad. I wish she'd been this invested in her therapy session.

As soon as we get home, Juliet unstraps her seatbelt and dashes into the house, leaving me in her dust. I gather our belongings, undo my seatbelt and slip out of the car, making my way wearily to the front door, grappling with my own bag to fish out my hand sanitizer. I deposit a good amount into my palms, rubbing it in, hoping this finally helps quiet my racing mind.

The house is empty. Owen is meeting his lawyer in town, and Portia is busy with her boxing class at the gym. I don't think I've ever had the estate all to myself before. Inside Juliet's room, her TV blares, and she bursts out laughing.

Well, almost to myself.

I quickly disable the alarm, my eardrums throbbing. Then I kick off my shoes and head straight for the kitchen. With Elise gone, we've been left to fend for ourselves when it comes to meals, and I'm not exactly a gourmet chef.

My stomach growls extra loud.

I grab a loaf of bread, along with lunch meat, mayo, and cheese. I'll make Juliet and me sandwiches for lunch with a handful of chips on the side, and maybe some baby carrots for added health benefits. I'm in the process of slathering mayo over a slice of bread when my nose crinkles up. *Is that cigarette smoke?*

I go back to spreading mayo on the bread, trying not to over-think it, when I'm suddenly hit with the smell again, only this time it's much stronger than before. I set the butterknife on the counter and drift down the hall. The cigarette smoke is getting stronger, especially the closer I get to the stairs.

Juliet.

I rush upstairs and bust into her bedroom, hoping to catch her in the act. She gasps, spinning around as I swing open the door. She's lounging in a bean bag chair, streaming YouTube onto her TV, and solving a Rubik's cube. "Are you smoking in here?"

She makes a face. "Ew, no, gross!"

I try to block out her morbid family portrait that looks like an ugly red gash on the wall and straighten my blouse. "Right, of course." I move back to the door, feeling ridiculous. "Sorry about that."

"But I smell it, too," she says before I leave.

I swivel around. "The cigarette smoke?"

She nods. "Yeah, it's coming from Vivienne's studio." She gives me a look. "It *always* smells like that."

"Okay, well, I'm making us sandwiches. You keep having fun." I shut her bedroom door and hurry into Vivienne's studio, where I'm immediately struck with a cloud of smoke. I cough, fanning in front of my nose. I search around, ripping white sheets from hidden photographs, and peering into cabinets. The mess I made of Odette's sculptures is gone, the shards swept away.

The window is pushed up halfway, as if someone cracked it open to let in some fresh air. A cigarette butt lies stamped out in the corner of the windowsill, still smoldering. I stare at it, trying to piece together who might have left it there. Portia doesn't smoke.

Does Owen?

I force the window shut, the glass chilly against my exposed forearms, and lock it into place. Vivienne was the only one who smoked in this house. And she's dead. Is Juliet lying to me? If she's capable of killing a bird, she's capable of sneaking cigarettes… Or am I being totally ridiculous?

My phone buzzes in my back pocket, and I grab it, clicking on the push notification from the SecureHome app. It's Portia, parking in the drive. I walk to the foyer to meet her, checking the cameras for movement around the studio to see whoever it was smoking in there, but there's nothing. In fact, there's no clear view of the window at all. Well, that's majorly frustrating…

"Hey," she says as she comes in, her cheeks flushed from exertion. She unties her tennis shoes and places them into the coat closet, looking at me expectantly. "So, how was the appointment?"

"It was... interesting."

"Uh-oh. That doesn't sound good." Portia hands me a pile of mail before making her way to the kitchen. She adds over her shoulder, "There's an invitation in there."

"An invitation to what?" I ask, following her. I sift through the pile of envelopes and flyers as Portia takes my place beside the kitchen counter. She continues to work on the sandwiches and grabs an extra plate for herself.

I spot the invitation right away. "Briar's Big Birthday Bash," I read in disbelief. "No, this is weird. Very thoughtful, but weird. The birthday bash was Vivienne's thing." Another thought strikes me, filling me with an overwhelming sense of joy. "She would die a second time if she knew her club member kiss-ups were throwing *me* a party."

Portia gives me a look. I know she probably wants to lecture me on karma and the harmful effects of putting negativity out into the universe, but instead, she says nothing and focuses on her sandwich.

One of the things I absolutely hated about sharing my November birthday month with Vivienne was how the celebrations always seemed to revolve around her. Since our birthdays were only a couple of days apart, we often ended up having joint birthday parties, which, honestly, felt like not having a birthday at all. Vivienne was never one to share the spotlight for too long. She always found a way to snatch it back again.

I can already feel my excitement mounting. This isn't usually my kind of thing, but it's a nice gesture. Plus, it will be good to get everybody out of the house. It feels a little like we've all been stowed away inside a bunker.

My pulse quickens as I tear open the envelope, my excitement turning to confusion, then shock. Inside is an old black-and-white glamour shot of Vivienne, posing in a fur coat and a string of pearls. It's jarring to see her like that, so beautiful and young, and even after everything, it tugs on my heartstrings a little. "Please join us for Vivienne Delphine Belville's 76th Big Birthday Bash," I read aloud, my heart sinking.

Portia's eyes widen as she chews her sandwich. "Oh, my gosh. Are you serious?" she says as she snatches the invitation away. "Let me see." She looks over the invitation and then the envelope, her fair brows crinkling. "There must be some mistake."

"I'm going to call Amira," I say, stepping into the parlor. She was one of Vivienne's closest friends and practically an aunt to us. Every year, she organized our mother's birthday party, making each celebration even more extravagant than the last. I dial her number, my fingers trembling as I wait for her to pick up, hoping she'll tell me the invitation is a sick joke, an exceptionally late April Fool's Day prank.

Portia is right behind me. "Speaker," she says, gesturing wildly at the phone. "Put her on speaker!"

I wave her away like an annoying mosquito, but she's relentless. With a sigh, I give in and switch the call to speaker mode.

"Hello?" Amira's raspy voice comes through the line. There's music in the background, and laughter. It's easy to imagine her with a martini in hand, mingling at some social event. Amira is the embodiment of a perpetual party girl, never quite outgrowing that phase.

"Amira, it's Briar," I say. "I got your invitation."

"Oh, you did?" Amira cries, clearly thrilled. "I hope it wasn't too presumptuous of me, after everything you and your sisters have been through. I just wanted to do something nice to help cheer you up, and what better way than a big celebration?"

"So, the party is... for me?"

"Well..." Amira hesitates. "Who else?"

"I think you sent me Vivienne's invitation instead. For her 76th annual birthday bash."

There's a long pause. "Oh, Briar, I'm so sorry," she says sincerely. "Really. It was a mix-up with the invitations. I had Vivienne's done months ago, and yours were more last minute. I should have double-checked before sending them out. I apologize." Before I can answer, she releases a frustrated groan. "I hope I didn't get all the invitations wrong. How embarrassing. Briar, dear, let me get back to you, I've got to call the print shop right away!"

The line goes dead.

Portia shrugs. "See? It was a mix-up. You'll be getting your party, after all."

"I'm not so sure I want one anymore," I admit, still clutching my phone.

Portia gives me a look as we walk back into the kitchen. "Oh, come on. Amira planned the whole thing for you."

"But it's tonight. Unless that's a mix-up, too."

"We haven't been out of this house for weeks. It might be fun." Portia finishes up the sandwiches as I mull over what to do. The last thing I want is to put on a brave and happy face when I feel more like hiding under a rock. Just the sight of my glamorous mother on that invitation has me feeling insecure all over again. Portia hands me a plate. "Can you take this up to Juliet? I'm going to shower." She heads to the stairs. "And we're going," she adds, making the decision for me.

"Wait," I say, following her. "I know this is kind of a weird and totally random question, but do you smoke? You know, cigarettes, like Vivienne did."

"Um, no." Portia pauses on the landing and raises an eyebrow at me. "Definitely not. Why do you ask?"

I wave a hand. "It's nothing." Because it probably *is* nothing. Plus, I should have known the answer. Miss my-body-is-my-temple would never smoke unless, of course, she were in the Brazilian rainforest and there was ayahuasca available. "Let's meet back up here later. I need to figure out what to wear to my birthday party."

31

THE WAITER OFFERS me a champagne flute and I down it in one gulp. It burns the back of my throat, the bubbles bursting out my nose and making my eyes water, but I'm desperate for anything to dull the horror because this birthday bash is the stuff of nightmares.

It's dark in here. The only source of light comes from the gilded chandeliers that float overhead, and they cast an eerie glow over the room. A jazz band performs onstage, the saxophone low and seductive. The tables have been removed, exposing the glossy black floor. The flickering candles are reflected in the marble like ethereal orbs.

My past is being blasted at me from every direction. Photos of me and my sisters cover the walls, horrifically edited photographs from the estate's gallery. Me as a baby eagle in a nest with tufts of red feathers on my head. Portia's face cracked open like an egg, yolk dripping out and puddling on the floor. Juliet with fireflies swarming her body so that she's lit up like a glow stick. It's like the world's worst art exhibit.

LED screen pillars stand around the room, flashing photo slideshows and playing old video footage. There are clips from *Star*

Sisters, my sisters and I dancing in perfect sync and singing our peppy pop songs while bouncing around the stage. I hear a lyric here and there and get annoyed at myself for singing along. *Why do they have to be so damn catchy?*

It's overwhelming for me, but even more for a little girl. Juliet grips my hand as our eyes adjust to the low lighting, overwhelmed by the music, the sheer amount of club members, the waiters as they rush around us with their silver trays. I'm grateful when she finds a group of her friends, and they're shepherded into another room to eat snacks and play games. If I had known it would be like this, I probably would've made up some excuse not to come.

"Amira, it's breathtaking," I say, hoping I come across as genuine, even though I'm cringing on the inside.

Amira pats my hand affectionately. Maybe it's the lack of light, but every time I see her, she looks twenty years younger. If I didn't know any better, I'd swear Vivienne and her friends were all vampires. It's more likely because she's married to one of the most successful plastic surgeons in Florida, and regularly gets work done. But the vampire theory, in my opinion, is more fun. "I'm so thrilled you like it," she says in her signature gravelly voice. She clasps my hand, her black eyes boring into me. "How are you, my love?"

"I'm okay..." I exchange a glance with Portia. "We're okay, right?"

Portia gives a *what-can-ya-do* look. "We're taking it day by day."

"Terrible business, isn't it?" Amira shakes her head and covers her mouth. The rings on her fingers glitter, the little bit of light in the room bouncing off the massive stones. "Just terrible. I really feel for you girls, I do. As long as I knew Vivienne, I never thought she'd ever be capable of something so horrific."

Just as she says it, a video clip of Vivienne interrupts the *Star Sisters* dancing on stage. It's a scene from one of her horror films. Vivienne, screaming and wielding a knife, slashing it violently at the camera with a wild look in her eyes like Glenn Close in *Fatal Attraction*. It catches us all off guard. My heart jumps into my throat and I stumble backwards into Portia. Amira gasps, blocking the screen with her arms. "I'm so sorry, I have no idea how that got in there," she shouts breathlessly.

I double over. I feel like my heart is about to explode out of my chest.

"Are you okay?" Portia asks. She touches my back, but I shake her off.

"Yeah, I'm fine." It comes out harsher than I intend, too defensive.

"Girls, really, I'm so sorry," Amira keeps repeating. "I swear I'm going to absolutely murder my party planner. After the initial blunder with the invitations, I explicitly instructed her to make sure the remainder of the event goes seamlessly."

"It's... It's okay," I stammer. My pulse is still thundering, and I place a hand on my chest to calm it. "I just need a moment."

Without looking back, I excuse myself and hurry to the bathroom. I have the door pushed halfway open when I hear voices coming from inside. "I knew Portia would snap one day. She's too high-strung. Smiling all the time. She's so fake. I can guarantee this whole thing was a set-up and she just wanted to see what it felt like to get away with murder."

I pause, hiding behind the door. I crack it open a little farther and peek inside. Addison and Paisley stand at the sink, touching up their makeup in the mirror. I wouldn't call us friends, but we've been friendly in the past. They brought over casseroles after Ted died. We played tennis together. We were in the same book club. We've rubbed elbows multiple times at the club.

"No way," Addison purrs as she applies a second coat of red lipstick, her highlighted blonde hair shining beneath the skylights. "My money's on Briar. She's always seemed like a loose cannon to me. Every time we talked, she complained about her mom. Talk about mommy issues."

Paisley snorts. She leans in closer to the mirror and tousles her chocolate-colored bangs with her manicured fingers. "I wouldn't put it past her."

They're exchanging theories about what they think really happened while we were held captive. It hurts, but it doesn't surprise me either. We live in a small town and people are bound to talk. I've overheard people whispering at the grocery store, the bank, even while I was in the waiting room at the dentist before my scheduled cleaning. Who cares if our psychotic mother kept us paralyzed so she could dress us up like dolls? No one is immune to gossip once tongues start wagging.

"But did you see the hottie she walked in with?" Addison drawls, and I realize she means Owen. "Do you think they're an item?"

"I doubt it," Paisley says. "Cousins, maybe?"

Addison sets her hands on her hips and smirks cruelly. "*Kissing* cousins. Their family is weird as shit. Reclusive shut-ins. Remember that Christmas party Vivienne threw the year before last? I felt like I was in *Grey Gardens*!"

"Not a cute look," Paisley agrees. "They've always given me the creeps."

Wounded, I slam open the door and step inside. Addison and Paisley startle, their shocked expressions gaping at me in the mirror. I stride over and wash my hands, relaxing as the cool water hits my wrists and flows between my fingers. I concentrate on obsessively lathering them with soap.

"Hey, it's been forever!" Addison says, a little too friendly and over-the-top. "You look sooo good!"

"Yeah, you look incredible," Paisley chimes in as she sets a comforting hand on my arm. "Given everything that happened. How are you?"

"Fine," I reply. I meet their gazes in the mirror and return their sickly-sweet smiles. "But why wouldn't I be fine? I got away with murder, right? No, actually, me and my sister did... after we orchestrated the whole thing."

The women look mortified. Their mouths hang open, eyes wide with panic. Addison recovers quickly. She's on my heels as I walk over to the paper towel dispenser and dry my hands. "We didn't mean anything by it, Briar."

"Just so you know, he's not my cousin," I say as I reach the door, casting a final pitying glance over my shoulder. "He's my fuck buddy."

I've never used the term *fuck buddy* before in my life, and I doubt I ever will again. But the look on their faces is priceless.

I leave them there, blinking in surprise. I don't care if it's not true. I don't care if it was totally lame and immature. And I really don't care what they tell people. I'm tired of caring what people think. I've invested too much time and energy worrying about it.

Back in the event room, I'm caught off guard to see the detective waving and walking toward me. *Oh God, what else can tonight throw at me?* I didn't recognize her at first because she's wearing a flowy gold gown and she's missing her gun and badge. At least from what I can see. She brushes her chestnut waves over one shoulder and smiles at me. "Hey," she says. She lifts her glass. "Happy birthday!"

I tuck a strand of hair behind my ear. This feels so awkward. I didn't expect to see her here at all. "Thanks."

"I hope this isn't weird," Detective Torres says, voicing my thoughts. "Amira's a family friend."

I smile. *Ah, makes sense. Who isn't Amira friends with?*

"And I've been meaning to stop by the estate and check on you and your sister, see how you've been holding up." She gestures at my hair, my dress. "I mean, you look great."

"Thanks. Um... Therapy," I say, blushing. "That's the secret. And a tight bond with my sisters. I don't think I could've made it through without them."

Yikes, I sound so cheesy. It's such a canned answer. But Detective Torres smiles. "You're lucky," she says. "My sister..." She averts her eyes, thinking, a troubled expression crossing her face. Then she takes another sip of champagne, swallowing hard. She breaks into a smile, raising the glass again. "This is really delicious."

"I know," I say, craving another.

Detective Torres winks at me. "I'm going to check out the dessert table. If I know Amira, there's bound to be chocolate. And not just any chocolate, but the good stuff!" She gives my shoulder a friendly pat and melts back into the crowd, singing the *Star Sisters* song that's playing right now. I swear, bubblegum pop is an infectious earworm nobody can escape.

Seeing the detective drags me right back to that ballroom, with my mother and Elise. Vivienne choking on her own blood at the foot of the stairs, Elise lying motionless in the center of the room, a faint smile on her face, finally at peace.

I shake off the gruesome memories, searching desperately for my next glass of champagne. I spin around, attempting to flag down a waiter. But no matter which way I turn, I come face to face with a younger version of myself wearing that robotic smile I used to plaster on, despite my growing hatred for performing. I never realized just how miserable I looked.

I barely finish the thought when it's interrupted by a familiar laugh. It's biting, cruel. My head snaps to the side, searching the crowd. Vivienne waves at me from across the room, her vindictive grin standing out against the blur of mingling guests.

I gasp and stumble into someone. "Hey," Owen says. He turns me around and takes me into his arms, steadying me. "You okay?"

I manage a nod, breathless. I twist my head, trying to figure out if what I saw was real or just another old video playing on the display screens.

I only calm down when I gaze up into Owen's concerned face. Now that I'm in his arms, I'm wondering if I should revoke my ban on the term *fuck buddy* because there's a large part of me wishing it were true. "I think I need some air."

Owen looks around, trying to find a clear path. "Okay, let's see..."

"There's a balcony," I tell him, pointing in the direction of the crowded bar. "That way."

He wraps a protective arm around my waist, leading me to the glass doors. I grab another champagne flute along the way, knocking it back, savoring the burn that heats my insides.

Once outside, I rush to the edge, taking in large gasps of fresh air. It's drizzling, the rain cool against my skin. Owen removes his suit jacket and drapes it over my shoulders. "Better?" he asks.

I nod, grateful. "Thanks." I stick my hands into the pockets, feeling for a packet of cigarettes or a lighter, but there's nothing. Owen doesn't strike me as a smoker, anyway. I would have smelled it on him before, and on the jacket now. If not Owen, then who? My shoulders droop. Yet another mystery for me to solve.

"It's claustrophobic in there, isn't it?"

"Yeah." I hug myself. Vivienne's knife-wielding performance is still playing inside my head. "It just feels so wrong. I shouldn't be here tonight. This was *her* thing."

Owen chuckles and shakes his head. "Don't make this about her, Briar. Tonight's your night."

He's right. Tonight *is* my night, and I'm letting her ruin it. I take a deep breath and square my shoulders, watching Owen as he gazes out across the green of the surrounding golf course. This is the first time I've really looked at him tonight, and he cleans up good. I'm used to him being a little rough around the edges, but in a suit and a crisp white button-down, I'm starting to notice what Portia was saying. He does look very *Bond*-esque, but not like the hero of the story. The sexy villain.

Suddenly, I'm wondering if he's noticed me tonight, how I've styled my hair into a sleek updo and spent almost an hour perfecting my makeup. With an eager, young sales associate's help, I selected an off-the-shoulder black dress with a daring side slit and strappy heels.

"You've been to hell and back," Owen goes on, leaning against the balcony railing. He takes a sip of his drink and raises it in a toast, the corner of his mouth quirking up. "I say, embrace it. You're a survivor. You deserve to be celebrated."

The sight of the champagne makes me feel sick. I can feel my stomach revolting and twisting, feel the champagne coming back up.

Oh, no.

I double over, vomiting into the potted plant in the corner of the balcony. "You're alright," Owen says as he brushes my hair back, keeping the strands away from my face. "I've got you."

"God," I groan, swiping at my mouth with the back of my hand. "I'm so sorry."

So much for spending a whole hour on my makeup. Drinking that fast was definitely a bad idea.

Owen rubs my back. "Don't apologize."

"I'm still a little out of it," I admit. And binging on cookies before we left probably didn't help. I remain crouched, trying not to sit back and ruin my dress on the wet balcony floor.

"I'll grab you some water," Owen says, reaching for the door. "Be right back."

I watch him go, embarrassed. The taste in my mouth is sour, and it burns the back of my throat. It burned much better going down. When Owen returns, I accept the glass gratefully, washing out my mouth.

"Should I drive you home?" he offers thoughtfully.

I'd love to go home. This all feels like a big fuss over nothing. I'm only one year older, who cares? My birthday never used to be important. It was always overshadowed by Vivienne's Big Birthday Bash. She let me think I was a part of it, but it was mainly all about her. And they're only throwing this for me now because she's gone. Because they've finally figured out what I've known all along. My mother was a monster.

But I also know it would be rude if I left early. Amira said there would be dinner and cake. Toasts and speeches. And I couldn't leave without my sisters.

"No, I can't. It wouldn't be right."

Owen nods. "Cool, then let's face it together. Come on. I'll do all the talking." He leads me back into the room, taking charge. He keeps one hand always on my lower back, my shoulder. A comforting reminder that he's not going anywhere, that he wants to support me. It's nice. Really nice.

He puts on a charming smile and makes easy conversation with all of Vivienne's friends, the stuck-up members of the club that always rub me the wrong way.

I'm shocked by how effortlessly he can tell a convincing lie. If I didn't know him, I'm sure he could easily fool me. He makes up a different story for each person he talks to. He runs a tech startup, he's a journalist who covers war zones, he's an engineer, a hobby pilot. No matter what anyone asks him, even the curveballs, somehow he always knows exactly what to say.

By the end of the night, I'm not only a little impressed, but I'm also turned on. Maybe it's the writer in him... or the criminal... but he never lost track of his lies, never lost the plot to his stories, even after creating so many of them. And I liked that he was there for me. I liked that every time I looked his way, he'd grin. A joke only the two of us shared. It was a different side to him I'd never seen before.

I keep thinking about it even later that night in bed, the desire he ignited still there. I fantasize about heading over there and slipping out of my clothes, climbing him like a tree. I groan as I turn over in bed and check the time. It's 2 a.m. *Why won't you just go to sleep, woman?*

I throw off my covers and pace around the room. Gaze out the window. There's a light on at the guesthouse. I want to go knock on his door but I'm hesitating. He could have fallen asleep with the lamp on. I don't want to disturb him. But when I see his shadow pass behind the curtains and I know that he's awake too, I slip on my robe and hurry downstairs into the humid night air.

32

I HESITATE BEFORE KNOCKING. I'm surprised at how nervous I am, but it's too late to run away. Owen answers, a lazy smile on his face. "Hey."

I peek over his shoulder. "Late-night writing session?"

Owen chuckles. He opens the door wider and nods toward his desk. There's a half-eaten apple and a small plate with crackers and cheese. "More like a late-night snack." He searches my face. I can tell by his frown that he senses my uneasiness. "Want to come in?"

"Sure." I step inside, my arms wrapped around my middle.

Owen offers me a friendly smile as he shuts the door. He sticks his hands into the pockets of his flannel pajama pants and comes to stand beside me. I like that he's taller than me, that I'd have to stand on my tiptoes to kiss him. I hope I'm not blushing from the thought. "How are you?" he asks. It's not just small talk. He genuinely wants to know. "Are you feeling better?"

"A little," I say, rubbing my arms. "But I can't sleep."

"Then don't." His blue eyes light up. "Stay with me. We'll play a board game." He goes over to the TV console and extends the bottom drawer. He picks up a box and holds it up for me to see. All the pieces rattle inside. "We've got Jenga and..." He lifts a larger box. "...Scrabble."

"Hmmm..." I tap my chin. "Jenga."

We spend the next hour huddled on the sofa, snacking on crackers and chips and having a blast with Jenga. I haven't laughed this much in forever. It feels freeing. Owen is horrible at this game. I keep asking if he's letting me win. He keeps denying it. "I swear," he laughs as he gathers the fallen pieces. I jump to help him, following him with the empty box and collecting nearby pieces with my free hand. "I'm trying my best."

"This is your best?" I say skeptically.

"The key word in that sentence was *trying*." He takes the box from me, closes it, and sets it into the drawer. "I vote we play Scrabble next."

"Hold on!" I protest, crossing my arms over my chest. "Don't I get a prize? I won at least ten times. Maybe more."

Owen puts the Scrabble box on the coffee table. "You only want to rub it in my face," he says, grinning at me. "Fine. What do you want? Now, remember, I only have a 20 in my wallet right now..."

"I don't want money," I laugh. "I want... an answer."

"That's a boring prize," Owen says, looking disappointed. "So, what's the question?"

I walk over to his desk and point to the picture I saw on that first day I tried to maul him with a kitchen knife. The one of me and Robert at the zoo. I'm standing on my father's feet and he's grasping both my hands. It's just the two of us, smiling at the camera. I hold it up and show Owen. "Why do you have this picture of me?"

Owen takes the photo and smiles down at it. "It's for the book."

"Yeah, I know. But why that one? Why not one of the photos from my mother's gallery?"

Owen swallows. He scratches at his Adam's apple. "I don't know. I guess because in those photos you look so..."

"Different," I guess. My heart sinks at the realization. "I used to be beautiful."

Owen stares at me. "I was going to say sad."

"Sad?"

"Yeah, in Vivienne's photos. There's no life in your eyes." He continues to admire the photograph in his hand. "This was the only one I found where you were actually smiling, where you seemed like you were enjoying yourself. A kid being a kid."

"Oh." I blink. "Why does it matter to you?"

"Because I care about you," he says earnestly. He watches me for a moment, his brow furrowed. "What do you mean you *used* to be beautiful?" He sets the picture back on the desk. "You're fucking gorgeous."

My mouth opens but no sound comes out. Owen exhales, the tension between us rising. I move in closer, tilting back my head, pushing up onto my tip toes, and he meets me halfway. We kiss softly at first. He's gentle with me, his hands trailing down my back, my hips, tangling in my hair. I want more of him. No, I *need* more of him. I'm so sick of holding back, constantly resisting.

I tear at his shirt, and he helps me shove it over his head. He peels off my robe, so that it falls to the floor, his hands moving down to my thighs, his fingers sliding beneath the hem of my nightgown. He squeezes my ass, forcing me closer to him. I part my lips, and he explores my mouth with his tongue. I forgot how good of a kisser he was. In fact, I think he's gotten better. "Please tell me you didn't learn that in prison," I whisper, and he chuckles huskily against my neck, the feeling of his hot breath on my bare skin driving me wild.

He brushes away the straps of my nightgown, and his mouth travels down to my breasts as he lifts me and carries me to his bed. It feels like my entire body is throbbing for him. I press myself against him, my legs wrapping tighter around his hips. I'm desperate to feel him on me, inside me, *everywhere*.

He lays me gently on the bed and spreads my legs, kneeling in front of me and applying painfully slow kisses up the length of my inner thighs. I gasp as he draws close and then cry out.

There's someone watching us from the window, their hair disheveled and their eyes wild. Owen sees me pointing frantically and jumps up. "What's wrong?" He shields me protectively and searches for whatever it is I saw.

But it's already gone.

"I saw someone!" I insist, my heart pounding painfully in my chest. My phone is buzzing on the floor in the pocket of my robe. Over and over again. It's the SecureHome app. I jump up from the bed and run over to it, clumsily punching in my passcode. There are at least ten push notifications, all with the same message: Motion detected.

I hastily get dressed, pointing at the window again. "There's someone out there!" I tell Owen as he goes to the window and peers outside.

"Who?"

"I don't know! I didn't get a good look at them."

Owen goes to the door. "I'll be right back," he says. He circles the guesthouse before walking up and down the length of the pool and around the side of the main house. I'm scared to be left alone, but I keep an eye on the open door as I click into the app and review the footage. I squint at the screen, looking for something. Anything. But there's nothing there.

My heart sinks and a stabbing pain ricochets through my gut, strong enough to bring me to my knees. I collapse onto the sofa, scrolling through different cameras and vantage points, rewinding the footage with shaking fingers.

I don't get it. If someone were out there, they would have been captured by the cameras, just like Owen is being now, unless they knew exactly where the blind spots were.

Maybe I saw my own reflection in the window. But then what motion did the app detect?

I pull down the push notifications and click on another one. The video begins to play, and I notice a large owl sitting in one of the magnolia trees. It opens its wings before soaring low over the pool and settling into a tree closer to the main house.

I breathe a sigh of relief, but I can't seem to shake the uneasy feeling, and my stomach feels even worse than before.

I don't know why it's suddenly hurting me again. Maybe it's the stress of the past couple of months finally catching up to me.

Owen returns a few moments later. "I didn't see anything," he says as he closes and locks the door.

"False alarm," I say, showing him the screen. Then I bury my face into my hands. "I'm so sorry."

"You have nothing to be sorry about." He sits beside me on the sofa and opens his arms, bringing me closer. "You're white as a sheet."

I rest my head against his chest and close my eyes, listening to the steady beat of his heart. I don't tell him what I thought I saw. A woman with blonde hair, her face hidden in the shadows...

It's unbelievable. Even beyond the grave, Vivienne is still the ultimate cock block. I exhale shakily, trying to relax as Owen strokes my hair.

I'm such a mess. What was I thinking coming over here? I guess it's been a while since I've slept with anyone. But just because Owen is here, and there's an attraction, doesn't mean we *should*. Especially when there's baggage and history and complicated emotions involved.

I used to rely on sex to cope before, and I can feel those old ways tiptoeing up again, trying to make a reappearance. It surprises me how much regular therapy has helped me. Ten years ago, I would have already ripped my clothes off without caring if some peeping Tom was watching us from outside the window. But now, at this point in my life, I've managed to replace sex with comfort food, work, and a compulsive need to clean. And I'd like to keep it that way.

This wouldn't just be meaningless sex for me and Owen. I can't simply slip out the next morning before he wakes up. Especially since we basically live together now.

Besides, it could potentially jeopardize our entire relationship, our friendship. We've only recently reconnected, and we're still trying to find stable footing. I value what we have, and I don't want to risk it all for one night together.

He needs a less neurotic partner. Someone who's not toting around a lifetime supply of trauma. A good Southern woman who'll bake him pies, assign Sundays to church, and rule over that beautiful house he's building and their brood of kids with a fair but iron fist.

And I know that's not me.

My shoulders droop as I pull away, the growing distance between us causing me physical pain. Every time I'm with him, it's like I'm a teenager again. Every nerve ending in my body, sizzling with desire, that lovesick puppy feeling that makes my knees go weak and my stomach flutter with butterflies. "I should go," I say quietly, avoiding his gaze.

Owen nods understandingly. "It's late," is all he says. He slips his shirt back over his head and strides over to the door, holding it open for me.

I'm hit with a wave of humid air, reeking of chlorine. The pool lights are on, glowing eerily below the surface, mystical refractions rippling across the magnolia trees, the palms. I blink out at the darkness, Owen watching me closely, his lips pressed together in a tight line. He swallows and reaches out, touching my elbow. His touch makes me shiver, the hairs on the nape of my neck standing on end, my nipples hardening inside my bra.

"Let me walk you." He smiles, a nostalgic look in his eyes. "Like old times."

I nod. "Okay."

It's not a far walk, but I'm not ready to leave him just yet. Shortly before the door, I swivel around and embrace him. He stiffens in surprise before relaxing into me, his strong arms encircling my waist, practically lifting me off the ground.

Everyone else is asleep and Vivienne isn't here to spy on us from the upstairs window anymore. I kind of want to gaze up at it and will her to appear, just so she can see us like this together, in each other's arms.

Owen buries his nose into my hair, breathing in my scent. One hand is pressed against the small of my back, holding me against him, and the other is tangled in my curls, gently gripping the strands. It's torture to pull away from him, but somehow I slip out of his grasp and move to the door.

Owen looks like a man defeated. I can see he wants me. I could *feel* that he wants me. But he's too much of a gentleman to push any further. He sighs softly, his chest rising and falling, putting his arms above his head in a desperate stretch as if he doesn't know what to do with himself. "Sleep well, okay? I'll see you in the morning."

"See you," I whisper with a tired smile as I step inside, using the glass door as a barrier between us.

"Briar?" Owen catches me before I can close the door.

"Yeah?"

"I'm glad you came back here."

I'm grateful it's dark because I'm pretty sure I'm blushing. "Goodnight, Owen."

33

My sneakers thump over the winding path bordered by towering topiary. The shrubs are meant to be animals—a pride of lions, a family of elephants, a pair of giraffes, but they're overgrown now. Neglected and deformed.

This is the first time I've gone running in weeks. It feels nice to be back in my jogging gear, music blasting in my ears. I fly around a bend and head in between the trees, pale sunlight streaming past the tangled canopy.

Thanks to all the caffeine I downed, I have more energy than I usually do this morning. I had trouble falling asleep last night. I kept thinking I was hearing footsteps in the hallway. I tried to chalk it up to the moisture in the air, the heat and humidity that loosens the floorboards, the paint, and everything else. There's also the fact this house is over two hundred years old. At this point, strange noises are inevitable.

And maybe I would have written it all off if it wasn't for the fact I thought I saw my mother's face peering through the guesthouse window last night. And then sometime around 4 in the morning, I could've sworn I smelled cigarette smoke. It seemed to slowly seep into my bedroom, hanging in the air.

It made me cough so violently that I went searching around the house for the source, but both of my sisters were sleeping, and I hightailed it back to bed once I realized the smell was coming from Vivienne's studio again.

I don't believe in ghosts. Especially not after I realized all those times I thought I was seeing Odette, I was actually high as a kite. But if anyone was going to come back and haunt me, it would definitely be my mother.

I slow my pace, hunching over as I catch my breath and wipe the sweat from my brow. From this distance, the house is mostly hidden by the trees, but the sunlight hitting the windows almost makes it look like the house is alive, quietly waiting until I draw closer to devour me.

I take a long drink from my water bottle before returning it to my fanny pack and readjusting my baseball cap, my eyes stuck to the menacing façade. Then I change directions and jog toward the guesthouse, planning on inviting Owen to join me for another cup of coffee. But I lunge behind a tree when I see him and Portia in the garden, talking and laughing together.

My cheeks redden as Portia leans in and whispers in his ear. Owen grins and places a hand on her arm. It lingers there a little too long before sliding downward. He takes her hand and squeezes it. I feel like he's squeezing my stomach, twisting my intestines, eviscerating me. Especially when Portia throws her arms around his neck and he catches her in an embrace. I slap a hand over my mouth and backtrack to the house.

I've seen enough.

Transcript from episode 22 of *Star Sisters*, "Sharing Is Caring", aired September 1997

The theme song plays and the title glitters across the screen and explodes into shooting stars. The stage is decorated like a park with large trees, a swing set, and a rock wall.

Briar (6), Portia (7), and Odette (11) are dressed in colorful outfits. Briar wears a cute denim overall dress with a tie-dye T-shirt. Portia wears a windbreaker and high-waisted jeans. Odette is in a T-shirt, denim shorts, and platform sneakers. A flannel shirt is tied around her waist. They carry sparkly backpacks.

The camera follows the girls as they head to the stage. They break into a high-energy dance routine. They're perfectly in sync.

Briar leads the group in singing a song about the importance of sharing. Her voice is surprisingly strong for her age. After the song, the girls hold hands and address the audience.

Briar: That was so much fun!

Portia: And we have so many more songs to share with you!

Odette rubs her belly.

Odette: I don't know about you guys, but I'm getting hungry!

Briar and Portia together: Snack time!
Cut to the kitchen of the Star Sisters' home.

Briar sits at the table, savoring a big slice of cake with blue and white icing and a red cherry on top. Portia enters the scene, her eyes lighting up. She skips over to the table.

Portia: Hey, can I have a bite?

Briar shields her slice with her hand.

Briar: Sorry, sis, but this slice is off-limits!

Portia raises an eyebrow and smirks, a mischievous glint in her eyes.

Portia: Oh, come on! You know what they say about sharing…

Briar hesitates before breaking into a grin.

Briar: You're right, Portia. Sharing is caring!

Briar gets up and cuts another slice of cake. She hands the plate to Portia, who smiles gratefully. The audience cheers in the background.

Portia: Thanks, Briar!

They both take a big bite of cake.

Briar: Mmm, I love cake!

Portia: You're the best sister in the world, Briar!

Briar: No, you are!

The sisters share a heartfelt smile.

The camera pans out as the sisters laugh together.

In this episode, the star sisters teach the audience valuable lessons about sharing. They share their toys with new friends at the park and let Ronnie, the mailman, borrow a favorite book. At the end of the show, they perform another song and dance number.

The camera pans to the live audience, where kids and parents sing along.

Briar, Portia, and Odette take their bows, thanking the audience for joining them. The three sisters hug tightly.

Credits roll as the theme song plays in the background.

End of transcript.

34

THE NEXT DAY, it's still dark when I sneak into my mother's bedroom. Nervously, I inch closer to the bed, shuddering at the sight of it. I was so sure I'd end up dying there, my body decaying all over the mattress. I head to her walk-in closet and flick on the lights, illuminating the spacious room, the marble floors and organized shelving systems, the massive chandelier that rains crystals.

I finger through Vivienne's gowns, slipping into something she hasn't been able to fit in for years. The form-fitting ivory silk feels luxurious and liberating on my skin, nothing like the modest neck-high, ankle-length dresses she made me wear.

I stride over to her vanity and take a seat, prying open her jewelry box. I pluck her pearls. *Mine.* I seize her diamond rings and emerald earrings. *Mine.* I slide on her favorite stilettos, the strand of fat saltwater pearls quivering between my breasts. Then I admire myself in the mirror. I look damn good—better than she ever did. I move to the enormous window, staring out at the sweeping property with its endless acres. *Everything is mine now.*

I descend the grand staircase, my hand resting elegantly on the polished railing. I walk into the dining room where I sit at the head of the table. It's stacked with homemade food. Biscuits with sausage gravy. Grits. Pancakes with pads of butter and warm maple syrup. It smells so incredible.

Portia comes downstairs a little while later. "Is that breakfast I smell?" she asks as she comes around the corner. She's in a serious gray pantsuit and black heels. I stare at her shoes, surprised. This is the first time I've seen her in anything other than sneakers or Birkenstocks since Odette's wake. She even wore sandals to my birthday.

She looks just as surprised to see my outfit of choice. "Wow!" she gasps, slapping me on the arm. "Hot mama! You look amazing!"

I smile. "Thanks."

"And hey, your hands look so much better. You stopped picking," she notices. "They're completely healed."

"Yeah, I don't really know why," I say with a shrug. "I just don't have the urge anymore."

"Speaking of urges..." Portia says as she runs playful fingers up my bare shoulder. "I've been dying to ask you. Did you spend the other night with our resident sexy convict?"

I narrow my eyes at her. "So, you think he's sexy?"

"Stop deflecting, Briar. Of course, I do. He's pretty much a GQ model." She sticks her tongue out at me. "I saw you from the window the other night. You and Owen... outside... by the pool..." She grins widely at me, drawing out the sentence like she's trying to jog my memory.

So someone *had* been watching us last night. I don't know why but the thought makes me feel a little uneasy. "Nothing happened. We were just talking."

Portia pouts, obviously disappointed. She glances around the dining table, at the empty seats. "Hey, where is Owen, anyway?"

I take a sip of my latte. "Why do you ask?"

"This isn't some kind of date? I thought that's why you're so dressed up."

"No. I just wanted to try something new."

"Well, you look great either way," Portia says. She snags a

biscuit from the table and her heels clack toward the kitchen. She returns a few seconds later. "Briar... Why is there a strange woman taking pictures of our kitchen? She says she works here now."

"She does," I confirm with a tight smile. I throw a dramatic hand into the air. "Meet Tara, Belville Estate's new housekeeper! I found her online last night, and she said she could start right away."

"You hired someone to replace Elise?" Portia asks, raising a skeptical brow. "Does this mean you changed your mind about the house stuff? I thought we already agreed that we're selling the estate. You told me you couldn't stand owning this place another minute."

"Maybe I changed my mind."

Portia holds up a hand, appearing dazed. "We'll unpack that later." She uses her half-eaten biscuit to point at the kitchen. "First of all, I'm pretty positive you hired a lurker. Second of all, next time you hire a housekeeper, maybe test her cooking skills first. These biscuits are rock solid, and I think she used olive oil instead of buttermilk. It's Southern sacrilege!"

I sigh. "Then I'll find someone else."

"Good," Portia says. "Let's start now!" She storms into the kitchen, and I can hear her fake friendly voice as she tries to get rid of Tara. "Hi, sorry, but there's been a mistake and we won't be requiring your services any longer. Um, please, don't take my picture. Yes, of course, you'll still get paid for today." She ushers the young woman with the neon pink hair through the parlor and out the front door, trying to stop her from snapping photos. "Follow me, this way. Let's put the cellphone away!"

Tara may not have been able to master the biscuit, but she sure as hell makes a damn good latte. I continue enjoying it as I wait for Portia to return but she stops short in the parlor.

"Did you replace the family photo above the mantel?" she asks, gesturing wildly at the new picture I've hung there instead. "There's a picture of you now!"

"That's just a placeholder," I assure her as I turn to look at her. I shake out my silky strands. I've covered it in hair spray and anti-frizz product and plastered my face with more makeup than I've worn in my entire life. "We can take a new family photo. A *better* one."

"Okay," Portia says, slowly blinking at me. "You're clearly going through something, but I don't have the time nor capacity to deal with it right now. Luke and I are playing nice and he's meeting me at the courthouse for the guardianship hearing in one hour, and I need you to watch Juliet for me. I went into her room and gave her a kiss goodbye, but she probably fell back asleep. Just check on her for me every now and then, okay? And for the love of Buddha, do not feed her those biscuits... or should I say projectiles?"

"Oh, right, the hearing!"

"Please tell me you didn't forget," Portia says. "You wrote me that character reference letter, didn't you?"

"Yes! It's on the table in the foyer." Portia takes the envelope and heads for the door, but I hurry after her. "Wait!" I stop her, grabbing her by the arm. She looks surprised, staring down at my fingers as they dig into her skin. I loosen my grip. "I wanted to ask you something."

"Yes?"

"What were you and Owen talking about yesterday?" Once it's out of my mouth, I realize how pathetically insecure I sound, but I still want to know the answer because it's been bugging me and I'll go crazy if I keep wondering.

Portia blinks. "Wait... are you serious? We were talking about you, Briar. Owen said he never got you something for your birthday. He asked me what you'd like, what you're into. He wants to do something special for you."

"Oh," I say, smiling, touched by the thought. "That's sweet."

"Is that the reason you're so dressed up?" Portia guesses, narrowing her eyes suspiciously at me. "Is this some kind of power play? A show of dominance? You're pulling a Vivienne!"

I scoff. "I am not!"

"You look and sound just like her!"

I bristle at the insult, crossing my arms defensively over my chest.

She gasps loudly when the rings on my fingers catch the light. "Hold on. Are you wearing her jewelry?" She claps her hands together and jumps in place. "Yes, yes, you are! I knew it! Those are her rings! And that's her pearl necklace. Is that her dress?"

I slap her hand away as she tugs at the silky fabric. "Look, forget it, I was just asking. Stop trying to change the subject."

"Don't worry, I'm not after your boyfriend." Portia softens. "But I'm sorry. I know you can't help it."

"What's that supposed to mean?"

"Well..." she continues, treading carefully. "If Luke cheated on me the way Ted cheated on you..." She shrugs her shoulders. "I'd be paranoid, too."

I'm breathless, the wind knocked out of me. I stop her again before she can reach for the door. "How dare you bring that up right now?"

"You're right, I'm sorry." Portia surprises me by bringing me in for a hug. "We'll talk about whatever you're going through when I get back. Promise me you'll meditate?"

"Portia..."

"Briar," she challenges, giving me a stern look.

I sigh. "Fine. But only for a minute."

"Ten minutes."

"Two."

"Five."

"Three."

"Deal." She smiles at me, grabbing an umbrella from the coat closet. "Wish me luck!"

"Good luck..."

I shut the door and lock it, resting my head against the cool wood. What am I doing? Allowing my mother to get inside my head like this. Again. *She's dead, she's dead, she's dead,* I remind myself. *She has no influence over you anymore!*

The rain picks up outside, setting my teeth on edge. I head upstairs to check on Juliet. She's tucked into her bed, piled beneath a poof of purple comforter. Her eyes are closed, her lashes fluttering as she blissfully dreams, her breathing low and even. I grab her remote from one of the bean bag chairs and crank down the volume to *Barbie: Life in the Dreamhouse*. Then I stand on my tiptoes and give my baby sister a loving kiss on the head, nudging her stuffed teddy back underneath her arm.

Quietly, I tiptoe out the door and downstairs. I pause at the bottom, turning my head to look down the long hall. My heart skips a beat when I catch a flicker of movement in the shadows, a swish of blonde hair.

I press a hand to my chest and slam my fist on the light switch. I walk up and down the hall, searching the corners, behind closed doors. There's no one here. No one at all. But I keep thinking I'm seeing her. What the hell is wrong with me? Why can't she just let me go? Why can't I?

Shaking my head, I look up at the photographs of Vivienne on the wall, and all of her paintings, and start bringing them down. One by one. Stacking them up against each other. I repeat my therapist's mantra inside my head: I am calm and in control, I am calm and in control, I am calm and in control.

I hold Vivienne's glamour shot, gripping the golden frame, glaring at her vicious eyes and blood-red lips. "I'm about to make you roll in your grave," I tell her. Then I set the alarm and slip out the back door.

35

BY THE TIME I reach the guesthouse, I'm soaked.

My hair is glued to my face. My dress is sticking to my skin. It's see-through from the rain. Before I can knock, the door swings open. Owen towers over me, his brow furrowed in confusion.

I don't explain myself. I wrap my arms around his neck and press my lips to his. He lifts me over the threshold, already knowing exactly what I want. Neither of us have to say a word. We don't even bother fully undressing. It's hurried and frantic. Like our lives depend on it.

He hoists me up onto his hips and I brace against the wall, both of us breathless as we struggle to remove his belt and pants in between kisses. His mouth travels everywhere—hovering over mine, trailing down my throat, nipping at my skin. It's total loss of control. When he finds my lips again, I taste the rain on him. The trees. The moss. The estate itself.

His hands slip under my soaked dress, hiking it up. He grinds against me, the hard length of him straining through his jeans. I moan into his mouth, tugging harder at the belt until it finally gives. As soon as he's free, he presses against the thin fabric of my panties, groaning at how wet I am, before tearing them apart with his hands. I hear the lace rip, watch as it falls to the floor in shreds.

"Fuck," he grunts as he enters me, and I gasp at how incredible this feels, at just how badly I've been craving this, and what a relief it is to finally give in.

Fuck is right, I think as he pushes in deeper, the pinches of pain delicious as he eases his entire length inside me. I spread my legs wider, encouraging him to take more of me, and he thrusts slowly. Tortuously. Taking his time with me. Savoring it. When he realizes he's driving me mad, he quickens his pace. The wall behind us shakes, framed pictures crashing down and shattering.

I see my mother's face on the floor, her smile distorted by the cracked glass, and I glare maliciously down at her as he fucks me harder. I dig my nails into his back, moaning as I come almost immediately, the position we're in supplying me with the perfect amount of friction. He watches me as I climax, my head lolling back, my body totally weak. It's so intense I see stars.

"I'm going to make you come again," he breathes as he carries me over to his desk and lays me across it, the rain making everything slippery. He tears away my dress, peeling the damp fabric off my skin, and I unclasp my bra, tossing it aside.

His eyes move hungrily over me as he removes his shirt and pants. Muted daylight pours in through the window, and I admire his body, thinking about how bad I've been wanting to climb him since we reunited.

I take his hand, exploring his fingers and thumb with my lips, gently sucking, and then nibbling his skin. Gripping my hips, he draws me closer, to the edge of the desk, and repositions my legs over his shoulders, spreading me to accommodate even more of him. I'm still so sensitive down there that the moment he starts thrusting, his fingers digging into my thighs, I can already feel my pleasure building again.

God, I haven't just missed sex like this. I *live* for sex like this.

Bang-your-brains-right-out-of-your-head sex, and two orgasms later, I notice Owen struggling to hold on, his lips parting in pleasure.

Before he releases, he slowly pulls out of me and grips a handful of my wet hair, bringing me upright for a deep kiss. He doesn't want to come yet. He won't let himself.

His strong hands glide down my hips, spinning me around until my ass presses up against him. I bend over the desk as he enters me again. I feel the warmth of his touch as his hand settles on my lower belly, guiding our bodies together.

I feel like I need this. Like I've been needing this for a while. I'm finally not focusing on anything other than how *amazing* this feels. No more tension, no more anxiety.

My head drops onto the desk as he hits my G-spot, eliciting sounds out of my mouth I've never made before. I'm on the verge of screaming. I slap a hand over my mouth, biting down on my palm to help stifle it.

I see stars again.

He surprises me by forcing me upright and pressing my back to his chest. He bites into my neck, my shoulder, his breath hot against my skin. His arms envelop me and one of his hands cups my breast while the other dips between my legs, his fingers working skillfully until he has me crying out.

When I feel like I'm about to tip over the edge, I stop him, grabbing his hand and leading him to the sofa. I nudge him back onto the cushions and straddle him. My fingers stroke through his chest hair, lingering on the dark numbers and shadowy crucifix along his pec, as I begin to rock my hips.

He exhales, and a soft moan escapes his lips, the sound driving me crazy. I take out every last bit of frustration I have on him. I picture my mother's enraged face, hoping she can see me now, loving that there's finally not a single thing she can do about this.

I'm the one in control.

I'm the one with the power.

I picture driving a knife into her over and over and over again—

straight into that icy cold heart of hers, twisting it, plunging it deeper.

Owen's face screws up and his breath grows ragged as he becomes fuller inside me. "Briar," he groans, his voice strained, and I know he's dangerously close.

"I want you to come inside me," I direct him, surprising myself, and he instantly obeys, gripping my hips tightly as he empties himself into me, the warmth seeping out onto my inner thighs.

I collapse on top of him, finding his mouth, our breaths merging. It takes him a while to recover, and for a moment, I think I've killed him, but once he does, he trails his fingertips along my sweaty back, pressing loving kisses against my face and neck. He buries his nose into my hair and holds me close to him. "I've been thinking about this moment for years..." he admits with a self-deprecating chuckle.

I smile, cuddling into him. "So, how was it?" I ask, our lips still brushing against each other.

"Let's just say," he groans huskily against my mouth, "it was worth every second of the wait."

"Remember our first time?"

"Yeah."

"In the woods after you proposed. You know," I say, walking my fingers playfully up his chest. "We're still technically engaged. I did say yes."

Owen grins, averting his gaze. "I think this is the part most men would run away."

"Why?" I tease him. "Am I making you sweat?"

He studies my face, twirling a strand of my hair around his finger. "I got you that ring," he says.

I prop up, looking at him. "You did?"

He nods. "Massive diamond. Four carats."

I slap a hand over my mouth. "Owen!"

"I was going to surprise you with it when you came home from college, but the police confiscated it along with the money… and drugs."

"I had no idea."

"It didn't feel like you anyway," he says, still playing with my hair. He tucks a strand behind my ear. "Too showy."

I smile. "You're right, but it's the thought that counts, and that was a *really* big thought."

I think about what could've been if I'd agreed to run away with Owen. Maybe he never would've gone to prison and I would've never met Ted or flailed so hard in my twenties like I did. Would we have already been married for ten-plus years now? With kids and the whole package?

After snuggling together for a while, he lifts me suddenly off the sofa and flings me over his shoulder, spanking my ass. He carries me to the shower. "You're about to get a whole lot wetter."

I shriek, laughing.

After a long, steamy shower session, Owen's in the kitchen brewing coffee and I'm in the living room, getting dressed and towel-drying my hair. I check around the desk for my bra, then the sofa, and between the cushions.

Owen comes over and hands me a mug. I thank him with a kiss. "This is nice," I tell him, and it really is. "It's like playing house."

"Stay for breakfast," he says, smiling, the edges of his blue eyes crinkling. "I'll whip us up some chocolate chip pancakes."

"You really know how to woo a girl, don't you?" I take a sip of coffee. It's delicious, and he's prepared it exactly how I like it. "Oh, shit. I can't stay actually," I realize, smacking my forehead. "Juliet's probably up by now, and I don't want her to get scared."

"No problem," Owen says, walking to the bedroom and kicking aside the broken picture frames so we don't step on the glass. "Let me get dressed. We can all have breakfast together."

"Perfect!" I turn around and scan the floor for my missing bra when my hip brushes against Owen's bag hanging from his desk chair. Papers slip out, flying everywhere. "Shit!" I run to catch them, singling out a file with a photo clipped to the front of it. Is that… my late husband's car?

Yes, I'm positive.

That's Ted's car. The Windsor Blue Bentley.

I spring forward and reach for the file, picking it off the ground. It's a police report. *The* police report from the day his body was found. The window of the Bentley is coated in an explosion of blood and brain matter. There's an outline of Ted's silhouette in the driver's seat, the back of his head blown out by the pistol he put in his mouth.

My heart is racing when Owen returns. He slips an arm around me and lifts my chin for another kiss. "What's that?" he asks against my lips, glancing at the file.

I pull away and hold up the police report.

His face pales. "Oh. That's… uh…" He scratches at his Adam's apple, forcing out a cough. "Research."

I shake my head, not understanding. "I thought you were working on a memoir for Vivienne."

"I am."

There's another paper on the ground between us. A book cover mockup, the title glaring up at me. **House of Horrors: The Belville Family Uncensored by Owen Greene.**

My heart drops. The walls feel like they're closing in around me. I pick it up and Owen reaches for me. "Briar…"

I chuckle bitterly. It's my immediate defense mechanism. Being a bitch is so much better than showing how heartbroken I really am. "House of horrors, huh?"

Owen presses a hand to his forehead. "It's a working title," he says finally, rubbing at his face, his mouth, his jaw. He looks lost. He never planned on me finding this. Never planned on telling me.

"So, this is what you were really working on?" I try to keep my voice even, try not to show the level of betrayal I feel. "Your way of getting your foot in the door, right?"

Owen's cheeks turn red. "It was just something I was exploring.

When that detective came around, she started talking about your husband's death, and how strange it was, and then after what happened with Vivienne, I saw an opportunity I couldn't pass up. Do you know how much money I could make with a book like this?"

"Money?" I scoff. "That's what this is about? I thought you never cared about any of that."

"Everyone cares about money, Briar. Especially people who grew up without it." He gives me a look. "*You* never had to go hungry."

I close my eyes, trying to hold in the tears. It's stopped raining now, but water still drips from the magnolia trees, sliding off the leaves and pattering against the windows. The sound fills the silence between us, making me nostalgic for happier times. Owen and I, perched below the magnolias—him reading his short stories to me. Bright-eyed and hopeful and barefoot, with a lopsided grin. My head resting against his shoulder.

"No, you're right about that," I say when I finally find the strength to look at him again. "I didn't. And I'm sorry that you did. But... Owen... you lied to me. You've been lying to me this whole time. Using me and my family as a launching pad for your writing career. Trying to sell some sensationalized piece of trash about my life!" I wave the paper at him. "It's my life, Owen. I'm human. Not some story you can twist to your advantage."

"It's not like that."

"All this time I thought you were helping me."

"I was!"

"You were helping yourself!"

"Briar, please..."

"When were you planning on telling me? When your book is flying off the shelves? Were you going to send me an autographed copy?"

"I was planning on telling you eventually. But I never found the right moment."

"Stop lying."

"I'm not." Owen reaches for me, and I step back. "Can I at least have my papers back? The police file?"

I throw the papers at him, everything except the police file. They bounce off his head. One page gets caught on his shoulder. A picture of Ted. Seeing them side by side, the similarities are glaring.

He's a carbon copy of him.

My stomach knots. He'd hidden it so well, but I should have known better. I think back to something Portia said. *You like the assholes.* Unfortunately for me, it's true. My type is, without a doubt, asshole. It's like I'm addicted to them, their toxicity, their ability to wreak havoc upon my life. And the most tragic part is I keep falling for them.

"Don't touch me," I warn him. I take the police report and tear it into pieces. Then I throw them at him, and they rain over the floor like sad-looking confetti. "There are your papers you care so much about!"

I'm disgusted with myself for sleeping with him. Catching feelings for him. Buying another man's promises and lies. Am I really that gullible?

"Do you know what?" I say, realizing what an idiot I am. "You were the first person I felt like I could trust in... forever. *Forever!* Do you know how badly my husband hurt me? My mother... and Elise? I mean, I can't trust anybody at all anymore, can I?"

"Briar, please. You can trust me," Owen says. "And I do care about you. A lot."

"If that were true, we wouldn't be having this conversation!" I fling at him. "This almost hurts worse than Ted. We've known each other since we were seven years old, and you have done nothing—*nothing*—but try to convince me that you'd always be there for me, no matter what!"

Owen winces. He looks like he wants to cut in and defend himself, but I quickly hold up a hand, stopping him.

"And I spent so many years blaming myself for you going to

prison, but you know what, that was on you! That was all you! And you didn't even try to reach out. After you said you would always make me feel loved and protected. You remember that, don't you?" I jab a finger at him. "*You* promised!"

"That was before," he shouts, startling me. He looks suddenly vicious, threatening. He stalks closer, his fists clenched. "Just because I was stuck in there doesn't mean I didn't move on. I thought of you every... single... day. I heard your laugh. I saw your smile. I dreamt of you." His face crumples. "But you weren't enough. I would lie in my cot and cry at night because I was scared shitless. I was just a kid. They strip you of your humanity in there. If you knew half the things I experienced..."

He searches my face, tears in his eyes.

"You don't even know," he says. "You can't even *relate* because you've had everything handed to you your entire life. You're so fucking spoiled, Briar."

"That's not fair. I can't believe you're turning this on me. The Owen I knew—"

"He's gone!" he shouts. "Don't you get that? I don't even know who I am anymore!"

"Yeah, well, I don't either!" I shoot back, standing my ground. We stare each other down for a moment. Neither of us moving.

Owen says this next part under his breath, "You turned out just like her."

"Excuse me?"

He doesn't have to say Vivienne's name. It's clear that's who he means. "I said you turned out just like her, and you don't even see it."

"How can you say that?"

"What happened to your husband, Briar?"

I stare at him, my heart pounding in my chest. "You don't get to ask me about him."

"So, you won't tell me the truth."

"You read the police report!"

"I want to hear your side of the story."

"*Fuck you.* Get out!"

Owen shakes his head. "Briar, we've both changed. That's the point! I don't know you anymore either… But we can find our way back to each other. If we just try. If you just hear me out."

"I did hear you out and I still want you to leave."

Owen exhales. His eyes are glassy as if he's about to cry. "I wasn't even sure if I was going to go through with the damn thing!" he shouts, his voice cracking. "I didn't want to mess this up. I didn't want to lose you all over again!"

"Well, it's too late now."

"I forgot what this feels like. I forgot what you do to me. You make me feel so… *helpless*. I can't even breathe when I'm around you. I can't think straight. I've felt it from the first moment I saw you, and I know you feel it too. Please don't make me go. I feel so guilty, especially now that I see how much I've hurt you."

"It's reassuring to know you have a conscience."

"I know this looks bad, but we can get through this."

I can't help but laugh. "I don't really see how. Who knows what else you've been lying to me about? That sob story you fed me about your father?"

It's meant to hurt him, and now I wonder if I've gone too far. But when all the color drains from Owen's face and he begins to stammer as if his brain suddenly short circuits, I see red. "Please tell me you're joking."

"It wasn't a complete lie," Owen says. "My cousin…" He stalls, scratching at the back of his head.

"Your cousin *what*?"

Owen coughs, the words jumbled. "He attempted suicide."

"Oh, my God!"

"I wanted you to feel comfortable opening up to me."

"You mean, you wanted to manipulate me. Trick me. Get more stories out of me for your precious book!"

Owen clenches his jaw. "Maybe it wasn't the best way to go about it."

"I'll say, you sociopath!" I turn away from him, desperately trying to hold back the tears. Owen reaches for me again, but I step back. "No," I protest. "No! You don't get to touch me anymore!"

"Wait..." Owen turns, listening for something. "Did you hear that?"

"Don't try to change the subject."

"No," Owen says, his expression serious. "I heard a splash."

It takes me a moment to process what he's saying, but then I hear something in the background, blaring like a siren. The house alarm.

I break into a cold sweat. "Juliet!"

36

Juliet floats face down in the water.

I run to the edge of the pool and plunge in at the same moment Owen does. We lift her onto the pool deck together and place her on her back. "Shit, shit, shit," I say, panicking as Owen starts performing CPR. "She's not breathing!"

Owen pauses chest compressions to administer mouth-to-mouth. I dial 911. My fingers are shaking uncontrollably and I'm trying not to hyperventilate again.

Owen curses when Juliet doesn't respond, his brow beading with sweat as he resumes chest compressions. This time, he applies more pressure. He pries open her mouth and forces air into her lungs before repeating the process all over again.

I'm in the middle of explaining to the 911 operator what's going on when Juliet's eyes suddenly snap open and she jerks forward, releasing a violent cough and gasping for air. Water shoots out of her mouth, splashing Owen and splattering over the pool deck. "Oh, thank God," I gasp, crying with relief. "She's okay."

An ambulance is already on its way. I hang up the phone and pull Juliet into my arms. She's crying too, frightened and in pain, her breathing shallow and ragged. I shower her face with kisses and hug her close to me.

Owen finally relaxes. He sits back, releasing a heavy exhale. I hate that I want to kiss and hug him too right now. For acting so quickly and for saving her life. I hate that he's ruined everything between us.

He reaches out to stroke Juliet's back. "I'm sorry, Briar," he says, sounding pitiful. "I am so sorry. This is all my fault."

No, it's mine. I was the one supposed to be watching her. I'm such a terrible big sister. She almost died on my watch.

"I mean it," he says. "I'm sorry. I'm an idiot, and I should've been honest with you from the start."

"Owen, please," I beg him. "Not right now."

Juliet clings to me, her bony arms digging painfully into my neck. I gently untangle her grip and give her a stern look. "What were you thinking, huh? You know you're not allowed near the pool unless there's an adult with you."

Did she just come outside to play and slip into the pool? Maybe she was searching for me after waking up to an empty house. Now I feel even more guilty than before. But there's something bugging me. Juliet's an excellent swimmer. The fact she fell in and couldn't make it out again is weird. Unless she hit her head...

I check her for any sign of injury. Then I take Juliet's chin and tilt her head in my direction, leaning closer. "Hold on. What's wrong with your eyes?" I demand.

Her pupils are massive, almost taking up the entire iris. Owen moves closer to get a better look. "What in the world..." He tries to get to the bottom of it. "Juliet, did you take medicine inside the house while your sister was gone?"

Juliet doesn't answer the question. Without warning, she lunges headfirst toward the edge of the pool. Owen catches her before she can dive back in, pulling her onto his lap and attempting to restrain her. She kicks and scratches at him, drawing blood. "What's gotten into you?"

Her head snaps in my direction. "Odette says we're all going to die."

My stomach drops. "What?"

"She's waiting for me in there." Juliet points to the rippling blue water, the waves reflected in her large pupils. She's staring at the water with this crazed look in her eyes, a creepy grin spreading across her face. Owen and I exchange a worried glance.

"What exactly is going on here?" Portia asks as she stomps across the lawn in her heels. She couldn't have arrived home from the courthouse at a worse time. She looks like a furious school principal about to drag me into her office and threaten expulsion.

She cocks a thumb over one shoulder, her cheeks flaring pink. "There's an ambulance outside." She starts jogging once she sees Juliet, soaked in pool water, gasping and shivering. "What the hell is this?"

She rips Juliet away from Owen and frantically searches her body, her head, her hands, everything, like a worried mother. "Juliet, baby. Are you alright? Talk to me." She shoots me a look that makes me instantly wither, and then directs it at Owen. "An explanation would be nice!"

"She fell into the pool," Owen explains.

Portia turns to me, and I sigh. "I only stepped out for a second."

Her mouth drops open. Once she's satisfied Juliet isn't in any immediate danger, she reaches down and takes her hand, asking softly, "Can you walk, sweetheart?" When Juliet nods, she helps her up off the ground and then glares down at us. She covers Juliet's ears and lowers her voice to a dangerous growl. "So, what are you saying? You were supposed to be watching her, but you wanted to get laid instead, and our sister almost drowned?" When I don't answer, Portia barks out an angry laugh. "Wow, wow, wow, Briar! You really win the sister of the year award!"

"You were the one trying to push us together!"

"Oh, my God. Don't you dare put this on me! You were

supposed to be watching her! Not ditch her for some guy. I mean, who even are you?"

She leads Juliet back to the house and I chase after them. "Trust me. I feel horrible!"

"Good," Portia snaps, swinging around to face me. I've never seen her this vicious. Portia has always been impossible to anger. The kind of person who takes everything in stride, goes with the flow. It's what makes her so amazing at her job. But this side of her is scary, and I know if I made her this mad, I seriously screwed up. "You should feel horrible. Juliet could have died! What were you even thinking? No, you weren't thinking. I'll tell you what was doing the thinking!"

"You're right," I say. "You're so right."

"There's something wrong with her eyes," Portia notices suddenly, panicking. She grasps Juliet's face and turns her head to each side. "Her pupils. Did you feed her something?"

"No!"

"Well, did she eat something?"

"I don't know."

"Unbelievable," Portia scoffs. "The judge just granted me guardianship. Do you want her to get taken away from us?"

"Of course not!"

"You're over thirty. Don't you think it's time to start acting like it?"

Ouch. But I deserve it. I deserve all of it. I follow her into the house, apologizing profusely. Portia comes to an abrupt halt in the kitchen, staring at the cookie jar. The lid is set aside, and crumbs scatter the countertop. We realize at the same time what happened.

After we escaped our mother, we emptied the whole house of food, cleaning out the fridge, the cabinets. But we forgot the cookie jar.

"You didn't get rid of the cookies?" Portia says slowly.

"They were sugar cookies, and I thought Owen made them with

Juliet," I explain. "I ate a couple the other night right before the... party."

Oh. So, that's why I was so sick that night...

"Juliet, sweetie, did you eat a cookie?" Portia coos, her face growing pale as she panics even more.

Juliet nods sheepishly. "I ate the rest of them," she whispers.

Portia glares at me. *If looks could kill.* She storms out of the house and meets the EMTs just as they're coming up to the door. I fill them in on what happened as Portia climbs into the back of the ambulance with Juliet. But when I try to climb in, Portia shoves me back, knocking the wind out of me. I'm shocked. She's never laid her hands on me before. She even raises her hand as if she's about to strike me in the face.

"Get out," she says. "I'm dead serious, Briar. I'm furious with you to a point where you might be better off outside this ambulance than in it. I honestly don't know what I'm capable of right now." She sets a protective hand over Juliet. "Just..." She sighs, shaking her head. "I'll text you later, okay?"

My shoulders sag as the doors slam shut. I back up as the ambulance pulls away, speeding out of the gate. When I turn around, Owen is standing on the front porch, waiting for me. "Briar..." he starts.

"Please, no. I can't," I say, shouldering past him. "I need to be alone right now." I move straight into the kitchen where I sweep up the cookie crumbs and dump them into the trash. Then, in a fit of rage, I toss the whole cookie jar into the garden, the porcelain shattering somewhere in the grass.

37

Hours later, I'm still cleaning. I soak the sponge in the soapy water a second time before wringing it out and going to town on the mantel in the parlor. I've been wanting to clean this thing since I arrived, and it's even more satisfying than I thought. It feels like my world has crumbled around me, but even if I can't fix everything, I can sure as hell make this place shine. I grit my teeth, putting my back into it.

Owen leans against the doorframe. He throws a thumb over his shoulder. "Just letting you know, I'm almost finished packing, and then I'll be out of here." He steps closer, testing the waters. He gestures to my cleaning project. "Can I help you with that?"

"No," I respond flatly.

"Oh, come on, Briar. Can we please talk about this? I don't want to leave on bad terms. I'm afraid... I'm afraid I'll never get to see you again." He sighs. "I *need* to see you again."

I close my eyes. God, he always knows exactly what to say to me. Because the thought of never seeing him again is almost too much to bear. I loved him once. I still do, even though I wish I didn't. I love him so much it hurts. But I'm damaged. Broken. We both are. We're not good for each other. Why can't he understand that?

"We did talk, and there's nothing more to discuss. You lied. You used me. You hurt me when I needed you the most, and unless you have a time machine to undo being a douchebag, then I think we're done here."

Owen opens his mouth to argue with me, but my cellphone cuts him off, blaring in my pocket. I answer it. "Portia?" I move into the ballroom, and Owen takes the hint, finally giving me some space.

"Hey," she says, obviously still pissed. I can hear the fast-paced sounds of the hospital in the background—the rush of voices, the echo of the intercom, the whirr of monitors. "We're going to be a little longer..."

I grasp the phone tighter. "How is she?"

"She's fine, but her blood pressure's a little high. They gave her some activated charcoal and fluids, and they want to keep monitoring her."

"Okay," I say, nodding. I'm relieved, but I know we're not out of the woods yet.

"I'll keep you updated, but I think we'll be good to come home tonight." There's a rustle on the other end of the line. "That's the doctor. Talk soon."

I slip my phone into my pocket and return to the parlor to finish cleaning. An hour passes. Two hours, maybe longer. I completely lose myself in it, until paint chips start sticking to the yellow part of the sponge. I frown, pulling back. *Maybe that's enough for now. At least until I buy some more paint.*

I'm in the middle of browsing color options on my phone when I step back and accidentally bump into a vase I had set aside while cleaning. It falls over and rolls away, crashing into the baseboard. It doesn't break, but something pops out of the neck. A small black object. I crouch down and pick it up, inspecting it. It looks like a flash drive, but wider and shorter, and there's a microphone.

Oh, my God. Seriously, Owen?

I run to the guesthouse, storming inside, holding the recording device up for Owen to see. I hurl it at his head, but he manages to catch it. "Spying on us too?"

Owen looks lost. "What are you talking about?"

I set my hands on my hips. "You know *exactly* what I'm talking about."

"No, I really don't." He examines the device, his brow furrowed. "I've never seen this before."

"It's a bug, isn't it?"

"Yeah, but I didn't put it in your house."

"Then who did?"

"Probably the police. They run surveillance jobs like that."

The police? But why would the detective bug our house? All of Vivienne's secrets are out. There's nothing left to monitor... is there?

I leave Owen and ransack the house, turning over framed photographs and flowerpots. I find one camera, then two. By the sixth camera, found hidden behind the extra toilet paper rolls in the spare bathroom, my pulse is racing.

I drop the camera to the ground, recoiling from it as it bounces and clatters over the hardwood floor. The ceiling creaks overhead and I stiffen, listening. It's the same noise I heard the other night when I couldn't sleep.

Footsteps.

With my heart in my throat, I tiptoe into the kitchen and steal my beloved butcher knife from the block. Then, holding it tight, I make my way upstairs.

The noises are coming from Vivienne's studio. Holding my breath, I step into the room and look around. I don't even know if anyone's up here, but my level of paranoia has reached its peak. The room is empty, but the window is wide open, and my eyes are tearing up from the amount of cigarette smoke in the air.

I cough and fan a hand in front of my nose as I follow the scent. It's not coming from the window, which was clearly opened as a way to mask the scent, but from the back of the studio. The smell gets stronger the closer I get to the wall, almost as if the smoke is coming from behind it. I spot something now I've never noticed before and I do a double take, wondering if I'm seeing things again.

There's a secret door here.

I press on the outer edges, and it cracks open, swinging to the side as I stumble back. "Holy shit!" I gasp in disbelief, blinking into the darkness. I blindly reach for the switch and flick it on, flooding the small compartment with light. A sculpture of Odette stands against the wall, the same one I obliterated with the mallet. But it's been painstakingly reconstructed. It almost looks as good as new, except her left eye is slightly lower than the right, her nose tilts too far, and her lips droop into a frown. She's missing some parts here and there, like a grotesque and incomplete puzzle.

Behind the sculpture, I see pictures of me and my family. News articles. Magazine clippings. Erected on the wall like some kind of sick shrine. There's even a family photo with Vivienne's face violently scratched out. I stumble forward, clutching my knife tighter.

Bloody towels are piled in the corner of the room, the metallic scent still lingering in the air. I bring my dress up over my nose as I walk to the supply closet, a navy blazer inside catching my attention. I recognize it instantly. It's the detective's. And there's a whole row of white sneakers at the bottom, one pair coated in dried blood.

I swallow, anxiously, as I push the navy blazer aside, and find a small collection of blonde wigs. "What the hell..."

Not far from that, a half-hidden gallon jug. I pick it up, my mouth running dry as I read the label: **Fresh Pork Blood. Keep Refrigerated.**

I drop the gallon, my panicked brain finally connecting all the dots. Detective Torres vandalized the gallery. She's been living inside our house. All those instances I sensed someone tampering with or moving my things—it wasn't my sisters or Elise.

And it was her, I realize now, who I saw that night, leering through the guesthouse window at Owen and me. I thought it looked like Vivienne because she'd been wearing a blonde wig. I can clearly picture the detective's face pressed close to the glass, her dark eyes stuck to us the whole time.

I move to the back of the room. There's a trio of monitors displaying live surveillance footage of the entire estate grounds. I cover my mouth, releasing a horrified groan into my hand. I feel violated thinking about how every move, every conversation, every intimate moment was recorded for her own personal sick pleasure. She was watching us the whole time, and we didn't even know it.

Old takeout containers litter the desk and the ground, spilling out from the overflowing metal bin. Beside the mess, an ashtray sits packed with stubbed cigarettes, reeking of the smell of smoke I'd noticed earlier. The cigarette butt I found on the windowsill was just a short walk away from this room. I didn't even know the detective smoked. She covered it up well.

My eyes land on a frumpy sleeping bag crammed in the corner. It's surrounded by a mess of crumbs and dirty plates and a bowl of moldy food. The stench slams into me, and I fight the urge to gag as it invades the fabric of my dress. So, *this* is where all the missing food has been going.

Keeping watch over my shoulder, I move to the desk and sit down, clicking through the monitors. "Wait. This can't be right," I say. Detective Torres has access to my SecureHome app?

A stream of code flashes over the screen and the room spins. She can control the footage in my app, selecting which cameras to put on a loop. So she could continue to sneak around the house, live under the same roof with us, and remain undetected.

I click on the video files, disgusted by the touchpad. It feels tacky, the sticky substance transferring to my fingers. I wish I had my hand sanitizer with me.

There are hundreds of videos here. My morning jogs. Our family dinners. Juliet dancing in her bedroom. Owen and I having sex. There's even footage of Vivienne and Elise's crime scene, blood and brains everywhere.

I cover my face, my whole body shaking. The detective is a *lurker*.

Something cold and hard touches the back of my head.

I freeze.

"Hand over the knife, Briar."

38

"Now, put your hands up, and turn around. Very slowly... and I mean slow."

I do as the detective says, swiveling around as slowly as possible. My phone peeks halfway out of my bra, and she snatches it, shutting it off before sliding it into her back pocket.

At first glance, I think she's wearing one of her wigs, but then I realize she's dyed her hair blonde and copied Vivienne's exact hairstyle. She's in jeans and a tank top, and I can clearly make out the realistic portrait tattoo of my mother on her left bicep.

"Oh, do you like it?" she asks, her dark eyes shining. "It's new! But I wish I would've waited longer because now I'm thinking about getting your face, Briar." She pushes the gun closer to me, the tip grazing my chin. I tense up, a knot forming in my stomach. "And you know what else? I always thought I'd look good as a redhead."

"What is this?" I whisper. If I keep my voice low, maybe she won't consider me a threat, won't pull the trigger.

Detective Torres sighs, keeping the gun pressed firmly against my head as she looks around. "You weren't supposed to see any of this."

There are bags under her eyes, like she hasn't been sleeping.

And there's something unhinged in them, too. It takes me a second to muster up the courage to ask the next question, my heart pounding so fast I can barely catch my breath. "Are you going to kill me?"

"I don't want to," she admits, looking sad. "But I never wanted any of this. I can't help that I'm so drawn to this family, to this house." Her grip trembles, her brown eyes welling with tears. "Ever since Odette died, I've been keeping a close eye on your family. When the police sent Martinez to investigate, I knew he was a skilled detective, but he didn't care about the Belville family. Not like I did. I mean, I've spent years studying your history!"

I knew it. I sensed it deep down, but I always wrote it off. It was weird to me how clueless the detective seemed about us when she literally grew up in the same town. Everyone in town knows who we are.

"Once he closed Odette's case, I felt that there was more going on here," Detective Torres continues. "And I had to find a way to become a part of your lives. So, in the middle of the night, I hopped the gate and set up my little operation in the storage room. I found it ages ago. I used to beg my parents to bring me here almost every weekend. I wanted to live here so bad. And then, years later, I bought the original blueprints for the estate at auction. This house has so many secret passages. Tunnels inside the walls, hidden compartments, sealed off wings..."

The detective glances at her Belville family shrine. "Your mother hadn't touched this storage room in decades. It was covered in cobwebs and rat shit. You'd be proud to know I tidied the place up, for the most part."

I glance at the moldy bowl of food again, wrinkling my nose.

"I bought the pig's blood a few days before I set up shop," she says, looking back at me, a sick smile on her face. "Can you believe you can purchase just about anything online? I threw it around the gallery. And since Martinez was already tied up with another case, I begged the lieutenant to let me take over, which he did. I was so excited. Until I realized the truth..."

I search her face, fearful. "About what?"

"Your mother. Can you believe the actress I idolized my entire life turned out to be such a bitch? You know that saying, 'Never meet your idols'? Well, it's true. And when I saw what she did to you and your sisters, I knew I had to get rid of her."

"You were the one who killed her?"

"I didn't have to. Elise, as usual, did all the heavy lifting. I had a plan worked out, but one morning, I reviewed the surveillance footage and saw that Elise had taken care of Vivienne for me. She even left a confession. Called the police, told us where to find the bodies. It was perfect. All I had to do was play my part as detective, and the case was open and shut, just like that."

I try to buy some time with questions, waiting for the chance to grab her gun, the knife, anything to have the upper hand. "So, all this time you were watching us?"

"For months," the detective says. "You know your mom was drugging Juliet, right?"

I gasp. "What?"

"Didn't you ever wonder why she was seeing things? Why her pupils always looked a little too big?"

I search my memory, but nothing comes to mind. Juliet's eyes were never as dilated as they were by the pool earlier, but maybe that's because Vivienne kept the doses small. Small enough her older sisters wouldn't notice.

"They thought it would keep her quiet," the detective says. "Keep her from realizing what was really going on. But kids are sponges, and that one's sharp. Smarter than they gave her credit for." She flips her blonde curls over one shoulder, frowning. "She reminds me of someone I used to know."

"Your sister?" I guess, drawing from our past conversations.

The detective looks at me, surprised. Maybe she thought I forgot about her little slip-up at my birthday party.

"Yeah, my sister," she confirms. "I lied to you that first time we met. I didn't move back to Gator Springs to care for my mom. I moved back for my sister. She was around Juliet's age when she died." She swallows painfully. "Leukemia."

"I'm so sorry," I say. Because I genuinely am. I know firsthand the pain of losing a sister.

"Me, too," she says softly. "It pushed me over the edge. I started losing it at work, in the interrogation room." She laughs, shaking her head. "I beat this rapist piece of shit so bad, I left him deaf in one ear."

"Grief makes you do crazy things," I say, hoping the fact I'm siding with her will get her to relax. Her grip on me loosens. The gun moves away from my head, the barrel scraping against my scalp.

"So does trauma. You know how it is, Briar," the detective says, and my stomach tightens as her words hit home. "That's why I have to take Juliet away from this place. It's a toxic environment, and it's rubbing off on her. She deserves a real chance."

My heart drops. The walls seem to close in. "A real chance at what?"

"At life."

"She's not your sister, Elena!" I snap before I can stop myself. The moment the words leave my mouth, I wish I could take them back. I see the hurt in her eyes, the tears that threaten to fall. Now is not the time to make her angry.

She clears her throat. "She's coming with me. I already planned everything," she says. "I already went through all this trouble."

I shake my head hard. "No, you can't take her."

The air feels suddenly thinner. My chest is tight, my pulse thudding in my throat. I look around the room, searching for a weapon. There's a lamp on the table, a heavy ceramic one. A fireplace poker. The corner of the marble countertop. My hands start to sweat and tremble.

"If you cared about your sister, you would let her go."

Oh, my God. She's serious. She really wants to take her.

"You're insane. You're unwell. You need help!" My voice is hoarse, shaking. "I won't let you take her."

"Yes, you will." The detective shoves me back, raising the gun again. Her finger hovers above the trigger. "Because you're not going to be around much longer."

"No, wait!" I shout, shielding my head and cowering. "You can't do this. It's murder! Kidnapping! The police will find you!"

"The police?" the detective says with an amused chuckle. "I *am* the police, Briar. Believe me, I know how to cover my tracks."

It feels hopeless. But if she really wanted me dead, she would've shot me from behind while I was still sitting at her computer.

I decide to make a run for it.

But something's wrong.

The detective's eyes turn pink, then red, as if they're slowly filling up with ink. A bloody tear runs down her cheek, and she jabs the gun at me. "Why are you looking at me like that?"

I stare in shock as darker blood drips from her nose, splashing onto her chest. She touches her nose, looks at her bloody fingers. "What the fuck?" The blood drips faster, falls harder. "What did you do?"

I back away, terrified, colliding with the wall. "I don't know! I didn't do anything!"

The detective grips her face. Her eyes are so red now they're almost black. Chunks of coagulated blood spill out of her mouth. She coughs and chokes. Tries to puke it up. "What the hell did you do to me?" she shouts, the sound wet and garbled.

"I didn't do anything!" I shout as she drops the gun and collapses at my feet. I'm shocked. Confused.

The detective isn't dead yet. She moans loudly, rolling around on the ground, convulsing.

The studio door opens and Juliet peeks around the corner. "You're back," I say, stupidly, and then as she skips inside, "I mean, get back! Stay back!" I rush forward to stop her, to shield her eyes, but I'm not fast enough.

Juliet kneels down beside the detective and pokes her with a curious finger. I hold my breath, not sure what to say or do, taken aback by her disregard for the gruesome scene. Then, without warning, Juliet brings the large blade with the golden hilt out from under her shirt and drives it into the detective's throat with both hands. Warm blood sprays me directly in the face, coats the floor, the ceiling, the walls. It happens so fast I barely have time to process it.

I'm gasping, short and quick, the taste of pennies on my tongue. Juliet looks up at me apologetically. "She told me she wanted to take me away," she says in a silvery voice, her eyes big and doe-like. I can see my own horrified reflection in them, the detective's blood all over my face.

I brace against the wall, almost climbing it, as my little sister comes closer.

"I gave her one of Mama's pretty flowers from her secret garden," Juliet explains. "I snuck in here earlier while she was away and sprinkled it over her potato chips." She covers her mouth, giggling. "She didn't even realize because it looked like seasoning!"

Portia appears in the doorway, and Juliet spins around to look at her. She holds up the bloodied knife like a trophy. "Can we hide her in the mirrors like Mama did?" she asks excitedly. "Or in the swamp like we did with Odette?"

39

Juliet's enthusiasm makes my blood run cold. I'm deathly silent, in pure shock, as she waves the murder weapon triumphantly around in the air.

The detective lies dead on the floor. A pool of blood collects beneath her, trickling between the floorboards. My mouth is open, my knees wobbly, as Juliet's words echo inside my head. *Or in the swamp like we did with Odette.*

"Please, say something," Portia whispers, and I shake my head, tears spilling over my cheeks. She hurries over to me and grasps my hand, but I yank away, angry and frightened.

"You lied to me." I touch my face, trying to wipe away the detective's blood, but it's caked on me, already drying down. "How could you?"

"I wanted to tell you," Portia insists. She's crying, staring at me with those big green eyes of hers, pleading with me to forgive her. "I did."

"You killed Odette!" I shout, losing it. "You knew this entire time what really happened and you said nothing!"

Portia nods, confirming my worst suspicions. She squeezes her eyes shut and covers her face. "Please don't hate me, Briar. I can't lose you, too."

"Was it all an act?"

"She was going to rip us apart," Portia explains, softening her voice as she tries to make me understand. She moves closer, catching me in her arms, not letting me go. "Don't you get it?" Her lower lip trembles violently as she clasps my face in her hands and forces me to look into her eyes. "She found out about Ryan."

I wince. "What?"

"Our idiot dealer showed up at the estate. He was demanding money, trying to get me to buy more blow. Odette assumed I'd fallen off the wagon. She sat me down to talk, to see if I needed help. It was all just a big misunderstanding. She wanted to talk to me about returning to rehab. She didn't want to see me ending up like Ryan, and I just snapped. I told her what really happened. I kept apologizing, telling her it was better her husband was dead because he treated her like garbage, but you should have seen the look on her face. It was like she didn't even recognize me. When I tried to backpedal, she didn't believe me. And then she ran upstairs, threatening to call the police, and I couldn't let that happen. Things turned physical."

The rust stains on the carpet. It wasn't rust.

It was really blood.

"I managed to take her cellphone away and shove her into your bedroom before she reached the stairs. I locked her in and tried to reason with her through the door. But she'd already made up her mind." Portia swallows hard, looking away. "Odette must have tried to climb out the window, because she fell and hit her head. Her leg was broken. She was totally out of it. Her head was bleeding *so* much. She begged me to take her to the hospital."

I grip my stomach, nauseous. "So you just left her to die?"

"You don't get it," Portia says. She extends a hand to Juliet, who takes it, still clutching the knife tightly. Blood droplets fall from the blade, splattering onto the floor below. "She wasn't strong enough to keep all those secrets. If she told anyone, we would lose everything. We could go to prison, even Odette. She'd known about Vivienne's murders for years. Admitting it might've made her an accessory. And Odette was so concerned about Juliet's well-being, but she didn't think ahead. Would Juliet really be happy in foster care, living with strangers? I tried explaining this to her, but she refused to calm down, to think rationally. I had no choice."

"You should've called an ambulance! You could've saved her! Did Vivienne—"

"Vivienne had nothing to do with Odette's death. Elise helped me move Odette to the swamp. We left her in the water and said a little prayer. She helped me cover it up. I always trusted that she wouldn't turn me in. I think in some twisted way, Elise wanted what was best for us. And if that meant covering up yet another family secret, the decision was easy for her. But she said something that night that stuck with me—that we were the monsters Vivienne created."

It feels like something inside me snaps. My last bit of sanity, maybe. I don't even know what to think anymore, what to feel.

"So you just let our sister drown?" I pull away from them. My legs feel weak beneath me. I'm seconds away from crashing to my knees. "That's cruel. That's *so* cruel, Portia. How could you?" The air whooshes out of me as I picture Odette's final moments—hurt and terrified, gasping in the murky swamp water as she struggled to stay afloat. "I can't believe this. I can't believe it was you this whole time!"

God. Poor Odette. That note she left me. She was trying to tell me what happened. Who was after her. But the paper was ruined, the ink swimming in her tears.

I can imagine now what the note actually said:

B,

Don't trust Portia. She's not who you think she is. She's a psychopath. She's trying to kill me. She killed my husband. I'm going to hide this somewhere for you to find. Please call the police. She took my phone and locked me in your room. If anything happens to me, I want Ryan's family to know the truth.

Please keep Juliet safe and stay away from her. I'm afraid you're next.

Please, please, please be careful.

I love you,

Odette

She was never trying to warn me about Vivienne.

She was trying to warn me about *Portia*.

"You had me worried there for a second, poking around. Getting Detective Torres to search the swamp." Portia nudges the detective's lifeless body with her foot. "But I was praying it would blow over."

"I trusted you..."

"I don't know why you're acting so surprised, Briar," Portia says, glaring at me. "It's not like you're completely innocent."

"That was different!" I insist. "Odette was—"

"Family?" she supplies. "They were family, too. Weren't they? At least by marriage."

I close my eyes, not wanting to compare what we did to Ted and Ryan to what Portia did to Odette.

Odette was innocent. Our older sister. Thoughtful and kind and patient. Ted and Ryan were *asking* for it. I cringe as the memories come flooding back. I cover my eyes, trying to block it out.

It's hard to believe I spent so many years making excuses for Ted, trying to make our relationship work. We even resorted to expensive therapists and couples' retreats, all planned and paid for by me, of course. It was only after Ted admitted that his family was broke, and they were only trying to keep up appearances that I realized why all my credit cards were maxed out and our joint bank account was in the negative. Even when the situation turned dire, he pushed and pushed for me to maintain the illusion. No matter how much I did for him, he was never satisfied.

When I threatened divorce, he threatened me back. *I'll drag you through the courts and bleed you for every penny. I'll go to the media and make up lies about you. I'll tell everyone you cheated, that you're doing drugs again.*

I backed down, but eventually, every time I saw his smug face, I wanted to die. Dinner at the club was a must for him, just to be seen. Over the expensive wine I paid for, he would say, "You know, Marcus just got a new pair of golf clubs. Carbon fiber. I could use a set like that..."

"I could too," I'd think, imagining myself beating him with them.

"You know, Jeremy just bought a Bentley. It's lime green." Shaking his head in disgust, he'd add, "Such bad taste. If I had a Bentley, it would be Windsor Blue. What do you think about that, honey? Briar, aren't you listening to me?"

"Hm?"

"I said..." He'd lean back and swish his wine, smirking. "Wouldn't I look sexy in a Bentley?"

At one point, I felt like his own personal ATM. And then it happened. Ted and Vivienne. I walked in on them one night at the condo. His head crammed between her thighs, blissfully unaware, while my own mother gazed up at me with this look on her face like, *I told you so. I told you he was a lying sack of shit.* Like some kind of twisted intervention. Shock therapy. I was already planning to leave Ted, but that night was the final straw.

One evening, Portia and I got him good and drunk. Then we drove him out to the Everglades, taking the back roads, parking our cars somewhere discreet. He was so out of it, he didn't know what was happening. I don't even think he felt it when the gun went off. There was a single shot, a splash of brains. I wiped my prints off of everything and planted his prints instead. Portia drove me home afterward, both of us still buzzing with adrenaline, still processing what had just happened.

We took care of Odette's husband, Ryan, shortly after. He seemed perfect on paper. Came from a wealthy family. Went to a good school. Was a doctor. Who knew he'd turn out to be such a verbally abusive prick behind closed doors? He had a history of cocaine use, and all we had to do was snowball from there. The drug is easy to find as long as you have the right connections. Whenever there was a family event, we'd sprinkle it into his drink, lace it along the fat of his steak. And when things weren't progressing as fast as we wanted, we slipped him a high enough dose to trigger a heart attack. Odette had no idea what we were doing, but we did it to protect her. Like sisters do.

I try not to dwell on how scared she must have been or the betrayal she likely felt in her final moments after discovering Portia was a killer. And I'm touched that she tried to warn me, unaware that I had a hand in the murder, too.

But Portia went too far. I would never have agreed to hurt her.

"You *are* a monster!" I fling at her, half-hearted.

"But so are you," Portia says. "After all, we are our mother's daughters. And you've already forgiven me. Because it's like Vivienne always said..." She brings me into her arms, refusing to let go. "We're a family. We're best when we're together."

Juliet gazes up at us, nodding, her eyes bright. "Together."

I begin to sob because she's right, I realize, as I sink into her shoulder and Juliet's head rests against the small of my back. Maybe my motive was never to protect Odette from Ryan, or myself from Ted—that sick urge always there, a constant parasite gnawing away at me, a craving for blood.

Maybe I just simply *wanted* to.

And how could I ever live without my sisters? They're the only ones who truly know me. Who share the same memories, the same upbringing. Who love and accept me. Even the dark parts.

We are the same. And without them, everything feels meaningless. I would *die* for them, even knowing they might turn on me next.

Now that I think about it... how could Odette be so careless, jeopardizing our entire existence like that? Every family has secrets. It's just a matter of learning how to live with them.

"Uh-oh," Juliet says, breaking away from us. She skips across the room and points at Owen with her bloody knife.

He stands in the doorway, his face unusually pale. He holds up his hands, looking directly at me. "I didn't hear or see anything."

Portia doesn't hesitate. A scary calm transforms her features. For a moment, she doesn't even look like herself anymore. She picks the detective's gun off the floor and shoots Owen in the legs. She's quick. A perfect shot.

Owen cries out, collapsing. "Briar, please," he groans, squirming in pain, his eyes wide as he falls onto his side and attempts to pull himself up again. It doesn't work. Blood gushes from his legs. "Don't do this! Please, don't do this. I love you. I always loved you!"

"I won't kill him," Portia says, handing me the gun. "Because you love him. But we both know he's a problem. So, what do we do?"

My sisters watch me expectantly. Owen's groaning grows louder and more desperate as I take my time, thinking it over. He pulls himself toward the door as I run the different scenarios through my head, trying to figure out what to tell the police once we eventually call them. "Let's do what we always do," I decide, placing my finger on the trigger. I'm trembling, but I force my arm to remain steady. "We'll stage a scene."

Pretty Dead Things **true-crime docuseries, released Friday, October 13, 2024, now available on multiple streaming services**

Aerial footage of Florida. The camera focuses on a signpost welcoming visitors to the small town of Gator Springs. Shots of the town center, the water tower, and the local coffee shop.

Cut to an interview with Briar and Portia Belville, seated on stools in a bright studio. Their hair and makeup are done, and they wear chic designer dresses.

Briar: We had a picturesque childhood. Fishing trips. Football games. Plenty of travel. Fame. All the toys a kid could want.

Portia: I remember she was always there. Our mother was so supportive. She'd be on stage with us, in the dressing room, making sure we had everything we needed. She made sure we felt loved and cared for.

Heartwarming pictures flicker across the screen, showing the three sisters and their mother, beaming with joy as they pose for the camera.

Interviewer: When did you realize something was wrong?

Briar: I found my sister's journal. The true story was so much scarier than we ever could've imagined.

Cut to camera 2.

Briar: Once we found the bodies, we knew we had to go to the police. But Elise wouldn't let us leave. She injected us with something. We trusted this woman. She was like a second mother to us. She helped raise us.

Pictures of Belville Estate's housekeeper, Elise Dowell, flash onscreen. In one photo, she's holding a baby Briar. In another, she's enjoying soft serve with the three girls at the estate. In a third picture, she hugs the girls on the set of Star Sisters.

Portia: We never imagined our mother would be capable of something like this.

A faded polaroid shows two smiling sisters in sundresses. Behind them, Vivienne stands in the doorway, her face hidden in the shadows.

Briar: She was the puppet master. She orchestrated everything. Elise would do whatever she asked. She was our mother's eyes and ears.

The interviewer shakes his head. He cups his chin and appears concerned yet sympathetic.

Interviewer: Who knew your mother, this successful and seemingly perfect actress, could have been hiding such a sinister past?

Briar: Mom sheltered us, which meant keeping us in the dark about everything. We knew she'd been married before, but that's it. She'd shut down if we asked about her past.

Interviewer: You two had no idea who your mother really was.

Briar and Portia shake their heads adamantly.

Briar and Portia together: No.

Portia: Our mother had plenty of boyfriends, but Robert was the only father we ever knew. And she took him from us.

Cut to an interview with Patricia Patel, Robert Wells' younger sister. She sits in her living room, wearing a turtleneck and a brown pencil skirt, a somber expression on her face.

Patricia: My phone rang, and it was the police. They wanted to know if I'd heard from Robert lately. I said, no, I haven't heard from him in months.

Cut to camera 2.

Patricia: It was like she was keeping him as a prisoner in his own home. He wasn't allowed to talk to friends, to other women. Not even his own sister.

The interviewer furrows his brow and strokes his chin.

Interviewer: And you were concerned.

Patricia: Oh, extremely. I was extremely concerned. There was no trace of him. It was like he vanished off the face of the earth.

Cut back to the studio.

Interviewer: Tell me about your sister, Odette, and what happened to her.

Briar: Odette was beautiful. Intelligent. Kind. She loved dancing. She danced with the Miami City Ballet for years. She was passionate about wildlife conservation. About nature. That was her purpose in life.

Portia: Odette went missing in August. None of us could reach her. No one knew where she went. Vivienne eventually found that one of the estate's airboats was gone. Odette left without telling anybody where she was going or why. Not us, not the people she worked with.

Interviewer: Was that typical behavior for your sister?

Briar: No, it was unlike her.

Cut to camera 2.

Portia: I remember sitting at the kitchen table and the police knocking on the door.

Interviewer: What were you thinking?

Portia: That something terrible was about to happen.

Suspenseful music plays.

Briar: We're sisters. We love each other. We're family.

Briar dabs at the corner of her eye with a tissue. Her voice becomes serious.

Briar: You never imagine the people closest to you are capable of hurting you.

Suspenseful music crescendos.

Cut to the grounds of the Belville Estate.

Detective Martinez steps out of his patrol car and walks along the swamp's edge. His golden badge catches the light coming through the trees. He kneels and points to the water.

Martinez: This is where we found the body. It was lying in the water, adjacent to the abandoned airboat. Almost as if it'd been thrown. Decomposition had already progressed.

Martinez faces the interviewer as he speaks.

Martinez: I remember thinking the scene didn't feel right. It looked like someone drove the boat out here and placed it there on purpose.

Interviewer: Were there tire marks?

Martinez: Yes, there were tire marks in the grass.

The interviewer taps his chin.

Interviewer: You felt that someone had staged the scene.

Martinez: My initial thought was that this was no accident. Yes.

Cut back to the studio.

Portia: Elena Torres showed up at the house shortly after Odette's wake. She introduced herself as a detective with the Gator Springs PD and let us know that she would be Martinez's replacement.

Briar: She portrayed herself as someone who had no idea who our mother was. She claimed she'd never seen any of her movies.

The interviewer smirks and tilts his head.

Interviewer: Little did you know…

Cut to camera 3.

Briar: She was intimidating, but friendly. We trusted her.

Portia: It was a mistake.

Cut to camera 2.

Interviewer: Your boyfriend emerged as the hero in this harrowing tale. Without him, you might not be here today, sharing your story.

Briar nods. A single tear drops down her cheek. She cradles her heavily pregnant belly, a protective hand guarding her unborn child.

Briar: I wish he could be here to witness the birth of his daughter. I've decided to name her Willa, after his grandmother. I know he would've been an amazing dad, and I've been so heartbroken since he passed. But I'm going to make sure she knows what kind of person her father was, how he saved us.

Portia takes her sister's hand and squeezes it tight. They share a sad smile.

Cut to footage of the Los Angeles skyline. The camera focuses on a beach at night, whitecaps washing onto the dark shore. A black SUV sits in the parking lot. Lieutenant Garcia with the LAPD sits in the driver's seat while the interviewer sits in the passenger seat.

Lieutenant Garcia (voiceover): I grew up obsessed with Hollywood. That's why I moved out here in the first place.

Cut to SUV interior.

Lieutenant Garcia: I was the detective assigned to Nils Hansen's case. It was huge at the time due to the big names involved. Famous actress meets musician heartthrob. They were newlyweds at the time of his disappearance, at the height of their celebrity.

Photographs and short interview clips from the era show the happy couple in their heyday.

Lieutenant Garcia: When I began the investigation, the first thing I did was ask around. You know, the usual questions. Did anyone have a grudge against him? Was there anyone looking to do him harm? No one wanted to talk to me. Until I started asking about his wife, Vivienne. Were they happy together? Did they ever argue? A close friend of his looked me in the eyes and told me, "He was absolutely terrified of her."

Video footage of the couple at a popular club in Hollywood. Vivienne has her arms wound tightly around Nils's neck. She has a dead look in her eyes as she stares down the camera.

Cut to the grounds of the Belville Estate. Drone footage of the gardens and burbling swamp.

Martinez (voiceover): I think she was convinced no one would ever find them. Who could've predicted something this heinous? But a lot happens behind closed doors.

Cut back to the studio.

Briar: We had no idea Detective Torres had… consumed one of our mother's flowers. Vivienne kept a secret garden with poisonous flowers she bred herself. She used to make iced tea from the petals and even put them in our grits. I think the detective was so obsessed with our family she must've seen Vivienne doing it and decided to try it herself. The coroner said the toxins caused internal bleeding. She hemorrhaged before we even realized what was happening.

Portia: After she killed Briar's boyfriend, she came after us. We tried to defend ourselves with a knife, but she was stronger. We were lucky the poison kicked in when it did. Otherwise… I don't think any of us would've made it out alive.

Footage is shown of the overgrown garden behind the Belville Estate.

Cut back to the studio.

Interviewer: There are theories online that the Belville sisters weren't victims at all—that you planned everything, that you covered up your mother's crimes. Maybe even helped her. What do you say to that?

Briar and Portia look at each other. They share a faint smile.

Briar: People love a good story. Let them believe whatever they want to believe. We know the truth. And that's all that matters.

A final picture of Vivienne and her daughters above the mantel, zooming in on their smiling faces, the image distorting and darkening.

Opening theme and title sequence begin.

Haunting images of the Belville Estate from the graveyard, gardens, and swamp are accompanied by eerie violin music. Vivienne's infamous photographs are animated. Vines crawl down her daughters' arms, sprouting red roses and thorns. Red wine spills, looking like a thick puddle of blood. A woman's manicured nails stroke along her string of pearls, a big emerald ring glittering on her finger. Missing person flyers and newspaper clippings with titles like The Belville Black Widows *and* Vanished Without a Trace. *Glamour shots of the Old Hollywood actress and footage of her daughters on* Star Sisters, *singing and dancing in matching outfits. Girls standing in the swamp, their hands tightly clasped, mud stuck to their legs and white gowns. A photograph of Odette smiling brightly, her eyes violently scratched out.*

Music ends.

Cut back to Briar in the studio, looking directly into the camera.

Briar: Let's start at the beginning.

THANK YOU FOR READING PRETTY DEAD THINGS!

Your feedback means the world to me, so please consider leaving me a review on Amazon or Goodreads.

livlowry.com/rate-pdt

ACKNOWLEDGMENTS

This book has been many years in the making. It's been a lot of daydreaming, planning and plotting, writing and rewriting. The final draft sounds nothing like the first draft I wrote years ago in an old notebook that was literally falling apart at the seams. I know it's not perfect, and I know I'm no Hemingway, but I'm so proud to finally bring this book into the world and share it with readers.

First, I'd like to thank my former agent, Aurora Fernandez at Trident Media Group, for taking a chance on me and my book, for your guidance, and for your support of my decision to pursue self-publishing.

Thank you to my beta readers for your invaluable feedback. You have made this book so much better.

Thank you to Stella for being my harshest critic. Thank you to Eve for being the best hype woman I could ever ask for. Thank you to my parents for always supporting me and raising me to be delusional enough to think I could ever do this as a career. It's harder than I thought, but I'll never give up. Thank you to my godparents for encouraging my writing from an early age, taking me to all those writing festivals and Barnes & Noble to further feed my book addiction. Thank you to my 4th-grade teacher, Mr. Jones, who read my creative writing assignment and told me it was very good, and I still think about that sometimes and smile. Thank you to my son—your cute little face is everything to me. I want to give you the world. Every single word I write is for you.

Thank you to my amazing husband, Frank, who never once stopped supporting me and has never once doubted me, even through the countless rejections. Thank you for taking those long walks with me, where we would brainstorm what happens next in the book. Thank you for being my fiercest champion.

And last but definitely not least, I want to say a huge thank you to my readers. I am so grateful for your support. Thank you, everyone.

AFTERWORD

Check out my website, where you can sign up for my newsletter, learn about future projects, and get updates on my book: www.livlowry.com

Follow me on TikTok @livlowryauthor

For business, media, or collaboration inquiries, you can reach me at olivia@livlowry.com.

If you come across any errors, inconsistencies, or typos I may have missed, please don't hesitate to reach out to me at olivia@livlowry.-com, and I'll correct them right away.

Thank you for reading!

ABOUT THE AUTHOR

Liv Lowry lives in Germany with her husband and her son. When she's not plotting her next thriller, she can usually be found reading true crime, exploring old castles, or sipping tea while dreaming up new ways to keep readers up at night.

tiktok.com/@livlowryauthor
amazon.com/author/liv-lowry
bookbub.com/authors/liv-lowry
goodreads.com/livlowryauthor
instagram.com/livlowryauthor
youtube.com/@livlowryauthor

Made in United States
North Haven, CT
02 February 2026

87932004R00200